Dance Class

Béka and Crip

PAPERCUTZ

New York

Dance Class Graphic Novels available from PAPERCUTZ™

DANCE CLASS graphic novels are also available digitally wherever e-books are sold.

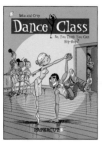

#1 "So, You Think You Can Hip-Hop?"

#2 "Romeos and Juliet"

#3 "African Folk Dance Fever"

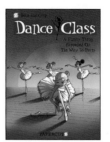

#4 "A Funny Thing Happened on the Way to Paris..."

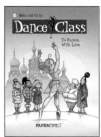

#5 "To Russia, With Love"

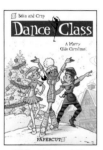

#6 "A Merry Olde Christmas"

#7 "School Night Fever"

#8 "Snow White and the Seven Dwarves"

#9 "Dancing in the Rain"

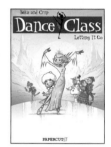

#10 "Letting It Go"

COMING SOON!

#11 "Dance With Me"

DANCE CLASS 3 IN 1 #1

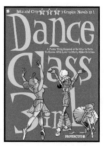

#1 DANCE CLASS 3 IN 1 #2

DANCE CLASS graphic novels are available for $10.99 each only in hardcover.
DANCE CLASS 3 IN 1 graphic novels are available for $14.99 each only in paperback.
Available from booksellers everywhere.
You can also order online from papercutz.com or call 1-800-886-1223, Monday through Friday, 9 - 5 EST.
MC, Visa, and AmEx accepted. To order by mail, please add $5.00 for postage and handling for first book
ordered, $1.00 for each additional book and make check payable to NBM Publishing. Send to: Papercutz,
160 Broadway, Suite 700, East Wing, New York, NY 10038.

Papercutz.com

Dance Class 3 in 1

Table of Contents

TOOTOOM
TOOM
TOOTOOM
TOOM

DANCE CLASS 3 IN 1
Originally published in France as Studio Danse [Dance Class] Volumes 4, 5, and 6
©2010-2012, 2020 BAMBOO ÉDITION.
www.bamboo.fr
All other editorial material © 2020 by Papercutz
www.papercutz.com

DANCE CLASS 3 IN 1 #2
"A Funny Thing Happened on the Way to Paris..."
"To Russia, With Love"
"A Merry Olde Christmas"

BÉKA — Writer
CRIP — Artist
MAËLA COSSON — Colorist
MARK McNABB — Production
JOE JOHNSON — Translation
TOM ORZECHOWSKI — Lettering
IZZY BOYCE-BLANCHARD — Editorial Intern
JEFF WHITMAN — Editor
JIM SALICRUP
Editor-in-Chief

Special thanks to CATHERINE LOISELET

ISBN: 978-1-5458-0482-7

Printed in China
July 2020

Papercutz books may be purchased for business or promotional use. For information on bulk purchases please
contact Macmillan Corporate and Premium Sales Department at (800) 221-7945 x5442.

Distributed by Macmillan
First Papercutz Printing

A Funny Thing Happened on the Way to Paris

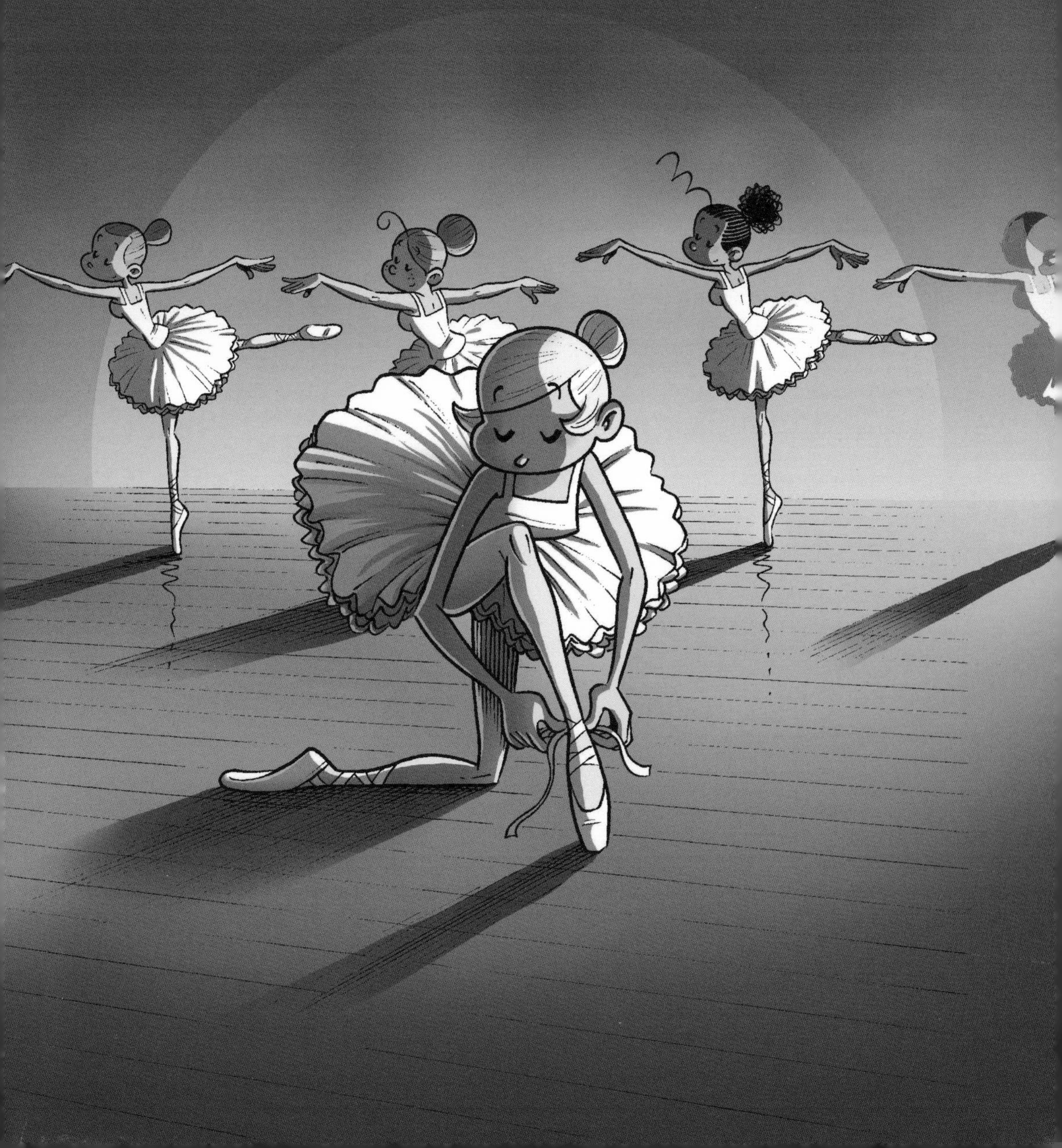

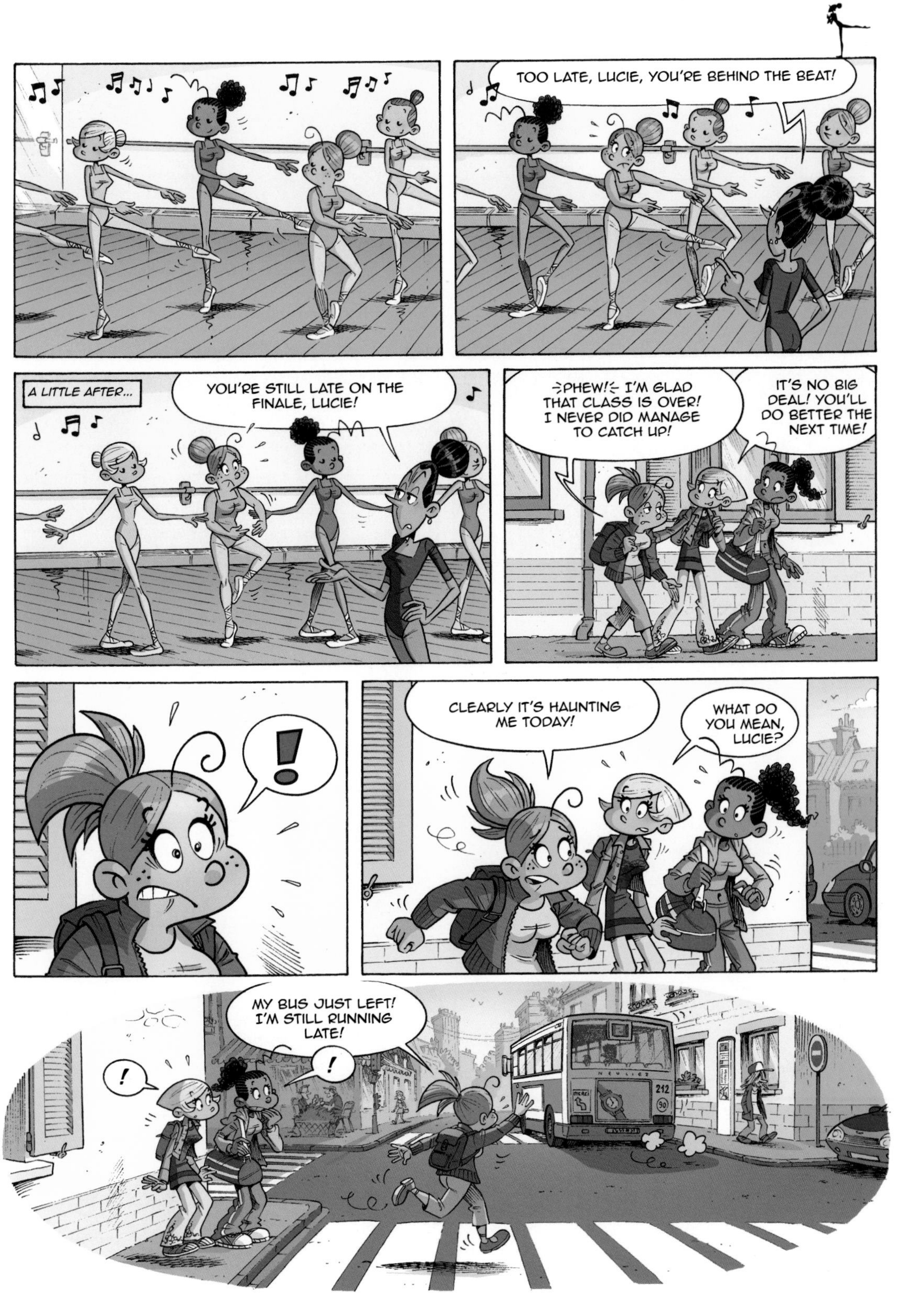
TOO LATE, LUCIE, YOU'RE BEHIND THE BEAT!
A LITTLE AFTER...
YOU'RE STILL LATE ON THE FINALE, LUCIE!
PHEW! I'M GLAD THAT CLASS IS OVER! I NEVER DID MANAGE TO CATCH UP!
IT'S NO BIG DEAL! YOU'LL DO BETTER THE NEXT TIME!
!
CLEARLY IT'S HAUNTING ME TODAY!
WHAT DO YOU MEAN, LUCIE?
MY BUS JUST LEFT! I'M STILL RUNNING LATE!
!
!
212

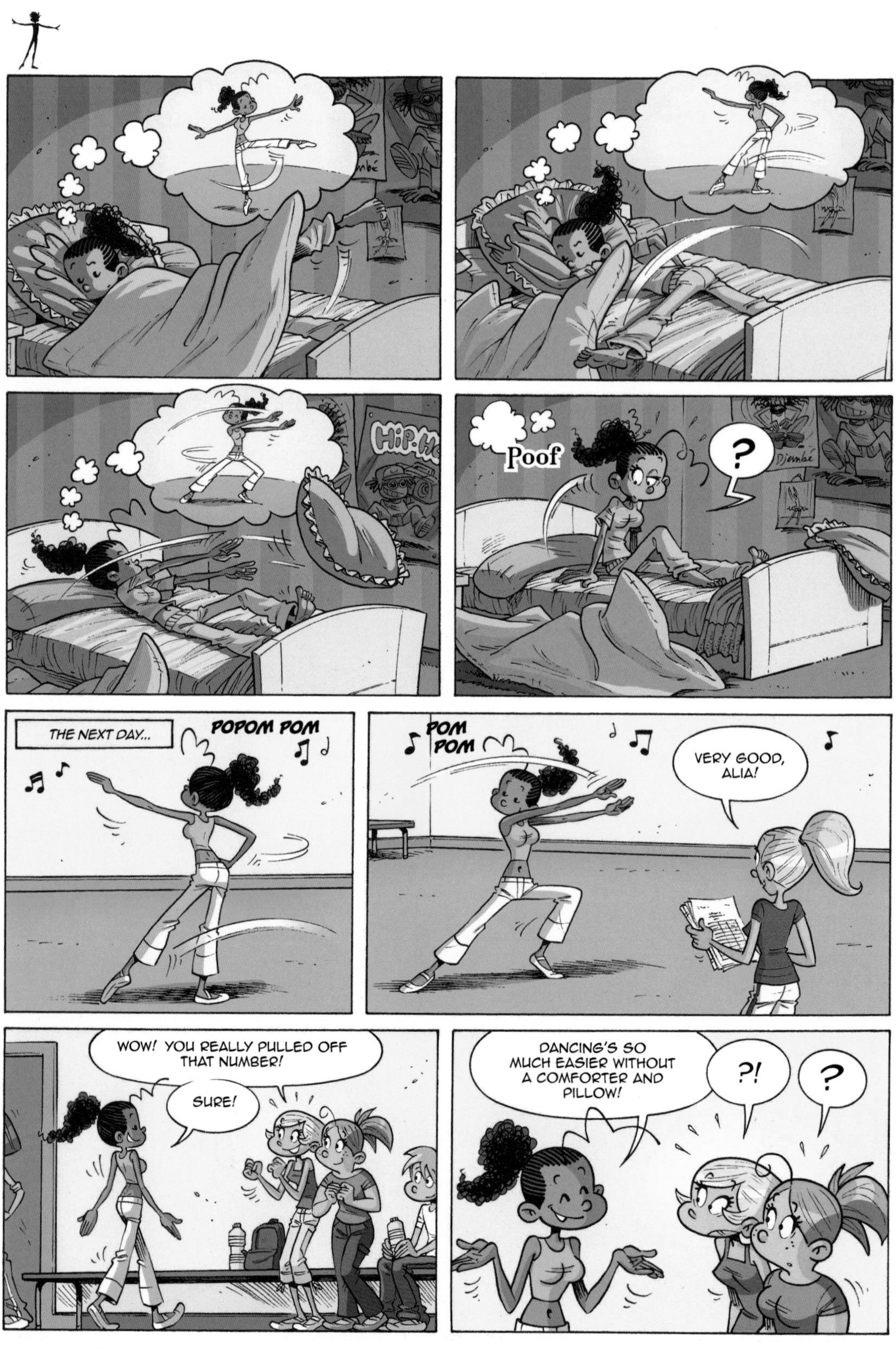
Poof
?
THE NEXT DAY...
POPOM POM
POM POM
VERY GOOD, ALIA!
WOW! YOU REALLY PULLED OFF THAT NUMBER!
SURE!
DANCING'S SO MUCH EASIER WITHOUT A COMFORTER AND PILLOW!
?!
?

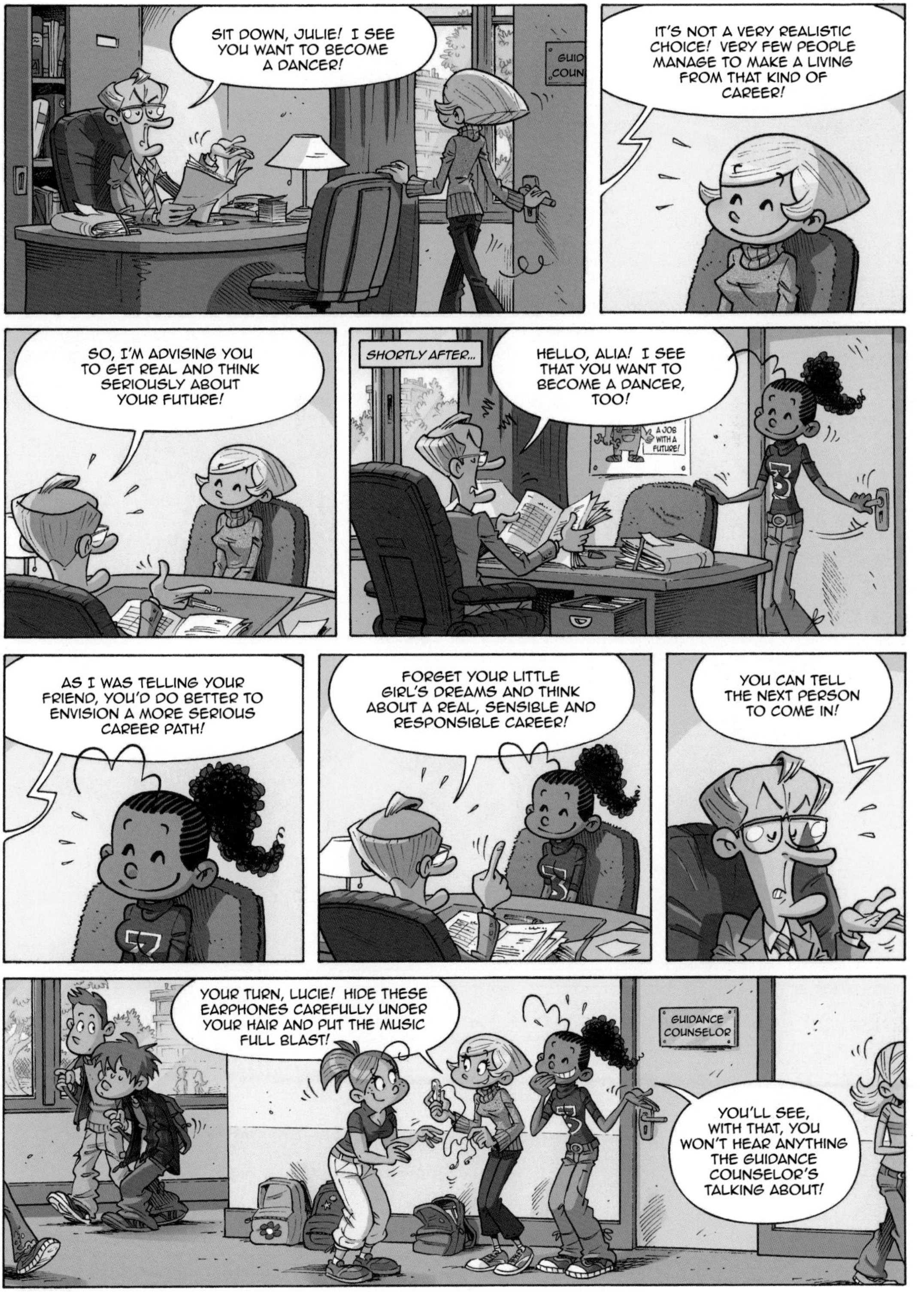
SIT DOWN, JULIE! I SEE YOU WANT TO BECOME A DANCER!
IT'S NOT A VERY REALISTIC CHOICE! VERY FEW PEOPLE MANAGE TO MAKE A LIVING FROM THAT KIND OF CAREER!
SO, I'M ADVISING YOU TO GET REAL AND THINK SERIOUSLY ABOUT YOUR FUTURE!
SHORTLY AFTER...
HELLO, ALIA! I SEE THAT YOU WANT TO BECOME A DANCER, TOO!
A JOB WITH A FUTURE!
AS I WAS TELLING YOUR FRIEND, YOU'D DO BETTER TO ENVISION A MORE SERIOUS CAREER PATH!
FORGET YOUR LITTLE GIRL'S DREAMS AND THINK ABOUT A REAL, SENSIBLE AND RESPONSIBLE CAREER!
YOU CAN TELL THE NEXT PERSON TO COME IN!
YOUR TURN, LUCIE! HIDE THESE EARPHONES CAREFULLY UNDER YOUR HAIR AND PUT THE MUSIC FULL BLAST!
GUIDANCE COUNSELOR
YOU'LL SEE, WITH THAT, YOU WON'T HEAR ANYTHING THE GUIDANCE COUNSELOR'S TALKING ABOUT!

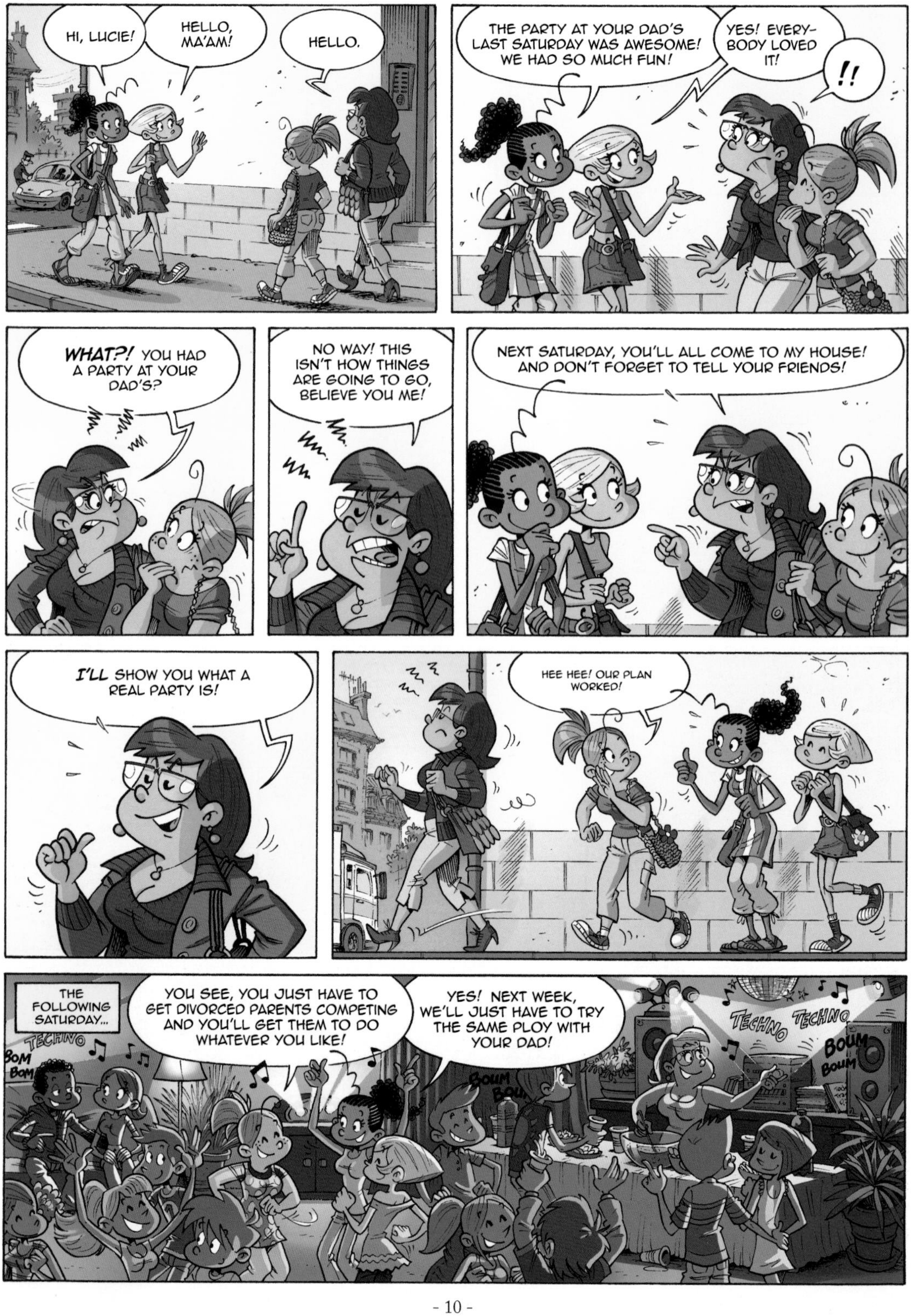

HI, LUCIE!
HELLO, MA'AM!
HELLO.
THE PARTY AT YOUR DAD'S LAST SATURDAY WAS AWESOME! WE HAD SO MUCH FUN!
YES! EVERY-BODY LOVED IT!
!!
WHAT?! YOU HAD A PARTY AT YOUR DAD'S?
NO WAY! THIS ISN'T HOW THINGS ARE GOING TO GO, BELIEVE YOU ME!
NEXT SATURDAY, YOU'LL ALL COME TO MY HOUSE! AND DON'T FORGET TO TELL YOUR FRIENDS!
I'LL SHOW YOU WHAT A REAL PARTY IS!
HEE HEE! OUR PLAN WORKED!
THE FOLLOWING SATURDAY...
YOU SEE, YOU JUST HAVE TO GET DIVORCED PARENTS COMPETING AND YOU'LL GET THEM TO DO WHATEVER YOU LIKE!
YES! NEXT WEEK, WE'LL JUST HAVE TO TRY THE SAME PLOY WITH YOUR DAD!
TECHNO
BOM BOM
TECHNO TECHNO
BOUM BOUM
BOUM BOUM

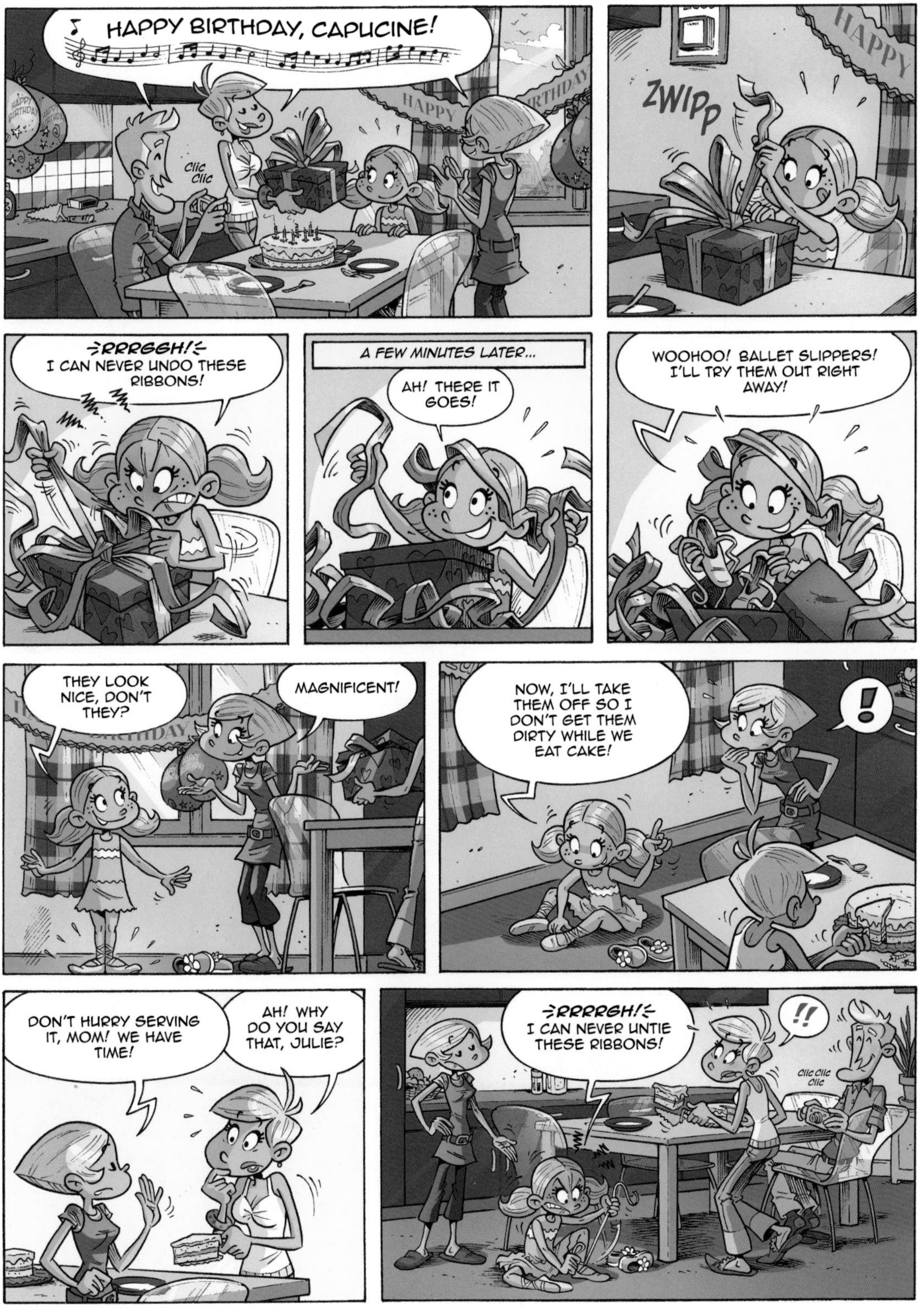
HAPPY BIRTHDAY, CAPUCINE!
Clic Clic
HAPPY BIRTHDAY
ZWIPP
HAPPY
RRRGGH! I CAN NEVER UNDO THESE RIBBONS!
A FEW MINUTES LATER...
AH! THERE IT GOES!
WOOHOO! BALLET SLIPPERS! I'LL TRY THEM OUT RIGHT AWAY!
THEY LOOK NICE, DON'T THEY?
MAGNIFICENT!
NOW, I'LL TAKE THEM OFF SO I DON'T GET THEM DIRTY WHILE WE EAT CAKE!
!
DON'T HURRY SERVING IT, MOM! WE HAVE TIME!
AH! WHY DO YOU SAY THAT, JULIE?
RRRRGH! I CAN NEVER UNTIE THESE RIBBONS!
!!
Clic Clic Clic

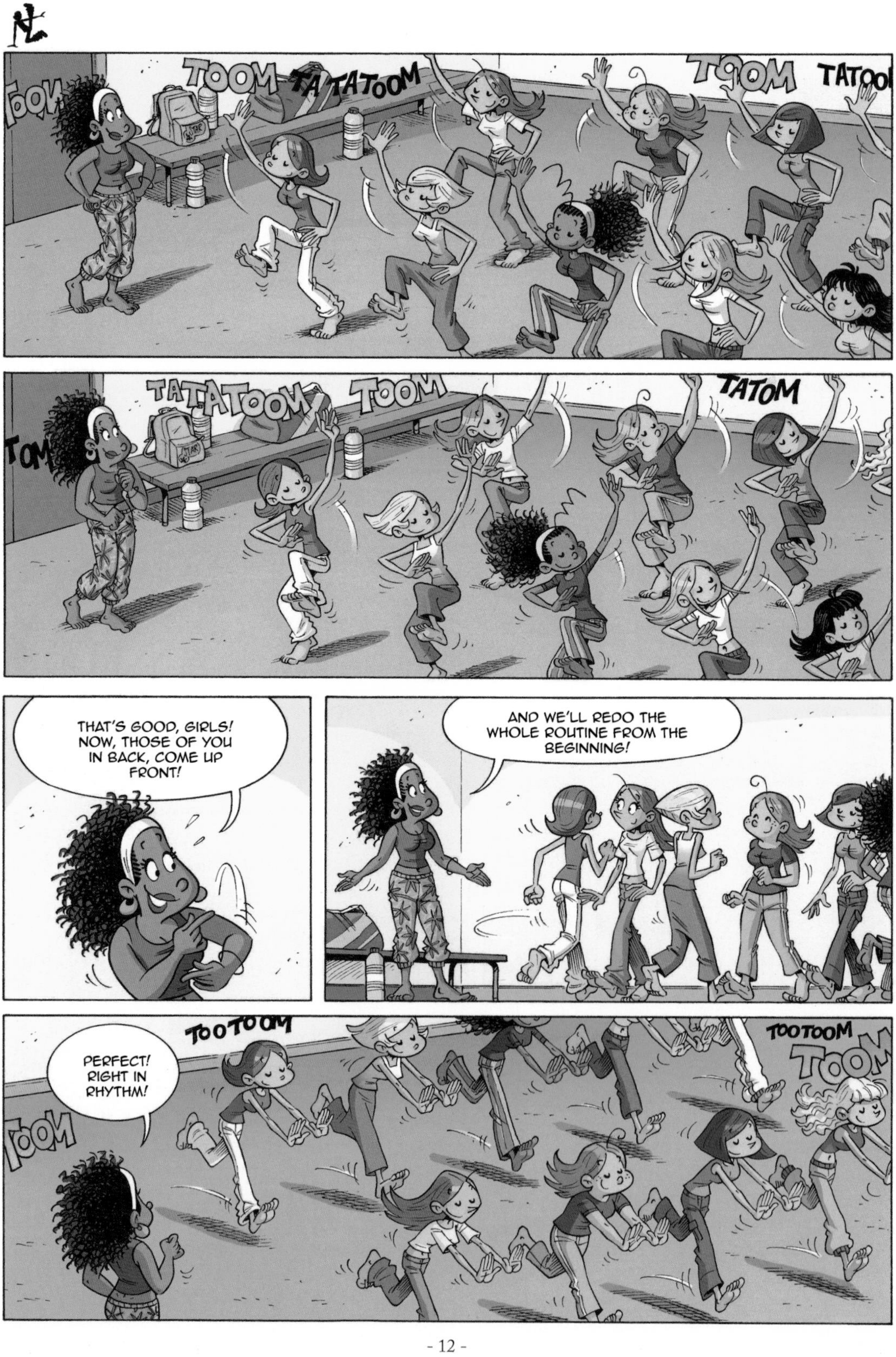
TOOM
TOOM TA TATOOM
TOOM TATOO
TOM
TATATOOM TOOM
TATOM
THAT'S GOOD, GIRLS! NOW, THOSE OF YOU IN BACK, COME UP FRONT!
AND WE'LL REDO THE WHOLE ROUTINE FROM THE BEGINNING!
TOOTOOM
TOOM
PERFECT! RIGHT IN RHYTHM!
TOOTOOM
TOOM

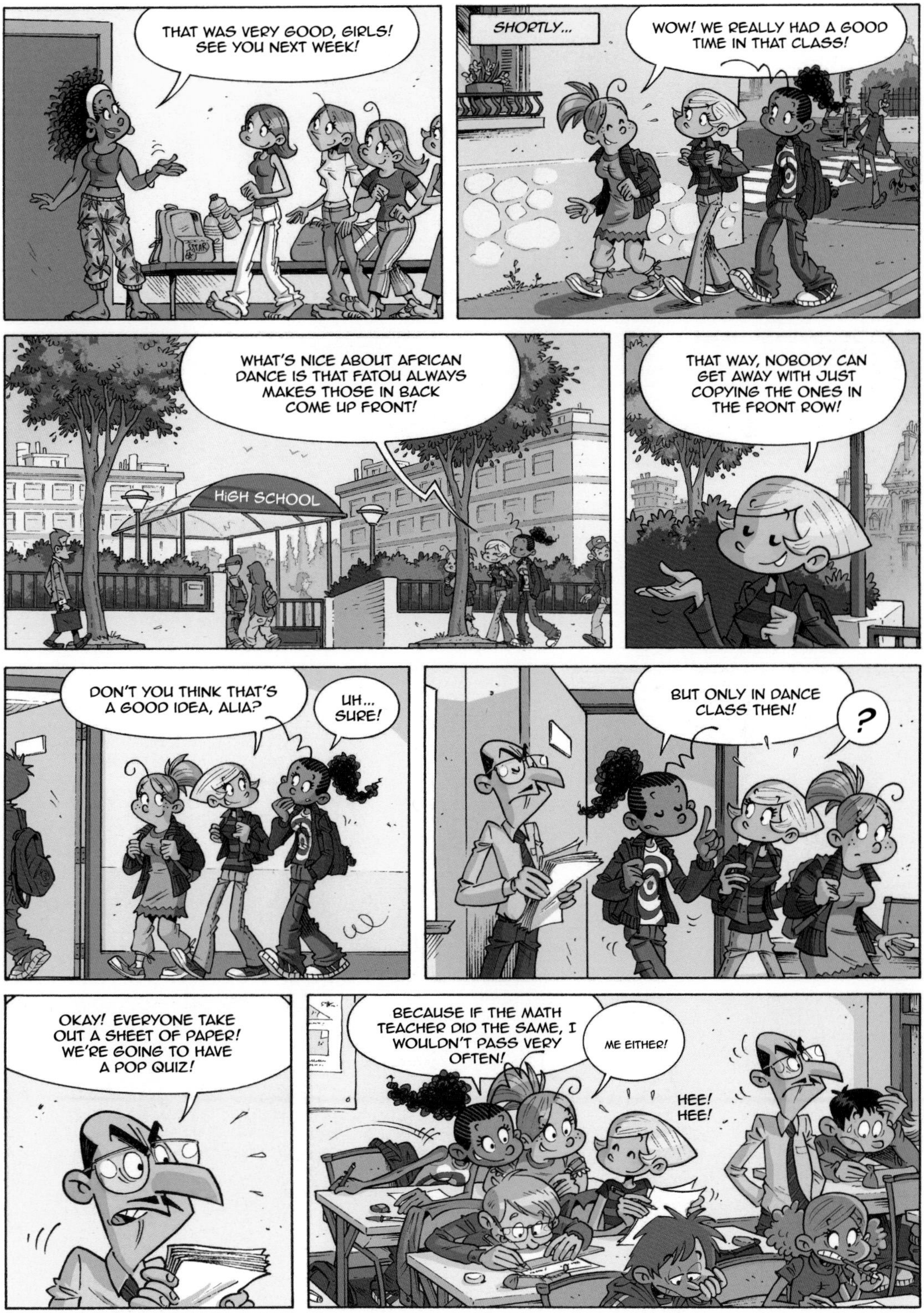
THAT WAS VERY GOOD, GIRLS! SEE YOU NEXT WEEK!
SHORTLY...
WOW! WE REALLY HAD A GOOD TIME IN THAT CLASS!
WHAT'S NICE ABOUT AFRICAN DANCE IS THAT FATOU ALWAYS MAKES THOSE IN BACK COME UP FRONT!
HIGH SCHOOL
THAT WAY, NOBODY CAN GET AWAY WITH JUST COPYING THE ONES IN THE FRONT ROW!
DON'T YOU THINK THAT'S A GOOD IDEA, ALIA?
UH... SURE!
BUT ONLY IN DANCE CLASS THEN!
?
OKAY! EVERYONE TAKE OUT A SHEET OF PAPER! WE'RE GOING TO HAVE A POP QUIZ!
BECAUSE IF THE MATH TEACHER DID THE SAME, I WOULDN'T PASS VERY OFTEN!
ME EITHER!
HEE! HEE!

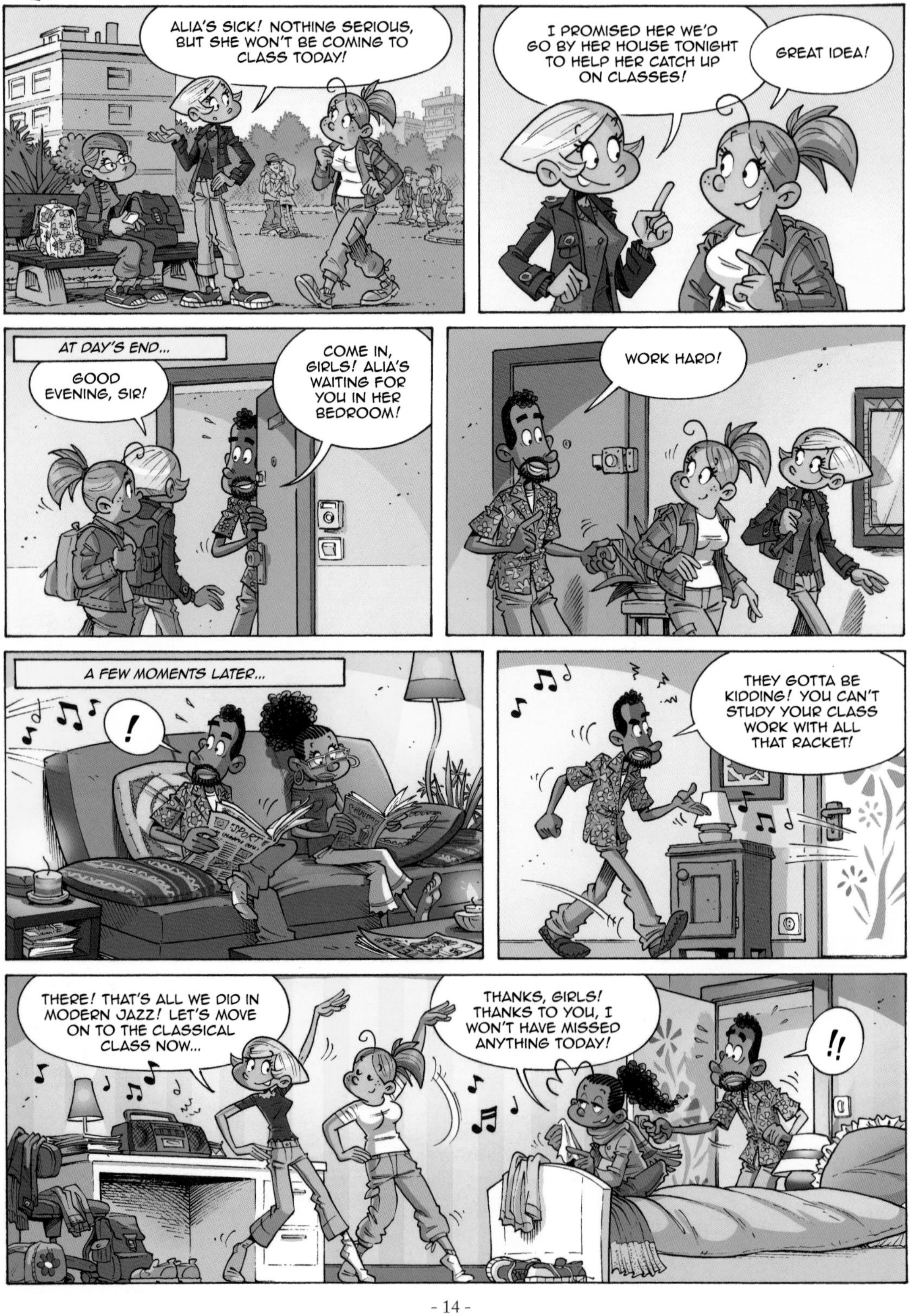
ALIA'S SICK! NOTHING SERIOUS, BUT SHE WON'T BE COMING TO CLASS TODAY!
I PROMISED HER WE'D GO BY HER HOUSE TONIGHT TO HELP HER CATCH UP ON CLASSES!
GREAT IDEA!
AT DAY'S END...
GOOD EVENING, SIR!
COME IN, GIRLS! ALIA'S WAITING FOR YOU IN HER BEDROOM!
WORK HARD!
A FEW MOMENTS LATER...
!
THEY GOTTA BE KIDDING! YOU CAN'T STUDY YOUR CLASS WORK WITH ALL THAT RACKET!
THERE! THAT'S ALL WE DID IN MODERN JAZZ! LET'S MOVE ON TO THE CLASSICAL CLASS NOW...
THANKS, GIRLS! THANKS TO YOU, I WON'T HAVE MISSED ANYTHING TODAY!
!!

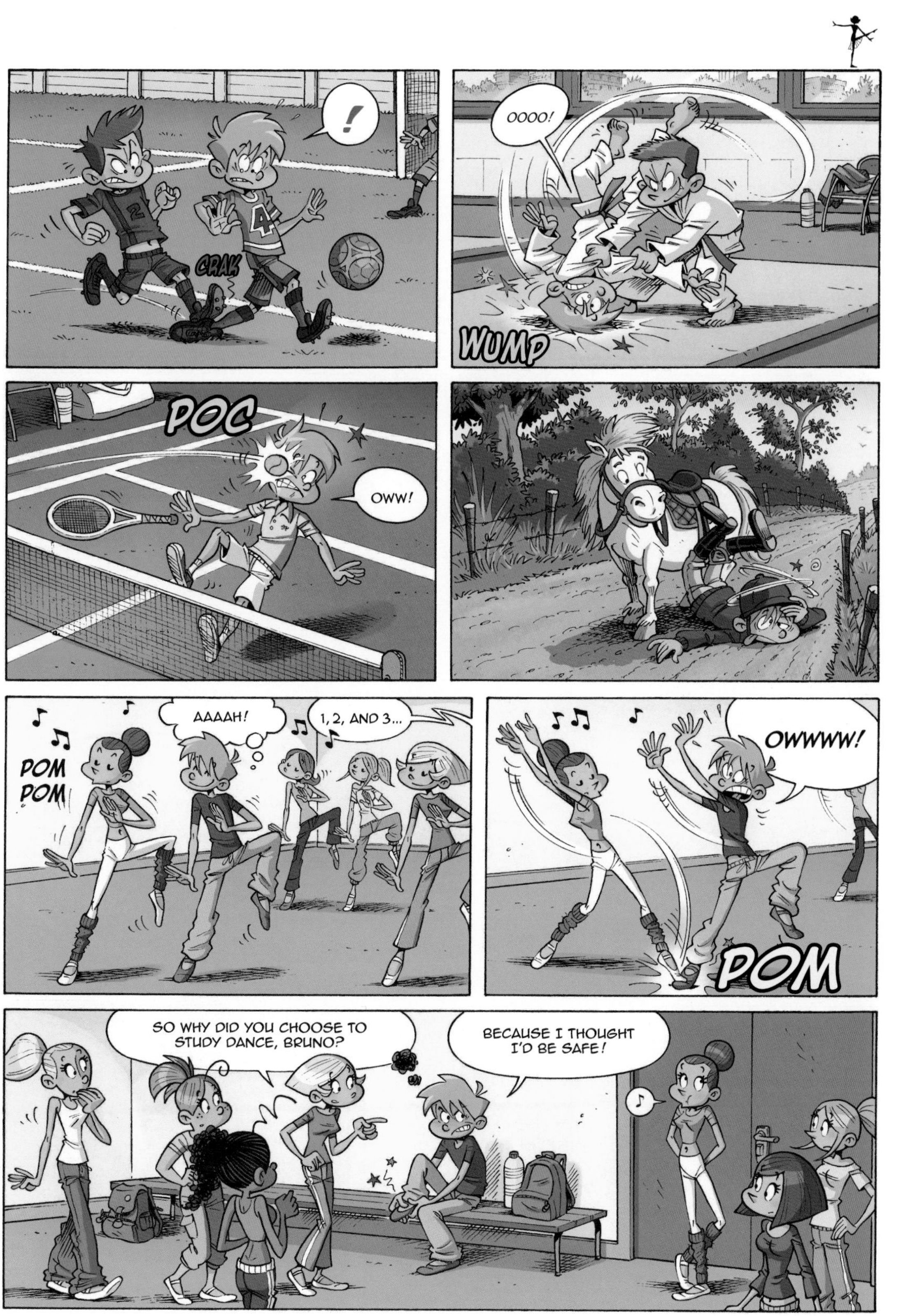
!
CRAK
OOOO!
WUMP
POC
OWW!
POM
POM
AAAAH!
1, 2, AND 3...
OWWWW!
POM
SO WHY DID YOU CHOOSE TO STUDY DANCE, BRUNO?
BECAUSE I THOUGHT I'D BE SAFE!

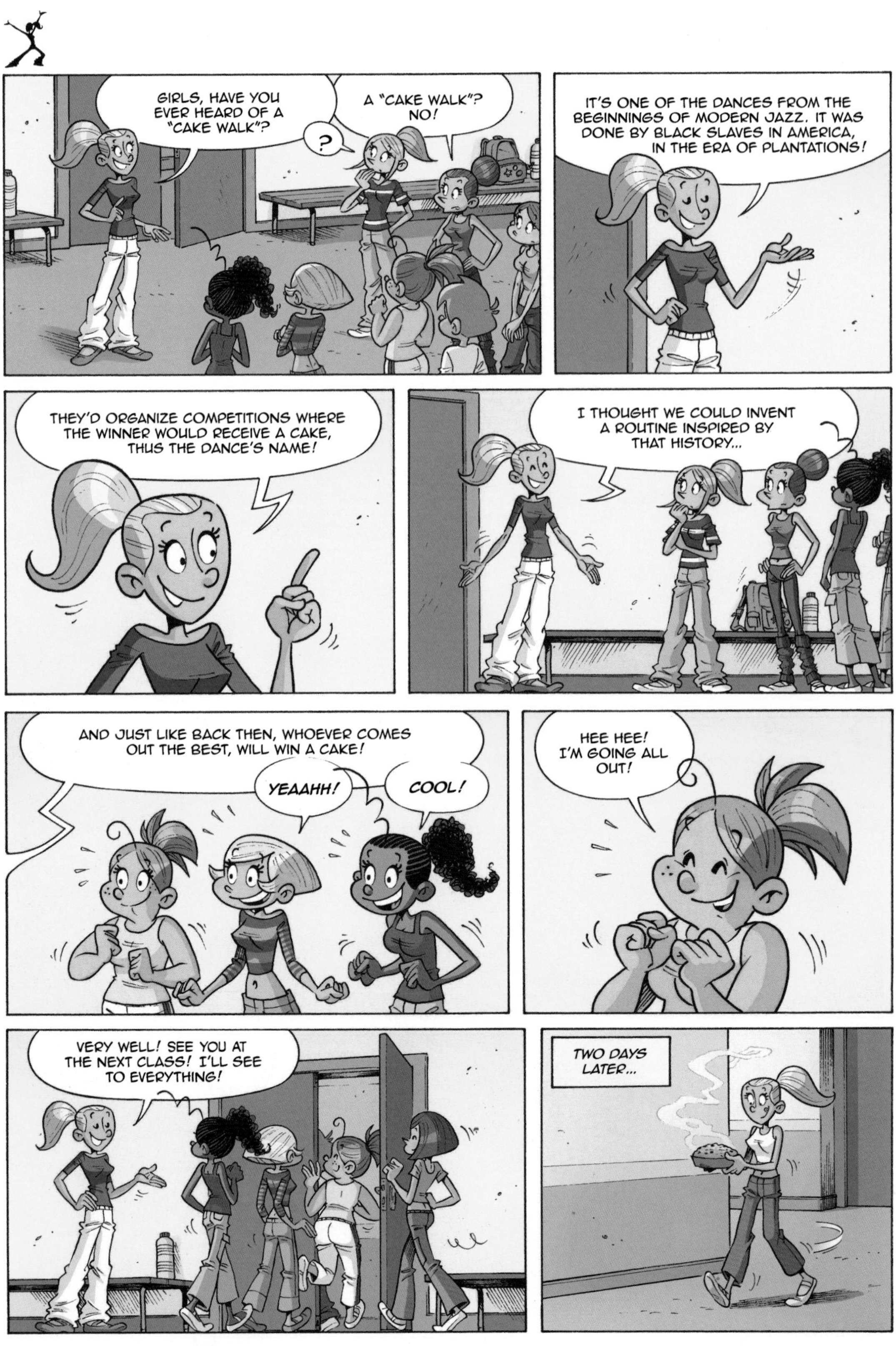
GIRLS, HAVE YOU EVER HEARD OF A "CAKE WALK"?
?
A "CAKE WALK"? NO!
IT'S ONE OF THE DANCES FROM THE BEGINNINGS OF MODERN JAZZ. IT WAS DONE BY BLACK SLAVES IN AMERICA, IN THE ERA OF PLANTATIONS!
THEY'D ORGANIZE COMPETITIONS WHERE THE WINNER WOULD RECEIVE A CAKE, THUS THE DANCE'S NAME!
I THOUGHT WE COULD INVENT A ROUTINE INSPIRED BY THAT HISTORY...
AND JUST LIKE BACK THEN, WHOEVER COMES OUT THE BEST, WILL WIN A CAKE!
YEAAHH!
COOL!
HEE HEE! I'M GOING ALL OUT!
VERY WELL! SEE YOU AT THE NEXT CLASS! I'LL SEE TO EVERYTHING!
TWO DAYS LATER...

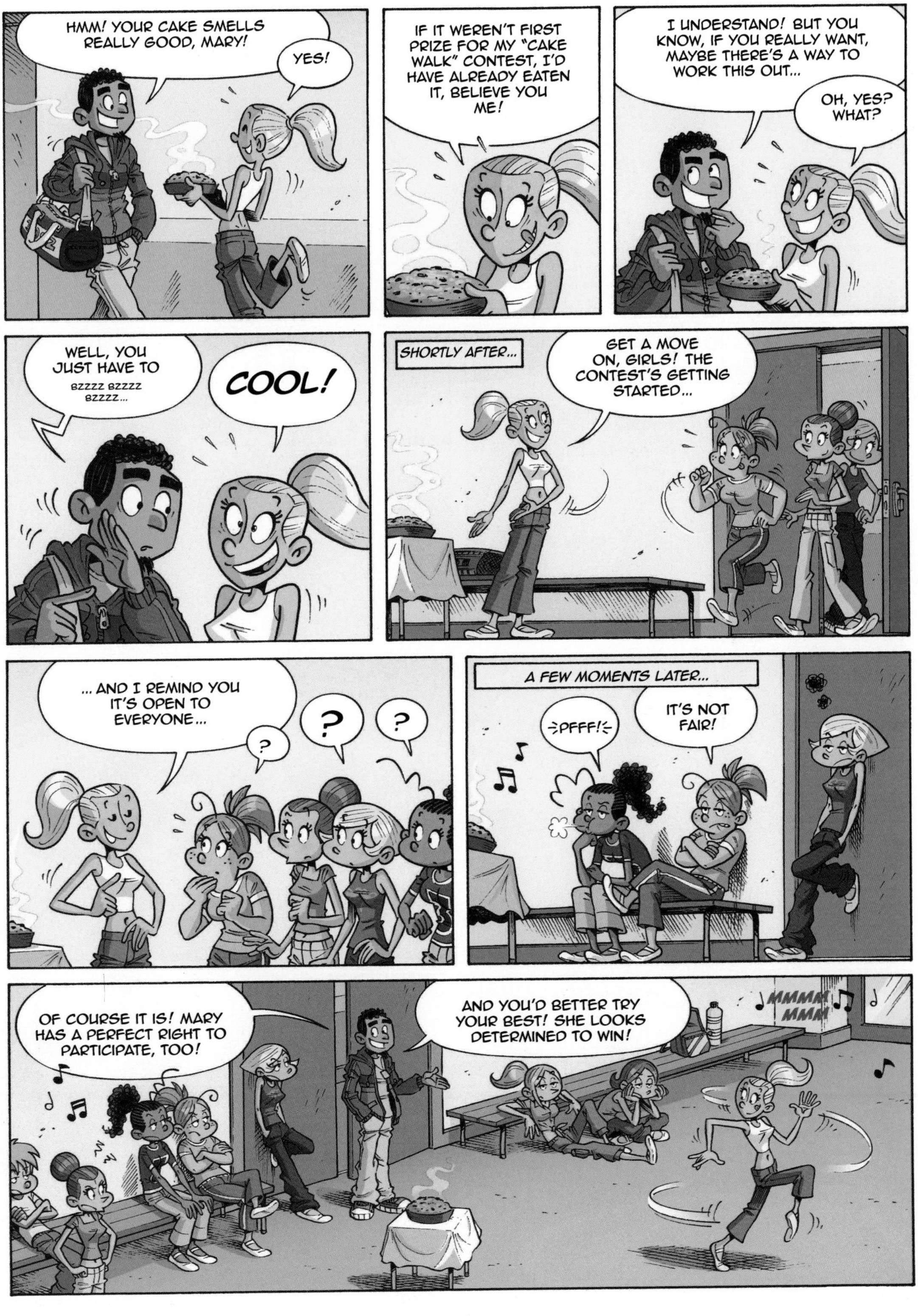
HMM! YOUR CAKE SMELLS REALLY GOOD, MARY!
YES!
IF IT WEREN'T FIRST PRIZE FOR MY "CAKE WALK" CONTEST, I'D HAVE ALREADY EATEN IT, BELIEVE YOU ME!
I UNDERSTAND! BUT YOU KNOW, IF YOU REALLY WANT, MAYBE THERE'S A WAY TO WORK THIS OUT...
OH, YES? WHAT?
WELL, YOU JUST HAVE TO BZZZZ BZZZZ BZZZZ...
COOL!
SHORTLY AFTER...
GET A MOVE ON, GIRLS! THE CONTEST'S GETTING STARTED...
... AND I REMIND YOU IT'S OPEN TO EVERYONE...
?
?
?
A FEW MOMENTS LATER...
PFFF!
IT'S NOT FAIR!
OF COURSE IT IS! MARY HAS A PERFECT RIGHT TO PARTICIPATE, TOO!
AND YOU'D BETTER TRY YOUR BEST! SHE LOOKS DETERMINED TO WIN!
MMMM MMM

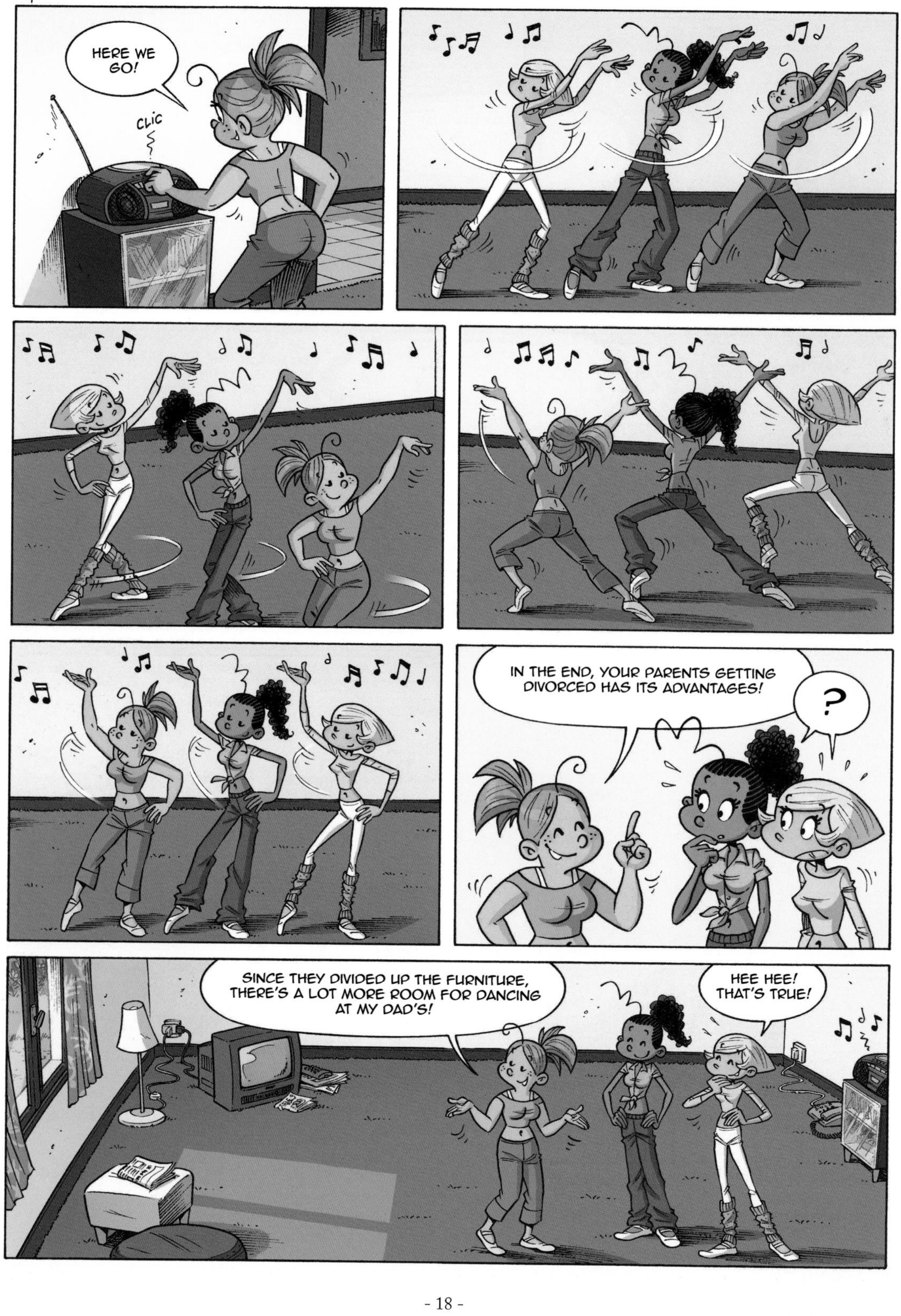
HERE WE GO!
CLIC
IN THE END, YOUR PARENTS GETTING DIVORCED HAS ITS ADVANTAGES!
?
SINCE THEY DIVIDED UP THE FURNITURE, THERE'S A LOT MORE ROOM FOR DANCING AT MY DAD'S!
HEE HEE! THAT'S TRUE!

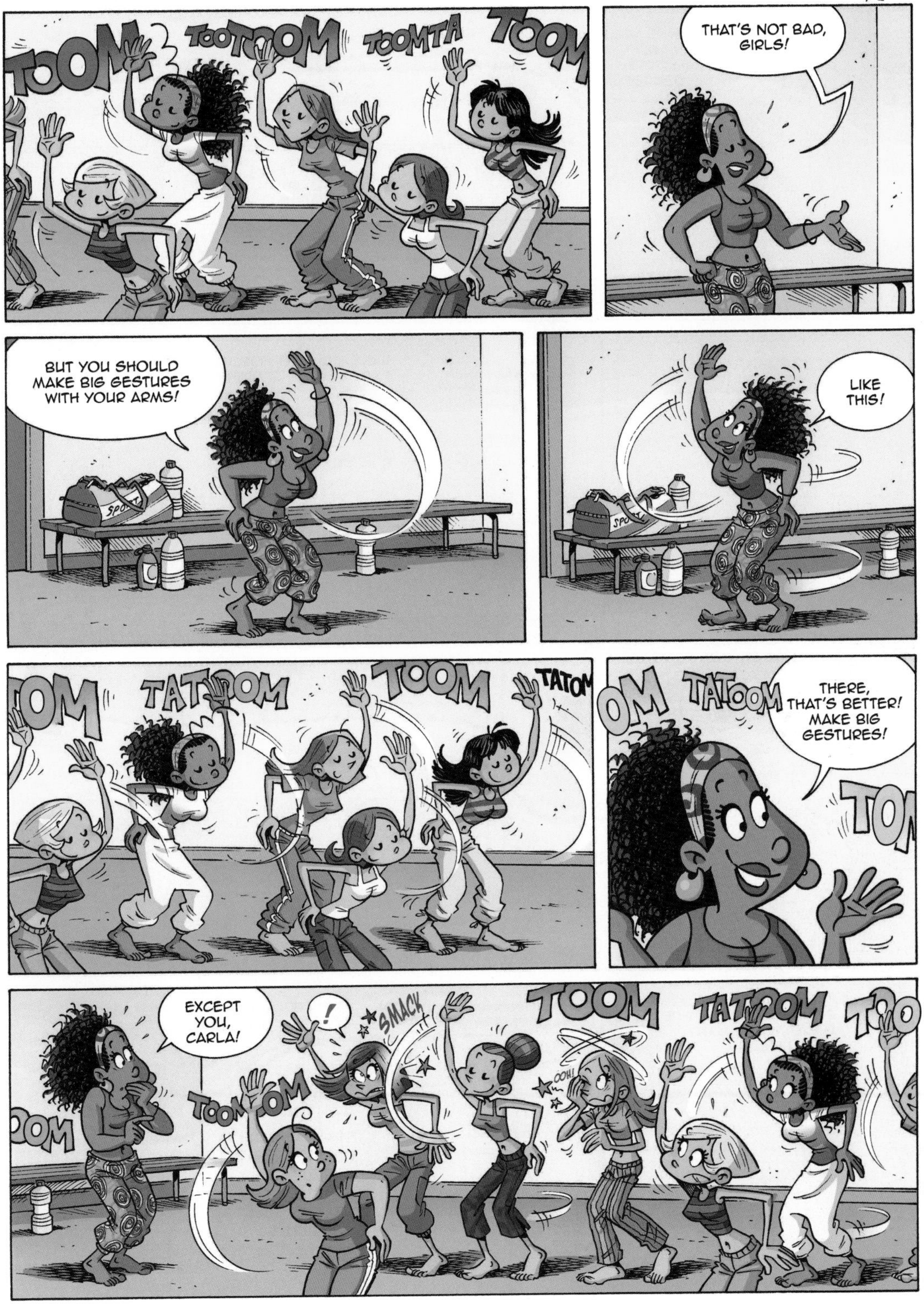
TOOM TOOTOOM TOOMTA TOOM
THAT'S NOT BAD, GIRLS!
BUT YOU SHOULD MAKE BIG GESTURES WITH YOUR ARMS!
LIKE THIS!
TOOM TATOOM TOOM TATOM
OM TATOOM
THERE, THAT'S BETTER! MAKE BIG GESTURES!
TOM
EXCEPT YOU, CARLA!
!
SMACK
OOH!
TOOM TATOOM TOO
OOM TOOMOM

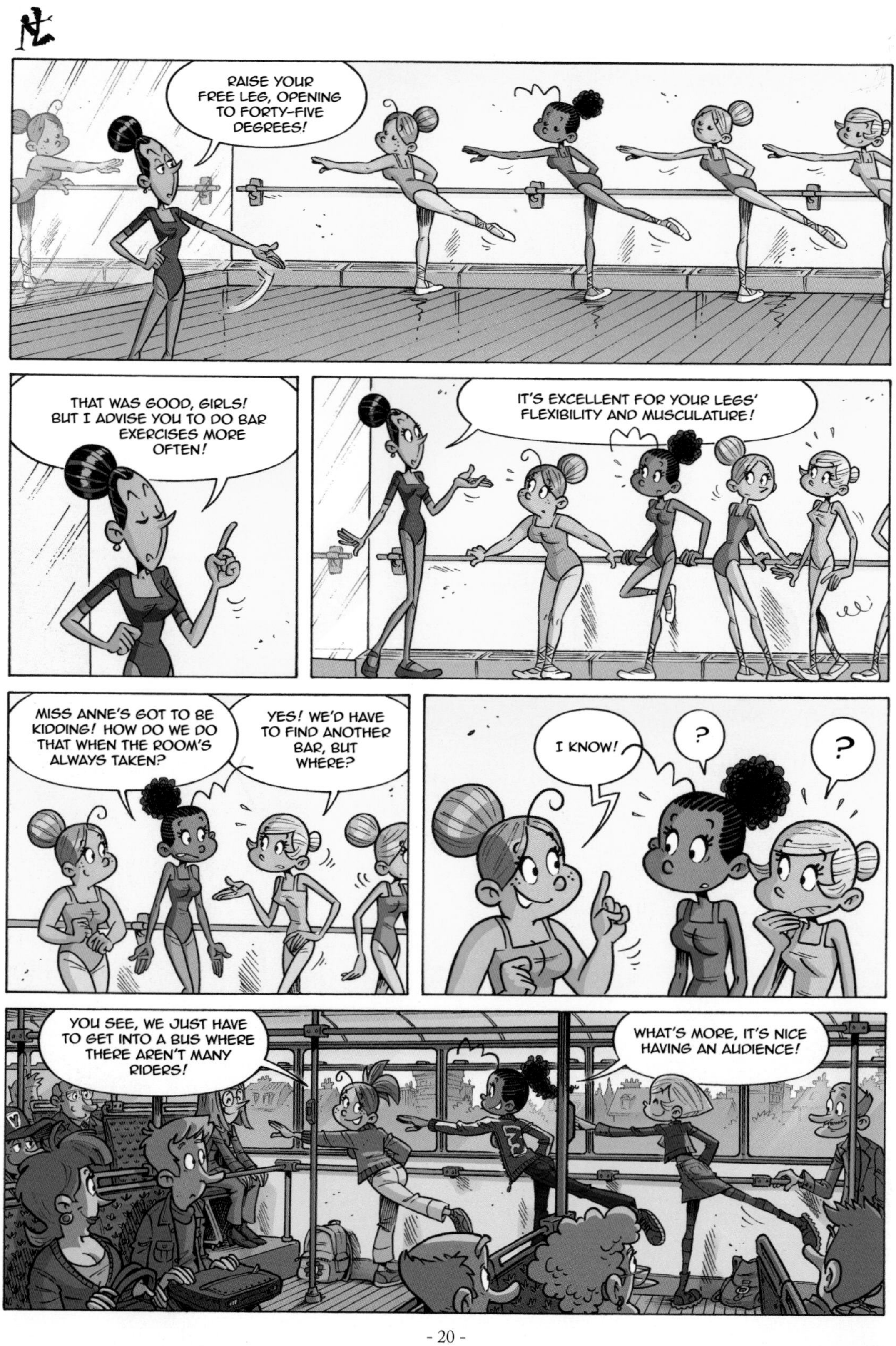
RAISE YOUR FREE LEG, OPENING TO FORTY-FIVE DEGREES!
THAT WAS GOOD, GIRLS! BUT I ADVISE YOU TO DO BAR EXERCISES MORE OFTEN!
IT'S EXCELLENT FOR YOUR LEGS' FLEXIBILITY AND MUSCULATURE!
MISS ANNE'S GOT TO BE KIDDING! HOW DO WE DO THAT WHEN THE ROOM'S ALWAYS TAKEN?
YES! WE'D HAVE TO FIND ANOTHER BAR, BUT WHERE?
I KNOW!
?
?
YOU SEE, WE JUST HAVE TO GET INTO A BUS WHERE THERE AREN'T MANY RIDERS!
WHAT'S MORE, IT'S NICE HAVING AN AUDIENCE!

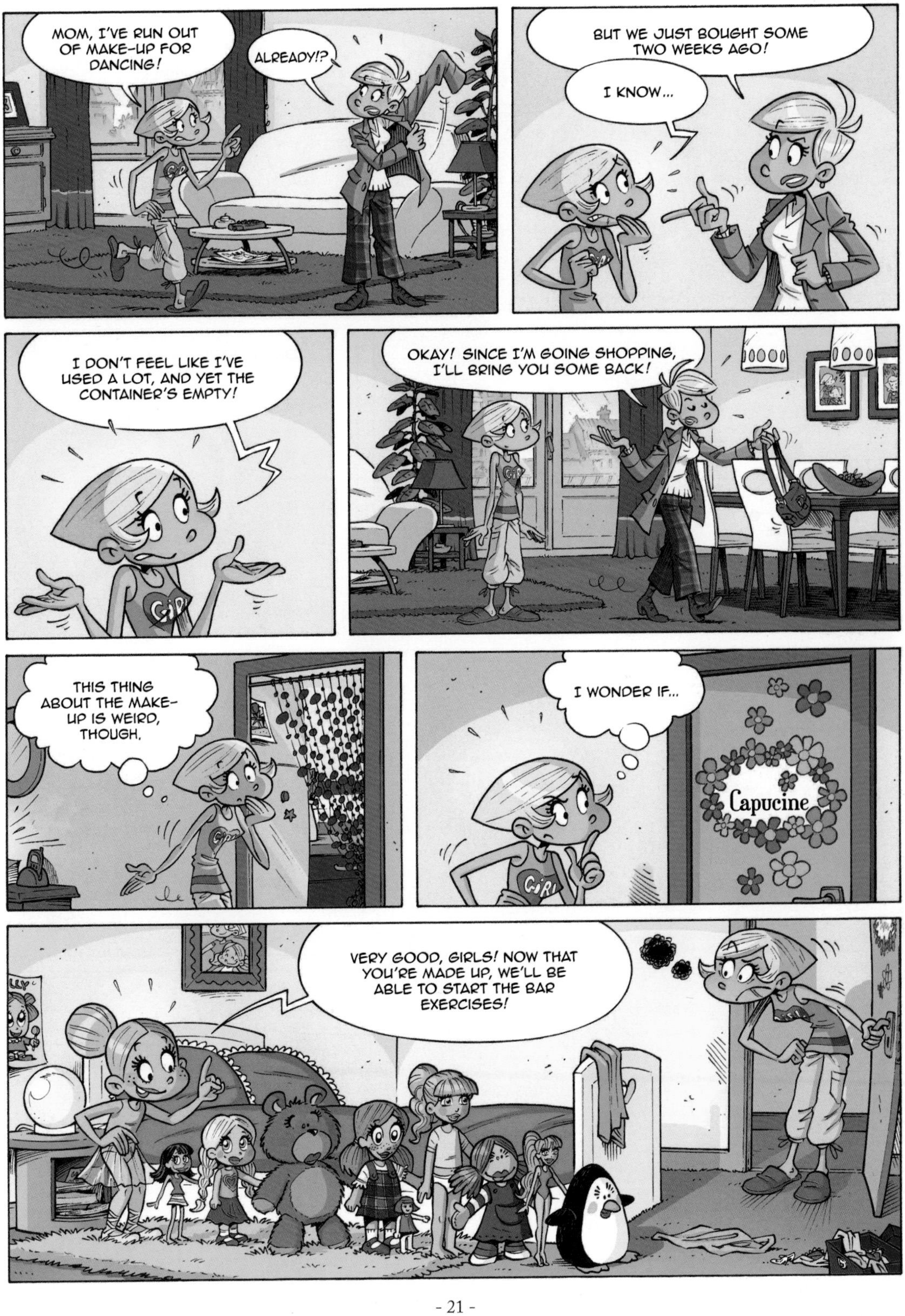
MOM, I'VE RUN OUT OF MAKE-UP FOR DANCING!
ALREADY!?
BUT WE JUST BOUGHT SOME TWO WEEKS AGO!
I KNOW...
I DON'T FEEL LIKE I'VE USED A LOT, AND YET THE CONTAINER'S EMPTY!
OKAY! SINCE I'M GOING SHOPPING, I'LL BRING YOU SOME BACK!
THIS THING ABOUT THE MAKE-UP IS WEIRD, THOUGH.
I WONDER IF...
Capucine
VERY GOOD, GIRLS! NOW THAT YOU'RE MADE UP, WE'LL BE ABLE TO START THE BAR EXERCISES!

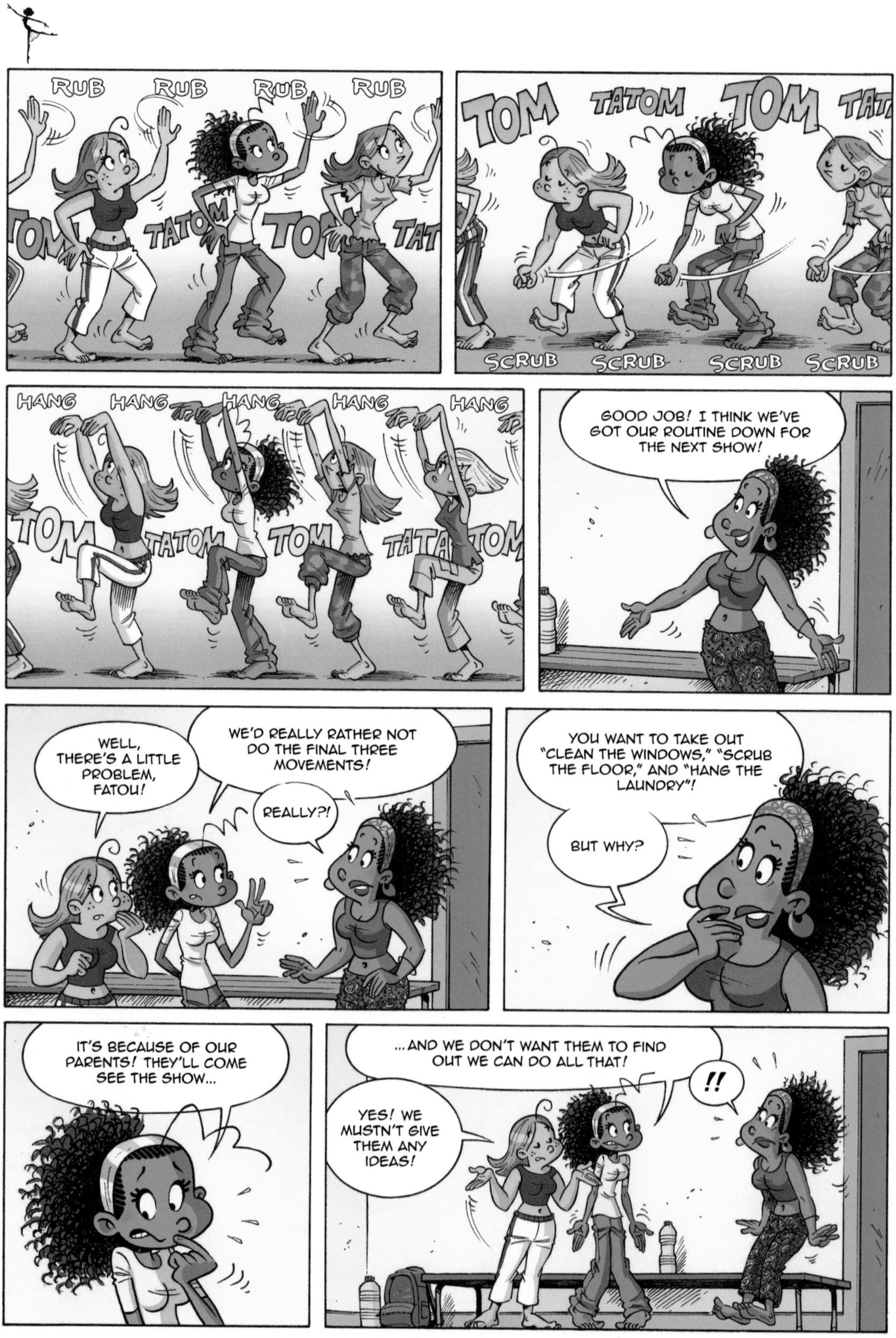
RUB RUB RUB RUB
TOM TATOM TOM TAT
TOM TATOM TOM TAT
SCRUB SCRUB SCRUB SCRUB
HANG HANG HANG HANG HANG
TOM TATOM TOM TATA TOM
GOOD JOB! I THINK WE'VE GOT OUR ROUTINE DOWN FOR THE NEXT SHOW!
WELL, THERE'S A LITTLE PROBLEM, FATOU!
WE'D REALLY RATHER NOT DO THE FINAL THREE MOVEMENTS!
REALLY?!
YOU WANT TO TAKE OUT "CLEAN THE WINDOWS," "SCRUB THE FLOOR," AND "HANG THE LAUNDRY"!
BUT WHY?
IT'S BECAUSE OF OUR PARENTS! THEY'LL COME SEE THE SHOW...
...AND WE DON'T WANT THEM TO FIND OUT WE CAN DO ALL THAT!
YES! WE MUSTN'T GIVE THEM ANY IDEAS!
!!

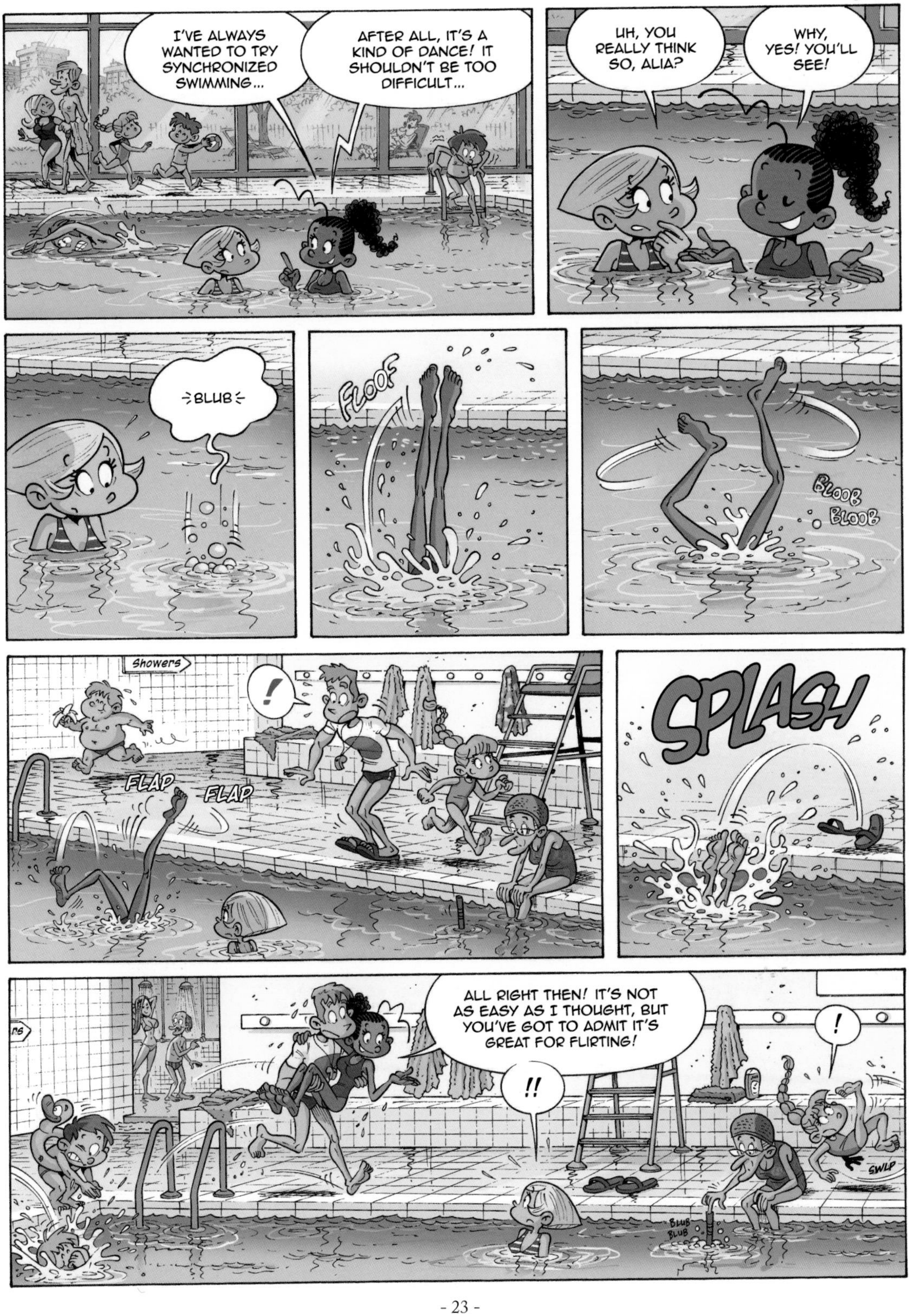

I'VE ALWAYS WANTED TO TRY SYNCHRONIZED SWIMMING...
AFTER ALL, IT'S A KIND OF DANCE! IT SHOULDN'T BE TOO DIFFICULT...
UH, YOU REALLY THINK SO, ALIA?
WHY, YES! YOU'LL SEE!
BLUB
FLOOF
BLOOB
BLOOB
Showers
!
FLAP
FLAP
SPLASH
ALL RIGHT THEN! IT'S NOT AS EASY AS I THOUGHT, BUT YOU'VE GOT TO ADMIT IT'S GREAT FOR FLIRTING!
!!
!
SWLP
BLUB
BLUB

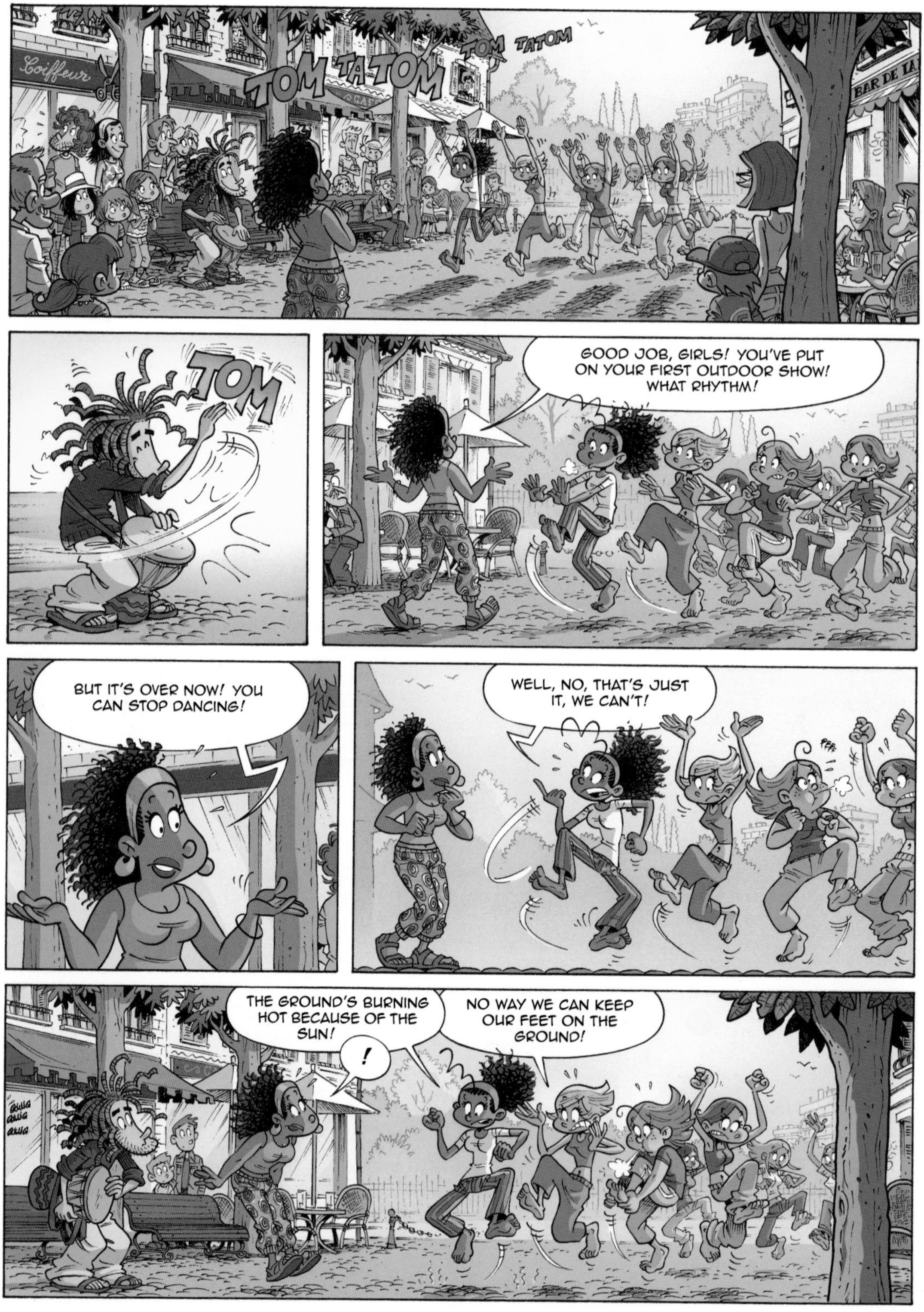
TOM TATOM
TOM TATOM
TOM
GOOD JOB, GIRLS! YOU'VE PUT ON YOUR FIRST OUTDOOR SHOW! WHAT RHYTHM!
BUT IT'S OVER NOW! YOU CAN STOP DANCING!
WELL, NO, THAT'S JUST IT, WE CAN'T!
THE GROUND'S BURNING HOT BECAUSE OF THE SUN!
!
NO WAY WE CAN KEEP OUR FEET ON THE GROUND!

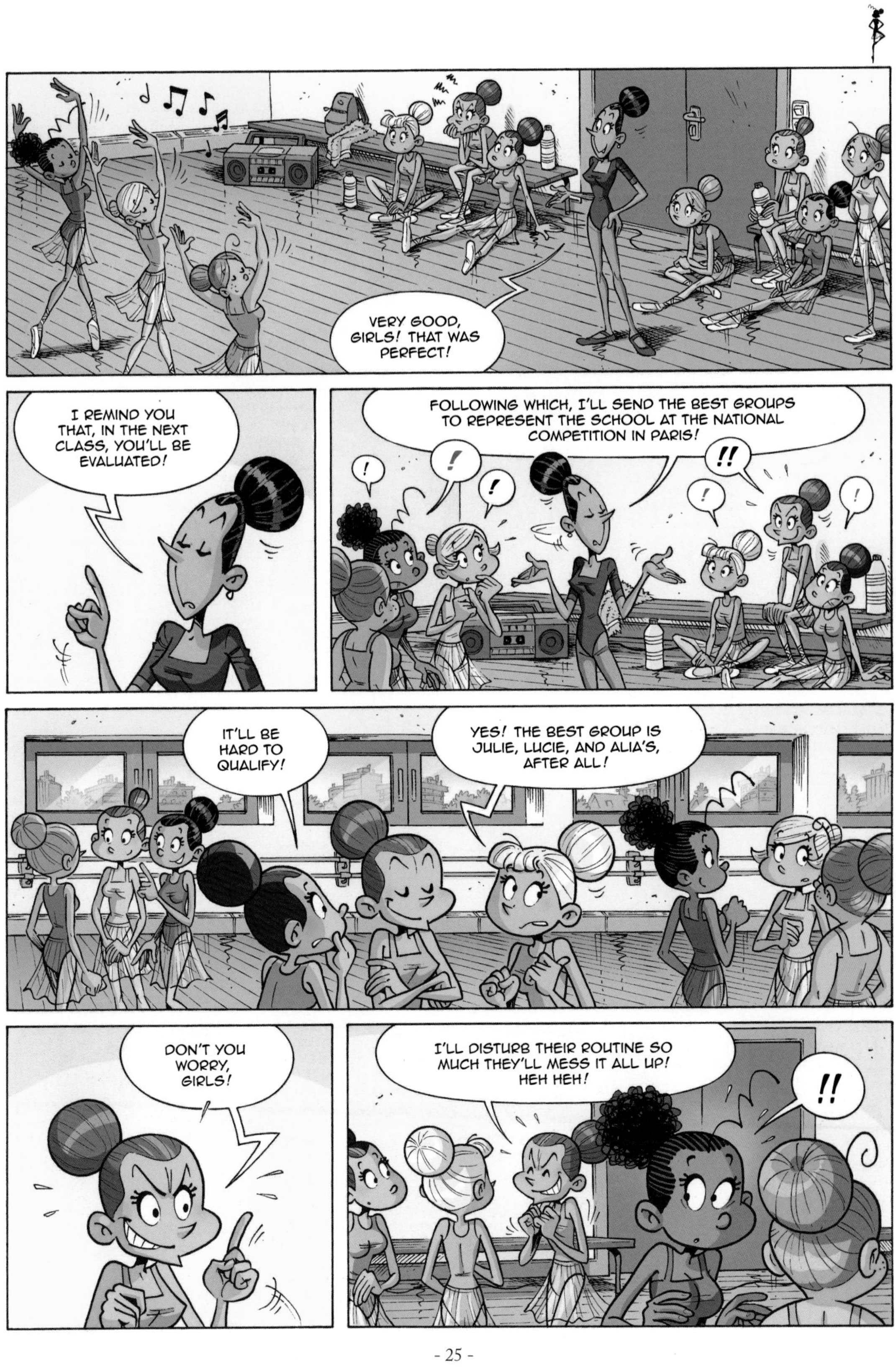
VERY GOOD, GIRLS! THAT WAS PERFECT!
I REMIND YOU THAT, IN THE NEXT CLASS, YOU'LL BE EVALUATED!
FOLLOWING WHICH, I'LL SEND THE BEST GROUPS TO REPRESENT THE SCHOOL AT THE NATIONAL COMPETITION IN PARIS!
!
!
!
!!
!
!
IT'LL BE HARD TO QUALIFY!
YES! THE BEST GROUP IS JULIE, LUCIE, AND ALIA'S, AFTER ALL!
DON'T YOU WORRY, GIRLS!
I'LL DISTURB THEIR ROUTINE SO MUCH THEY'LL MESS IT ALL UP! HEH HEH!
!!

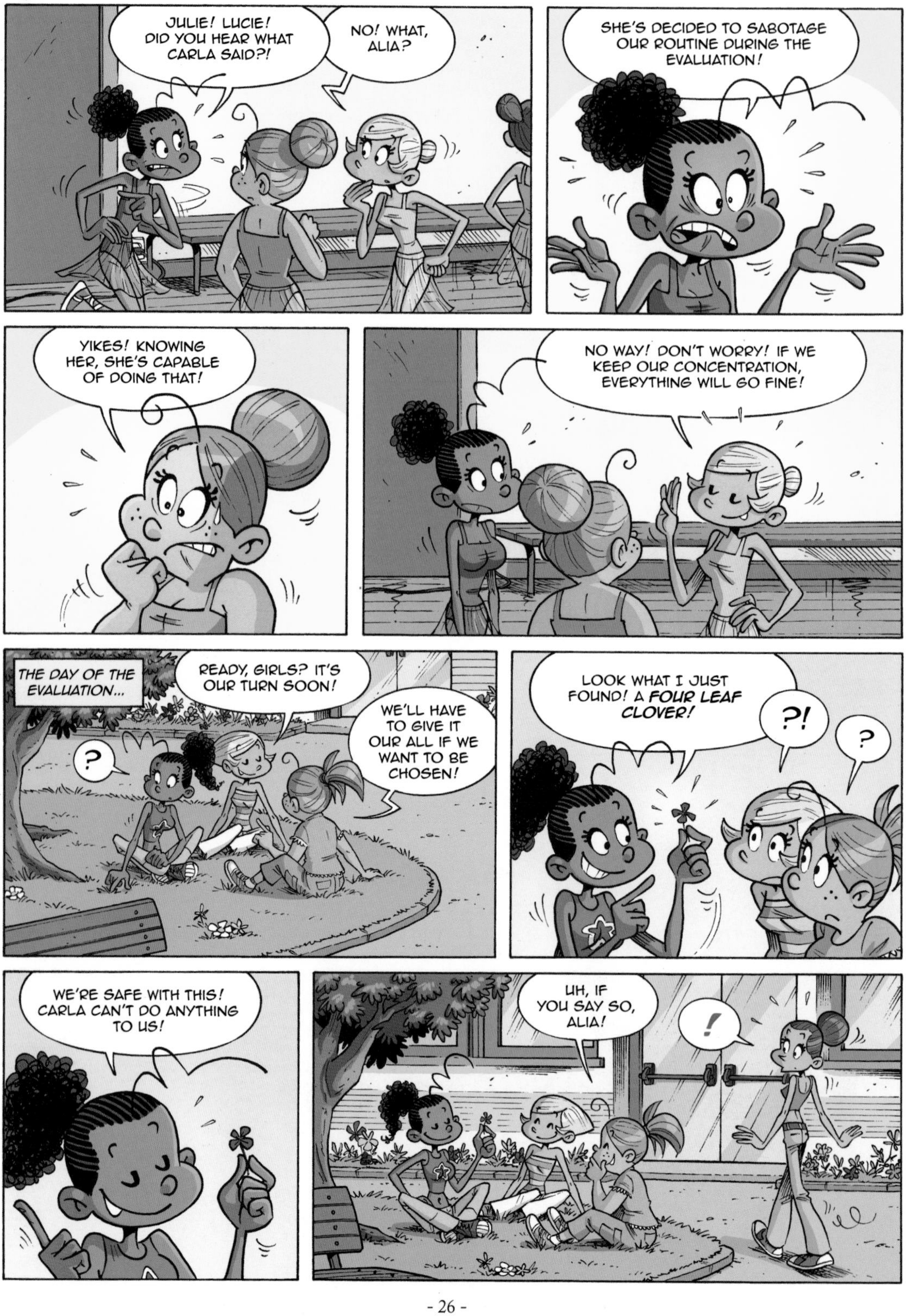
JULIE! LUCIE! DID YOU HEAR WHAT CARLA SAID?!
NO! WHAT, ALIA?
SHE'S DECIDED TO SABOTAGE OUR ROUTINE DURING THE EVALUATION!
YIKES! KNOWING HER, SHE'S CAPABLE OF DOING THAT!
NO WAY! DON'T WORRY! IF WE KEEP OUR CONCENTRATION, EVERYTHING WILL GO FINE!
THE DAY OF THE EVALUATION...
READY, GIRLS? IT'S OUR TURN SOON!
?
WE'LL HAVE TO GIVE IT OUR ALL IF WE WANT TO BE CHOSEN!
LOOK WHAT I JUST FOUND! A FOUR LEAF CLOVER!
?!
?
WE'RE SAFE WITH THIS! CARLA CAN'T DO ANYTHING TO US!
UH, IF YOU SAY SO, ALIA!
!

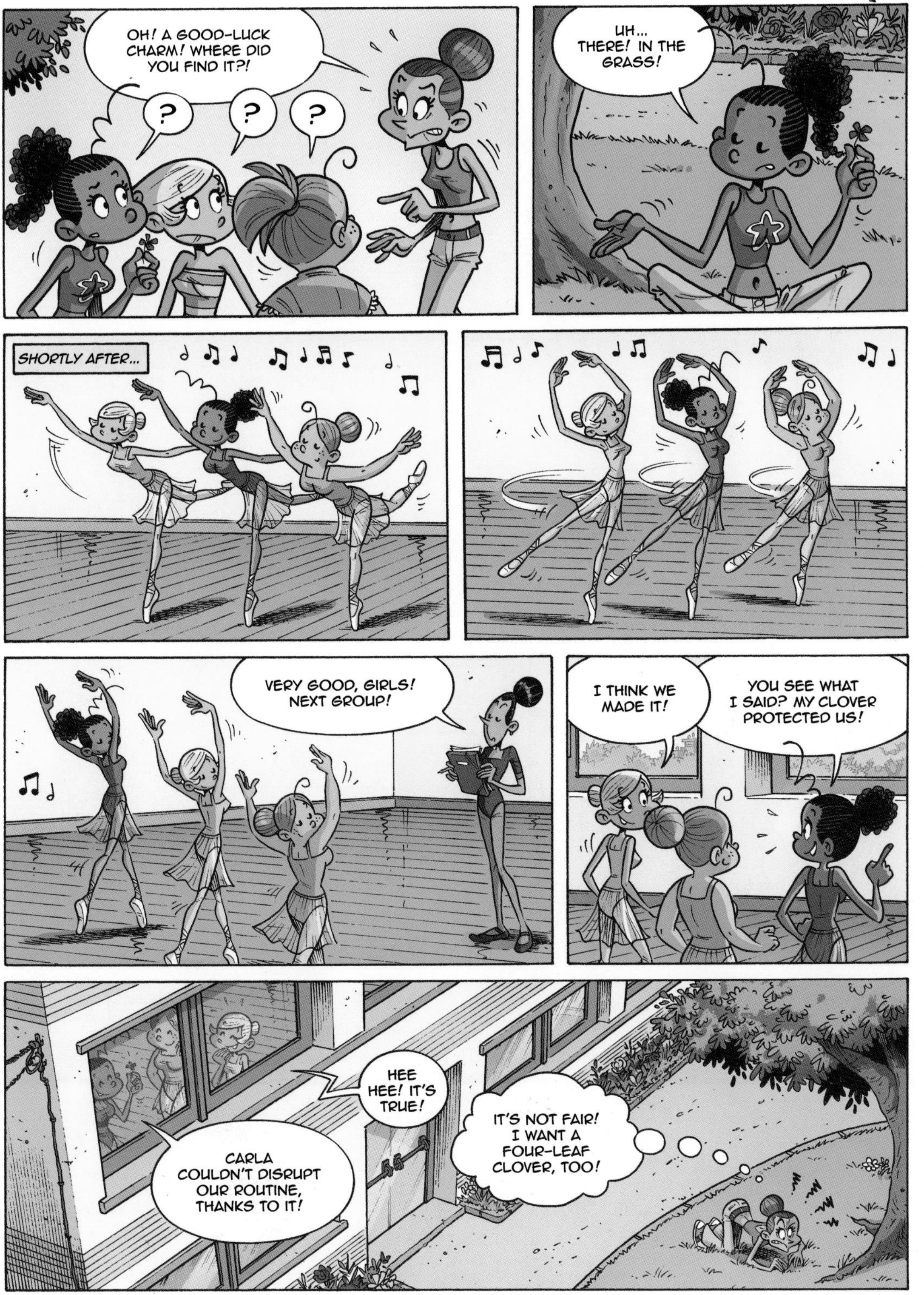
OH! A GOOD-LUCK CHARM! WHERE DID YOU FIND IT?!
?
?
?
UH... THERE! IN THE GRASS!
SHORTLY AFTER...
VERY GOOD, GIRLS! NEXT GROUP!
I THINK WE MADE IT!
YOU SEE WHAT I SAID? MY CLOVER PROTECTED US!
CARLA COULDN'T DISRUPT OUR ROUTINE, THANKS TO IT!
HEE HEE! IT'S TRUE!
IT'S NOT FAIR! I WANT A FOUR-LEAF CLOVER, TOO!

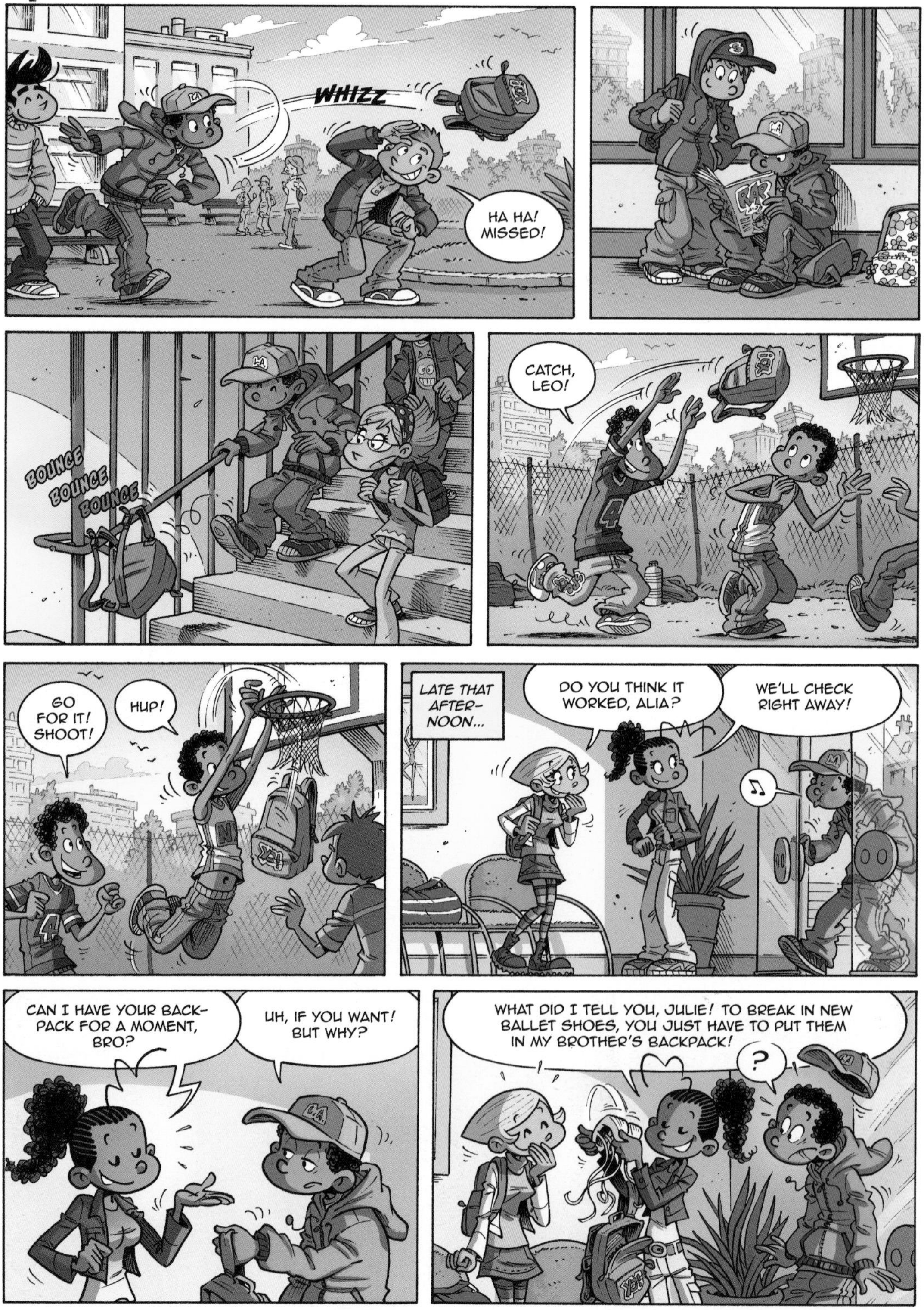
WHIZZ
HA HA! MISSED!
BOUNCE
BOUNCE
BOUNCE
CATCH, LEO!
GO FOR IT! SHOOT!
HUP!
LATE THAT AFTERNOON...
DO YOU THINK IT WORKED, ALIA?
WE'LL CHECK RIGHT AWAY!
♫
CAN I HAVE YOUR BACKPACK FOR A MOMENT, BRO?
UH, IF YOU WANT! BUT WHY?
WHAT DID I TELL YOU, JULIE! TO BREAK IN NEW BALLET SHOES, YOU JUST HAVE TO PUT THEM IN MY BROTHER'S BACKPACK!
?

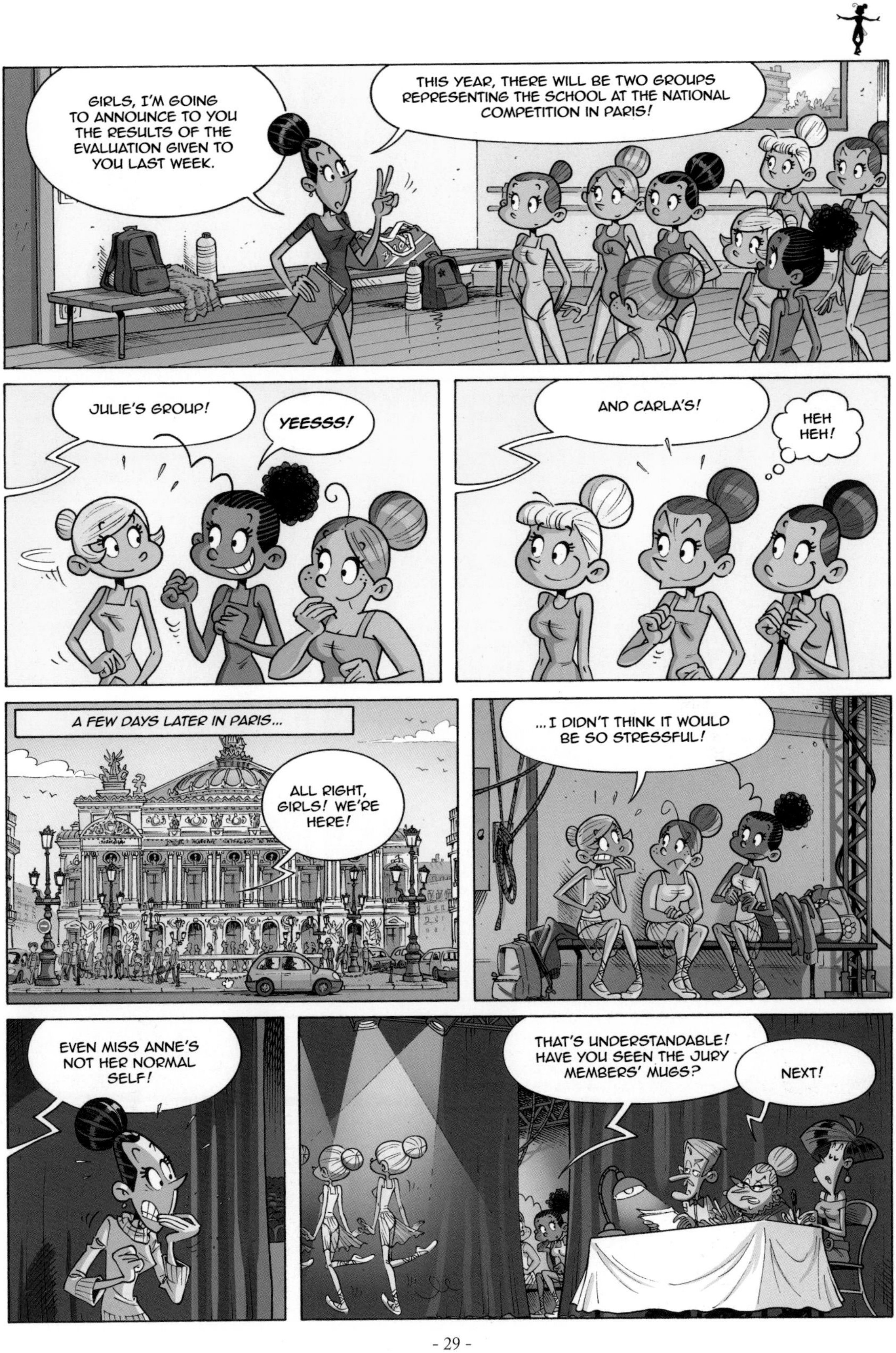
GIRLS, I'M GOING TO ANNOUNCE TO YOU THE RESULTS OF THE EVALUATION GIVEN TO YOU LAST WEEK.
THIS YEAR, THERE WILL BE TWO GROUPS REPRESENTING THE SCHOOL AT THE NATIONAL COMPETITION IN PARIS!
JULIE'S GROUP!
YEESSS!
AND CARLA'S!
HEH HEH!
A FEW DAYS LATER IN PARIS...
ALL RIGHT, GIRLS! WE'RE HERE!
...I DIDN'T THINK IT WOULD BE SO STRESSFUL!
EVEN MISS ANNE'S NOT HER NORMAL SELF!
THAT'S UNDERSTANDABLE! HAVE YOU SEEN THE JURY MEMBERS' MUGS?
NEXT!

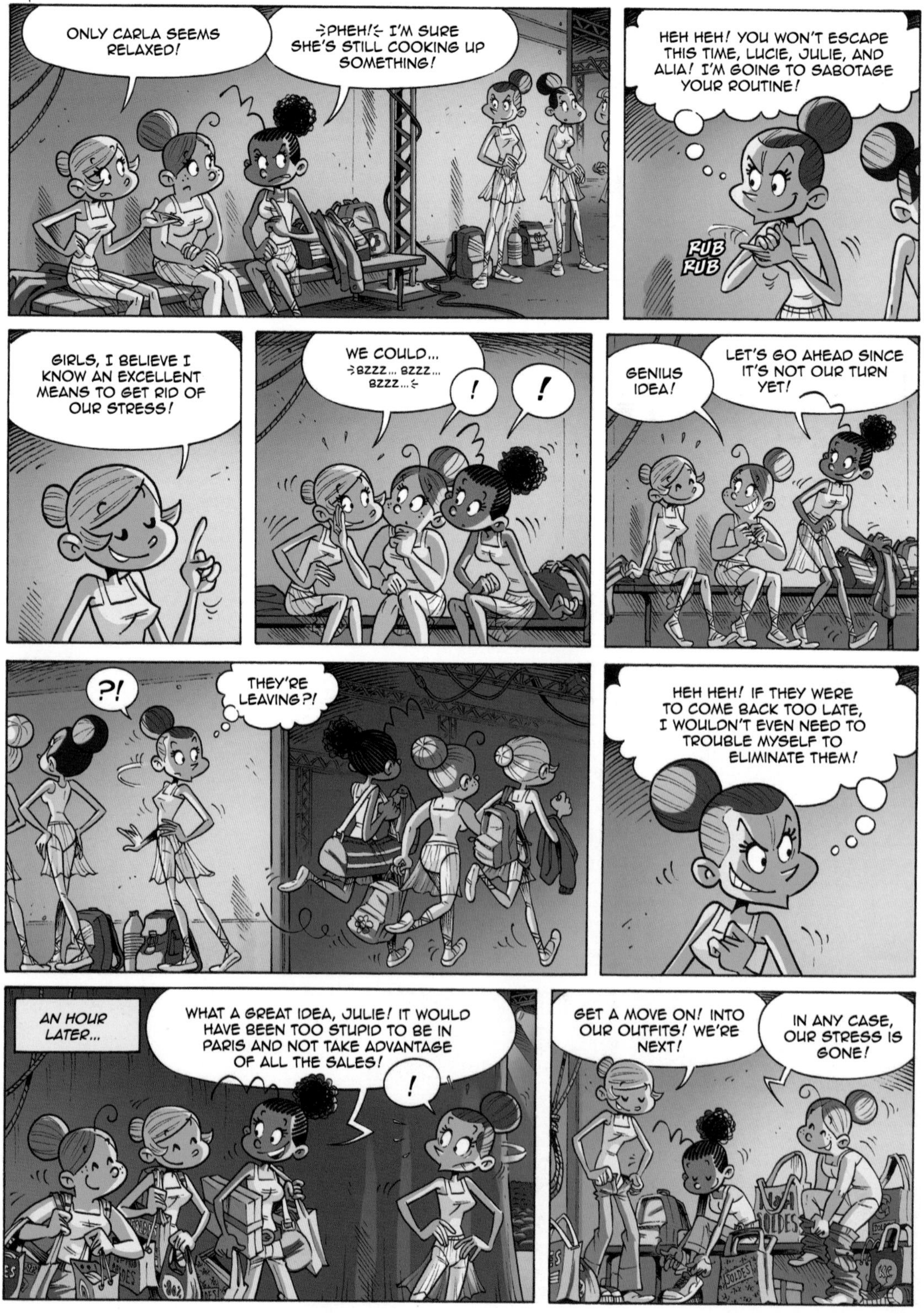
ONLY CARLA SEEMS RELAXED!
PHEH! I'M SURE SHE'S STILL COOKING UP SOMETHING!
HEH HEH! YOU WON'T ESCAPE THIS TIME, LUCIE, JULIE, AND ALIA! I'M GOING TO SABOTAGE YOUR ROUTINE!
RUB RUB
GIRLS, I BELIEVE I KNOW AN EXCELLENT MEANS TO GET RID OF OUR STRESS!
WE COULD... BZZZ... BZZZ... BZZZ...
!
!
GENIUS IDEA!
LET'S GO AHEAD SINCE IT'S NOT OUR TURN YET!
?!
THEY'RE LEAVING?!
HEH HEH! IF THEY WERE TO COME BACK TOO LATE, I WOULDN'T EVEN NEED TO TROUBLE MYSELF TO ELIMINATE THEM!
AN HOUR LATER...
WHAT A GREAT IDEA, JULIE! IT WOULD HAVE BEEN TOO STUPID TO BE IN PARIS AND NOT TAKE ADVANTAGE OF ALL THE SALES!
!
GET A MOVE ON! INTO OUR OUTFITS! WE'RE NEXT!
IN ANY CASE, OUR STRESS IS GONE!

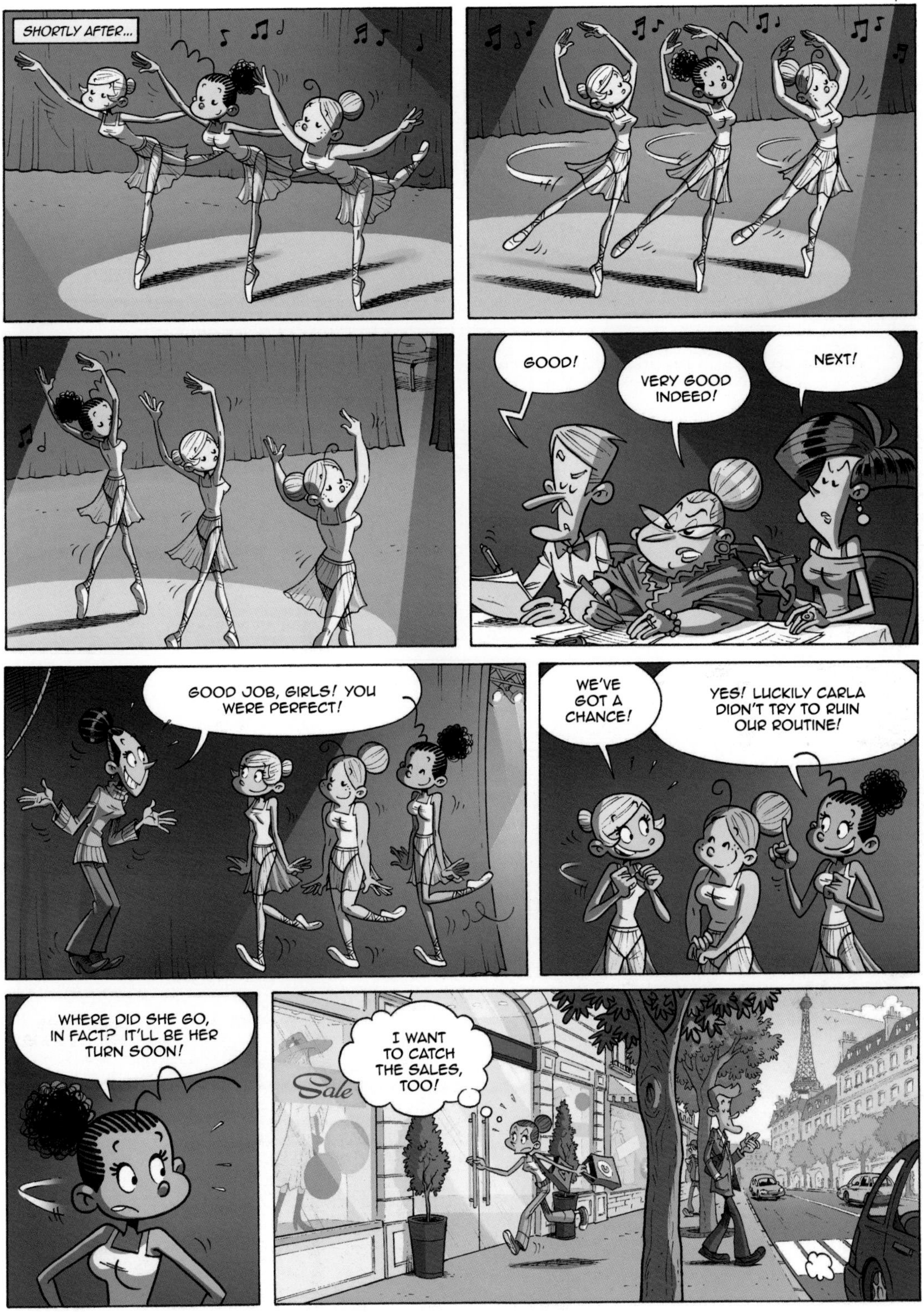

SHORTLY AFTER...
GOOD!
VERY GOOD INDEED!
NEXT!
GOOD JOB, GIRLS! YOU WERE PERFECT!
WE'VE GOT A CHANCE!
YES! LUCKILY CARLA DIDN'T TRY TO RUIN OUR ROUTINE!
WHERE DID SHE GO, IN FACT? IT'LL BE HER TURN SOON!
I WANT TO CATCH THE SALES, TOO!
Sale

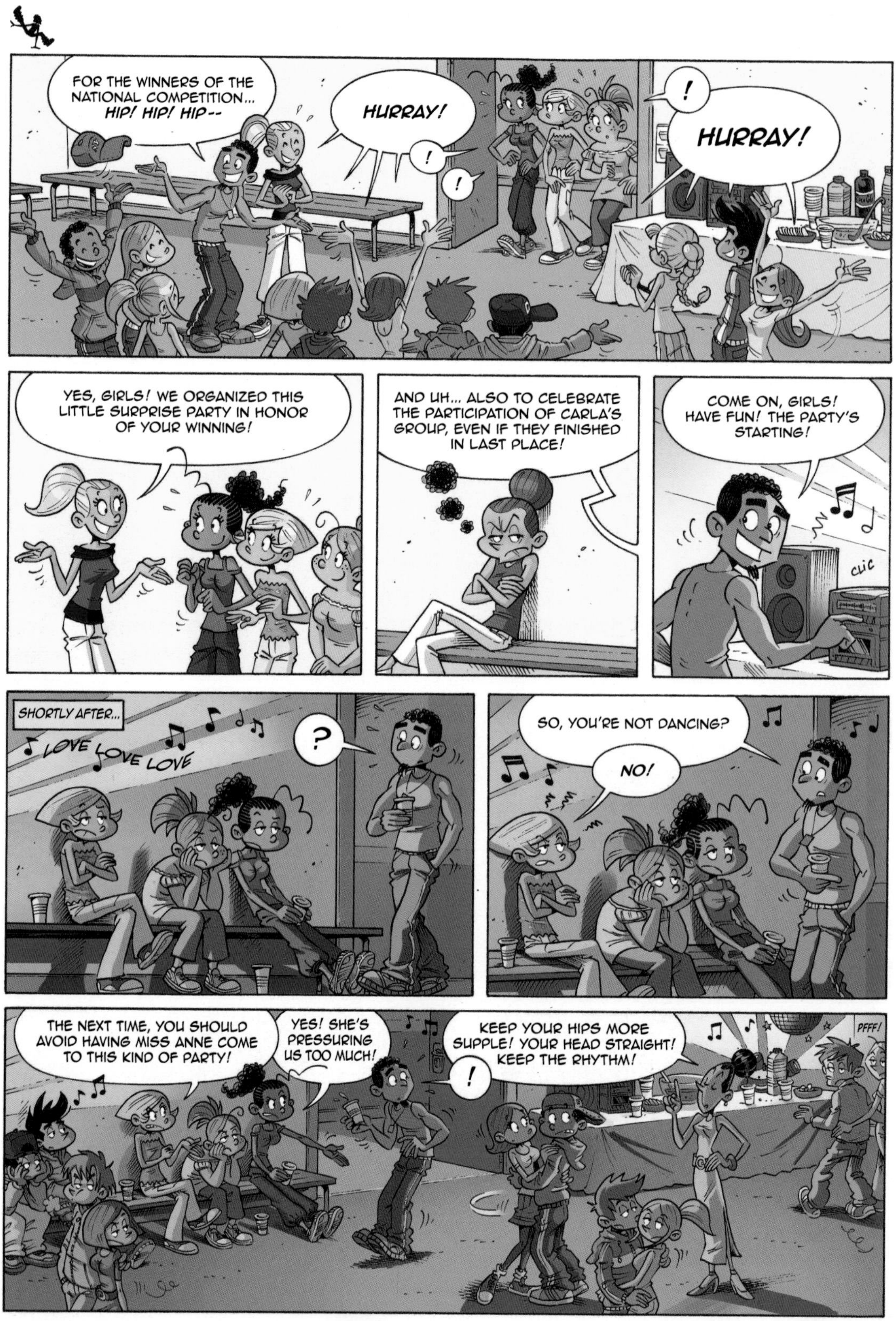
FOR THE WINNERS OF THE NATIONAL COMPETITION... HIP! HIP! HIP--
HURRAY!
!
!
!
HURRAY!
YES, GIRLS! WE ORGANIZED THIS LITTLE SURPRISE PARTY IN HONOR OF YOUR WINNING!
AND UH... ALSO TO CELEBRATE THE PARTICIPATION OF CARLA'S GROUP, EVEN IF THEY FINISHED IN LAST PLACE!
COME ON, GIRLS! HAVE FUN! THE PARTY'S STARTING!
CLIC
SHORTLY AFTER...
LOVE LOVE LOVE
?
SO, YOU'RE NOT DANCING?
NO!
THE NEXT TIME, YOU SHOULD AVOID HAVING MISS ANNE COME TO THIS KIND OF PARTY!
YES! SHE'S PRESSURING US TOO MUCH!
KEEP YOUR HIPS MORE SUPPLE! YOUR HEAD STRAIGHT! KEEP THE RHYTHM!
!
PFFF!

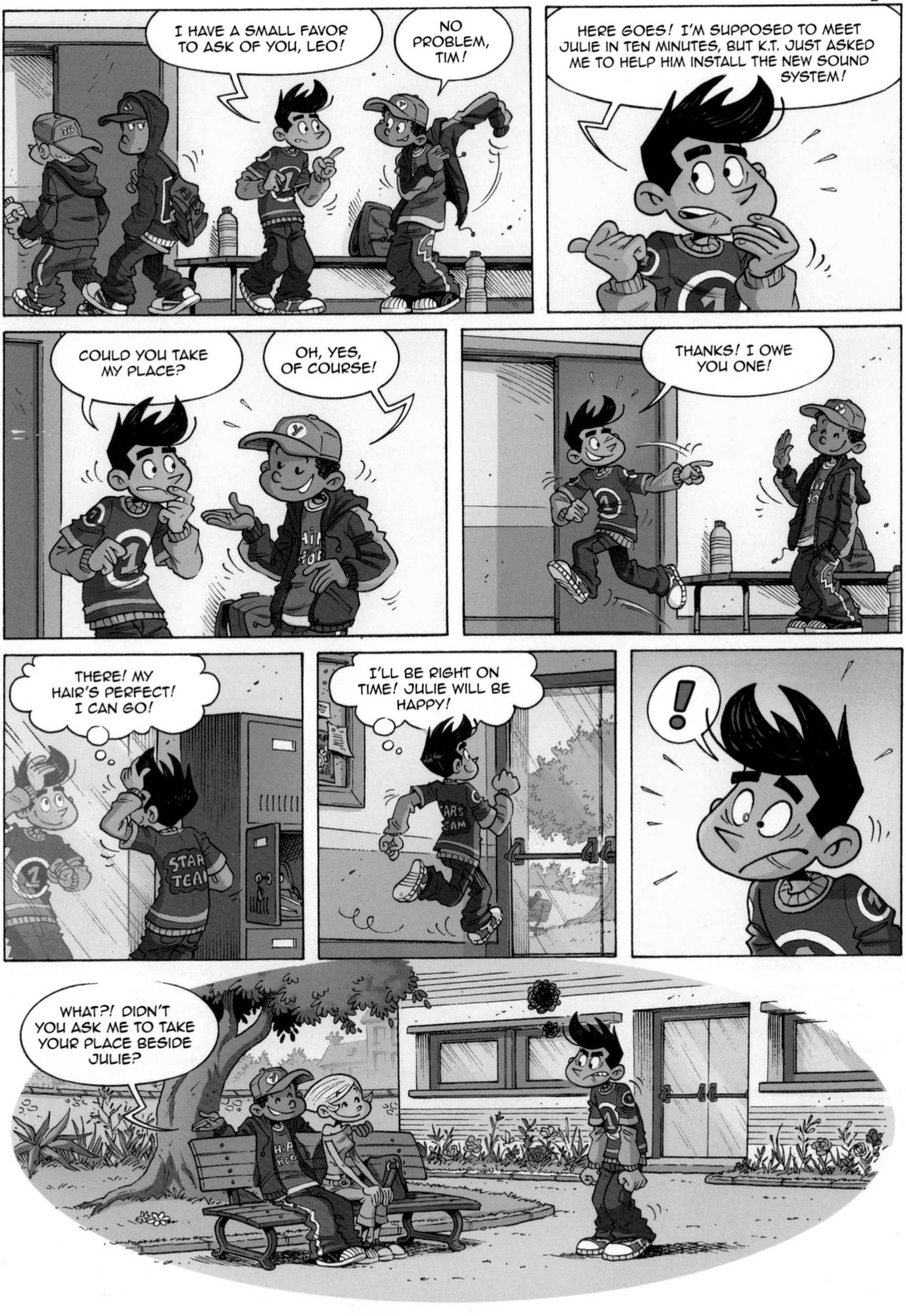
I HAVE A SMALL FAVOR TO ASK OF YOU, LEO!
NO PROBLEM, TIM!
HERE GOES! I'M SUPPOSED TO MEET JULIE IN TEN MINUTES, BUT K.T. JUST ASKED ME TO HELP HIM INSTALL THE NEW SOUND SYSTEM!
COULD YOU TAKE MY PLACE?
OH, YES, OF COURSE!
THANKS! I OWE YOU ONE!
THERE! MY HAIR'S PERFECT! I CAN GO!
I'LL BE RIGHT ON TIME! JULIE WILL BE HAPPY!
!
WHAT?! DIDN'T YOU ASK ME TO TAKE YOUR PLACE BESIDE JULIE?

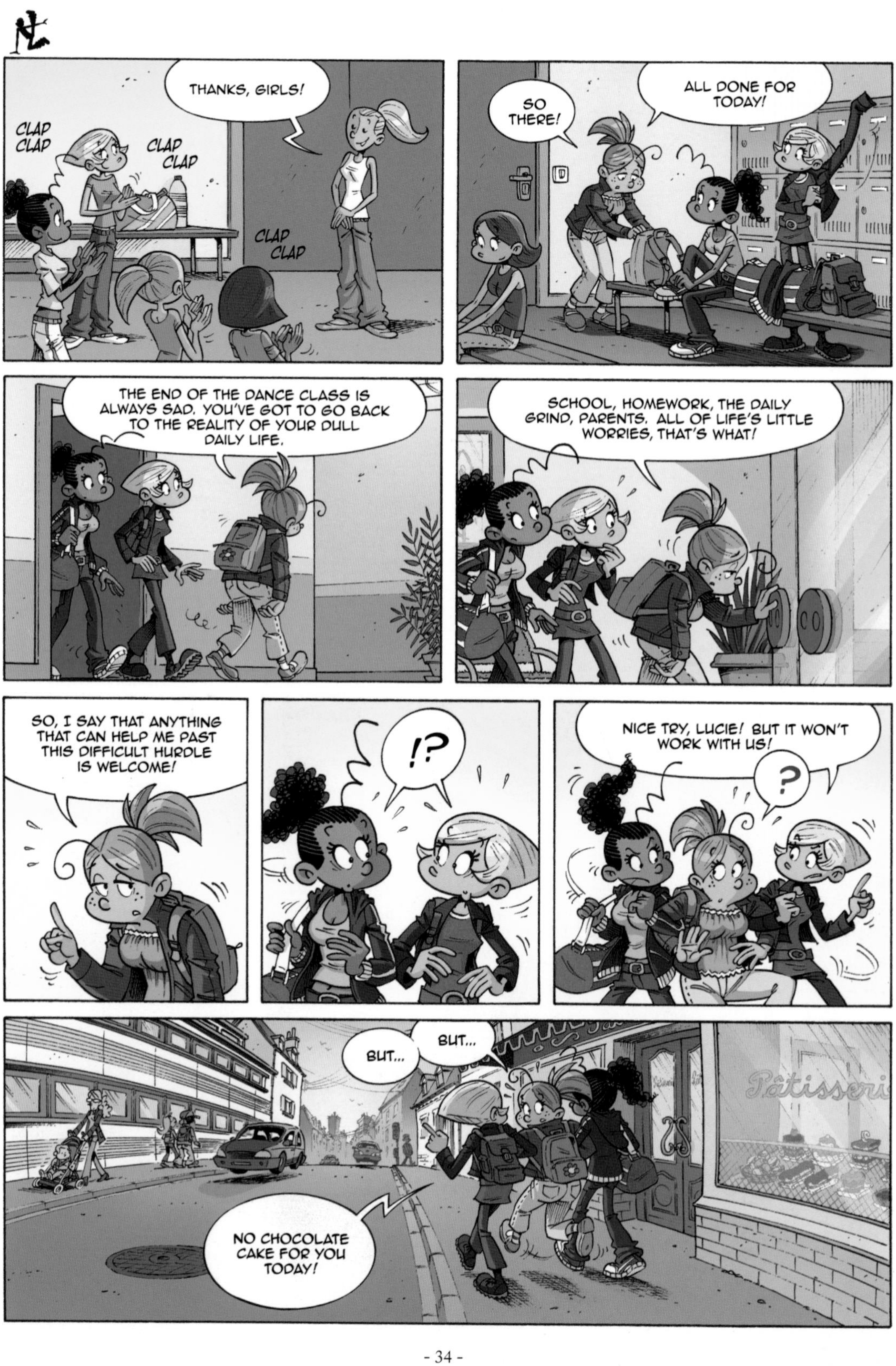
CLAP CLAP
CLAP CLAP
CLAP CLAP
THANKS, GIRLS!
SO THERE!
ALL DONE FOR TODAY!
THE END OF THE DANCE CLASS IS ALWAYS SAD. YOU'VE GOT TO GO BACK TO THE REALITY OF YOUR DULL DAILY LIFE.
SCHOOL, HOMEWORK, THE DAILY GRIND, PARENTS. ALL OF LIFE'S LITTLE WORRIES, THAT'S WHAT!
SO, I SAY THAT ANYTHING THAT CAN HELP ME PAST THIS DIFFICULT HURDLE IS WELCOME!
!?
NICE TRY, LUCIE! BUT IT WON'T WORK WITH US!
?
BUT...
BUT...
NO CHOCOLATE CAKE FOR YOU TODAY!
Pâtisserie

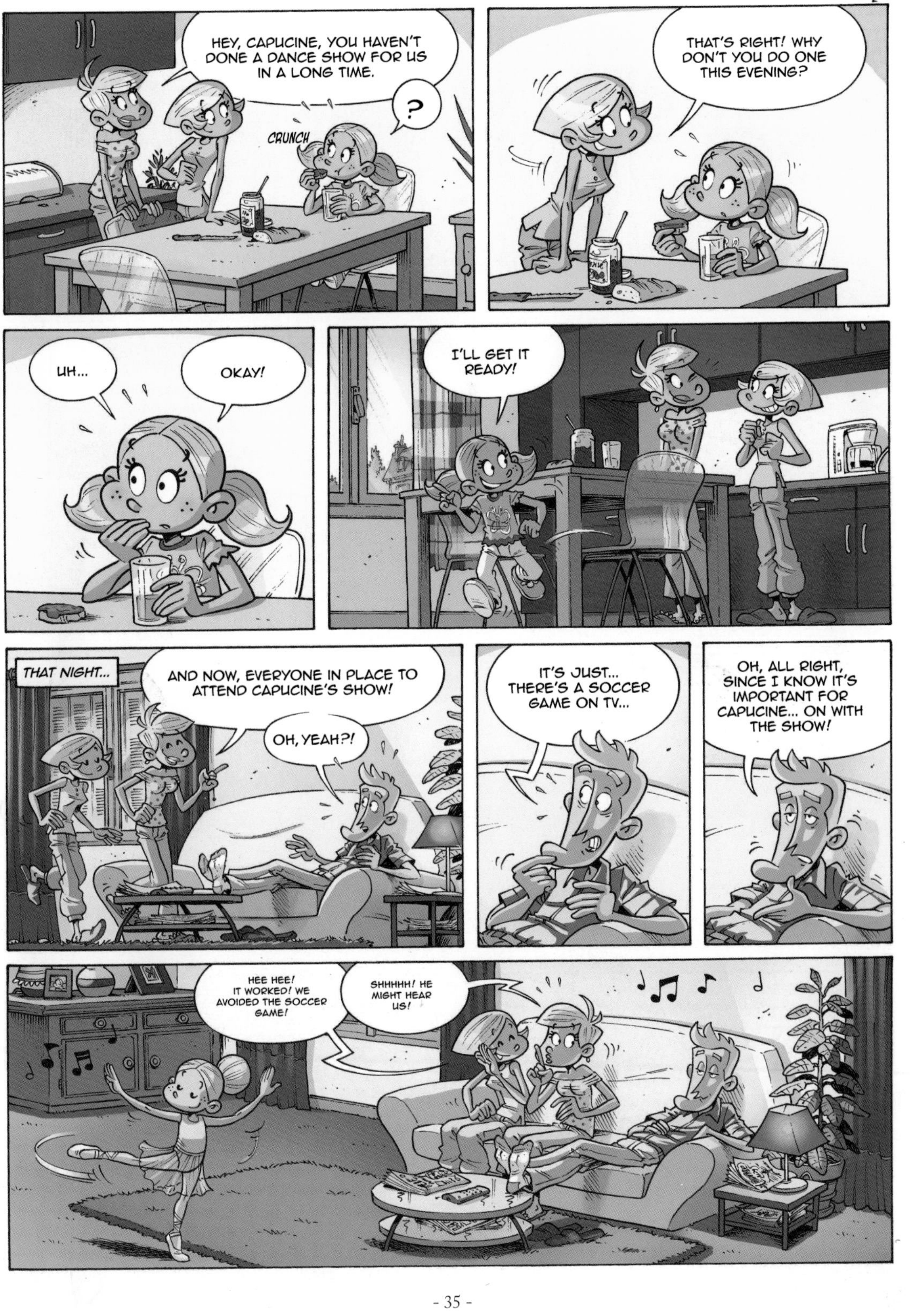
HEY, CAPUCINE, YOU HAVEN'T DONE A DANCE SHOW FOR US IN A LONG TIME.
?
CRUNCH
THAT'S RIGHT! WHY DON'T YOU DO ONE THIS EVENING?
UH...
OKAY!
I'LL GET IT READY!
THAT NIGHT...
AND NOW, EVERYONE IN PLACE TO ATTEND CAPUCINE'S SHOW!
OH, YEAH?!
IT'S JUST... THERE'S A SOCCER GAME ON TV...
OH, ALL RIGHT, SINCE I KNOW IT'S IMPORTANT FOR CAPUCINE... ON WITH THE SHOW!
HEE HEE! IT WORKED! WE AVOIDED THE SOCCER GAME!
SHHHHH! HE MIGHT HEAR US!

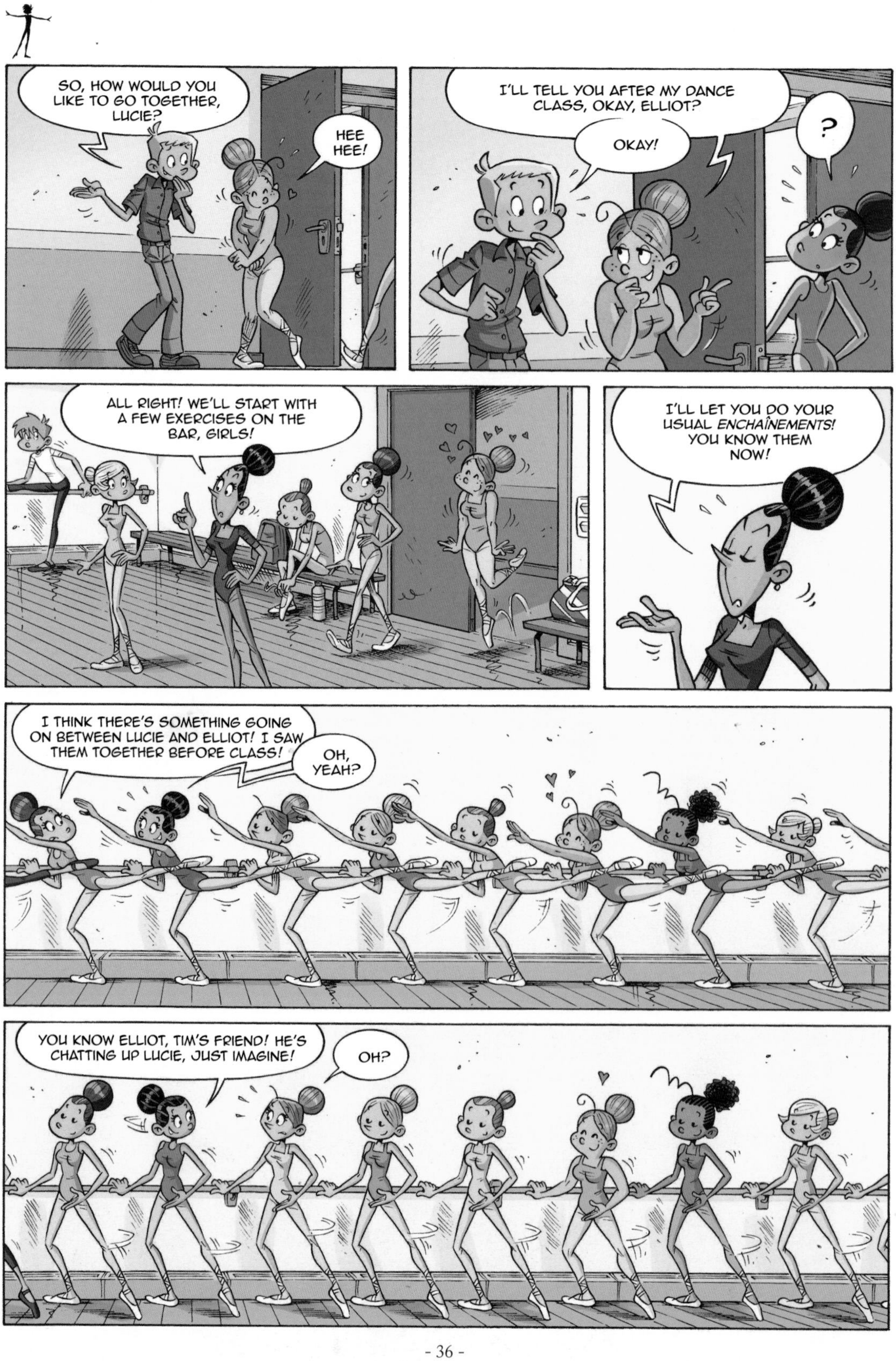
SO, HOW WOULD YOU LIKE TO GO TOGETHER, LUCIE?
HEE HEE!
I'LL TELL YOU AFTER MY DANCE CLASS, OKAY, ELLIOT?
OKAY!
?
ALL RIGHT! WE'LL START WITH A FEW EXERCISES ON THE BAR, GIRLS!
I'LL LET YOU DO YOUR USUAL *ENCHAÎNEMENTS!* YOU KNOW THEM NOW!
I THINK THERE'S SOMETHING GOING ON BETWEEN LUCIE AND ELLIOT! I SAW THEM TOGETHER BEFORE CLASS!
OH, YEAH?
YOU KNOW ELLIOT, TIM'S FRIEND! HE'S CHATTING UP LUCIE, JUST IMAGINE!
OH?

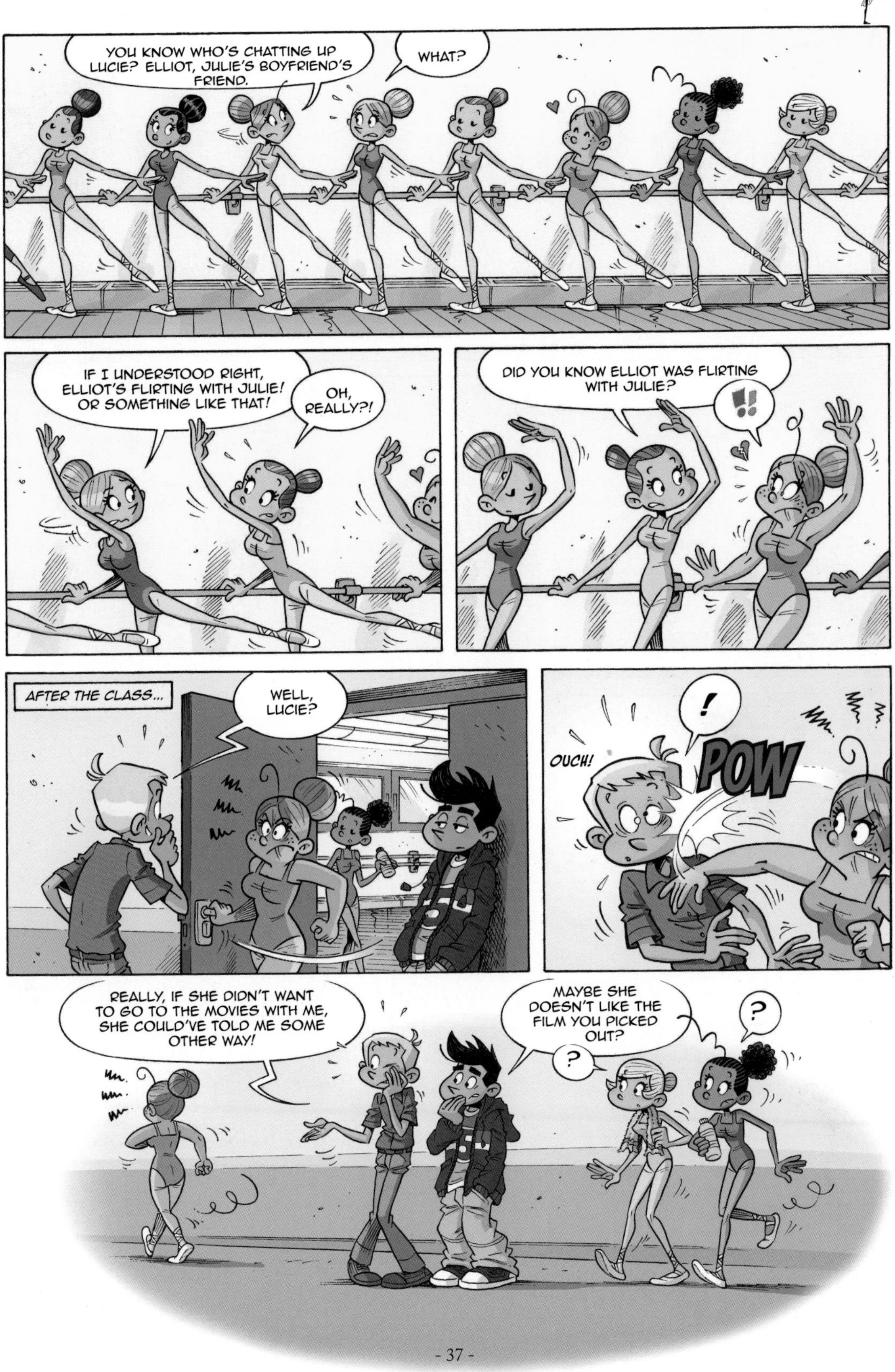

YOU KNOW WHO'S CHATTING UP LUCIE? ELLIOT, JULIE'S BOYFRIEND'S FRIEND.
WHAT?
IF I UNDERSTOOD RIGHT, ELLIOT'S FLIRTING WITH JULIE! OR SOMETHING LIKE THAT!
OH, REALLY?!
DID YOU KNOW ELLIOT WAS FLIRTING WITH JULIE?
!!
AFTER THE CLASS...
WELL, LUCIE?
OUCH!
!
POW
REALLY, IF SHE DIDN'T WANT TO GO TO THE MOVIES WITH ME, SHE COULD'VE TOLD ME SOME OTHER WAY!
MAYBE SHE DOESN'T LIKE THE FILM YOU PICKED OUT?
?
?

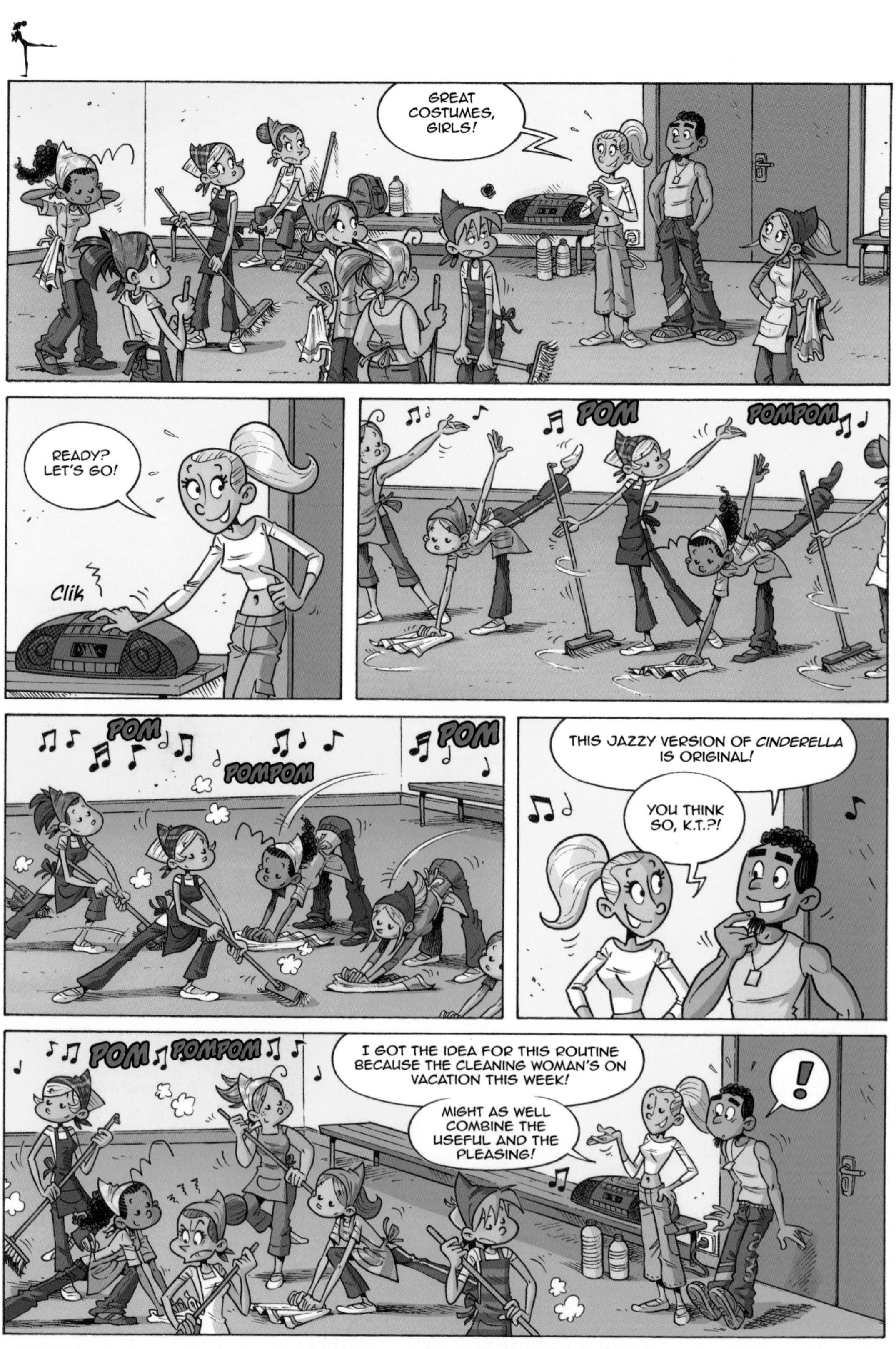
GREAT COSTUMES, GIRLS!
READY? LET'S GO!
Clik
POM
POMPOM
POM
POMPOM
POM
THIS JAZZY VERSION OF *CINDERELLA* IS ORIGINAL!
YOU THINK SO, K.T.?!
POM
POMPOM
I GOT THE IDEA FOR THIS ROUTINE BECAUSE THE CLEANING WOMAN'S ON VACATION THIS WEEK!
MIGHT AS WELL COMBINE THE USEFUL AND THE PLEASING!
!

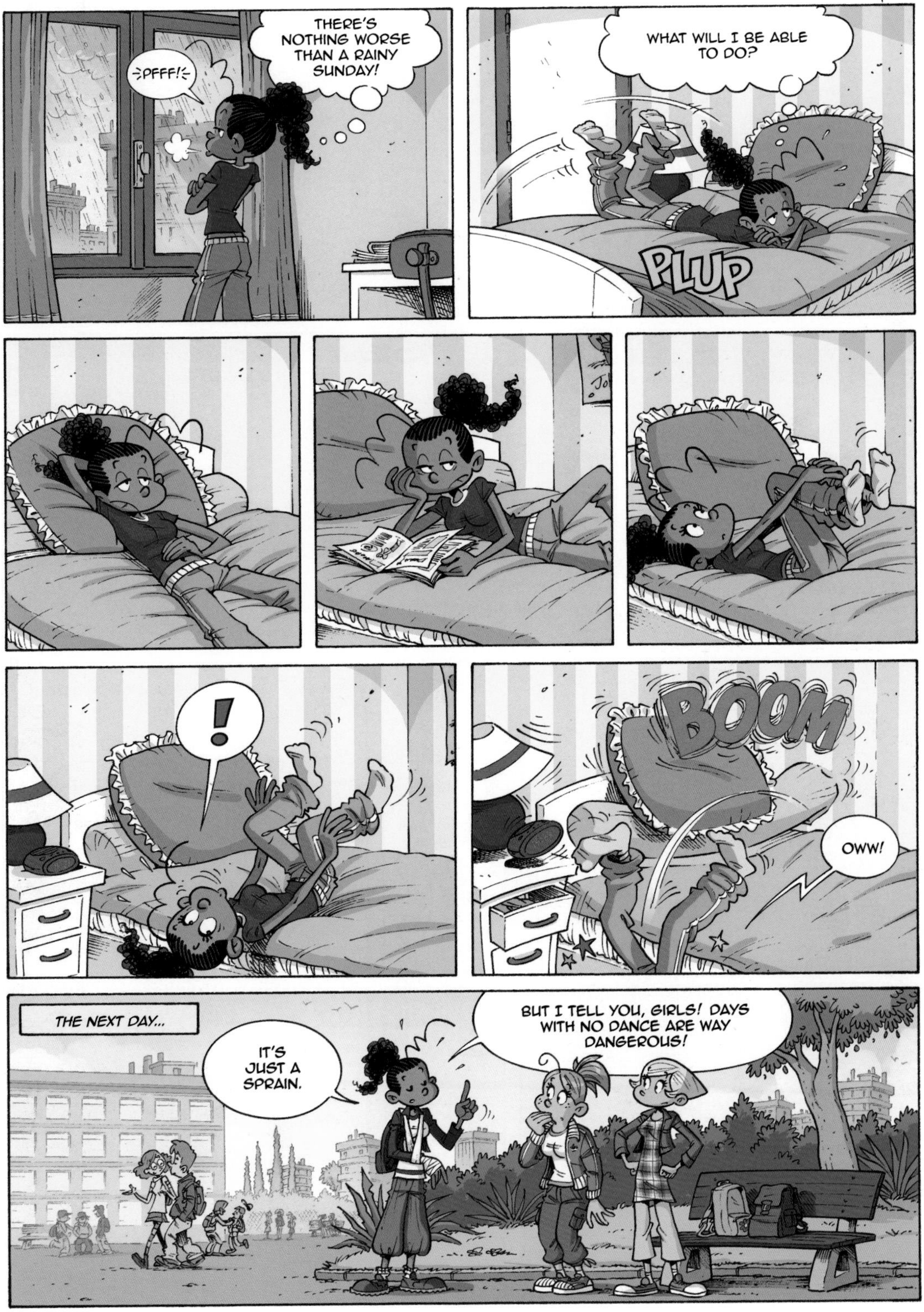
PFFF!
THERE'S NOTHING WORSE THAN A RAINY SUNDAY!
WHAT WILL I BE ABLE TO DO?
PLUP
!
BOOM
OWW!
THE NEXT DAY...
IT'S JUST A SPRAIN.
BUT I TELL YOU, GIRLS! DAYS WITH NO DANCE ARE WAY DANGEROUS!

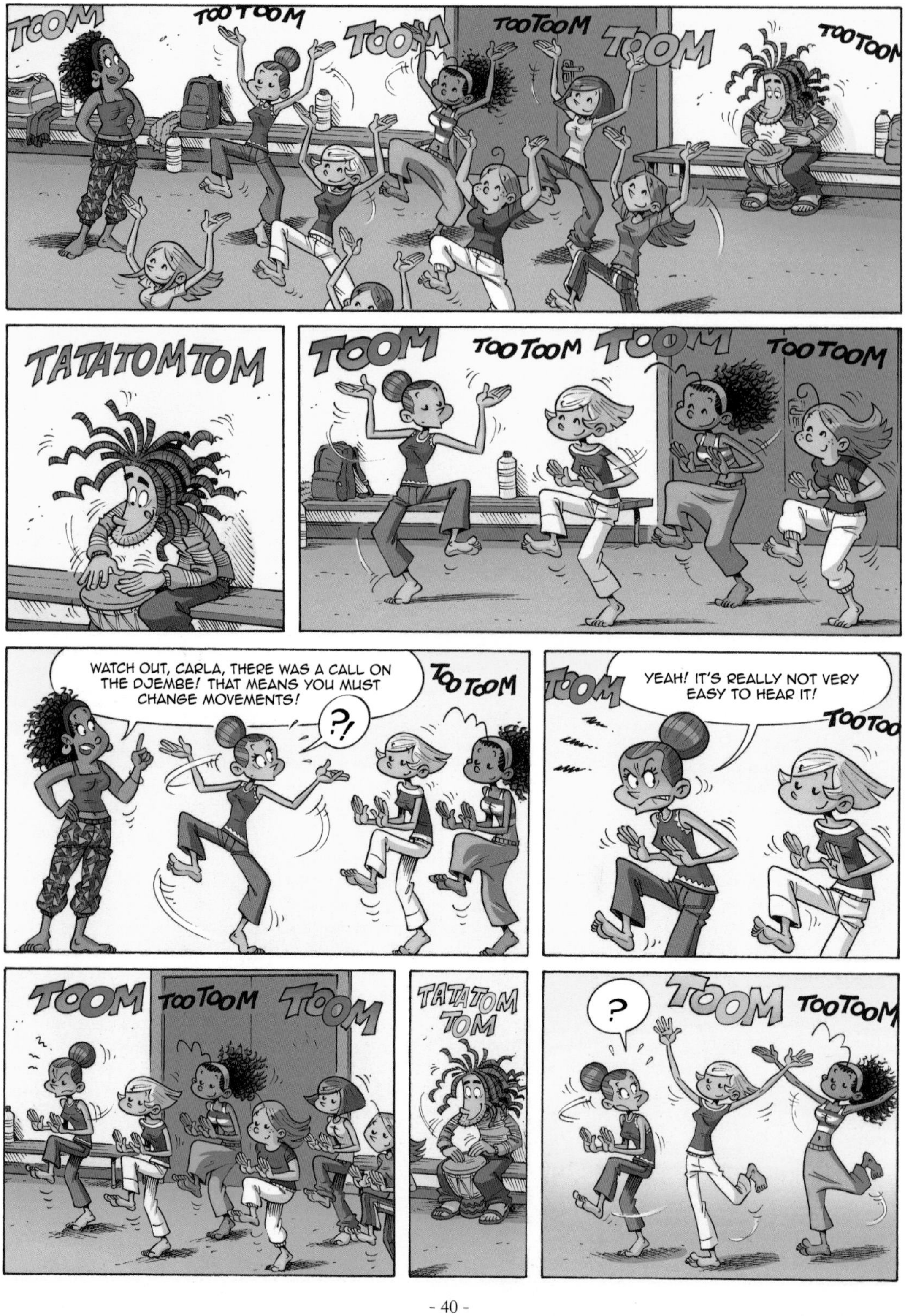
TOOM
TOOTOOM
TOOM
TOOTOOM
TOOM
TOOTOOM
TATATOMTOM
TOOM
TOOTOOM
TOOM
TOOTOOM
WATCH OUT, CARLA, THERE WAS A CALL ON THE DJEMBE! THAT MEANS YOU MUST CHANGE MOVEMENTS!
?!
TOOTOOM
YEAH! IT'S REALLY NOT VERY EASY TO HEAR IT!
TOOM
TOOM
TOOTOOM
TOOM
TATATOM TOM
?
TOOM
TOOTOOM

TOOM
TOOTOOM
TOO

YES! I KNOW, FATOU! I MISSED THE CALL AGAIN!

TRY TO BE MORE ATTENTIVE SO YOU CAN REACT TO WHAT YOU HEAR!

TOOM
TOOTOOM
TOOM

TOOTOOM
TELEELOOLEELOO
TOOM

!

?
TOOM
TOOTOOM
ZOOM

WHY IS CARLA CHANGING MOVEMENTS? THERE WASN'T ANY CALL!

YES! THERE WAS ONE!

ON HER CELLPHONE! SHE NEVER TURNS IT OFF DURING CLASSES!

!

AND SHE CAN HEAR THOSE KIND OF CALLS COME WHAT MAY!

?

HELLO-O-O...

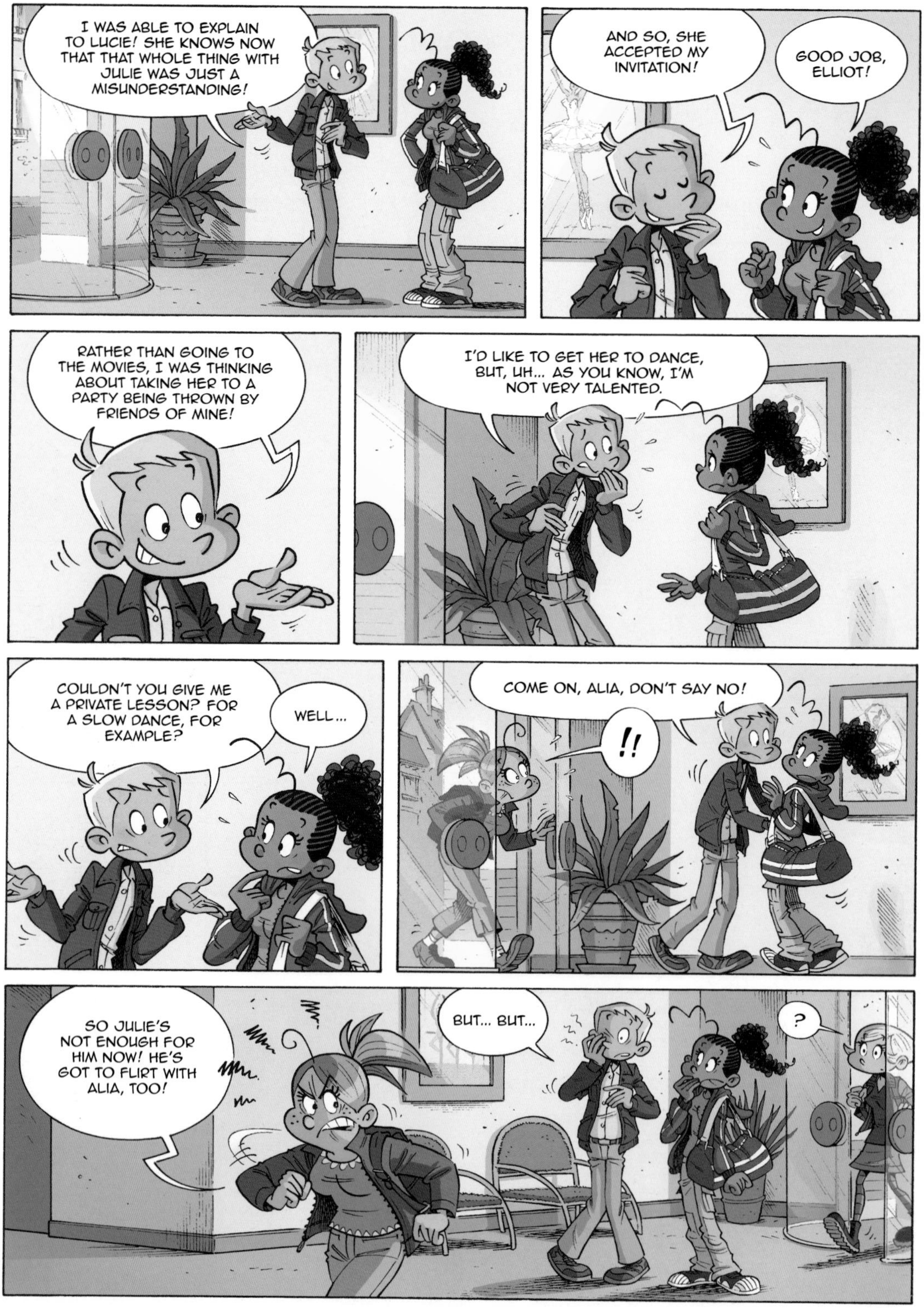
I WAS ABLE TO EXPLAIN TO LUCIE! SHE KNOWS NOW THAT THAT WHOLE THING WITH JULIE WAS JUST A MISUNDERSTANDING!
AND SO, SHE ACCEPTED MY INVITATION!
GOOD JOB, ELLIOT!
RATHER THAN GOING TO THE MOVIES, I WAS THINKING ABOUT TAKING HER TO A PARTY BEING THROWN BY FRIENDS OF MINE!
I'D LIKE TO GET HER TO DANCE, BUT, UH... AS YOU KNOW, I'M NOT VERY TALENTED.
COULDN'T YOU GIVE ME A PRIVATE LESSON? FOR A SLOW DANCE, FOR EXAMPLE?
WELL...
COME ON, ALIA, DON'T SAY NO!
!!
SO JULIE'S NOT ENOUGH FOR HIM NOW! HE'S GOT TO FLIRT WITH ALIA, TOO!
BUT... BUT...
?

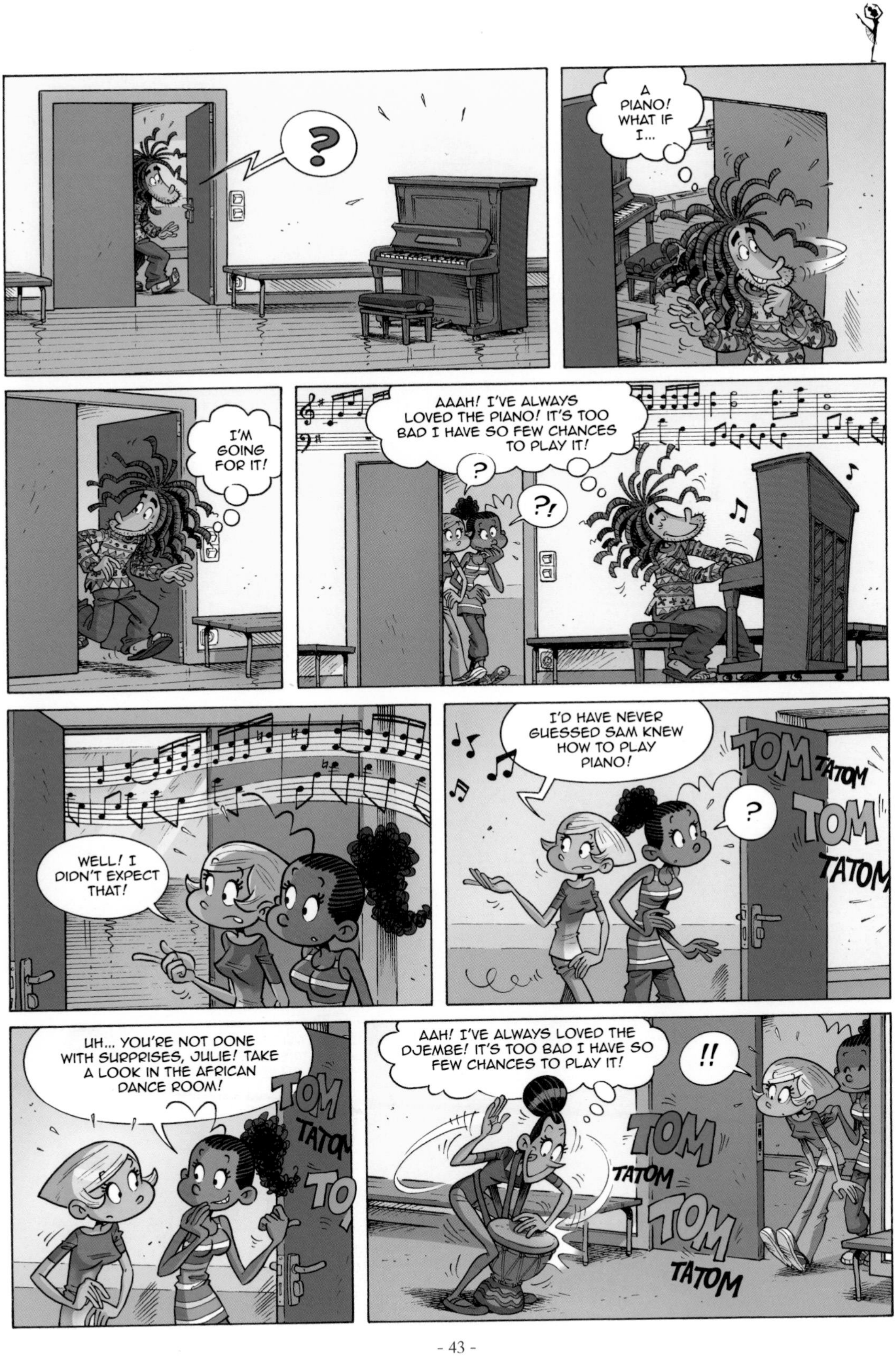
?
A PIANO! WHAT IF I...
I'M GOING FOR IT!
AAAH! I'VE ALWAYS LOVED THE PIANO! IT'S TOO BAD I HAVE SO FEW CHANCES TO PLAY IT!
?
?!
WELL! I DIDN'T EXPECT THAT!
I'D HAVE NEVER GUESSED SAM KNEW HOW TO PLAY PIANO!
?
TOM TATOM TOM TATOM
UH... YOU'RE NOT DONE WITH SURPRISES, JULIE! TAKE A LOOK IN THE AFRICAN DANCE ROOM!
AAH! I'VE ALWAYS LOVED THE DJEMBE! IT'S TOO BAD I HAVE SO FEW CHANCES TO PLAY IT!
!!
TOM TATOM TOM TATOM

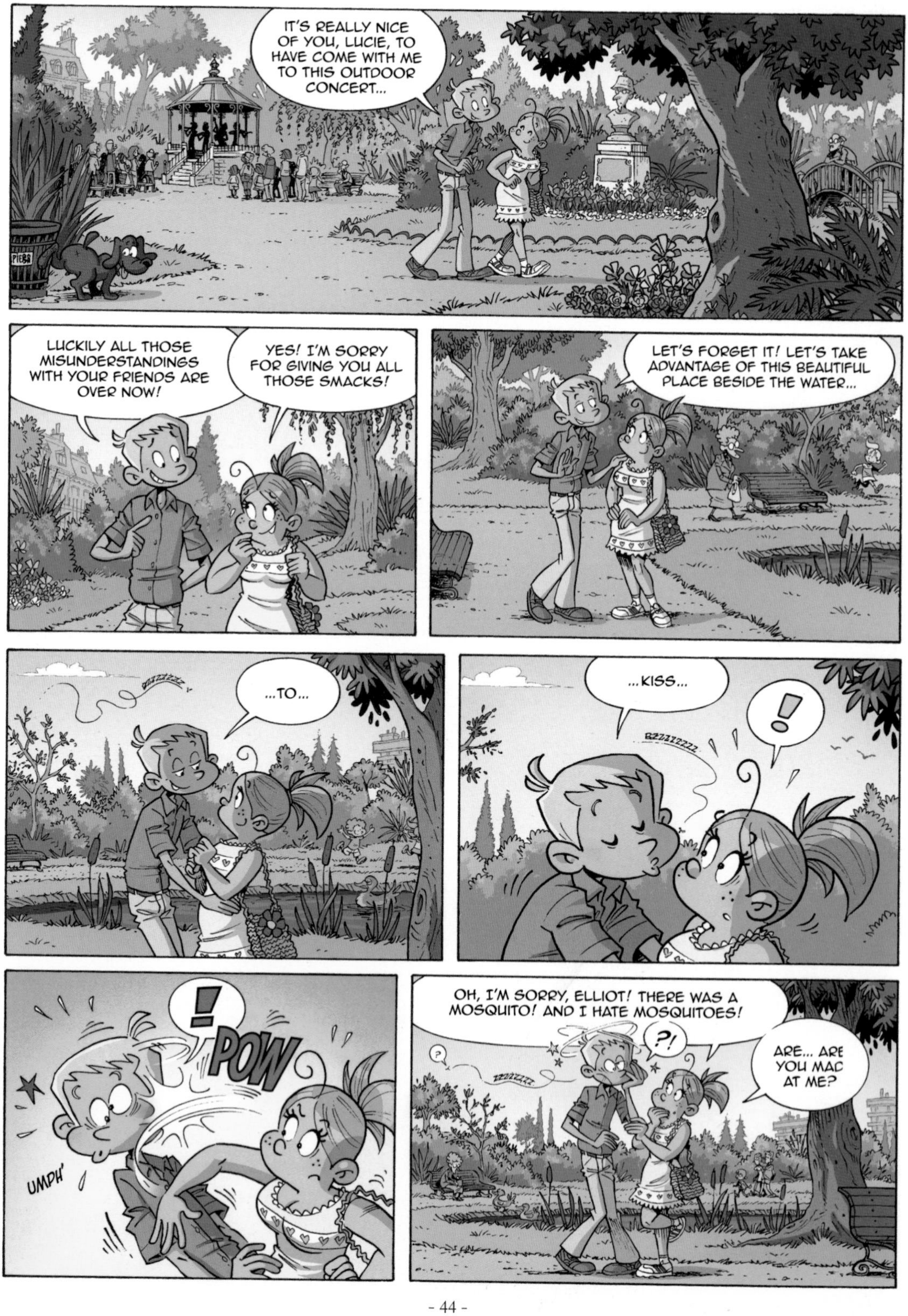
IT'S REALLY NICE OF YOU, LUCIE, TO HAVE COME WITH ME TO THIS OUTDOOR CONCERT...
LUCKILY ALL THOSE MISUNDERSTANDINGS WITH YOUR FRIENDS ARE OVER NOW!
YES! I'M SORRY FOR GIVING YOU ALL THOSE SMACKS!
LET'S FORGET IT! LET'S TAKE ADVANTAGE OF THIS BEAUTIFUL PLACE BESIDE THE WATER...
...TO...
...KISS...
BZZZZZZZZ
!
!
POW
UMPH'
OH, I'M SORRY, ELLIOT! THERE WAS A MOSQUITO! AND I HATE MOSQUITOES!
?!
?
ARE... ARE YOU MAD AT ME?

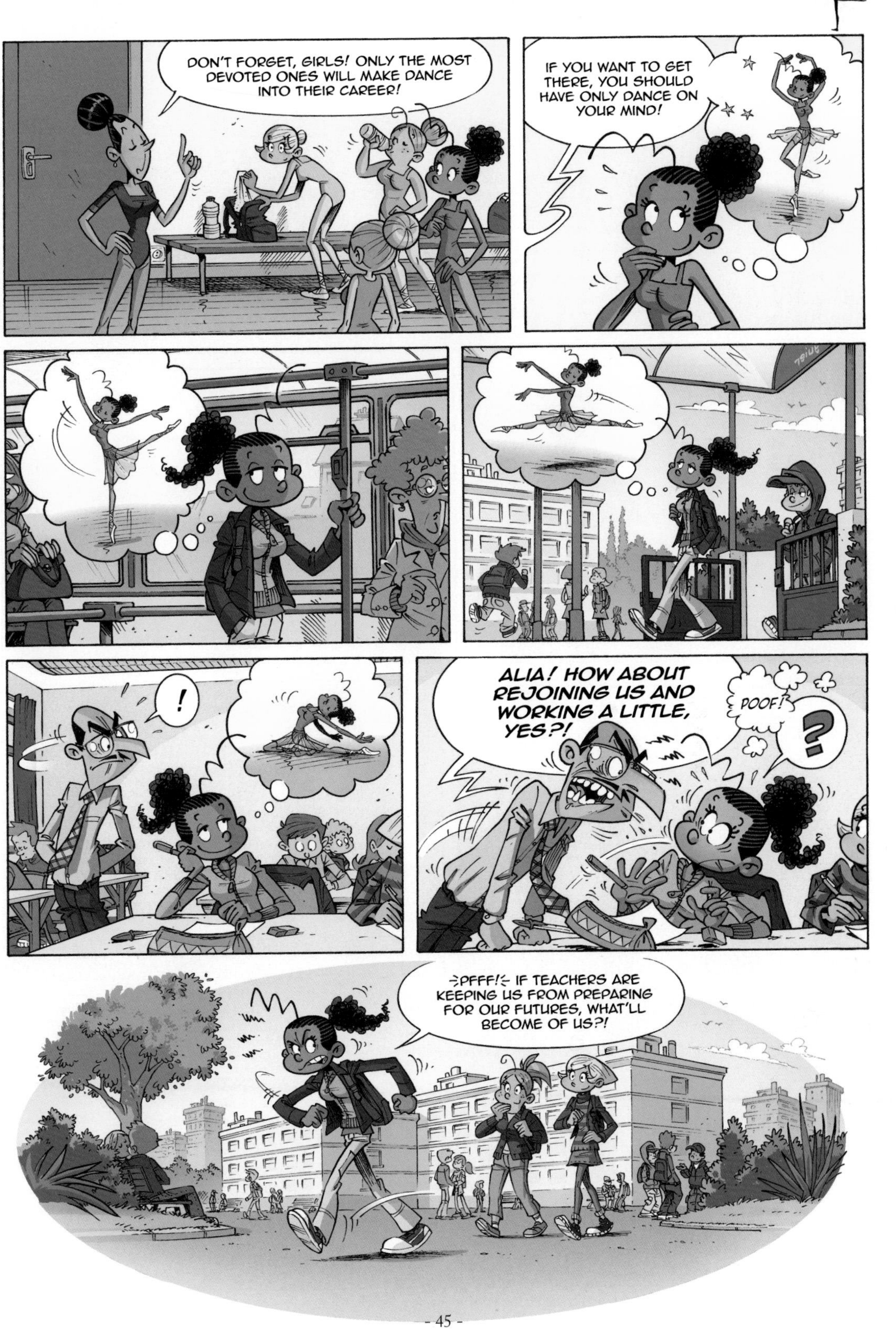

DON'T FORGET, GIRLS! ONLY THE MOST DEVOTED ONES WILL MAKE DANCE INTO THEIR CAREER!
IF YOU WANT TO GET THERE, YOU SHOULD HAVE ONLY DANCE ON YOUR MIND!
!
ALIA! HOW ABOUT REJOINING US AND WORKING A LITTLE, YES?!
POOF!
?
PFFF! IF TEACHERS ARE KEEPING US FROM PREPARING FOR OUR FUTURES, WHAT'LL BECOME OF US?!

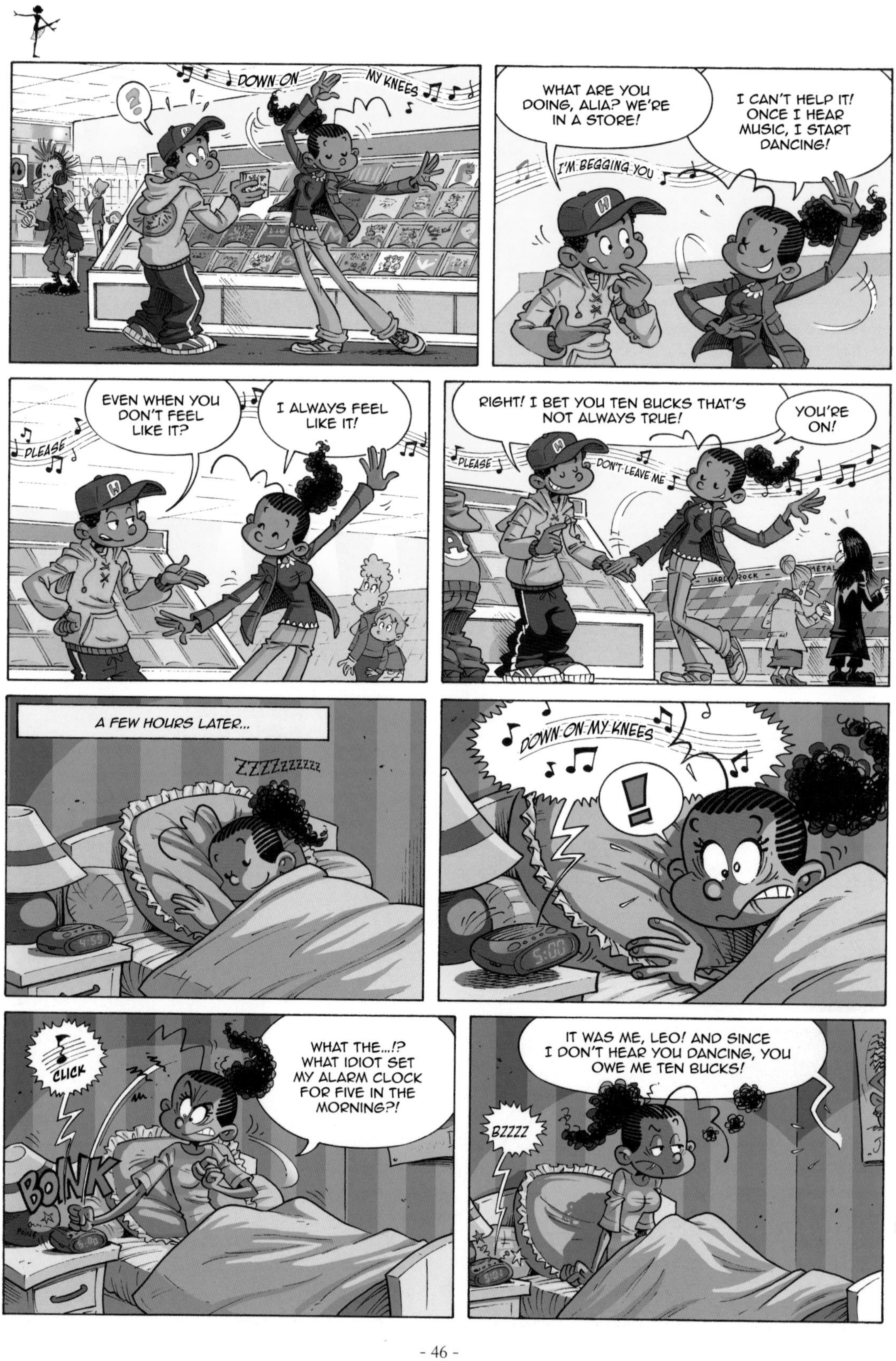
DOWN ON
MY KNEES
?
WHAT ARE YOU DOING, ALIA? WE'RE IN A STORE!
I CAN'T HELP IT! ONCE I HEAR MUSIC, I START DANCING!
I'M BEGGING YOU
EVEN WHEN YOU DON'T FEEL LIKE IT?
I ALWAYS FEEL LIKE IT!
PLEASE
RIGHT! I BET YOU TEN BUCKS THAT'S NOT ALWAYS TRUE!
YOU'RE ON!
PLEASE
DON'T LEAVE ME
HARD ROCK
METAL
A FEW HOURS LATER...
ZZZZzzzzzz
DOWN ON MY KNEES
!
CLICK
BOINK
WHAT THE...!? WHAT IDIOT SET MY ALARM CLOCK FOR FIVE IN THE MORNING?!
BZZZZ
IT WAS ME, LEO! AND SINCE I DON'T HEAR YOU DANCING, YOU OWE ME TEN BUCKS!

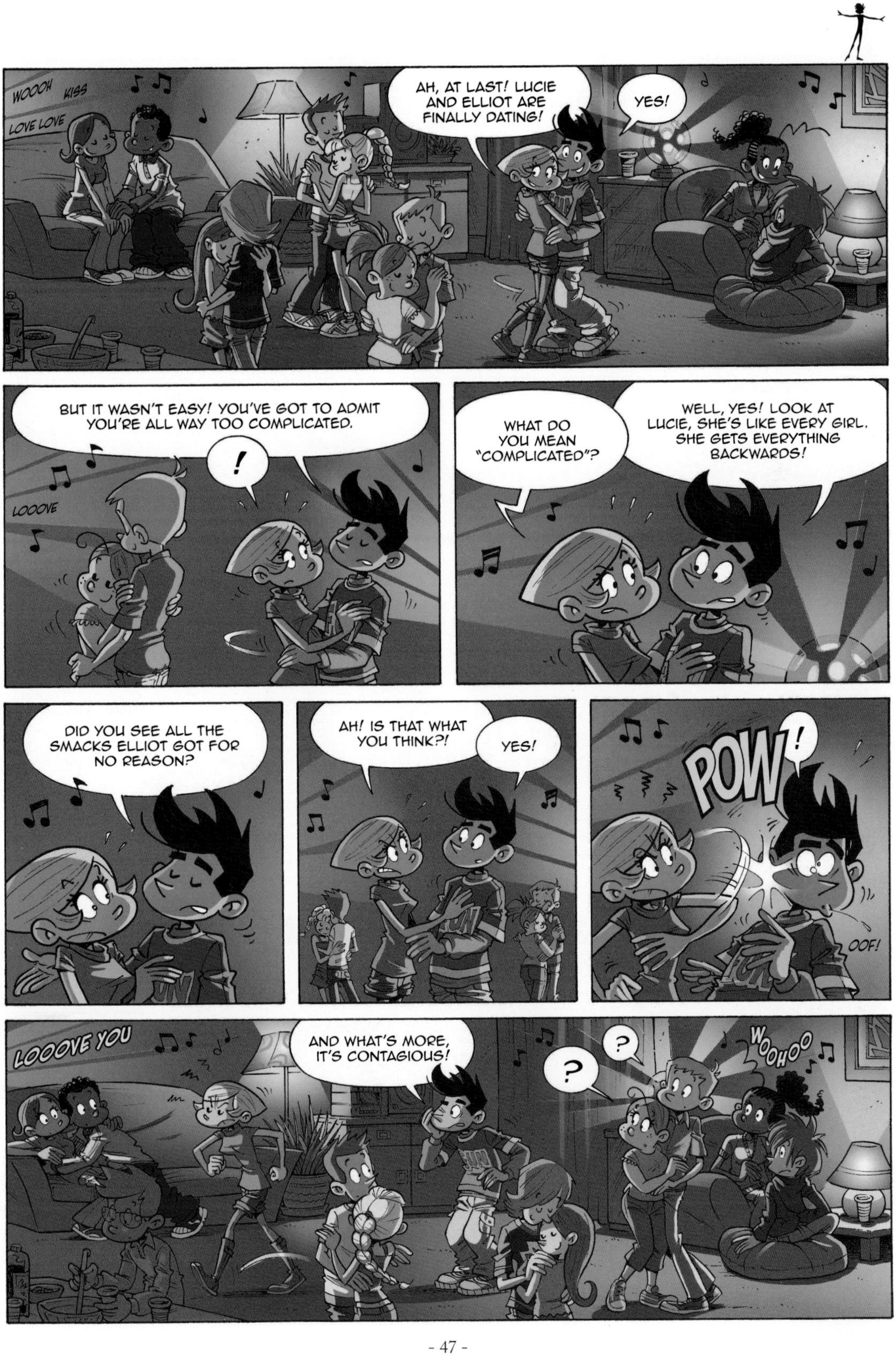
WOOOH
KISS
LOVE LOVE
AH, AT LAST! LUCIE AND ELLIOT ARE FINALLY DATING!
YES!
BUT IT WASN'T EASY! YOU'VE GOT TO ADMIT YOU'RE ALL WAY TOO COMPLICATED.
!
LOOOVE
WHAT DO YOU MEAN "COMPLICATED"?
WELL, YES! LOOK AT LUCIE, SHE'S LIKE EVERY GIRL. SHE GETS EVERYTHING BACKWARDS!
DID YOU SEE ALL THE SMACKS ELLIOT GOT FOR NO REASON?
AH! IS THAT WHAT YOU THINK?!
YES!
POW
!
OOF!
LOOOVE YOU
AND WHAT'S MORE, IT'S CONTAGIOUS!
?
?
WOOHOO

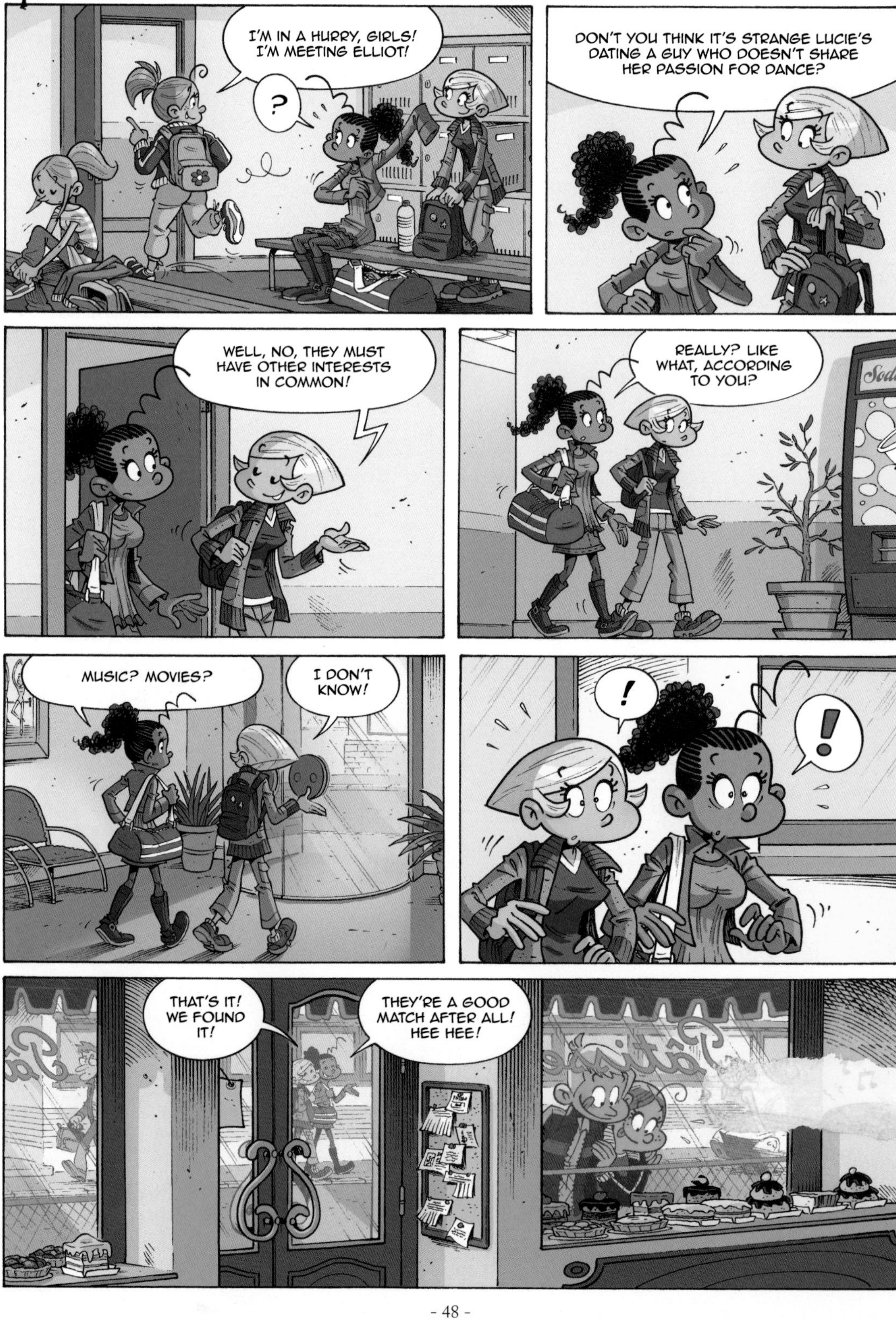
I'M IN A HURRY, GIRLS! I'M MEETING ELLIOT!
?
DON'T YOU THINK IT'S STRANGE LUCIE'S DATING A GUY WHO DOESN'T SHARE HER PASSION FOR DANCE?
WELL, NO, THEY MUST HAVE OTHER INTERESTS IN COMMON!
REALLY? LIKE WHAT, ACCORDING TO YOU?
Soda
MUSIC? MOVIES?
I DON'T KNOW!
!
!
THAT'S IT! WE FOUND IT!
THEY'RE A GOOD MATCH AFTER ALL! HEE HEE!

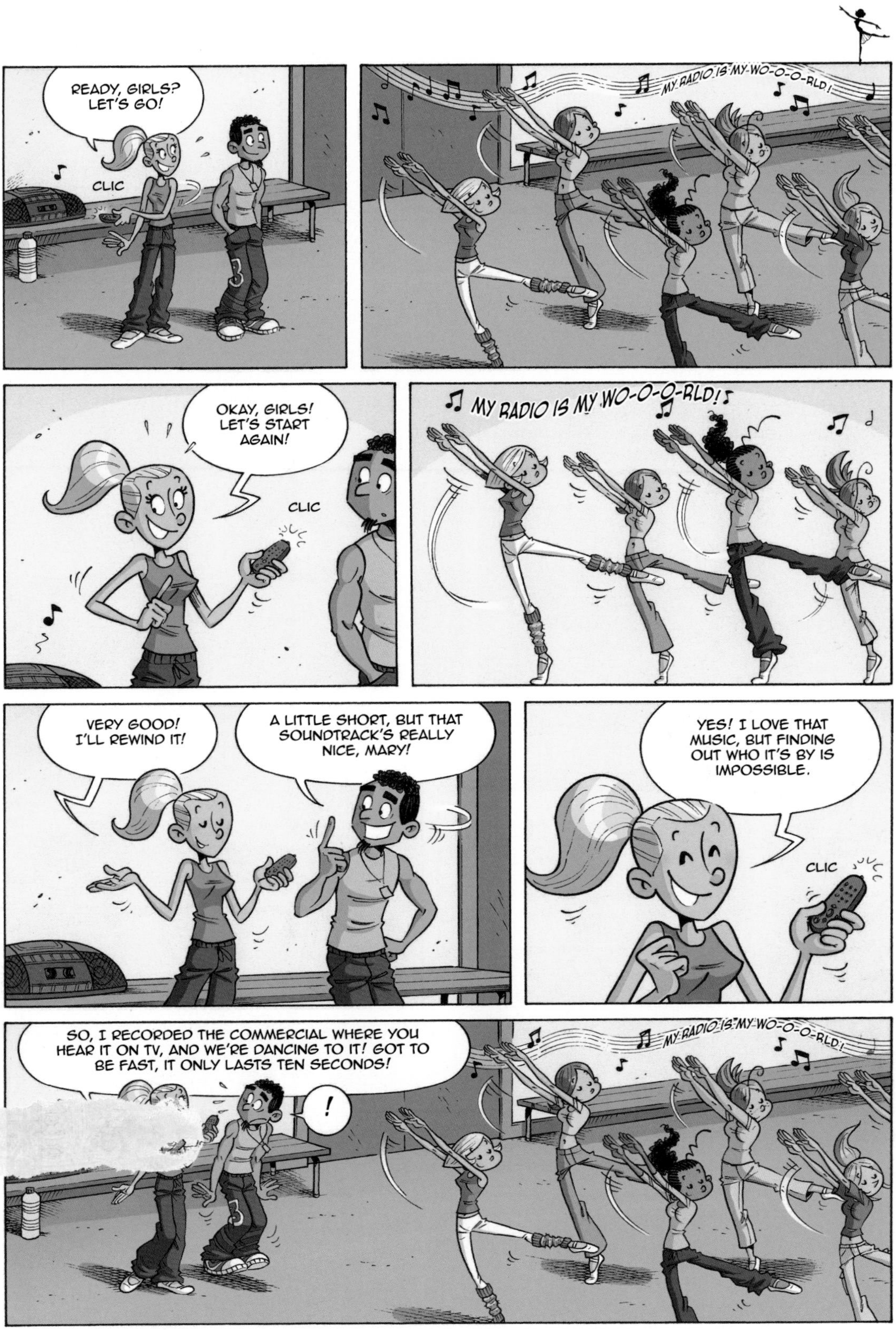
READY, GIRLS? LET'S GO!
CLIC
MY RADIO IS MY WO-O-O-RLD!
OKAY, GIRLS! LET'S START AGAIN!
CLIC
MY RADIO IS MY WO-O-O-RLD!
VERY GOOD! I'LL REWIND IT!
A LITTLE SHORT, BUT THAT SOUNDTRACK'S REALLY NICE, MARY!
YES! I LOVE THAT MUSIC, BUT FINDING OUT WHO IT'S BY IS IMPOSSIBLE.
CLIC
SO, I RECORDED THE COMMERCIAL WHERE YOU HEAR IT ON TV, AND WE'RE DANCING TO IT! GOT TO BE FAST, IT ONLY LASTS TEN SECONDS!
!
MY RADIO IS MY WO-O-O-RLD!

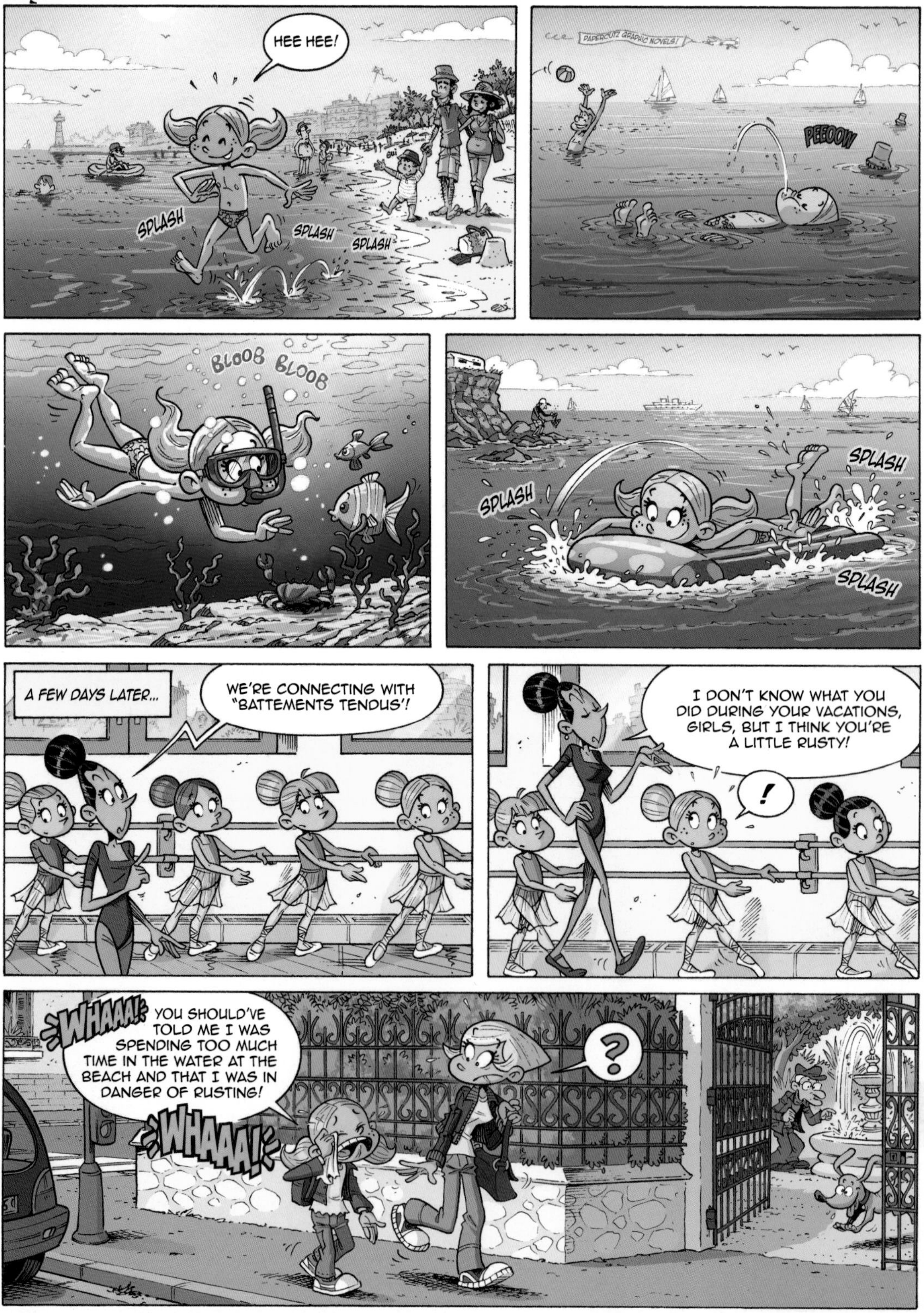

HEE HEE!
SPLASH
SPLASH
SPLASH
PAPERCUTZ GRAPHIC NOVELS!
PEEOOW
BLOOB BLOOB
SPLASH
SPLASH
SPLASH
A FEW DAYS LATER...
WE'RE CONNECTING WITH "BATTEMENTS TENDUS"!
I DON'T KNOW WHAT YOU DID DURING YOUR VACATIONS, GIRLS, BUT I THINK YOU'RE A LITTLE RUSTY!
!
WHAAA!
YOU SHOULD'VE TOLD ME I WAS SPENDING TOO MUCH TIME IN THE WATER AT THE BEACH AND THAT I WAS IN DANGER OF RUSTING!
WHAAA!
?

To Russia, With Love

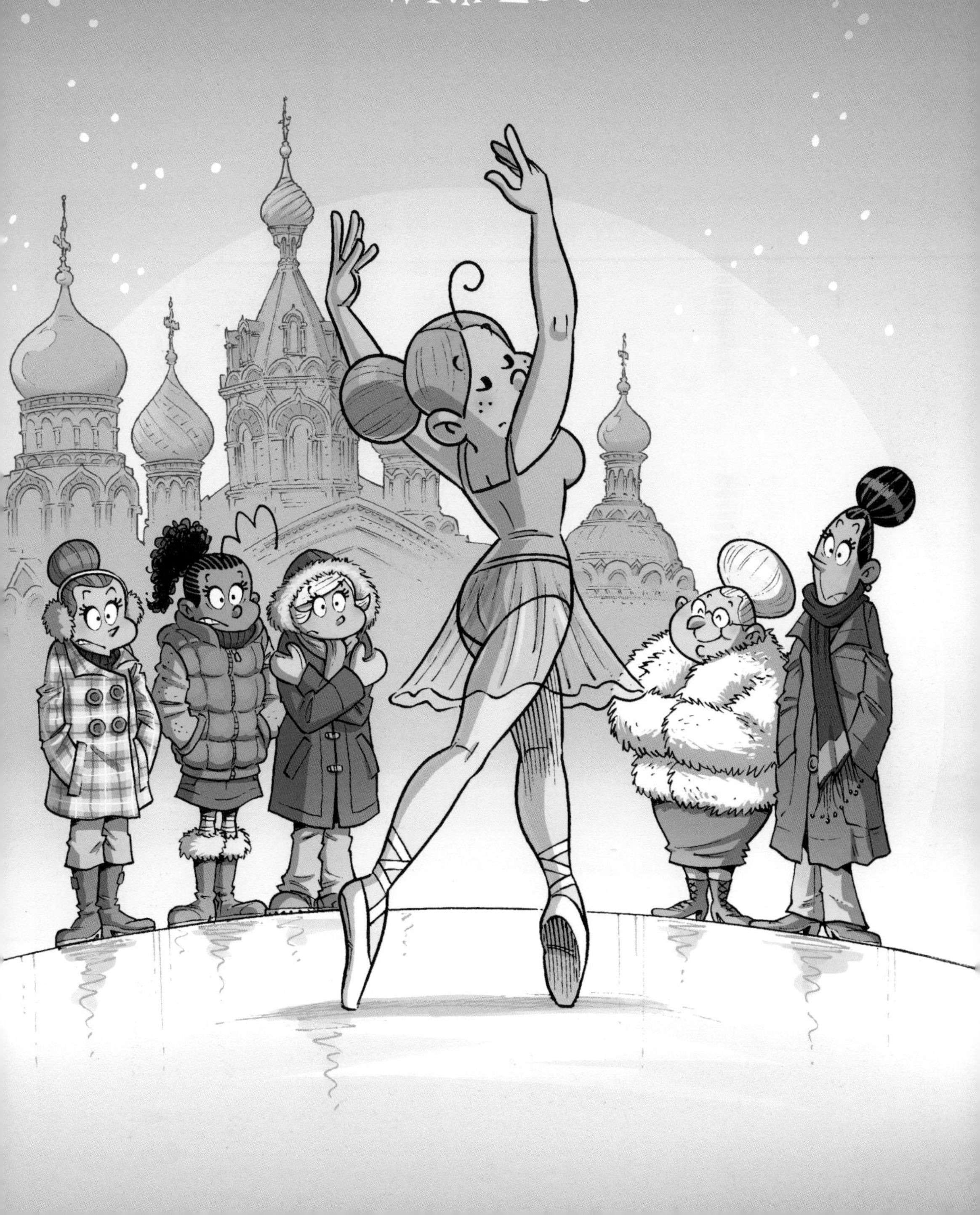

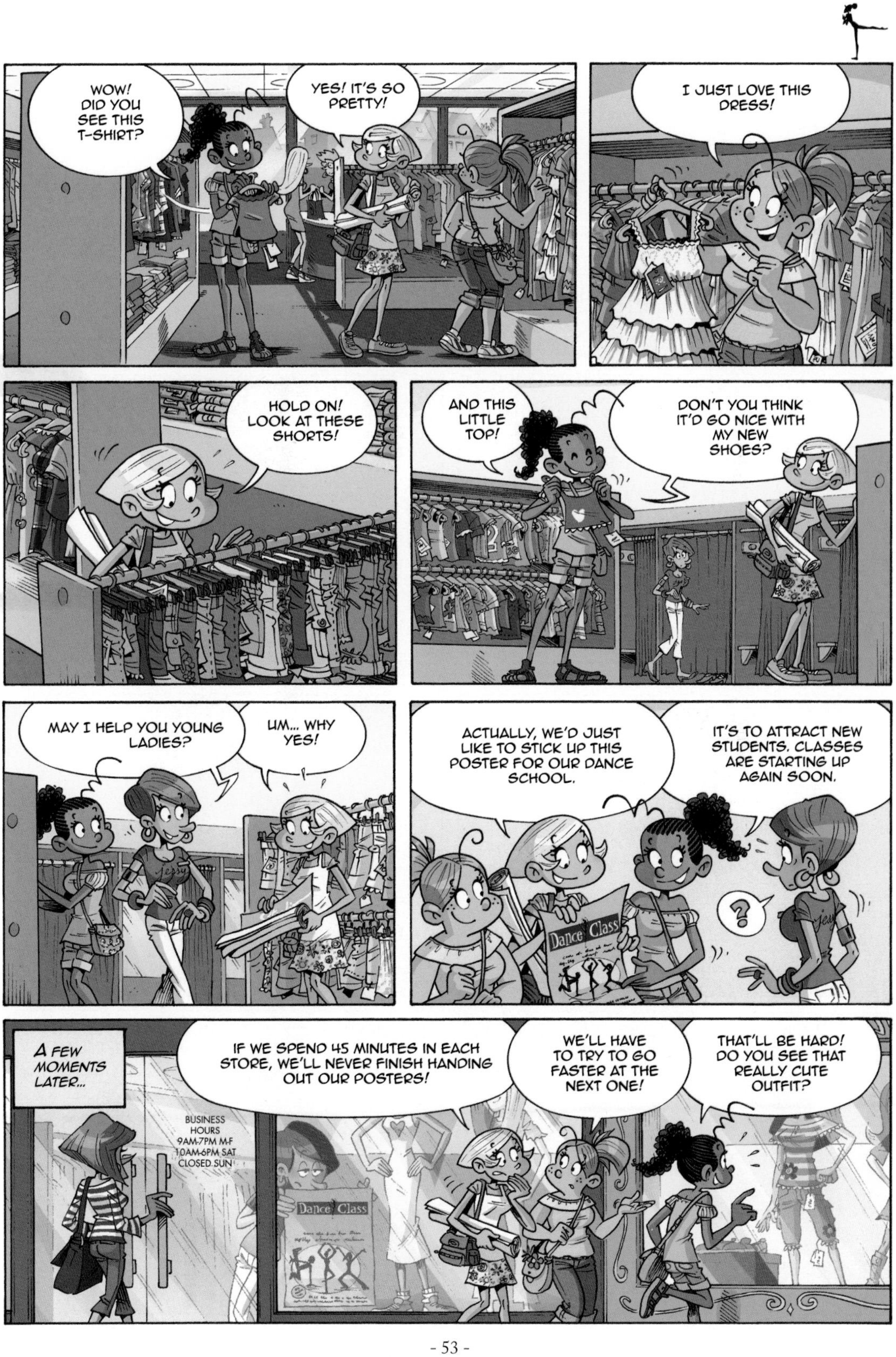

WOW! DID YOU SEE THIS T-SHIRT?
YES! IT'S SO PRETTY!
I JUST LOVE THIS DRESS!
HOLD ON! LOOK AT THESE SHORTS!
AND THIS LITTLE TOP!
DON'T YOU THINK IT'D GO NICE WITH MY NEW SHOES?
MAY I HELP YOU YOUNG LADIES?
UM... WHY YES!
ACTUALLY, WE'D JUST LIKE TO STICK UP THIS POSTER FOR OUR DANCE SCHOOL.
IT'S TO ATTRACT NEW STUDENTS. CLASSES ARE STARTING UP AGAIN SOON.
?
Dance Class
A FEW MOMENTS LATER...
IF WE SPEND 45 MINUTES IN EACH STORE, WE'LL NEVER FINISH HANDING OUT OUR POSTERS!
WE'LL HAVE TO TRY TO GO FASTER AT THE NEXT ONE!
THAT'LL BE HARD! DO YOU SEE THAT REALLY CUTE OUTFIT?
BUSINESS HOURS 9AM-7PM M-F 10AM-6PM SAT CLOSED SUN
Dance Class

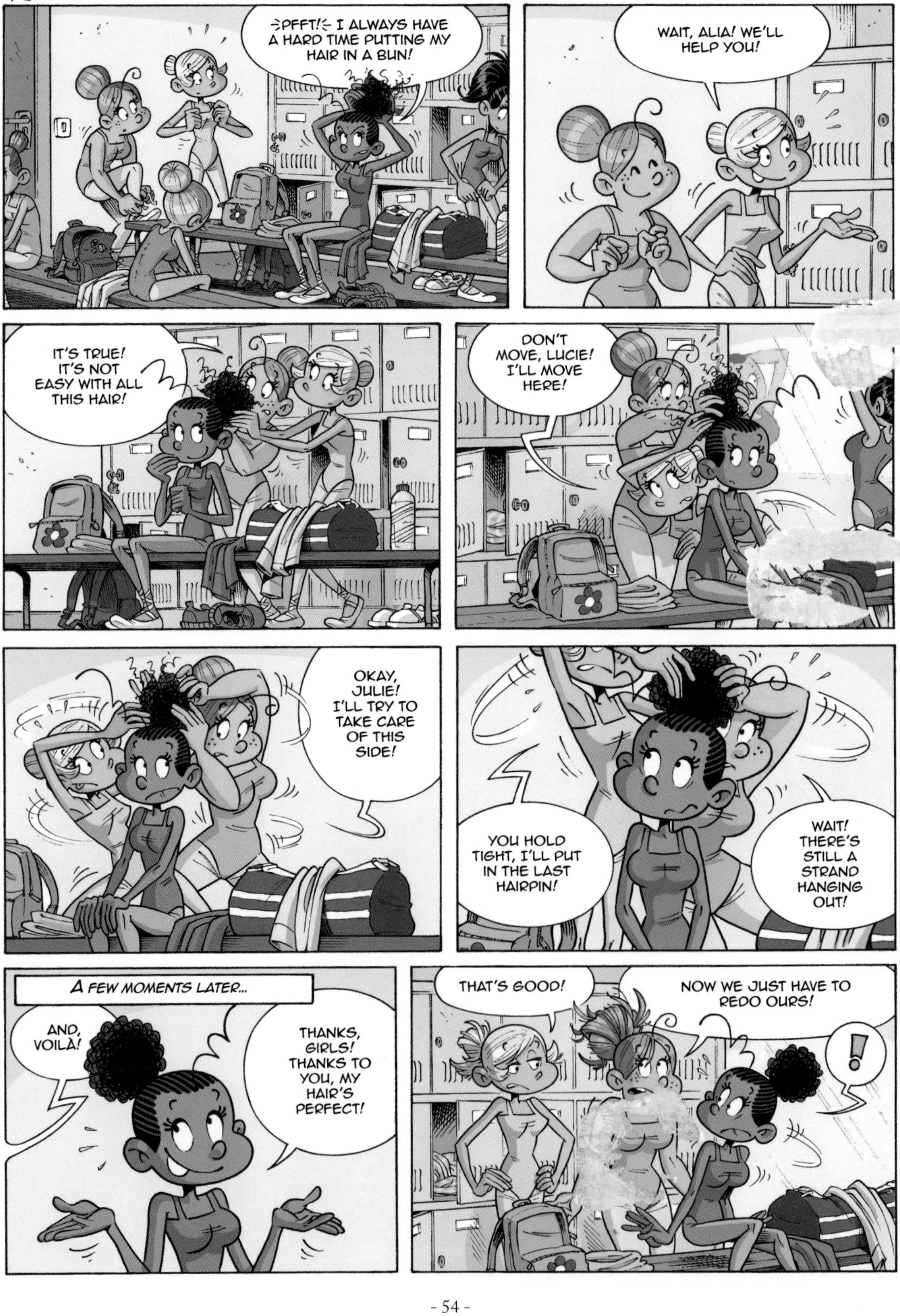

PFFT! I ALWAYS HAVE A HARD TIME PUTTING MY HAIR IN A BUN!
WAIT, ALIA! WE'LL HELP YOU!
IT'S TRUE! IT'S NOT EASY WITH ALL THIS HAIR!
DON'T MOVE, LUCIE! I'LL MOVE HERE!
OKAY, JULIE! I'LL TRY TO TAKE CARE OF THIS SIDE!
YOU HOLD TIGHT, I'LL PUT IN THE LAST HAIRPIN!
WAIT! THERE'S STILL A STRAND HANGING OUT!
A FEW MOMENTS LATER...
AND, VOILÀ!
THANKS, GIRLS! THANKS TO YOU, MY HAIR'S PERFECT!
THAT'S GOOD!
NOW WE JUST HAVE TO REDO OURS!
!

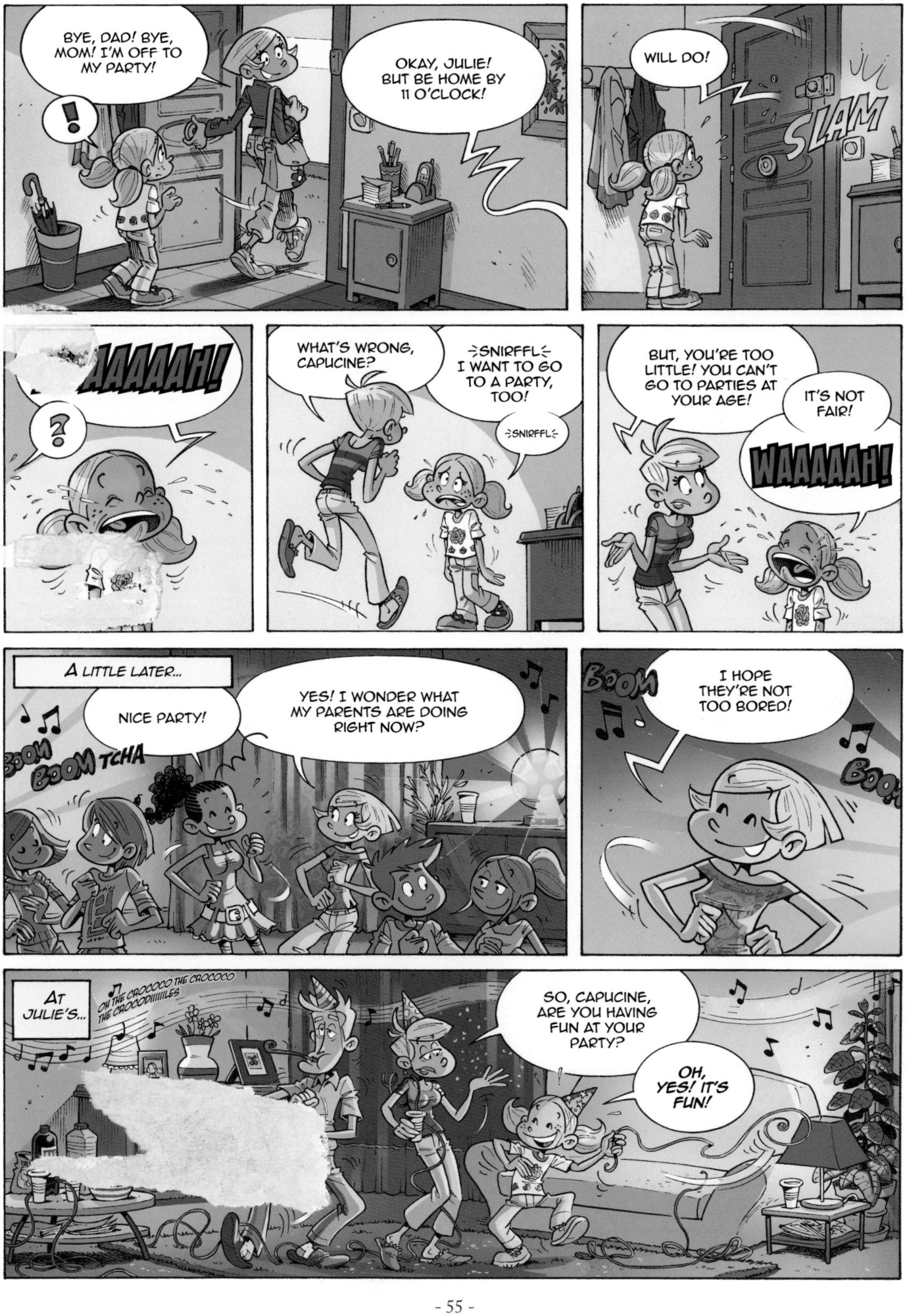
BYE, DAD! BYE, MOM! I'M OFF TO MY PARTY!
!
OKAY, JULIE! BUT BE HOME BY 11 O'CLOCK!
WILL DO!
SLAM
AAAAAH!
?
WHAT'S WRONG, CAPUCINE?
SNIRFFL I WANT TO GO TO A PARTY, TOO!
SNIRFFL
BUT, YOU'RE TOO LITTLE! YOU CAN'T GO TO PARTIES AT YOUR AGE!
IT'S NOT FAIR!
WAAAAAH!
A LITTLE LATER...
NICE PARTY!
YES! I WONDER WHAT MY PARENTS ARE DOING RIGHT NOW?
BOOM BOOM TCHA
BOOM
I HOPE THEY'RE NOT TOO BORED!
AT JULIE'S...
OH THE CROCOCO THE CROCOCO THE CROCODIIIIIILES
SO, CAPUCINE, ARE YOU HAVING FUN AT YOUR PARTY?
OH, YES! IT'S FUN!

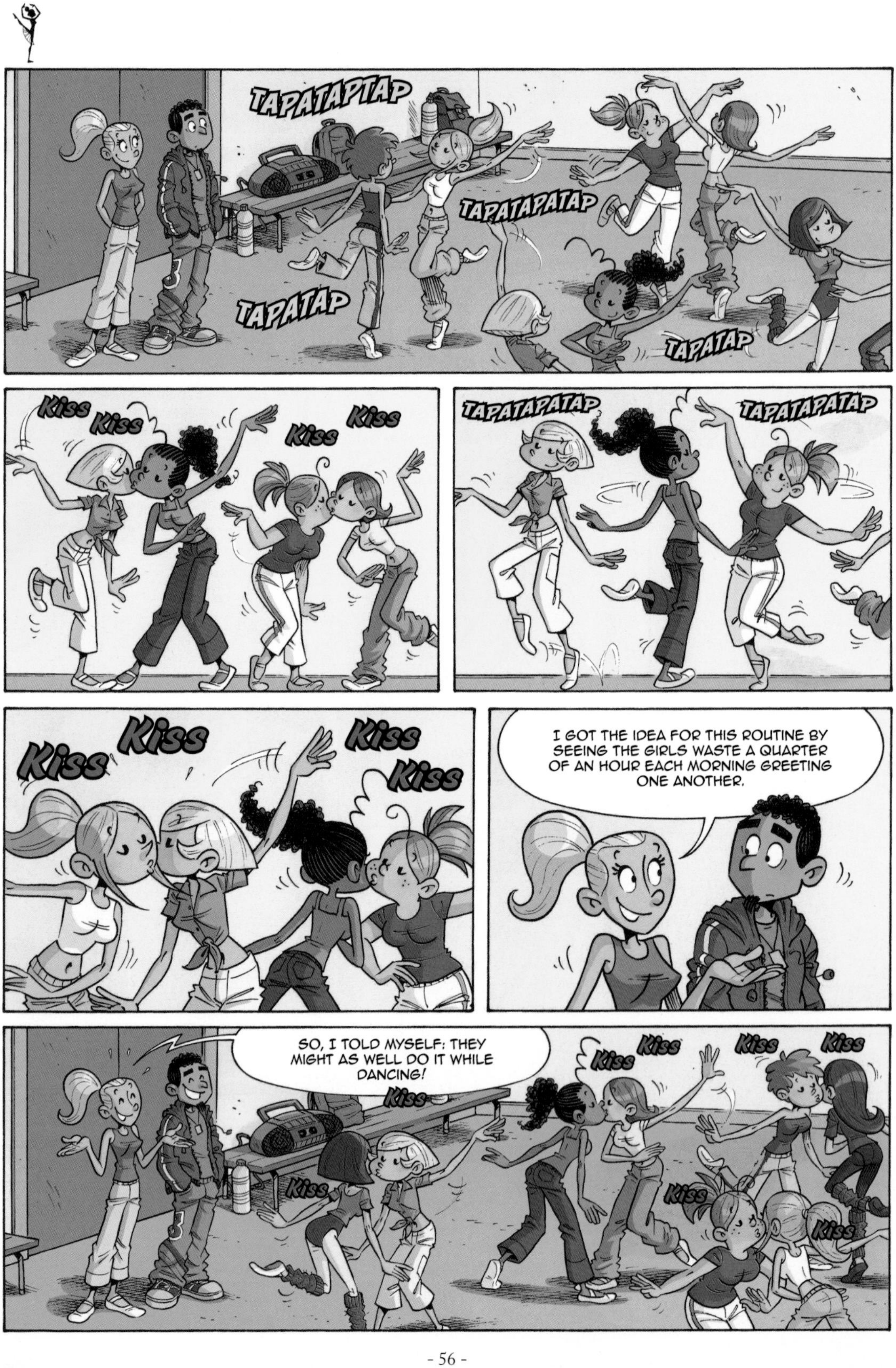
TAPATAPTAP
TAPATAPATAP
TAPATAP
TAPATAP
Kiss
Kiss
Kiss
Kiss
TAPATAPATAP
TAPATAPATAP
Kiss
Kiss
Kiss
Kiss
I GOT THE IDEA FOR THIS ROUTINE BY SEEING THE GIRLS WASTE A QUARTER OF AN HOUR EACH MORNING GREETING ONE ANOTHER.
SO, I TOLD MYSELF: THEY MIGHT AS WELL DO IT WHILE DANCING!
Kiss
Kiss
Kiss
Kiss
Kiss
Kiss
Kiss
Kiss

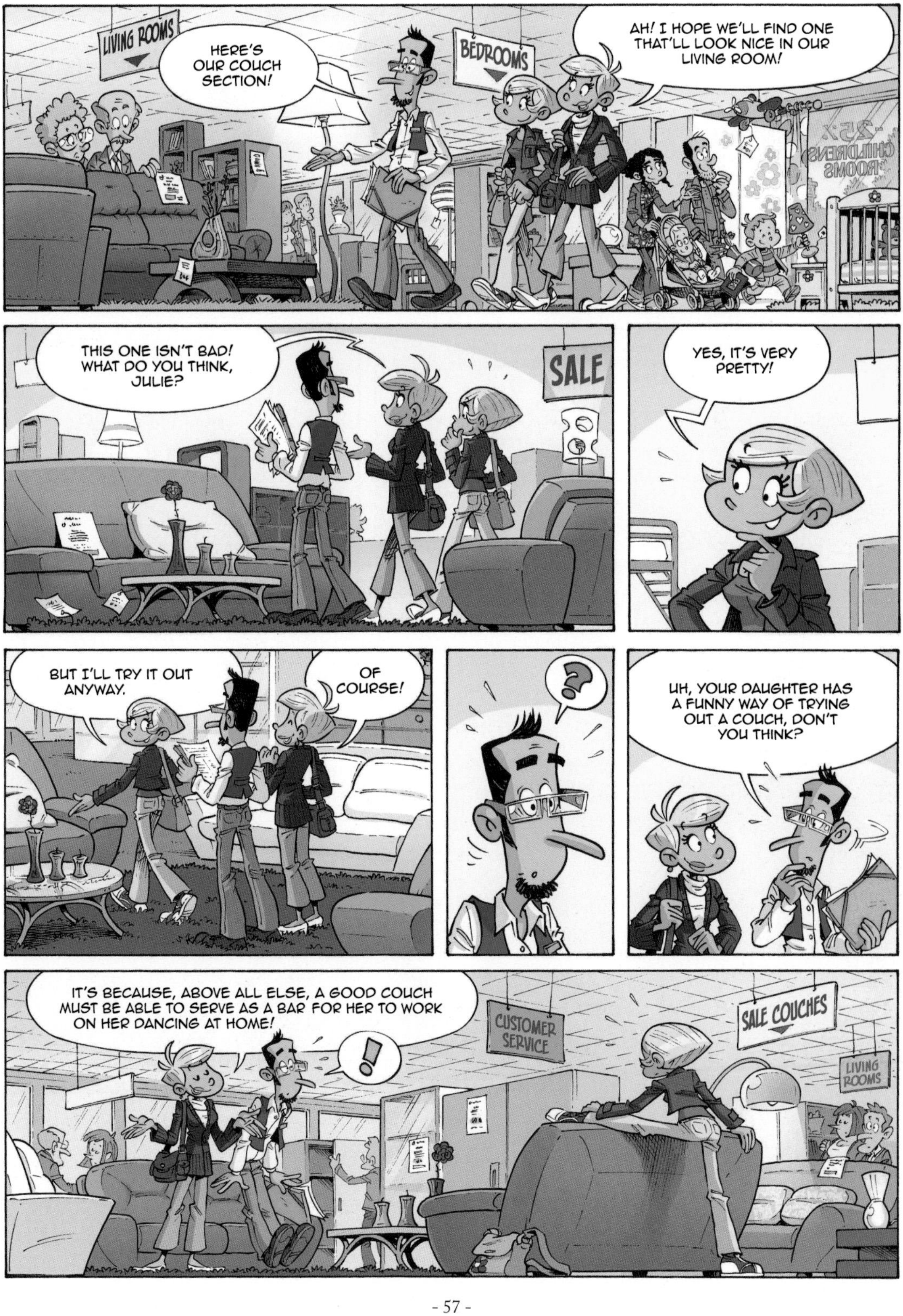

LIVING ROOMS
HERE'S OUR COUCH SECTION!
BEDROOMS
AH! I HOPE WE'LL FIND ONE THAT'LL LOOK NICE IN OUR LIVING ROOM!
THIS ONE ISN'T BAD! WHAT DO YOU THINK, JULIE?
SALE
YES, IT'S VERY PRETTY!
BUT I'LL TRY IT OUT ANYWAY.
OF COURSE!
?
UH, YOUR DAUGHTER HAS A FUNNY WAY OF TRYING OUT A COUCH, DON'T YOU THINK?
IT'S BECAUSE, ABOVE ALL ELSE, A GOOD COUCH MUST BE ABLE TO SERVE AS A BAR FOR HER TO WORK ON HER DANCING AT HOME!
!
CUSTOMER SERVICE
SALE COUCHES
LIVING ROOMS

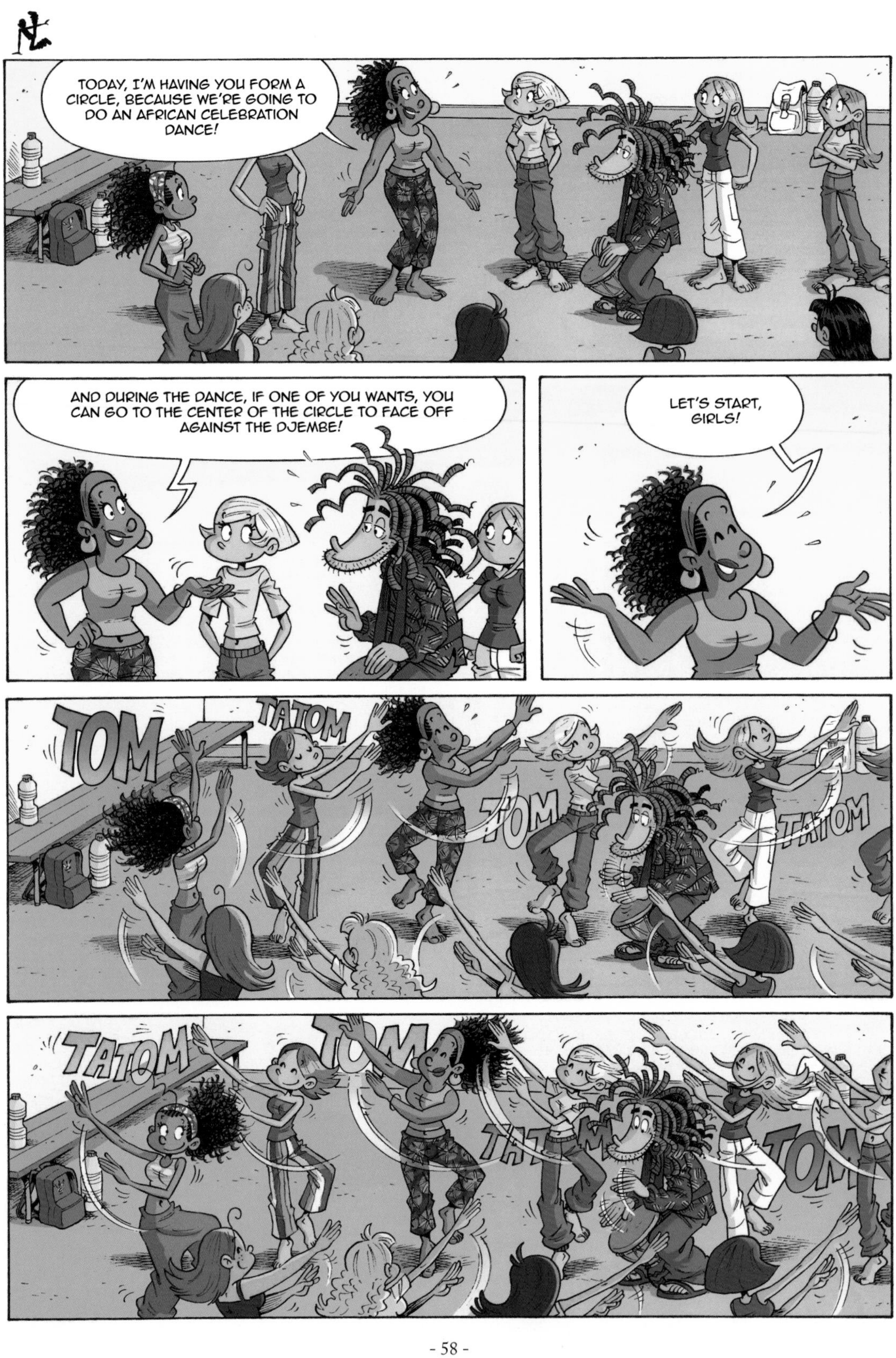
TODAY, I'M HAVING YOU FORM A CIRCLE, BECAUSE WE'RE GOING TO DO AN AFRICAN CELEBRATION DANCE!
AND DURING THE DANCE, IF ONE OF YOU WANTS, YOU CAN GO TO THE CENTER OF THE CIRCLE TO FACE OFF AGAINST THE DJEMBE!
LET'S START, GIRLS!
TOM
TATOM
TOM
TATOM
TATOM
TOM
TATOM
TOM

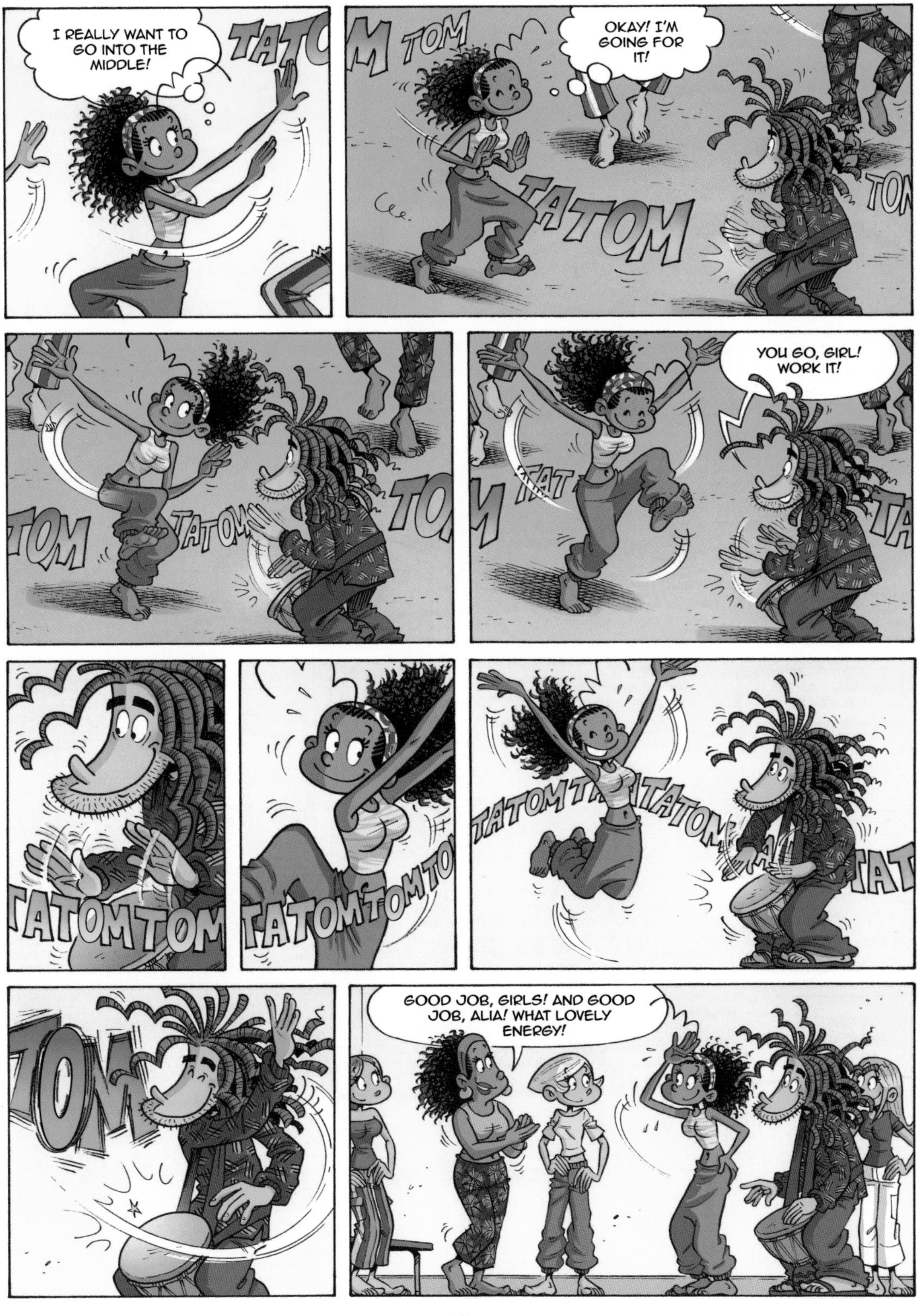
I REALLY WANT TO GO INTO THE MIDDLE!
TATOM
TOM
OKAY! I'M GOING FOR IT!
TATOM
TOM
TATOM
TOM
TAT
YOU GO, GIRL! WORK IT!
TA
TATOMTOM
TATOMTOMTOM
TATOMTATATOM
TAT
TOM
GOOD JOB, GIRLS! AND GOOD JOB, ALIA! WHAT LOVELY ENERGY!

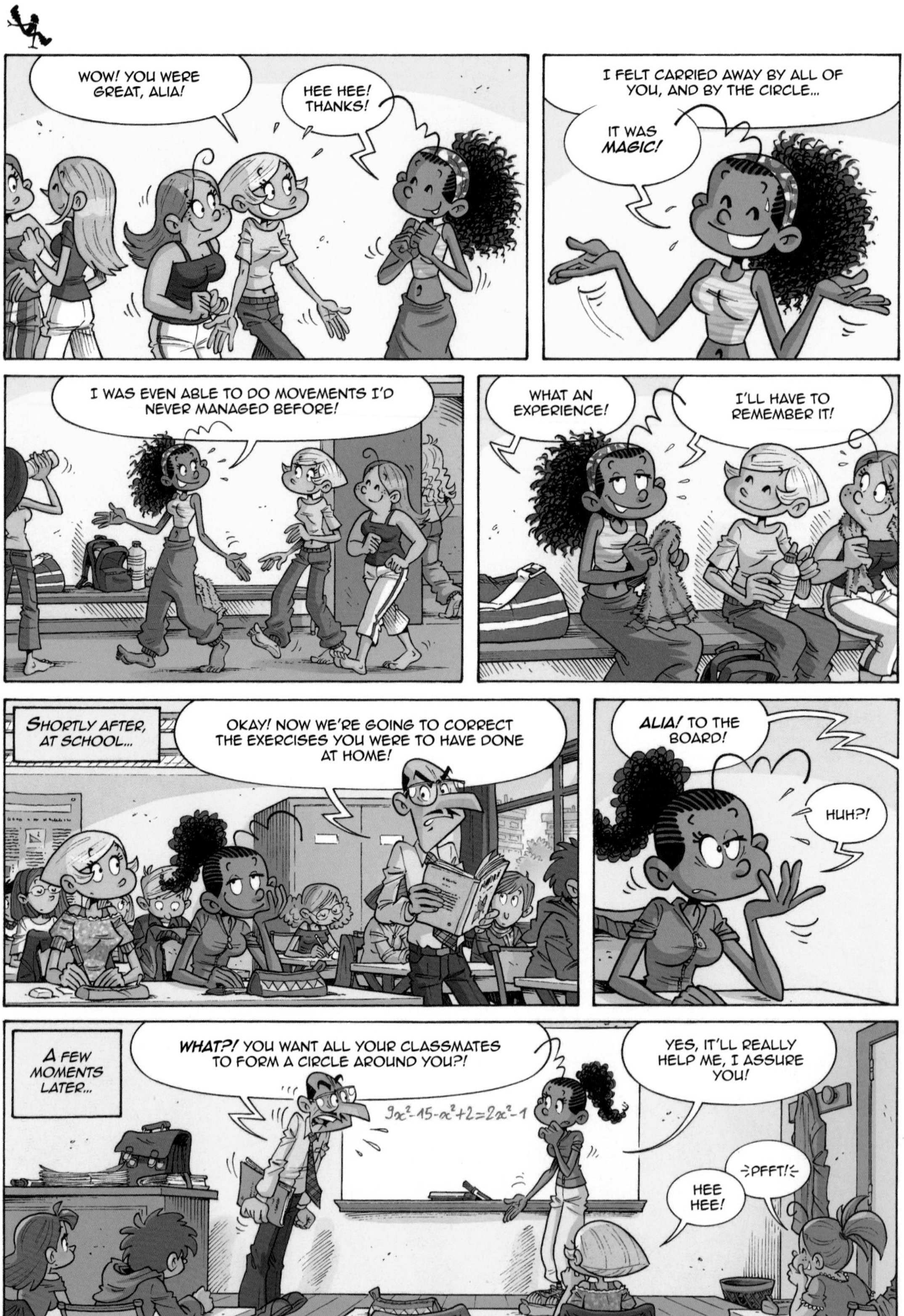

WOW! YOU WERE GREAT, ALIA!
HEE HEE! THANKS!
I FELT CARRIED AWAY BY ALL OF YOU, AND BY THE CIRCLE...
IT WAS MAGIC!
I WAS EVEN ABLE TO DO MOVEMENTS I'D NEVER MANAGED BEFORE!
WHAT AN EXPERIENCE!
I'LL HAVE TO REMEMBER IT!
SHORTLY AFTER, AT SCHOOL...
OKAY! NOW WE'RE GOING TO CORRECT THE EXERCISES YOU WERE TO HAVE DONE AT HOME!
ALIA! TO THE BOARD!
HUH?!
A FEW MOMENTS LATER...
WHAT?! YOU WANT ALL YOUR CLASSMATES TO FORM A CIRCLE AROUND YOU?!
$9x^2-15-x^2+2=2x^2-1$
YES, IT'LL REALLY HELP ME, I ASSURE YOU!
HEE HEE!
PFFT!

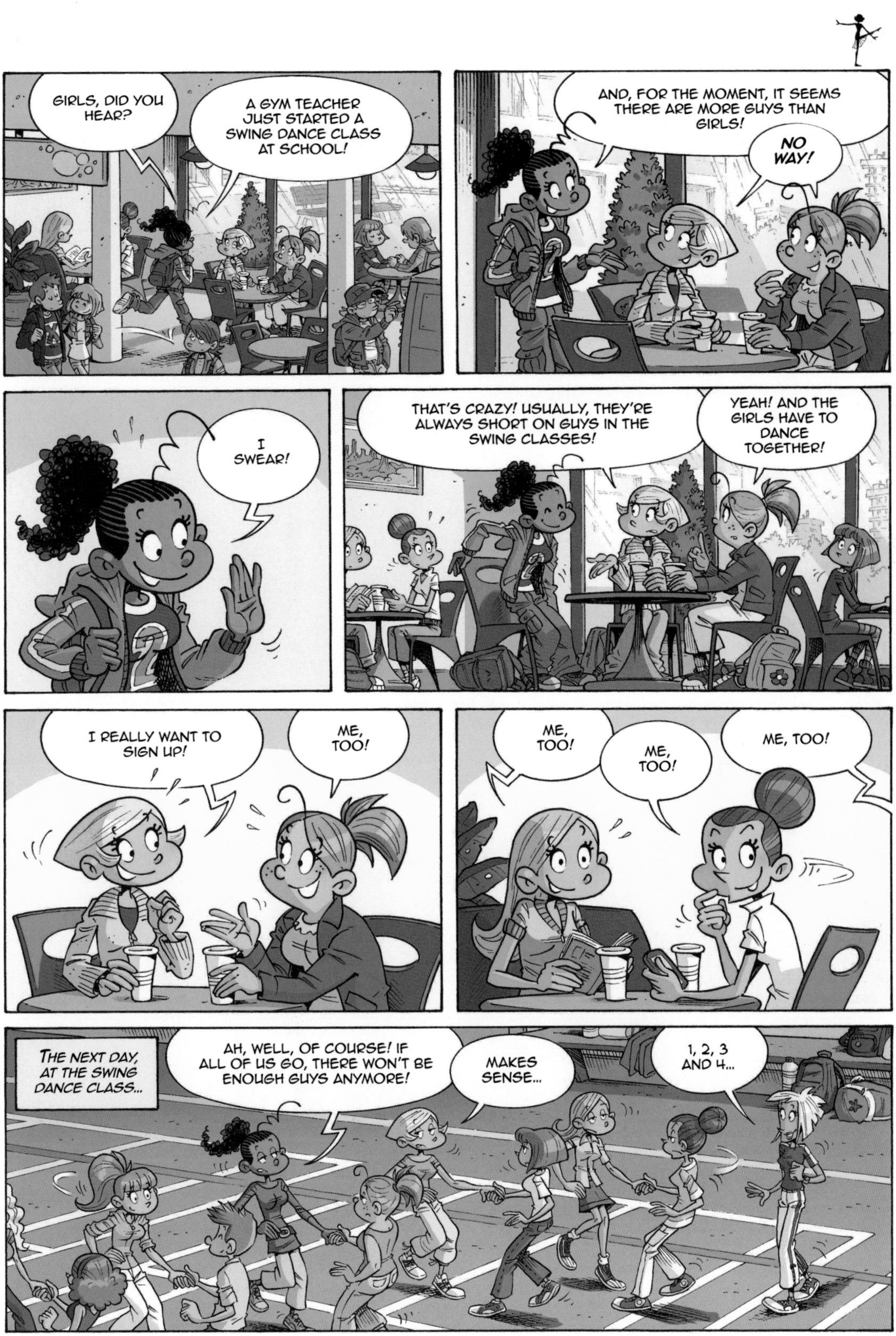

GIRLS, DID YOU HEAR?
A GYM TEACHER JUST STARTED A SWING DANCE CLASS AT SCHOOL!
AND, FOR THE MOMENT, IT SEEMS THERE ARE MORE GUYS THAN GIRLS!
NO WAY!
I SWEAR!
THAT'S CRAZY! USUALLY, THEY'RE ALWAYS SHORT ON GUYS IN THE SWING CLASSES!
YEAH! AND THE GIRLS HAVE TO DANCE TOGETHER!
I REALLY WANT TO SIGN UP!
ME, TOO!
ME, TOO!
ME, TOO!
ME, TOO!
THE NEXT DAY, AT THE SWING DANCE CLASS...
AH, WELL, OF COURSE! IF ALL OF US GO, THERE WON'T BE ENOUGH GUYS ANYMORE!
MAKES SENSE...
1, 2, 3 AND 4...

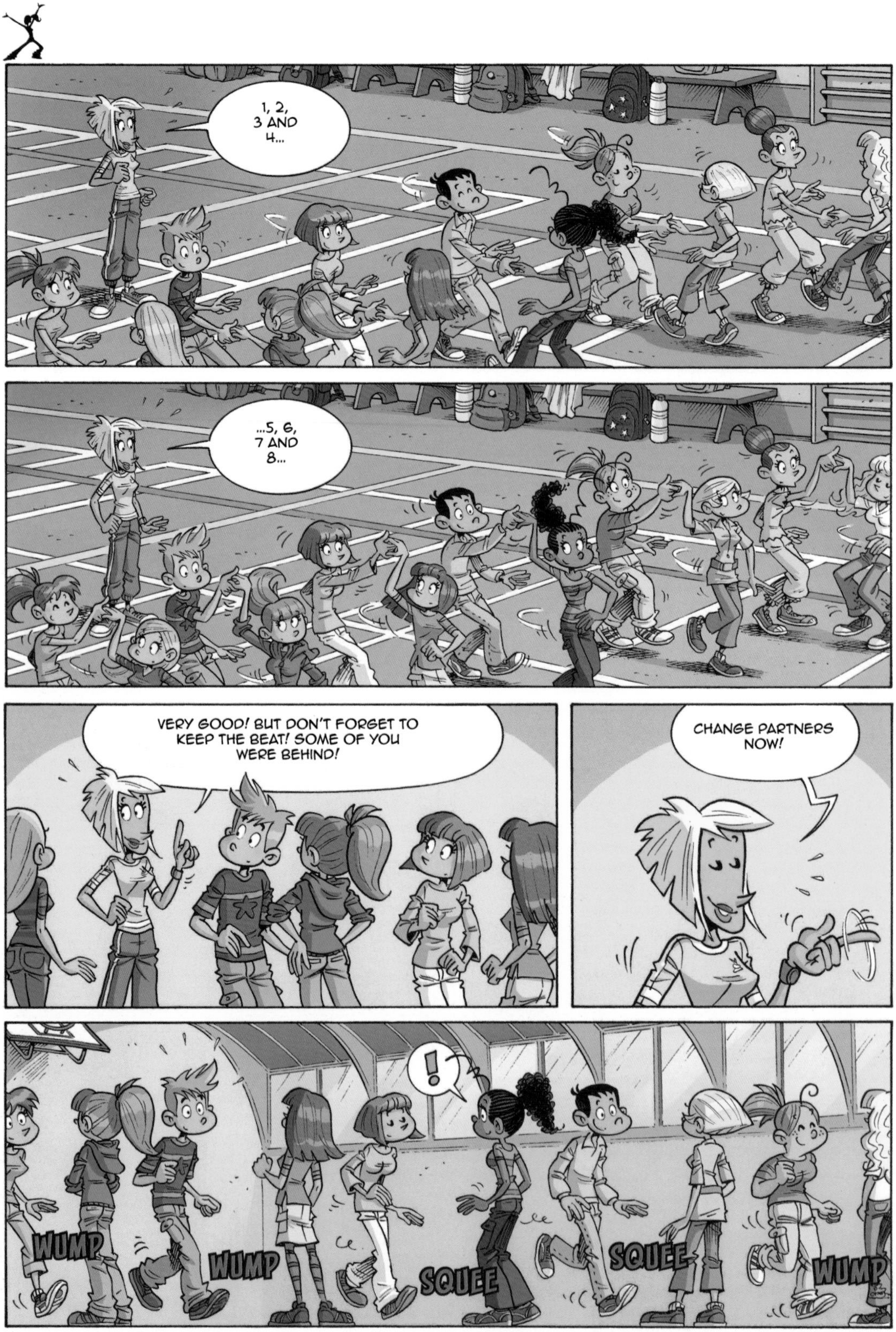
1, 2, 3 AND 4...
...5, 6, 7 AND 8...
VERY GOOD! BUT DON'T FORGET TO KEEP THE BEAT! SOME OF YOU WERE BEHIND!
CHANGE PARTNERS NOW!
!
WUMP
WUMP
SQUEE
SQUEE
WUMP

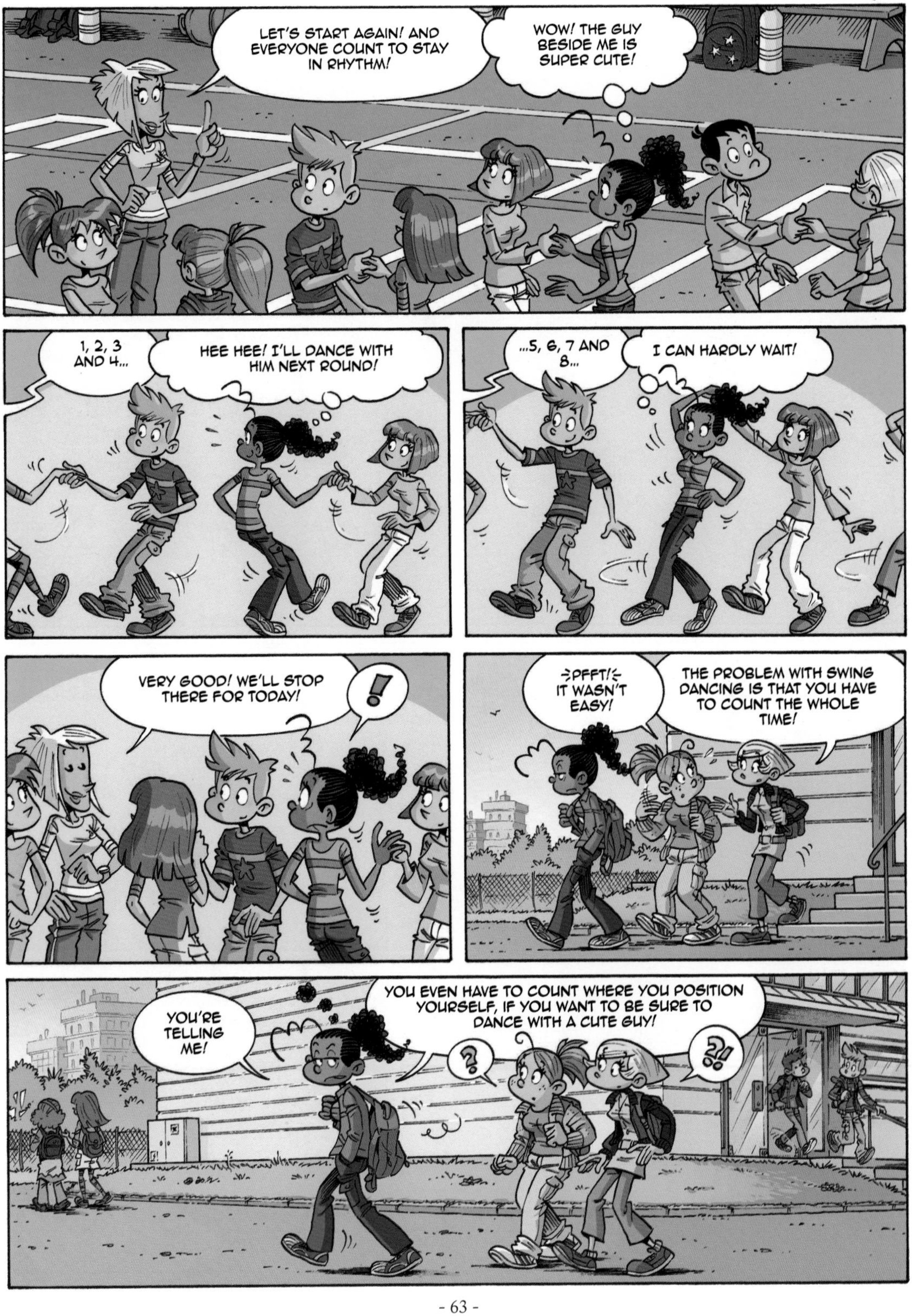

LET'S START AGAIN! AND EVERYONE COUNT TO STAY IN RHYTHM!
WOW! THE GUY BESIDE ME IS SUPER CUTE!
1, 2, 3 AND 4...
HEE HEE! I'LL DANCE WITH HIM NEXT ROUND!
...5, 6, 7 AND 8...
I CAN HARDLY WAIT!
VERY GOOD! WE'LL STOP THERE FOR TODAY!
!
PFFT! IT WASN'T EASY!
THE PROBLEM WITH SWING DANCING IS THAT YOU HAVE TO COUNT THE WHOLE TIME!
YOU'RE TELLING ME!
YOU EVEN HAVE TO COUNT WHERE YOU POSITION YOURSELF, IF YOU WANT TO BE SURE TO DANCE WITH A CUTE GUY!
?
?!

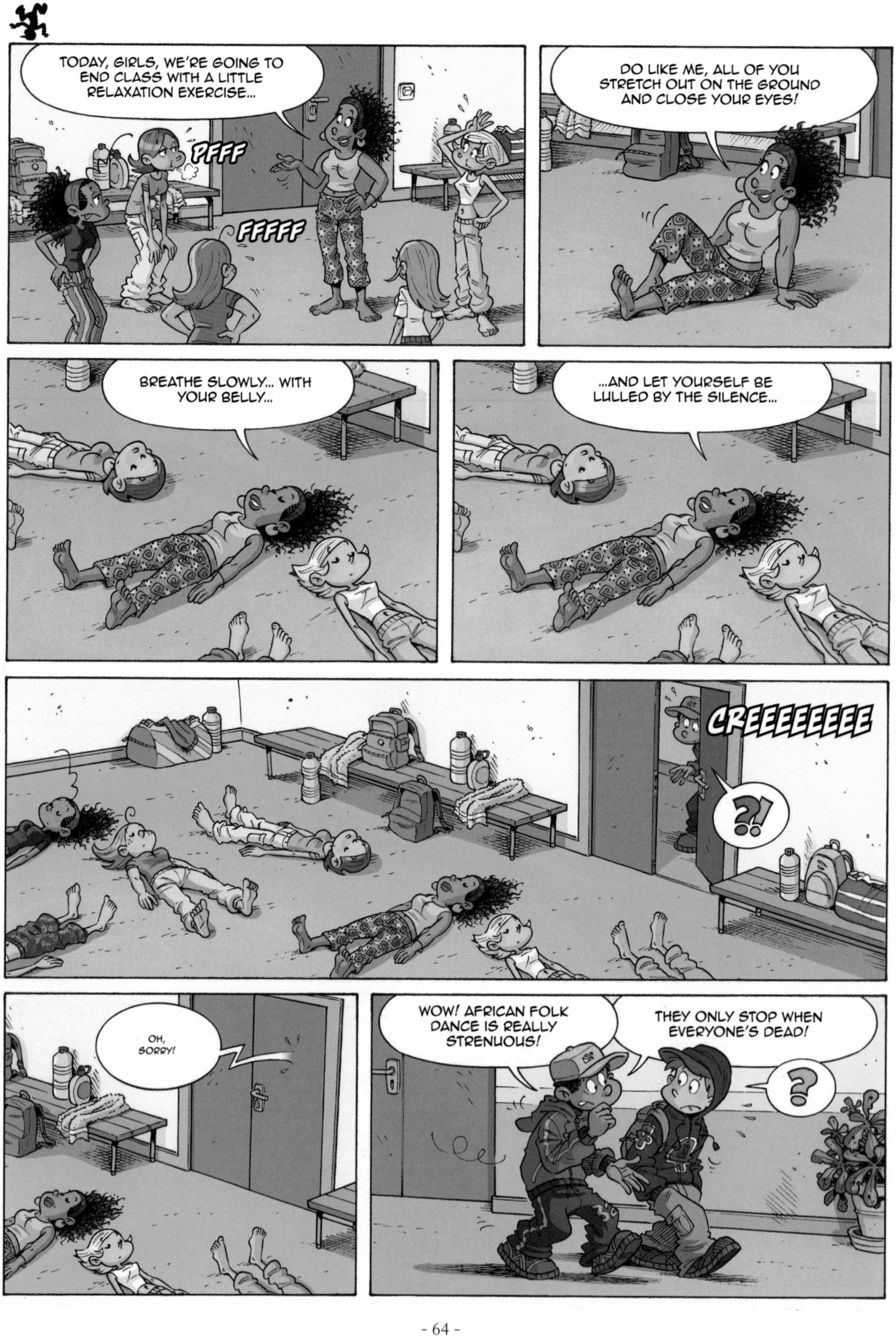
TODAY, GIRLS, WE'RE GOING TO END CLASS WITH A LITTLE RELAXATION EXERCISE...
PFFF
FFFFF
DO LIKE ME, ALL OF YOU STRETCH OUT ON THE GROUND AND CLOSE YOUR EYES!
BREATHE SLOWLY... WITH YOUR BELLY...
...AND LET YOURSELF BE LULLED BY THE SILENCE...
CREEEEEEEE
?!
OH, SORRY!
WOW! AFRICAN FOLK DANCE IS REALLY STRENUOUS!
THEY ONLY STOP WHEN EVERYONE'S DEAD!
?

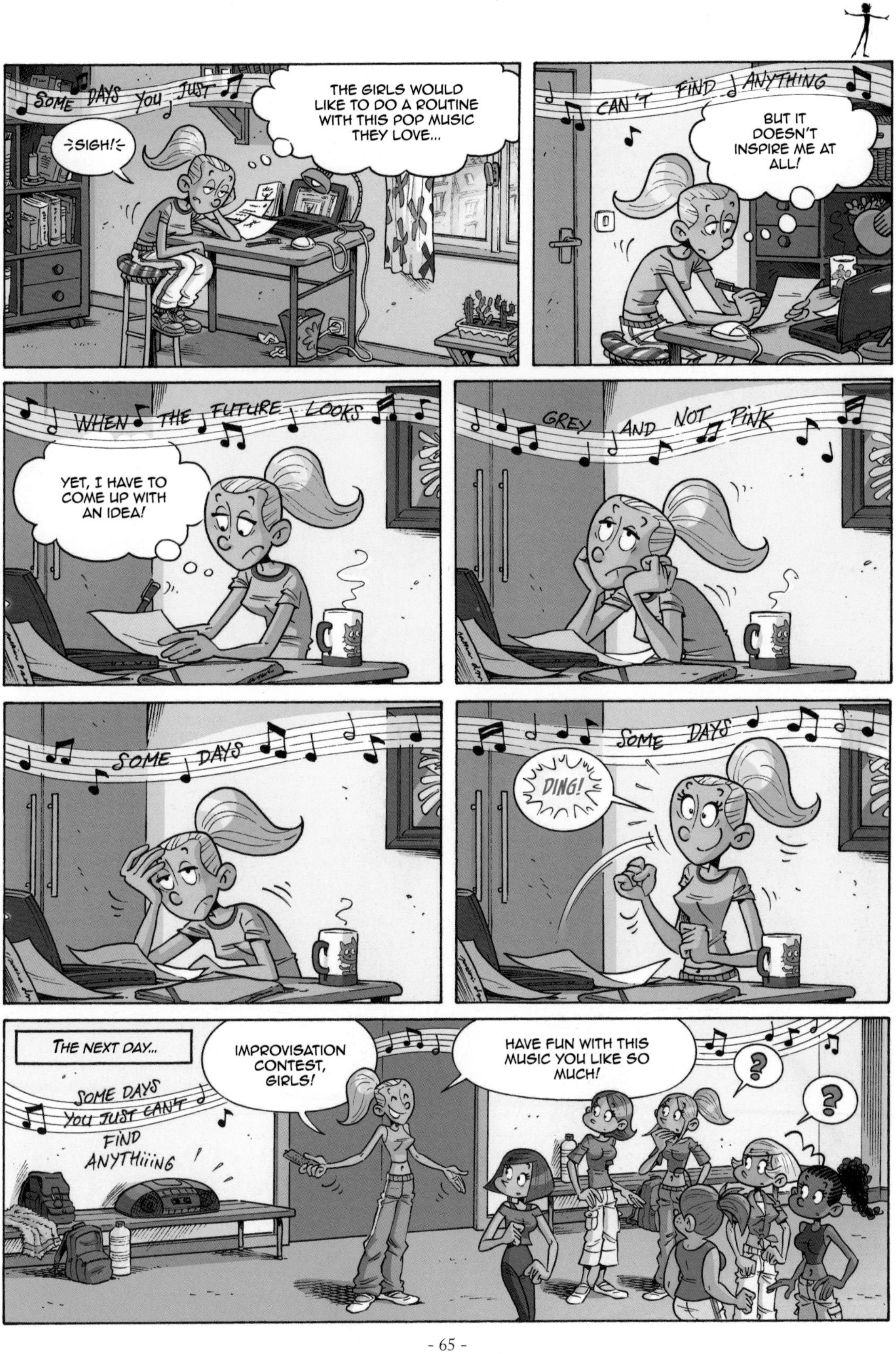
SOME DAYS YOU JUST
SIGH!
THE GIRLS WOULD LIKE TO DO A ROUTINE WITH THIS POP MUSIC THEY LOVE...
CAN'T FIND ANYTHING
BUT IT DOESN'T INSPIRE ME AT ALL!
WHEN THE FUTURE LOOKS
YET, I HAVE TO COME UP WITH AN IDEA!
GREY AND NOT PINK
SOME DAYS
SOME DAYS
DING!
THE NEXT DAY...
IMPROVISATION CONTEST, GIRLS!
HAVE FUN WITH THIS MUSIC YOU LIKE SO MUCH!
SOME DAYS YOU JUST CAN'T FIND ANYTHiiiNG
?
?

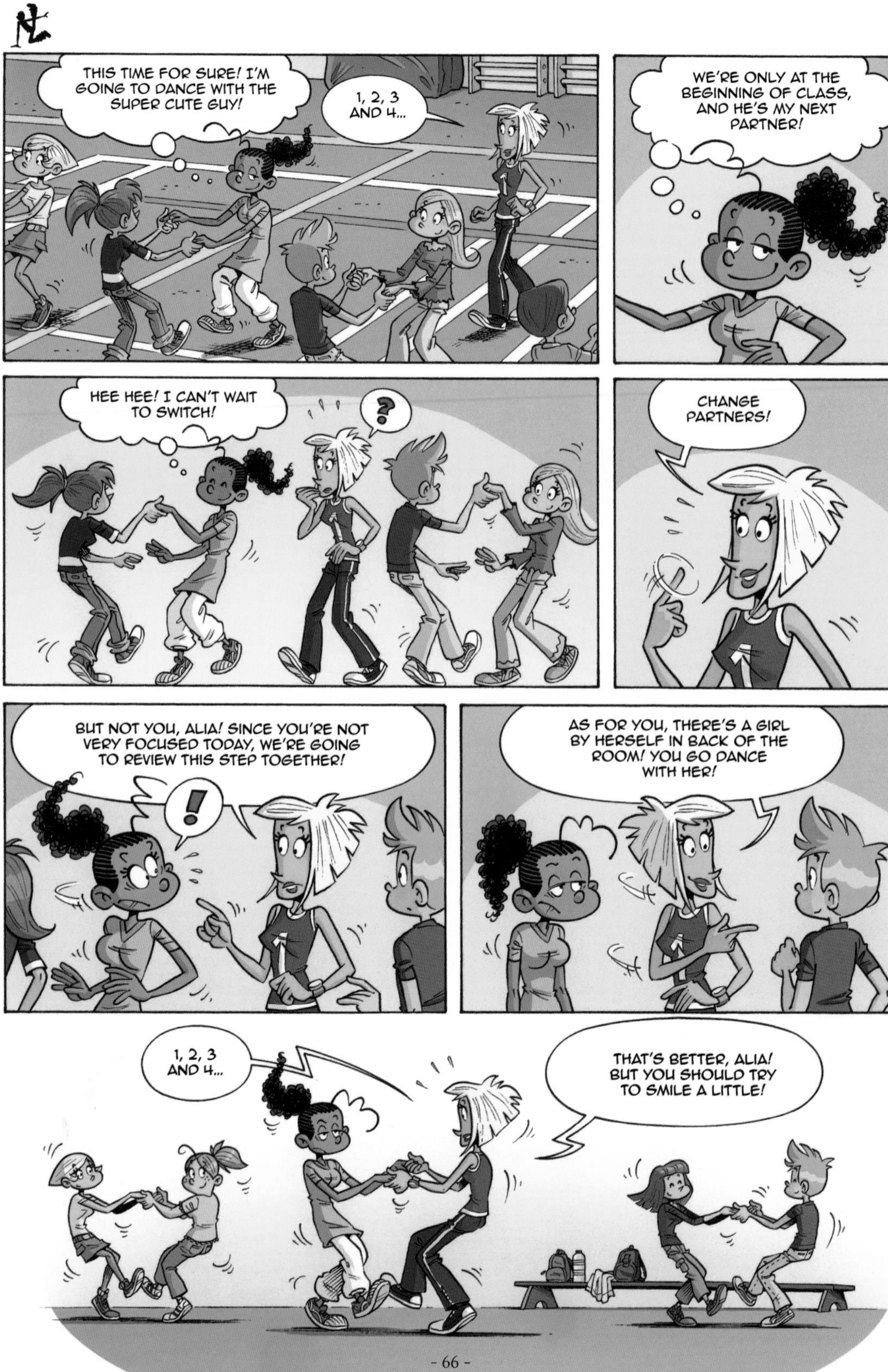

THIS TIME FOR SURE! I'M GOING TO DANCE WITH THE SUPER CUTE GUY!
1, 2, 3 AND 4...
WE'RE ONLY AT THE BEGINNING OF CLASS, AND HE'S MY NEXT PARTNER!
HEE HEE! I CAN'T WAIT TO SWITCH!
?
CHANGE PARTNERS!
BUT NOT YOU, ALIA! SINCE YOU'RE NOT VERY FOCUSED TODAY, WE'RE GOING TO REVIEW THIS STEP TOGETHER!
!
AS FOR YOU, THERE'S A GIRL BY HERSELF IN BACK OF THE ROOM! YOU GO DANCE WITH HER!
1, 2, 3 AND 4...
THAT'S BETTER, ALIA! BUT YOU SHOULD TRY TO SMILE A LITTLE!

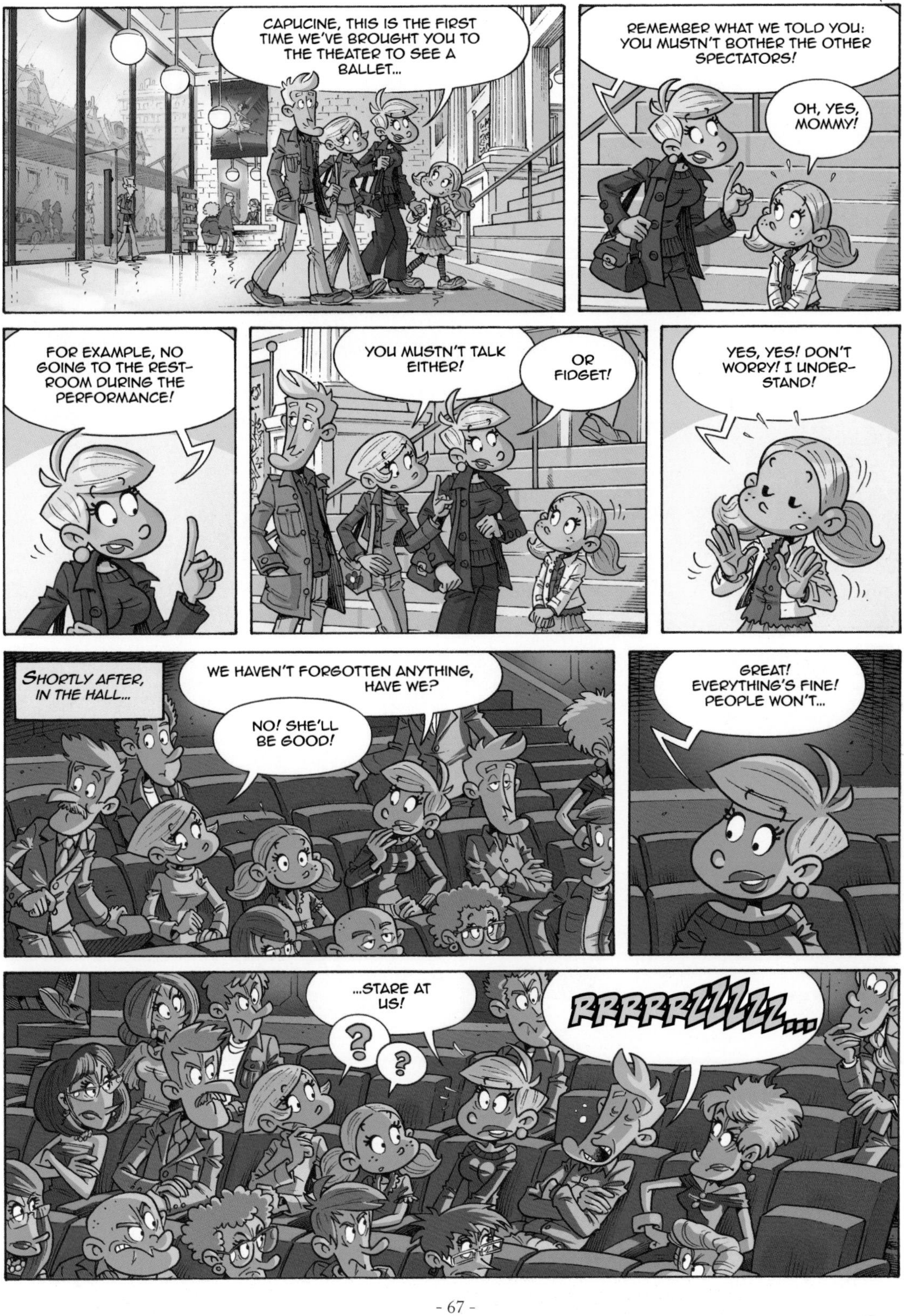

CAPUCINE, THIS IS THE FIRST TIME WE'VE BROUGHT YOU TO THE THEATER TO SEE A BALLET...
REMEMBER WHAT WE TOLD YOU: YOU MUSTN'T BOTHER THE OTHER SPECTATORS!
OH, YES, MOMMY!
FOR EXAMPLE, NO GOING TO THE REST-ROOM DURING THE PERFORMANCE!
YOU MUSTN'T TALK EITHER!
OR FIDGET!
YES, YES! DON'T WORRY! I UNDER-STAND!
SHORTLY AFTER, IN THE HALL...
WE HAVEN'T FORGOTTEN ANYTHING, HAVE WE?
NO! SHE'LL BE GOOD!
GREAT! EVERYTHING'S FINE! PEOPLE WON'T...
...STARE AT US!
?
?
RRRRRZZZZZ...

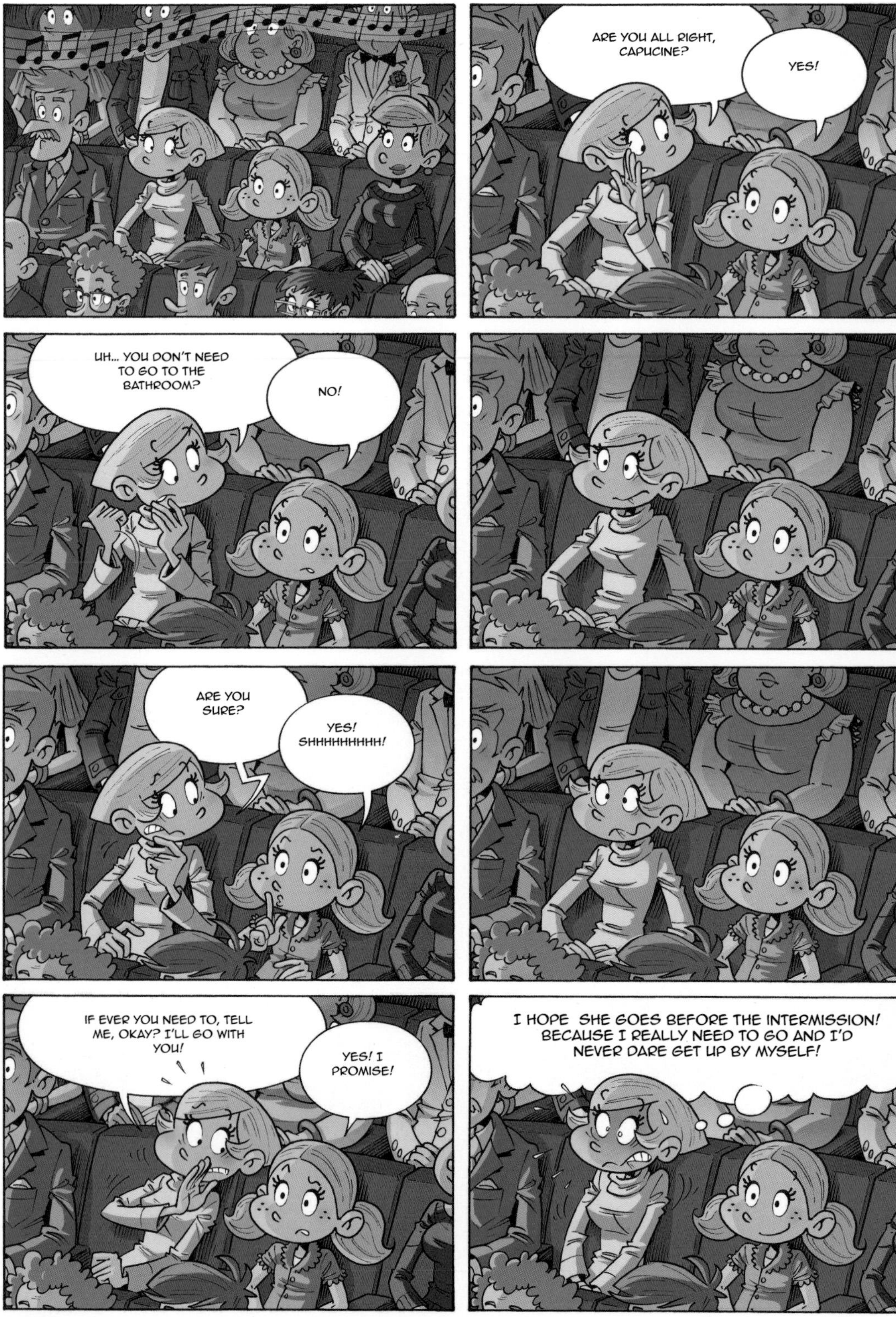

ARE YOU ALL RIGHT, CAPUCINE?
YES!
UH... YOU DON'T NEED TO GO TO THE BATHROOM?
NO!
ARE YOU SURE?
YES! SHHHHHHHHHH!
IF EVER YOU NEED TO, TELL ME, OKAY? I'LL GO WITH YOU!
YES! I PROMISE!
I HOPE SHE GOES BEFORE THE INTERMISSION! BECAUSE I REALLY NEED TO GO AND I'D NEVER DARE GET UP BY MYSELF!

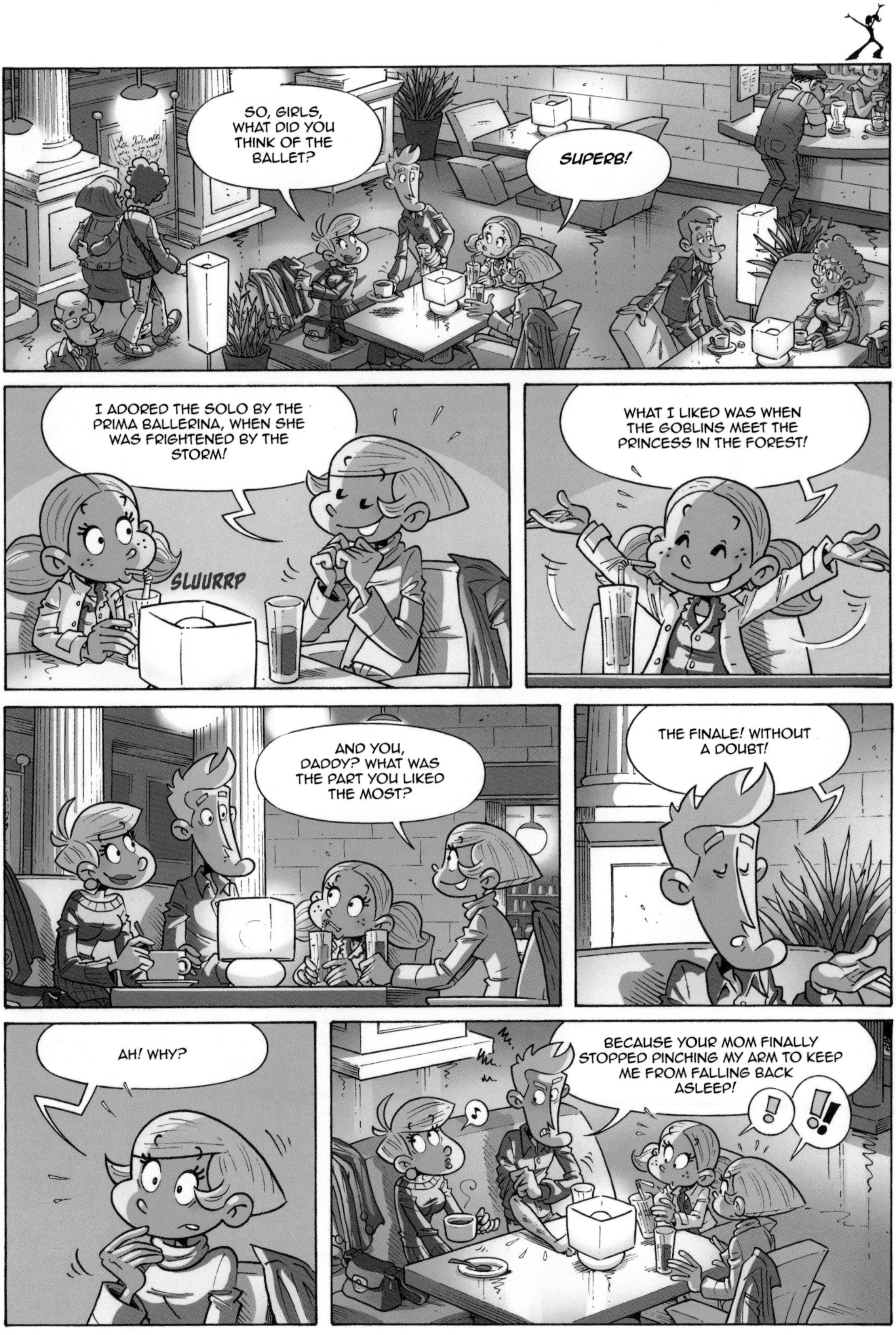
SO, GIRLS, WHAT DID YOU THINK OF THE BALLET?
SUPERB!
I ADORED THE SOLO BY THE PRIMA BALLERINA, WHEN SHE WAS FRIGHTENED BY THE STORM!
SLUURRP
WHAT I LIKED WAS WHEN THE GOBLINS MEET THE PRINCESS IN THE FOREST!
AND YOU, DADDY? WHAT WAS THE PART YOU LIKED THE MOST?
THE FINALE! WITHOUT A DOUBT!
AH! WHY?
BECAUSE YOUR MOM FINALLY STOPPED PINCHING MY ARM TO KEEP ME FROM FALLING BACK ASLEEP!
!
!!

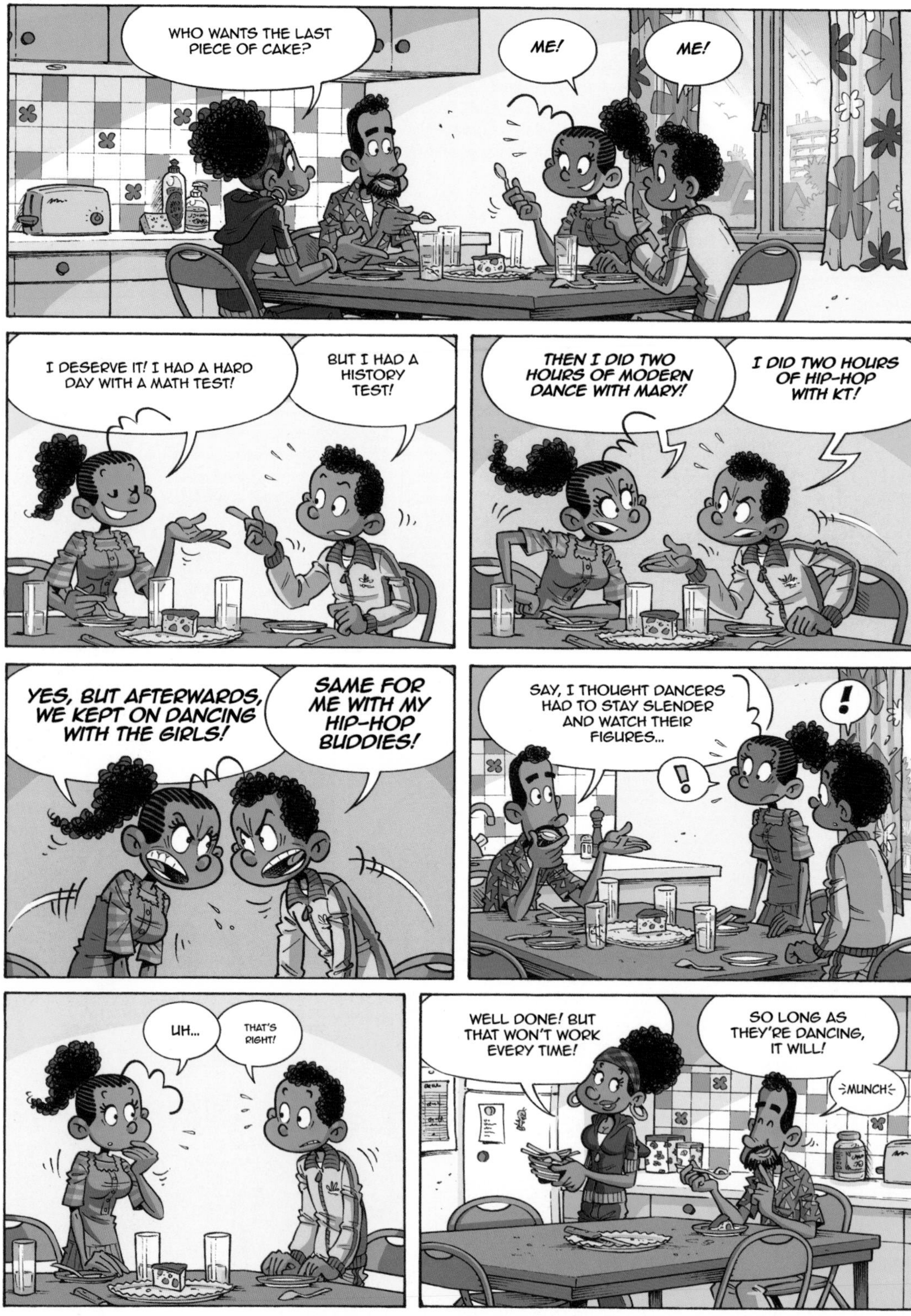
WHO WANTS THE LAST PIECE OF CAKE?
ME!
ME!
I DESERVE IT! I HAD A HARD DAY WITH A MATH TEST!
BUT I HAD A HISTORY TEST!
THEN I DID TWO HOURS OF MODERN DANCE WITH MARY!
I DID TWO HOURS OF HIP-HOP WITH KT!
YES, BUT AFTERWARDS, WE KEPT ON DANCING WITH THE GIRLS!
SAME FOR ME WITH MY HIP-HOP BUDDIES!
SAY, I THOUGHT DANCERS HAD TO STAY SLENDER AND WATCH THEIR FIGURES...
!
!
UH...
THAT'S RIGHT!
WELL DONE! BUT THAT WON'T WORK EVERY TIME!
SO LONG AS THEY'RE DANCING, IT WILL!
MUNCH

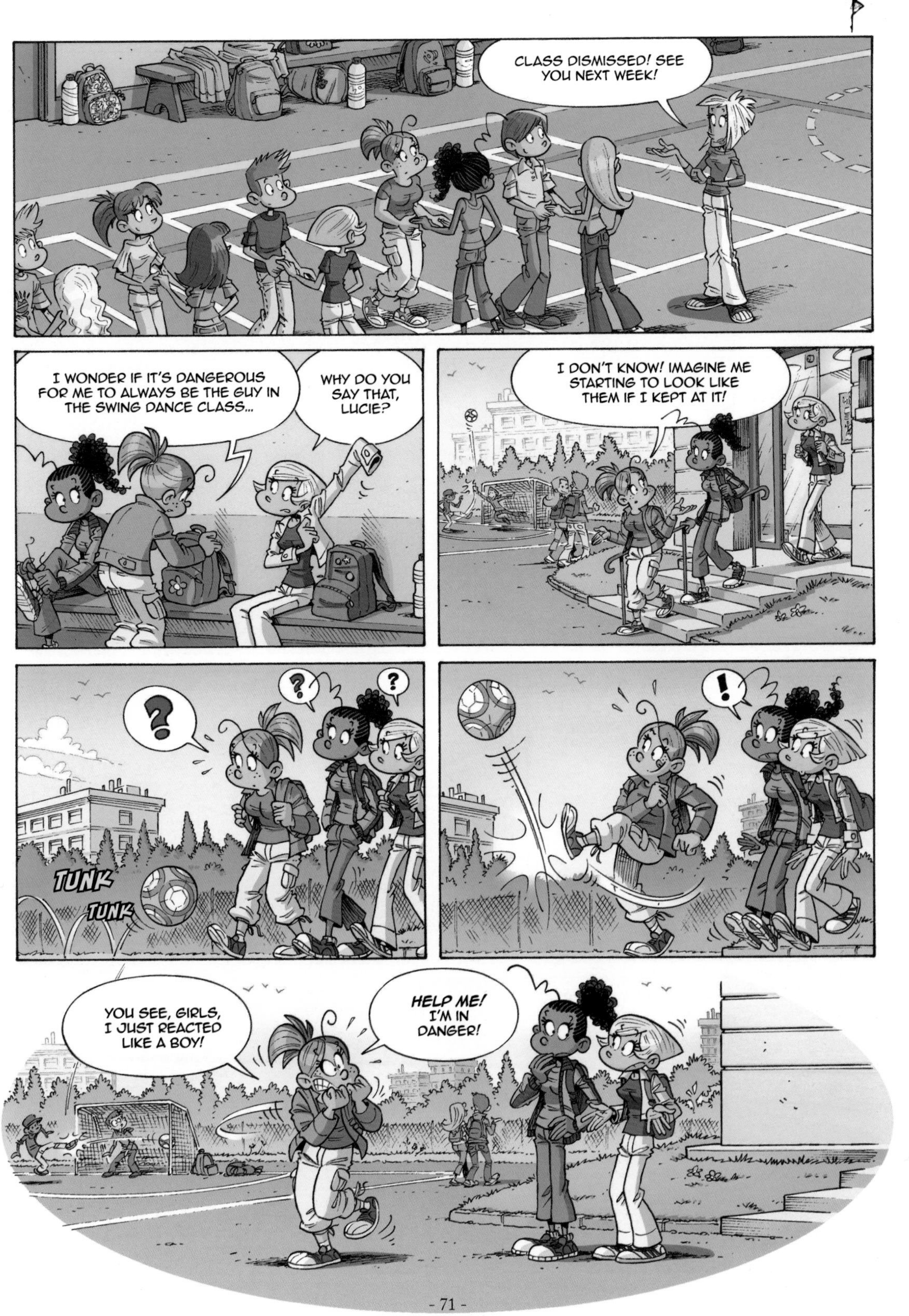
CLASS DISMISSED! SEE YOU NEXT WEEK!
I WONDER IF IT'S DANGEROUS FOR ME TO ALWAYS BE THE GUY IN THE SWING DANCE CLASS...
WHY DO YOU SAY THAT, LUCIE?
I DON'T KNOW! IMAGINE ME STARTING TO LOOK LIKE THEM IF I KEPT AT IT!
?
?
?
TUNK
TUNK
!
YOU SEE, GIRLS, I JUST REACTED LIKE A BOY!
HELP ME! I'M IN DANGER!

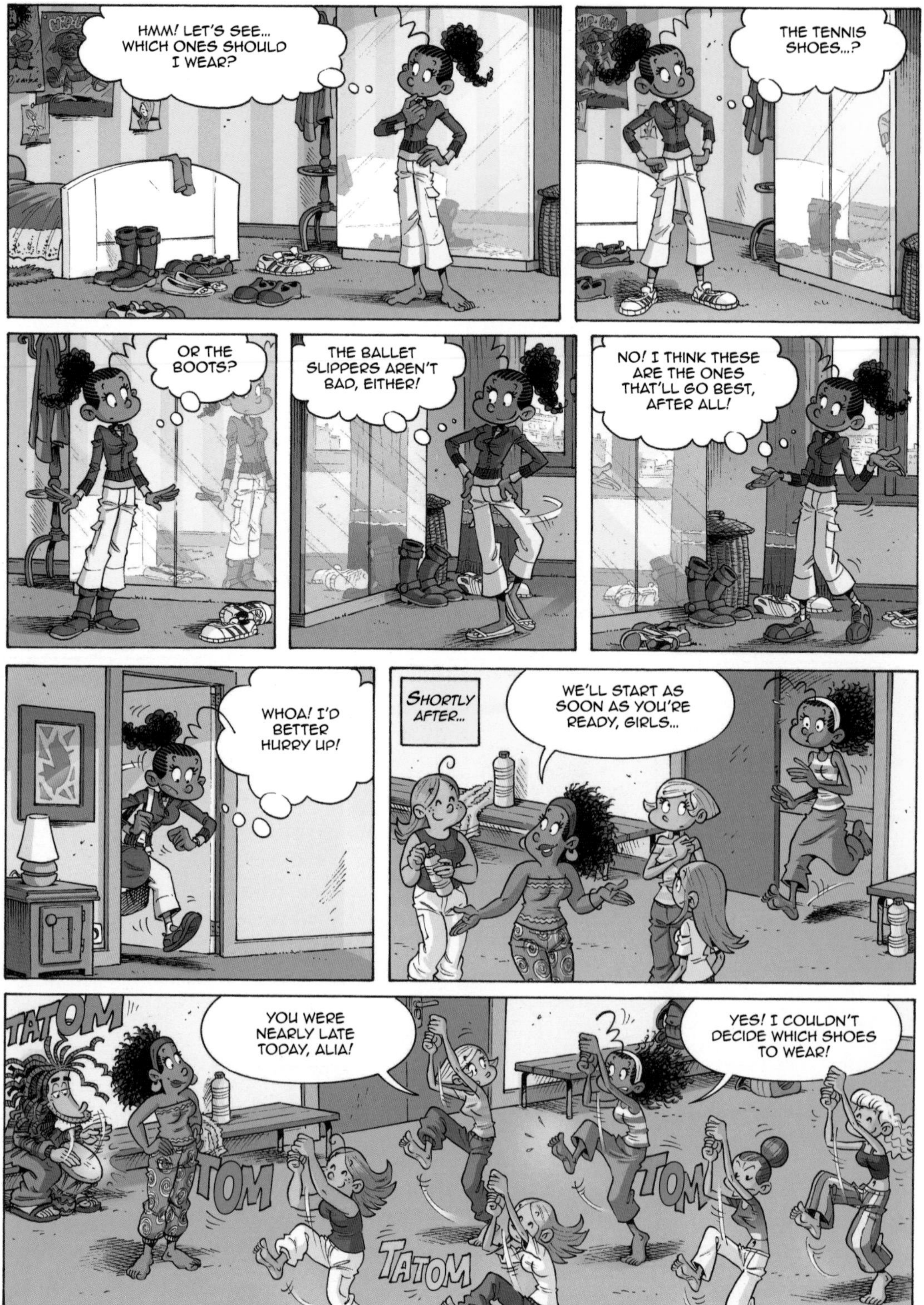
HMM! LET'S SEE... WHICH ONES SHOULD I WEAR?
THE TENNIS SHOES...?
OR THE BOOTS?
THE BALLET SLIPPERS AREN'T BAD, EITHER!
NO! I THINK THESE ARE THE ONES THAT'LL GO BEST, AFTER ALL!
WHOA! I'D BETTER HURRY UP!
SHORTLY AFTER...
WE'LL START AS SOON AS YOU'RE READY, GIRLS...
TATOM
YOU WERE NEARLY LATE TODAY, ALIA!
YES! I COULDN'T DECIDE WHICH SHOES TO WEAR!
TOM
TOM
TATOM

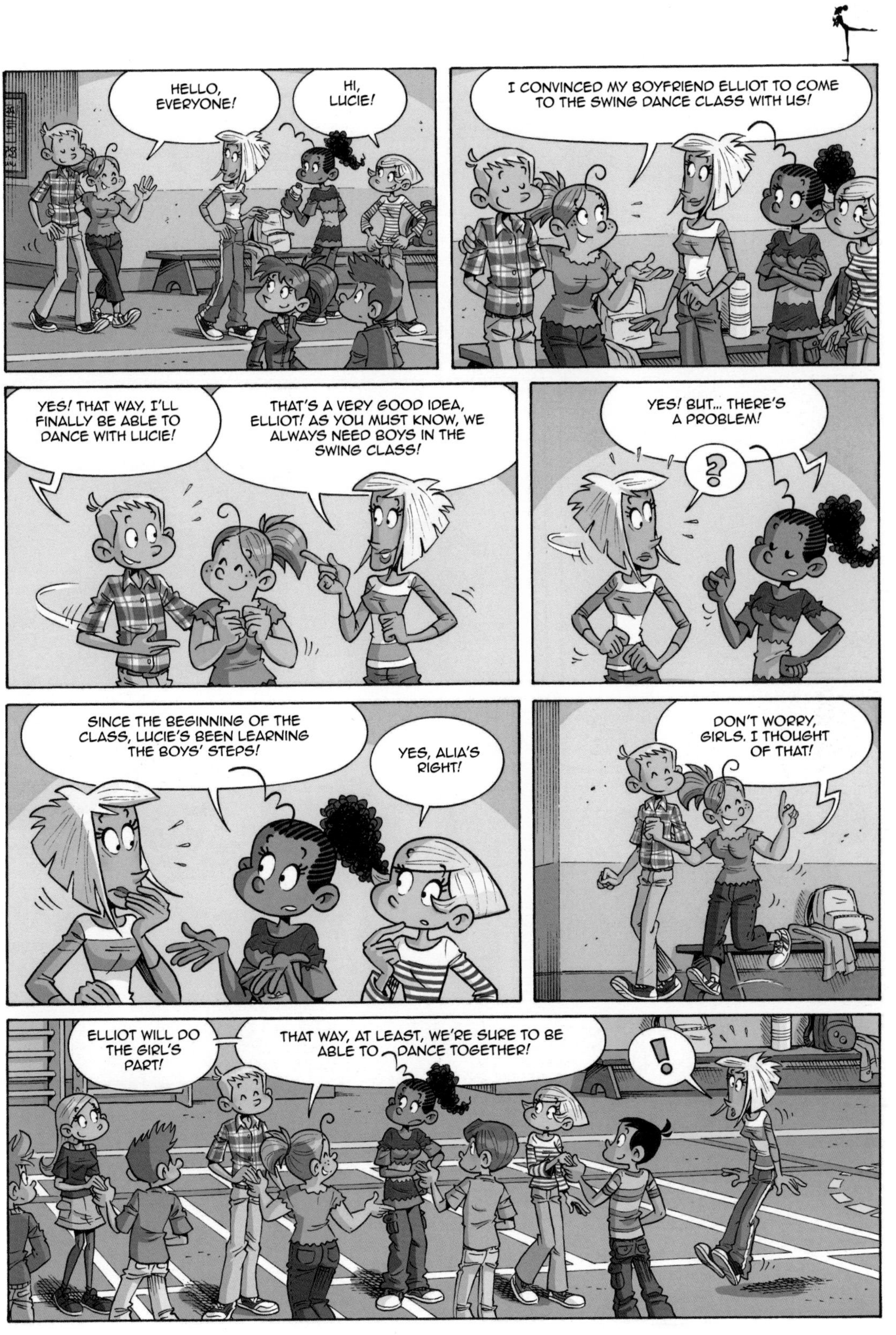

HELLO, EVERYONE!
HI, LUCIE!
I CONVINCED MY BOYFRIEND ELLIOT TO COME TO THE SWING DANCE CLASS WITH US!
YES! THAT WAY, I'LL FINALLY BE ABLE TO DANCE WITH LUCIE!
THAT'S A VERY GOOD IDEA, ELLIOT! AS YOU MUST KNOW, WE ALWAYS NEED BOYS IN THE SWING CLASS!
YES! BUT... THERE'S A PROBLEM!
?
SINCE THE BEGINNING OF THE CLASS, LUCIE'S BEEN LEARNING THE BOYS' STEPS!
YES, ALIA'S RIGHT!
DON'T WORRY, GIRLS. I THOUGHT OF THAT!
ELLIOT WILL DO THE GIRL'S PART!
THAT WAY, AT LEAST, WE'RE SURE TO BE ABLE TO DANCE TOGETHER!
!

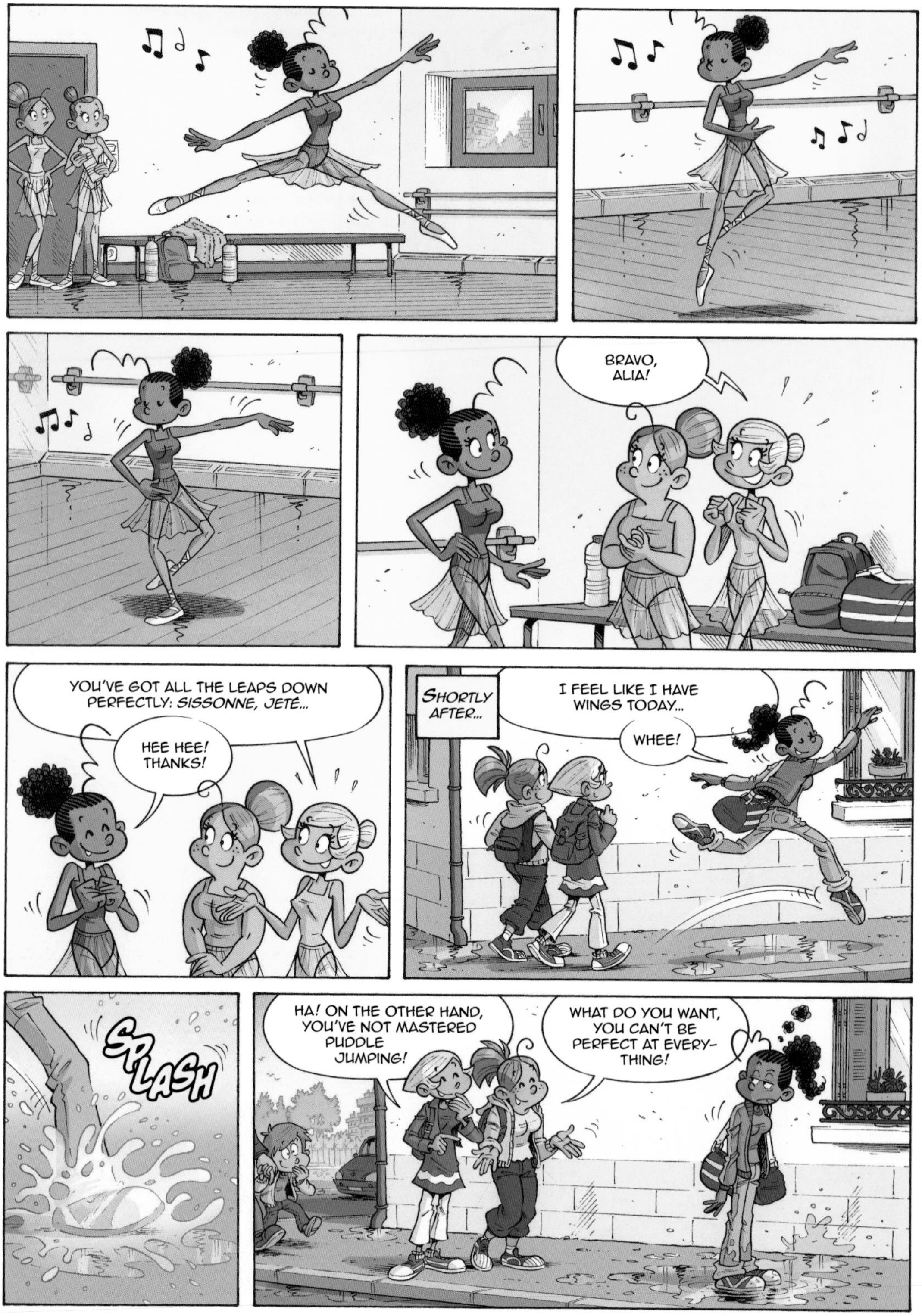
BRAVO, ALIA!
YOU'VE GOT ALL THE LEAPS DOWN PERFECTLY: *SISSONNE, JETÉ*...
HEE HEE! THANKS!
SHORTLY AFTER...
I FEEL LIKE I HAVE WINGS TODAY...
WHEE!
SPLASH
HA! ON THE OTHER HAND, YOU'VE NOT MASTERED PUDDLE JUMPING!
WHAT DO YOU WANT, YOU CAN'T BE PERFECT AT EVERY-THING!

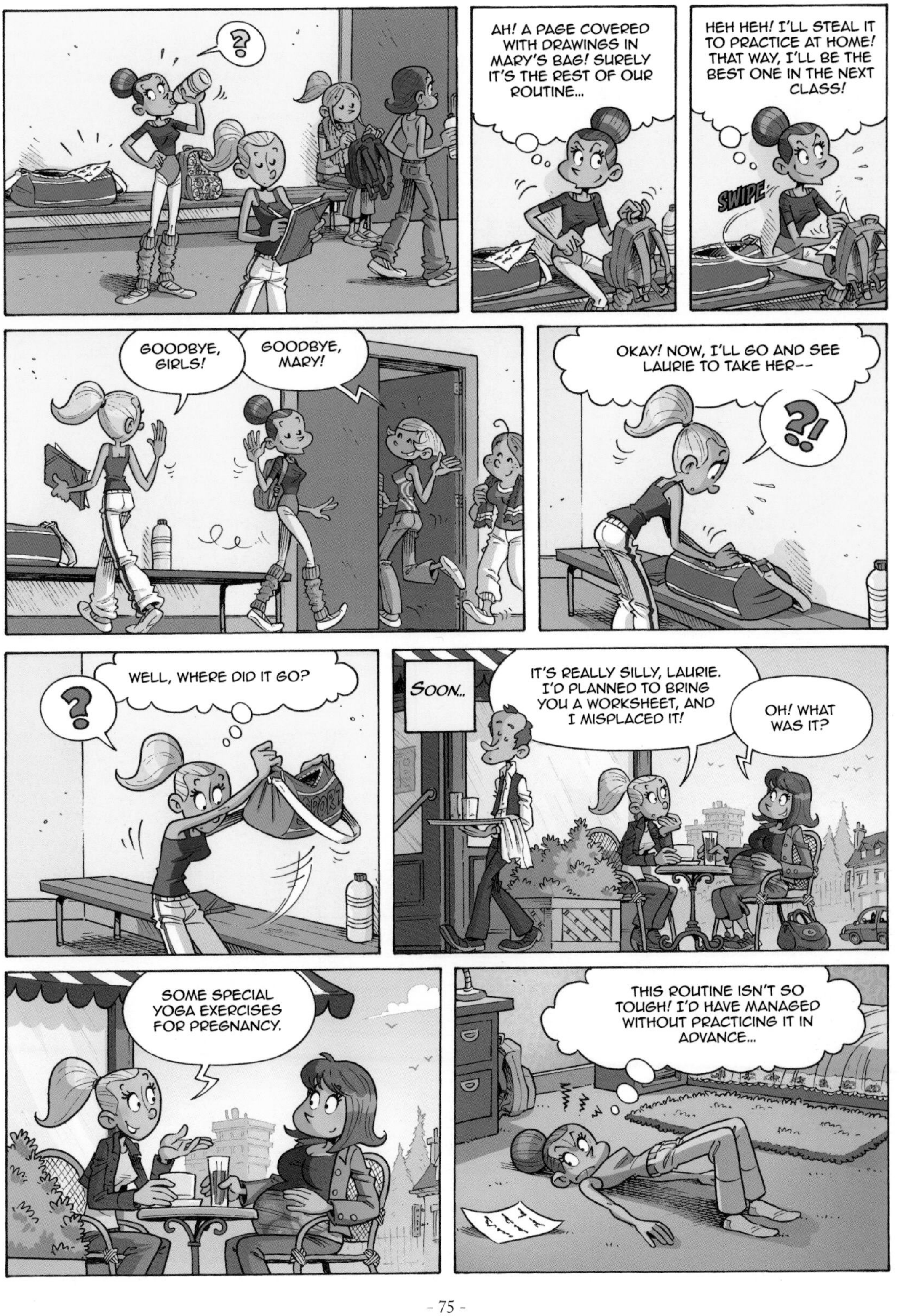
?
AH! A PAGE COVERED WITH DRAWINGS IN MARY'S BAG! SURELY IT'S THE REST OF OUR ROUTINE...
HEH HEH! I'LL STEAL IT TO PRACTICE AT HOME! THAT WAY, I'LL BE THE BEST ONE IN THE NEXT CLASS!
SWIPE
GOODBYE, GIRLS!
GOODBYE, MARY!
OKAY! NOW, I'LL GO AND SEE LAURIE TO TAKE HER--
?!
WELL, WHERE DID IT GO?
?
SOON...
IT'S REALLY SILLY, LAURIE. I'D PLANNED TO BRING YOU A WORKSHEET, AND I MISPLACED IT!
OH! WHAT WAS IT?
SOME SPECIAL YOGA EXERCISES FOR PREGNANCY.
THIS ROUTINE ISN'T SO TOUGH! I'D HAVE MANAGED WITHOUT PRACTICING IT IN ADVANCE...

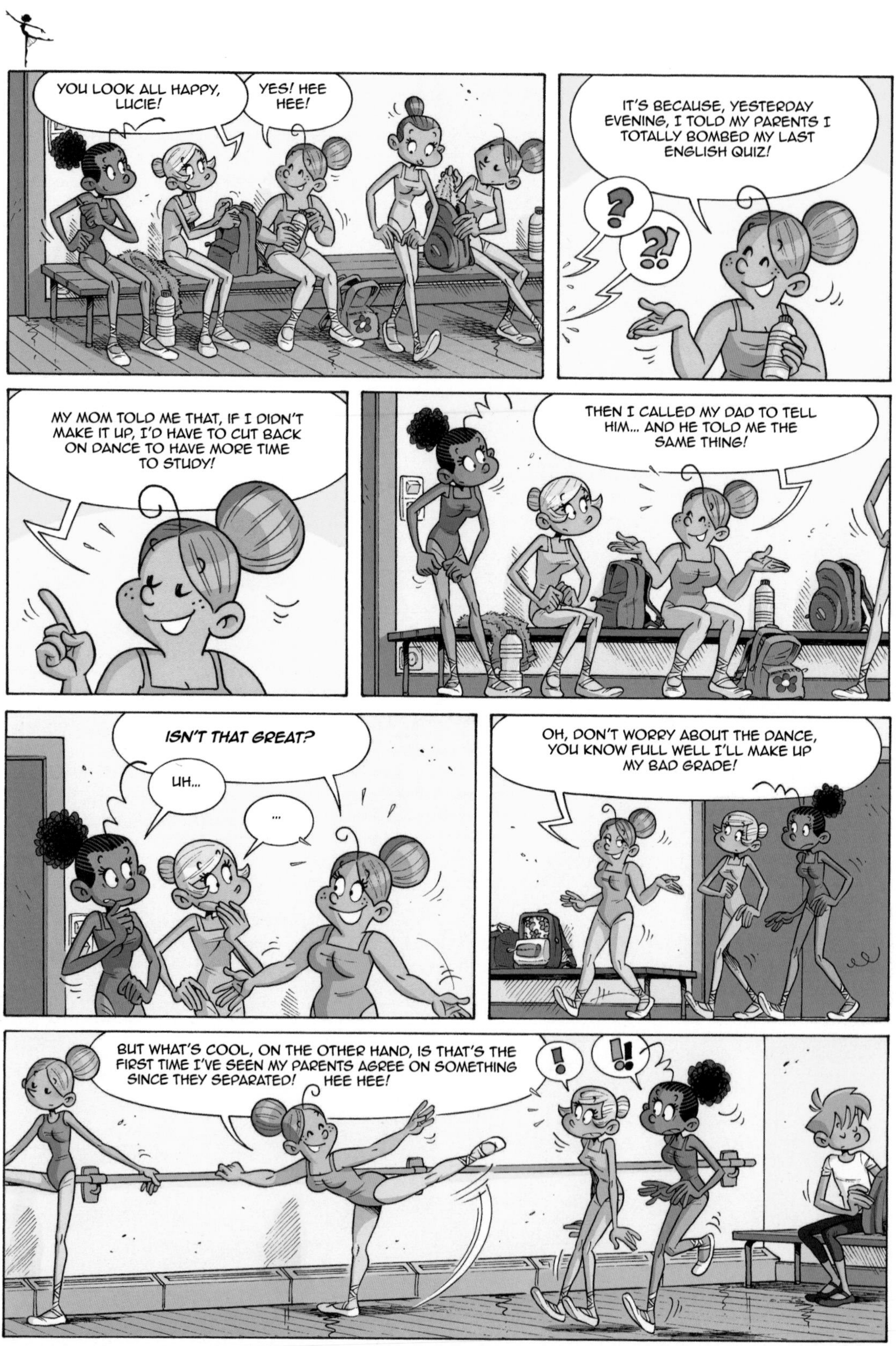

YOU LOOK ALL HAPPY, LUCIE!
YES! HEE HEE!
IT'S BECAUSE, YESTERDAY EVENING, I TOLD MY PARENTS I TOTALLY BOMBED MY LAST ENGLISH QUIZ!
?
?!
MY MOM TOLD ME THAT, IF I DIDN'T MAKE IT UP, I'D HAVE TO CUT BACK ON DANCE TO HAVE MORE TIME TO STUDY!
THEN I CALLED MY DAD TO TELL HIM... AND HE TOLD ME THE SAME THING!
ISN'T THAT GREAT?
UH...
...
OH, DON'T WORRY ABOUT THE DANCE, YOU KNOW FULL WELL I'LL MAKE UP MY BAD GRADE!
BUT WHAT'S COOL, ON THE OTHER HAND, IS THAT'S THE FIRST TIME I'VE SEEN MY PARENTS AGREE ON SOMETHING SINCE THEY SEPARATED! HEE HEE!
!
!!

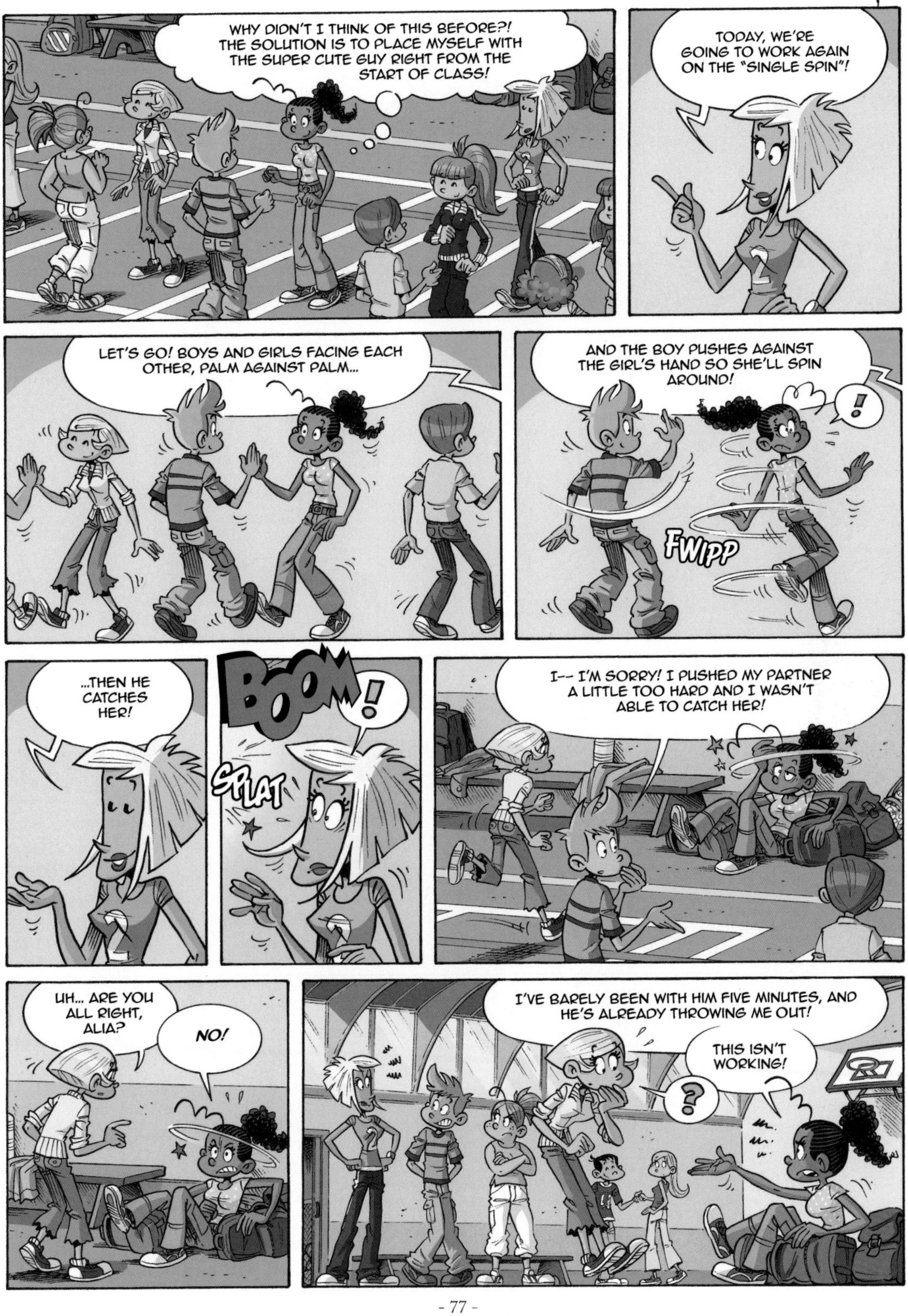
WHY DIDN'T I THINK OF THIS BEFORE?! THE SOLUTION IS TO PLACE MYSELF WITH THE SUPER CUTE GUY RIGHT FROM THE START OF CLASS!
TODAY, WE'RE GOING TO WORK AGAIN ON THE "SINGLE SPIN"!
LET'S GO! BOYS AND GIRLS FACING EACH OTHER, PALM AGAINST PALM...
AND THE BOY PUSHES AGAINST THE GIRL'S HAND SO SHE'LL SPIN AROUND!
!
FWIPP
...THEN HE CATCHES HER!
BOOM
!
SPLAT
I-- I'M SORRY! I PUSHED MY PARTNER A LITTLE TOO HARD AND I WASN'T ABLE TO CATCH HER!
UH... ARE YOU ALL RIGHT, ALIA?
NO!
I'VE BARELY BEEN WITH HIM FIVE MINUTES, AND HE'S ALREADY THROWING ME OUT!
THIS ISN'T WORKING!
?

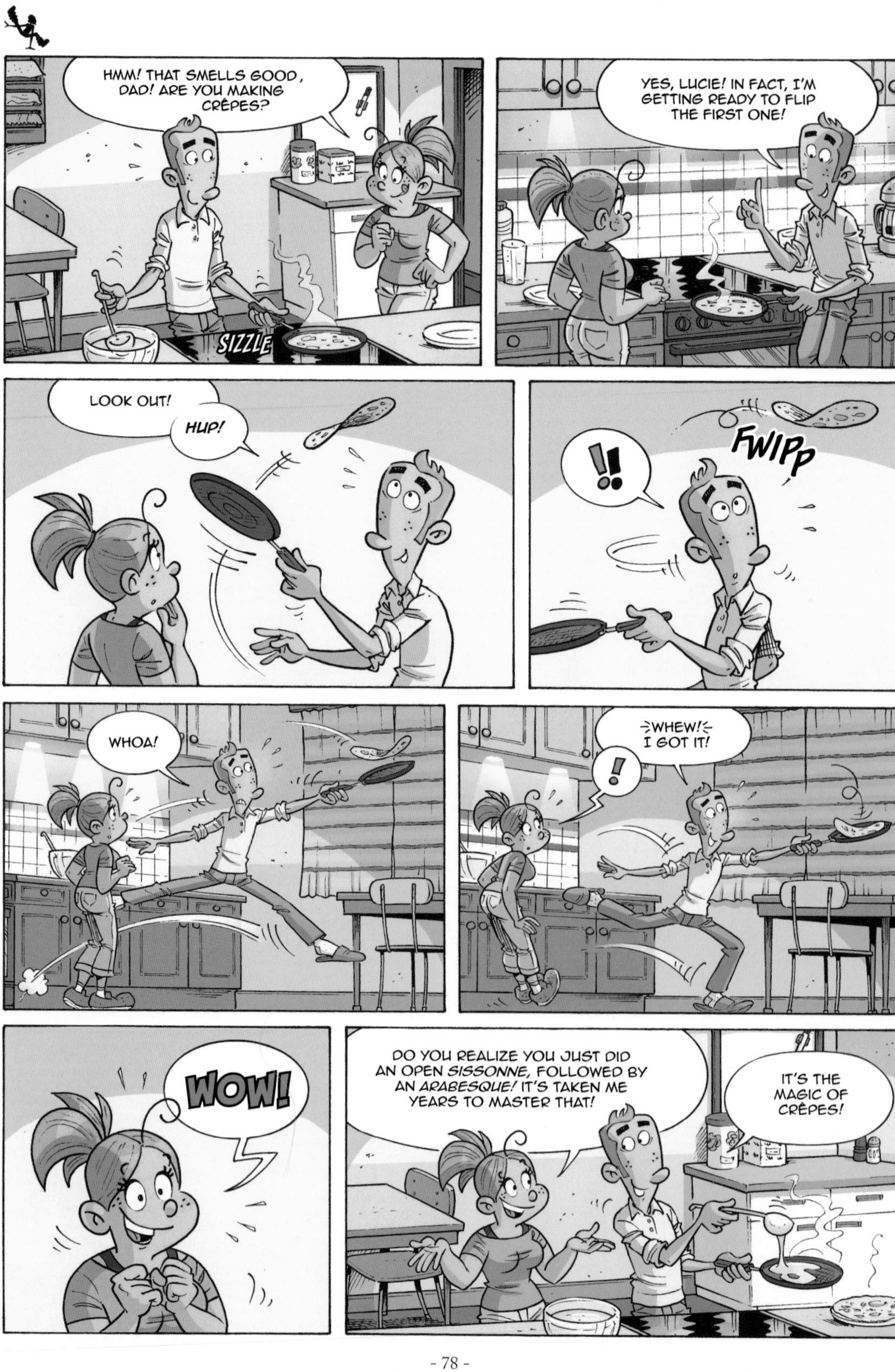
HMM! THAT SMELLS GOOD, DAD! ARE YOU MAKING CRÊPES?
SIZZLE
YES, LUCIE! IN FACT, I'M GETTING READY TO FLIP THE FIRST ONE!
LOOK OUT!
HUP!
!!
FWIPP
WHOA!
!
WHEW! I GOT IT!
WOW!
DO YOU REALIZE YOU JUST DID AN OPEN *SISSONNE*, FOLLOWED BY AN *ARABESQUE*! IT'S TAKEN ME YEARS TO MASTER THAT!
IT'S THE MAGIC OF CRÊPES!

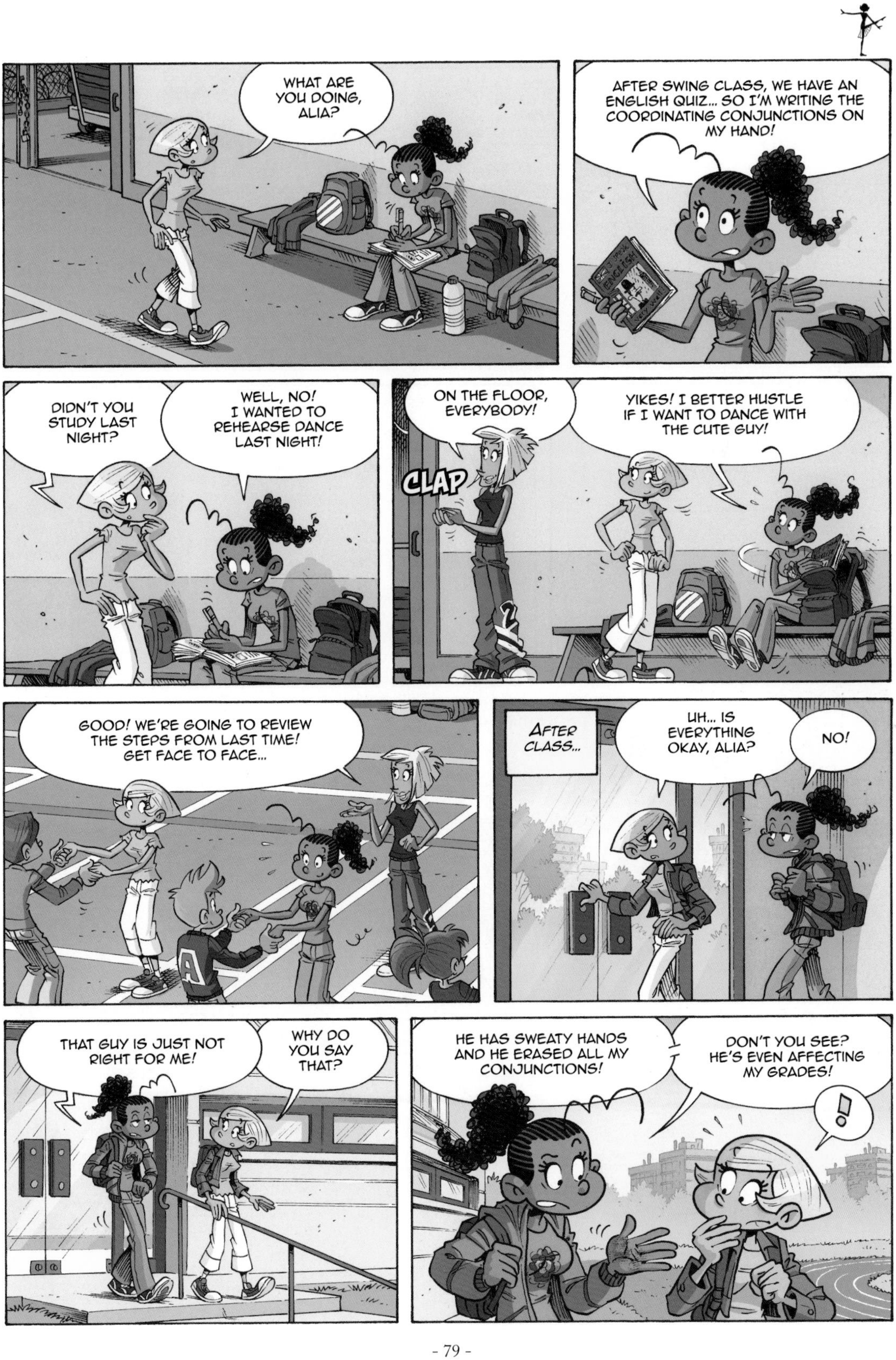
WHAT ARE YOU DOING, ALIA?
AFTER SWING CLASS, WE HAVE AN ENGLISH QUIZ... SO I'M WRITING THE COORDINATING CONJUNCTIONS ON MY HAND!
ENGLISH
DIDN'T YOU STUDY LAST NIGHT?
WELL, NO! I WANTED TO REHEARSE DANCE LAST NIGHT!
ON THE FLOOR, EVERYBODY!
CLAP
YIKES! I BETTER HUSTLE IF I WANT TO DANCE WITH THE CUTE GUY!
GOOD! WE'RE GOING TO REVIEW THE STEPS FROM LAST TIME! GET FACE TO FACE...
AFTER CLASS...
UH... IS EVERYTHING OKAY, ALIA?
NO!
THAT GUY IS JUST NOT RIGHT FOR ME!
WHY DO YOU SAY THAT?
HE HAS SWEATY HANDS AND HE ERASED ALL MY CONJUNCTIONS!
DON'T YOU SEE? HE'S EVEN AFFECTING MY GRADES!
!

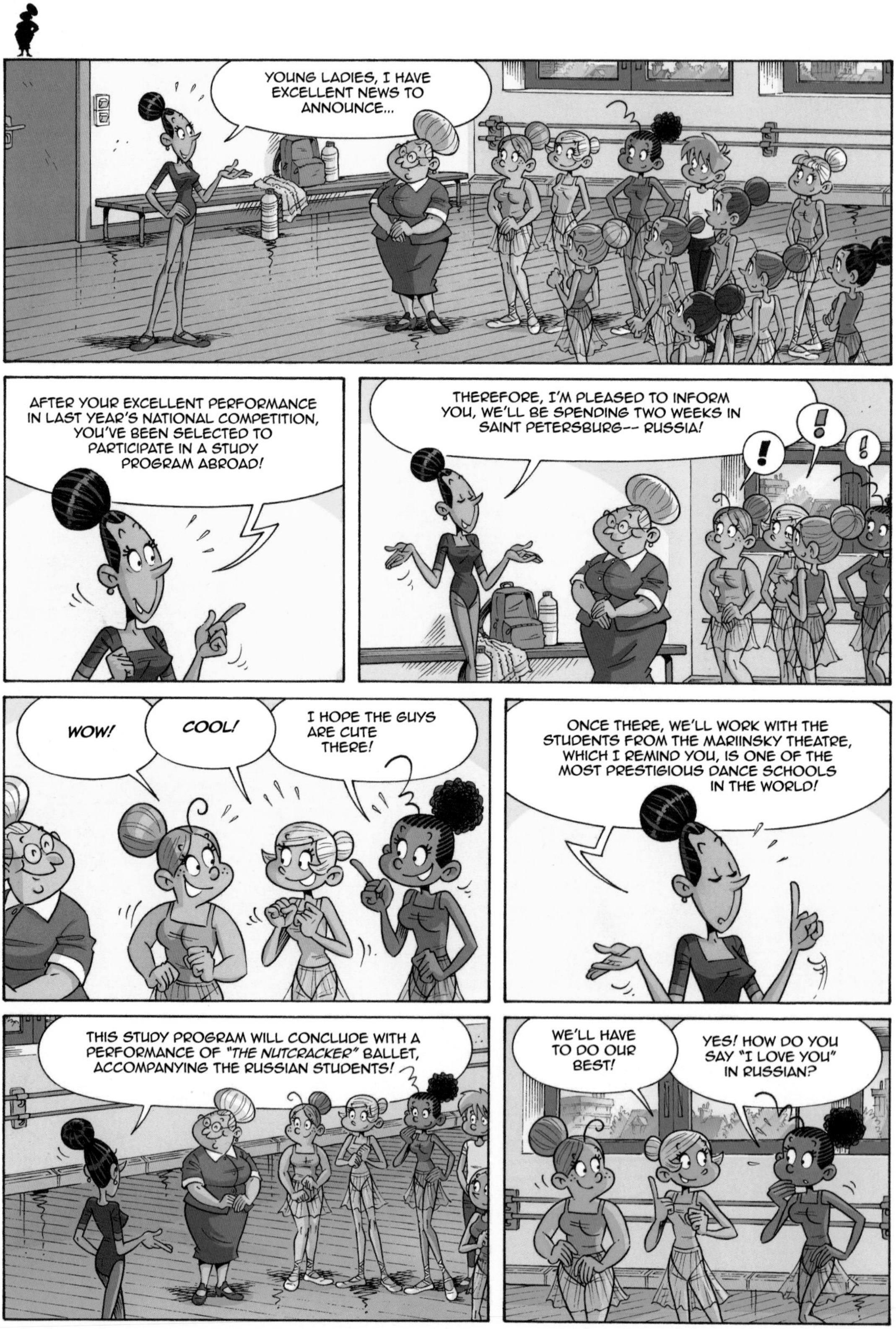
YOUNG LADIES, I HAVE EXCELLENT NEWS TO ANNOUNCE...
AFTER YOUR EXCELLENT PERFORMANCE IN LAST YEAR'S NATIONAL COMPETITION, YOU'VE BEEN SELECTED TO PARTICIPATE IN A STUDY PROGRAM ABROAD!
THEREFORE, I'M PLEASED TO INFORM YOU, WE'LL BE SPENDING TWO WEEKS IN SAINT PETERSBURG-- RUSSIA!
!
!
!
WOW!
COOL!
I HOPE THE GUYS ARE CUTE THERE!
ONCE THERE, WE'LL WORK WITH THE STUDENTS FROM THE MARIINSKY THEATRE, WHICH I REMIND YOU, IS ONE OF THE MOST PRESTIGIOUS DANCE SCHOOLS IN THE WORLD!
THIS STUDY PROGRAM WILL CONCLUDE WITH A PERFORMANCE OF *"THE NUTCRACKER"* BALLET, ACCOMPANYING THE RUSSIAN STUDENTS!
WE'LL HAVE TO DO OUR BEST!
YES! HOW DO YOU SAY "I LOVE YOU" IN RUSSIAN?

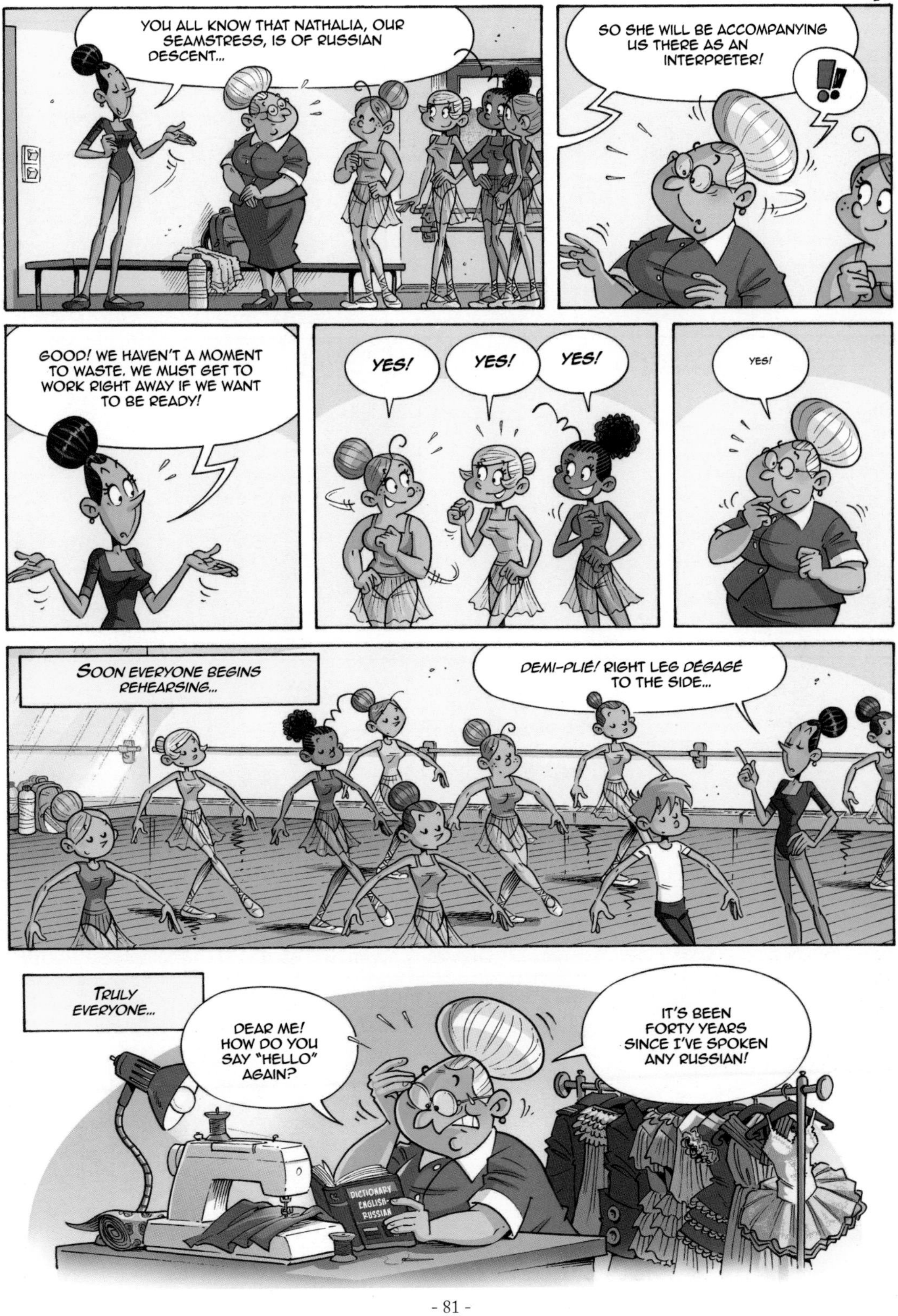

YOU ALL KNOW THAT NATHALIA, OUR SEAMSTRESS, IS OF RUSSIAN DESCENT...
SO SHE WILL BE ACCOMPANYING US THERE AS AN INTERPRETER!
!!
GOOD! WE HAVEN'T A MOMENT TO WASTE. WE MUST GET TO WORK RIGHT AWAY IF WE WANT TO BE READY!
YES!
YES!
YES!
YES!
SOON EVERYONE BEGINS REHEARSING...
DEMI-PLIÉ! RIGHT LEG DÉGAGÉ TO THE SIDE...
TRULY EVERYONE...
DEAR ME! HOW DO YOU SAY "HELLO" AGAIN?
IT'S BEEN FORTY YEARS SINCE I'VE SPOKEN ANY RUSSIAN!
DICTIONARY ENGLISH-RUSSIAN

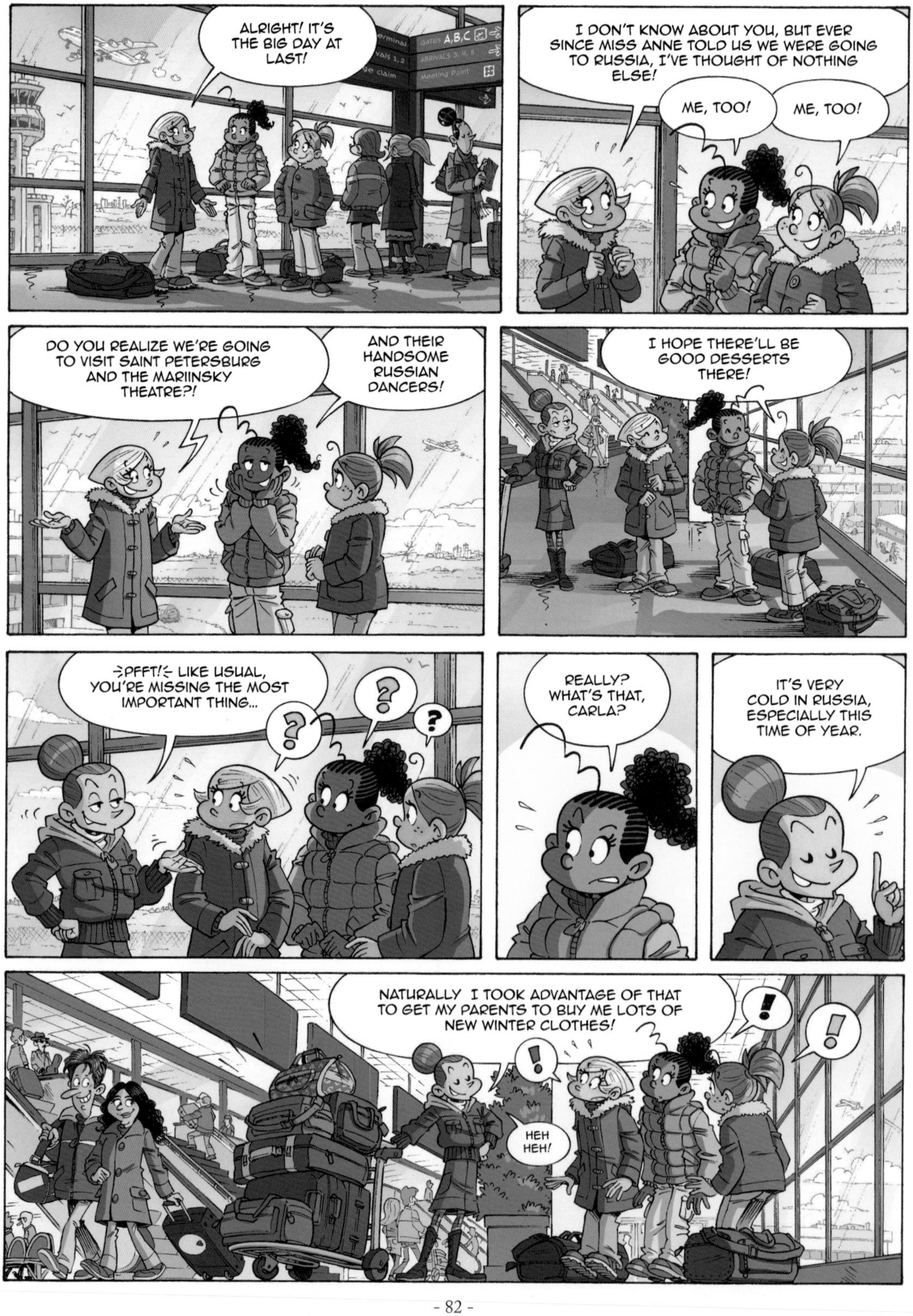
ALRIGHT! IT'S THE BIG DAY AT LAST!
I DON'T KNOW ABOUT YOU, BUT EVER SINCE MISS ANNE TOLD US WE WERE GOING TO RUSSIA, I'VE THOUGHT OF NOTHING ELSE!
ME, TOO!
ME, TOO!
DO YOU REALIZE WE'RE GOING TO VISIT SAINT PETERSBURG AND THE MARIINSKY THEATRE?!
AND THEIR HANDSOME RUSSIAN DANCERS!
I HOPE THERE'LL BE GOOD DESSERTS THERE!
PFFT! LIKE USUAL, YOU'RE MISSING THE MOST IMPORTANT THING...
?
?
REALLY? WHAT'S THAT, CARLA?
IT'S VERY COLD IN RUSSIA, ESPECIALLY THIS TIME OF YEAR.
NATURALLY I TOOK ADVANTAGE OF THAT TO GET MY PARENTS TO BUY ME LOTS OF NEW WINTER CLOTHES!
!
!
!
HEH HEH!

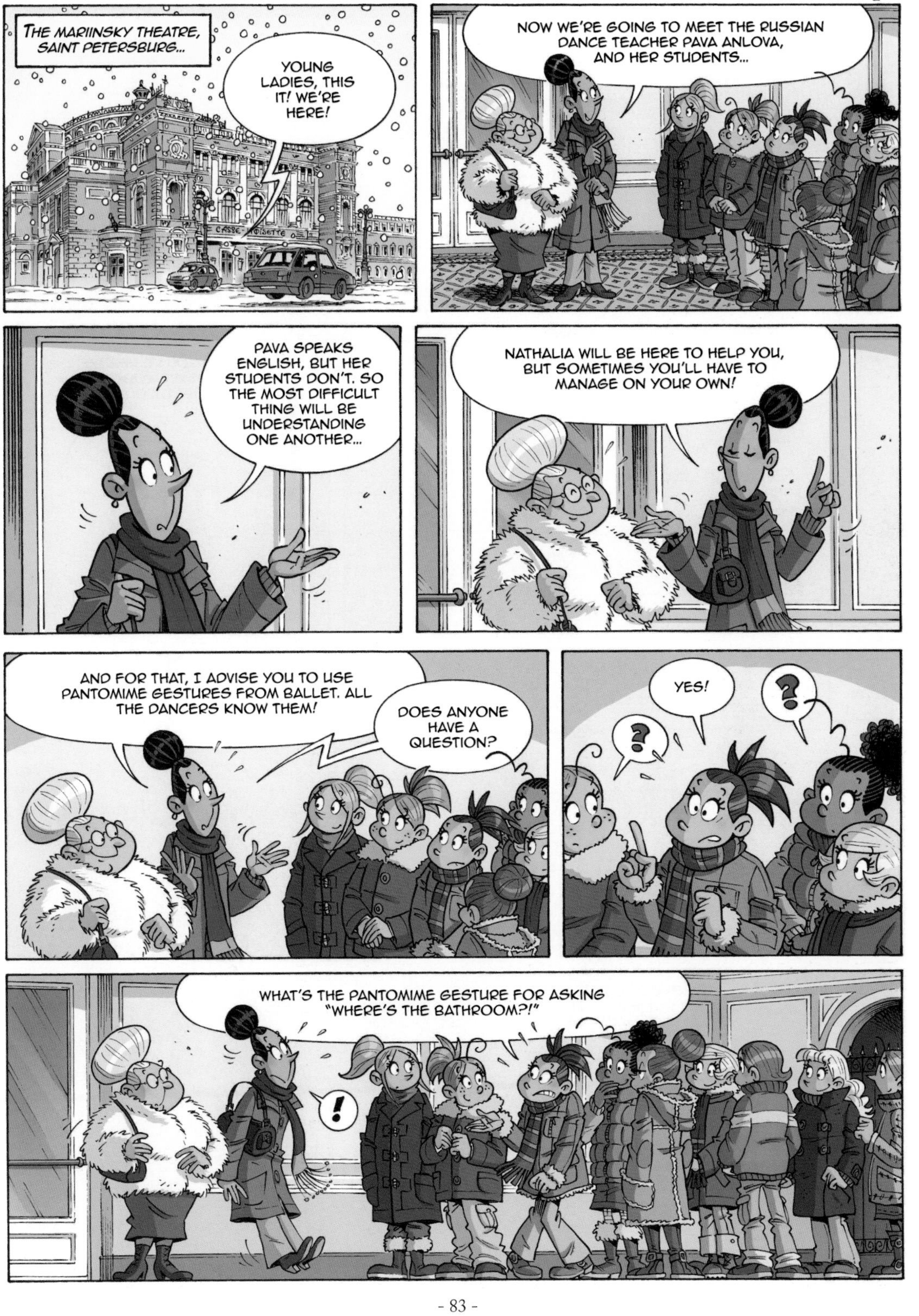
THE MARIINSKY THEATRE, SAINT PETERSBURG...
YOUNG LADIES, THIS IT! WE'RE HERE!
NOW WE'RE GOING TO MEET THE RUSSIAN DANCE TEACHER PAVA ANLOVA, AND HER STUDENTS...
PAVA SPEAKS ENGLISH, BUT HER STUDENTS DON'T. SO THE MOST DIFFICULT THING WILL BE UNDERSTANDING ONE ANOTHER...
NATHALIA WILL BE HERE TO HELP YOU, BUT SOMETIMES YOU'LL HAVE TO MANAGE ON YOUR OWN!
AND FOR THAT, I ADVISE YOU TO USE PANTOMIME GESTURES FROM BALLET. ALL THE DANCERS KNOW THEM!
DOES ANYONE HAVE A QUESTION?
?
YES!
?
WHAT'S THE PANTOMIME GESTURE FOR ASKING "WHERE'S THE BATHROOM?!"
!

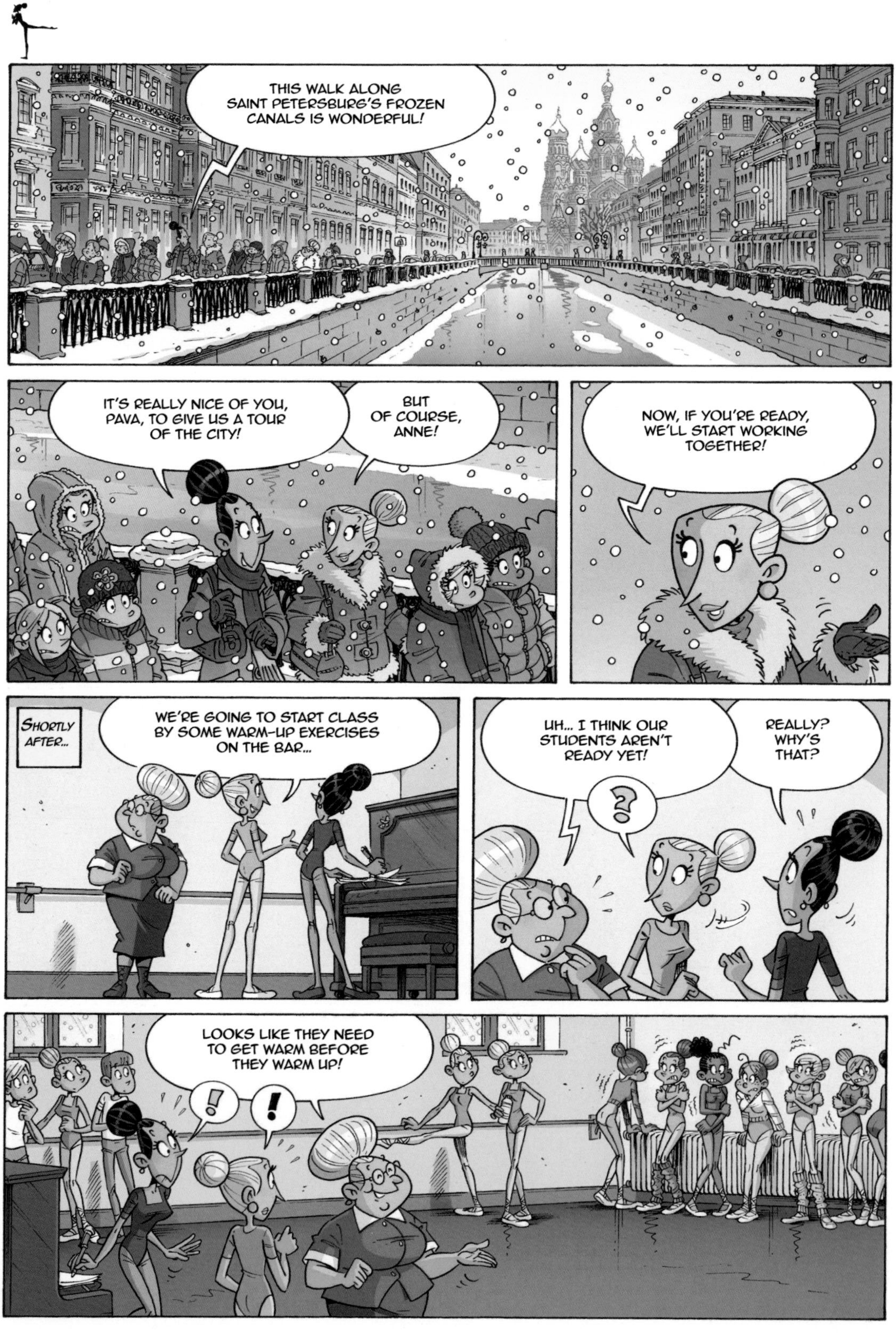
THIS WALK ALONG SAINT PETERSBURG'S FROZEN CANALS IS WONDERFUL!
IT'S REALLY NICE OF YOU, PAVA, TO GIVE US A TOUR OF THE CITY!
BUT OF COURSE, ANNE!
NOW, IF YOU'RE READY, WE'LL START WORKING TOGETHER!
SHORTLY AFTER...
WE'RE GOING TO START CLASS BY SOME WARM-UP EXERCISES ON THE BAR...
UH... I THINK OUR STUDENTS AREN'T READY YET!
?
REALLY? WHY'S THAT?
LOOKS LIKE THEY NEED TO GET WARM BEFORE THEY WARM UP!
!
!

Panel 1:
- DID YOU SEE THAT GUY? HE'S SO HANDSOME! I'M GOING GO TALK TO HIM!
- <THAT'S A PRETTY AMERICAN GIRL! I'M GØING OVER TO GØ SEE HER. >*

Panel 2:
- HELLO, I'M ALIA!
- <HELLØ, I'M NIKØLAI!>

Panel 3:
- DO YOU UNDERSTAND ME?
- <DØ YØN UNDERSTAND RUSSIAN?>

Panel 4:
- I THINK YOU'RE VERY CUTE AND I TOLD MYSELF THAT MAYBE...
- <YØN ARE VERY PRETTY AND I THØNGHT THAT...>

Panel 5:
- WELL, WOULD YOU BE INTERESTED IN SEEING ME AFTER REHEARSAL?
- <MAYBE WE CØNLD GØ ØNT TØGETHER ØNCE CLASS IS ØVER?>

Panel 6:
- UH...
- UH...

Panel 7:
- SO ALIA, HOW'S IT GOING WITH YOUR RUSSIAN SWEETIE?
- DON'T EVEN ASK!

Panel 8:
- HE DOESN'T UNDERSTAND ANYTHING ABOUT WHAT I'M FEELING! WE'RE JUST NOT RIGHT FOR ONE ANOTHER!

*TRANSLATED FROM THE RUSSIAN.

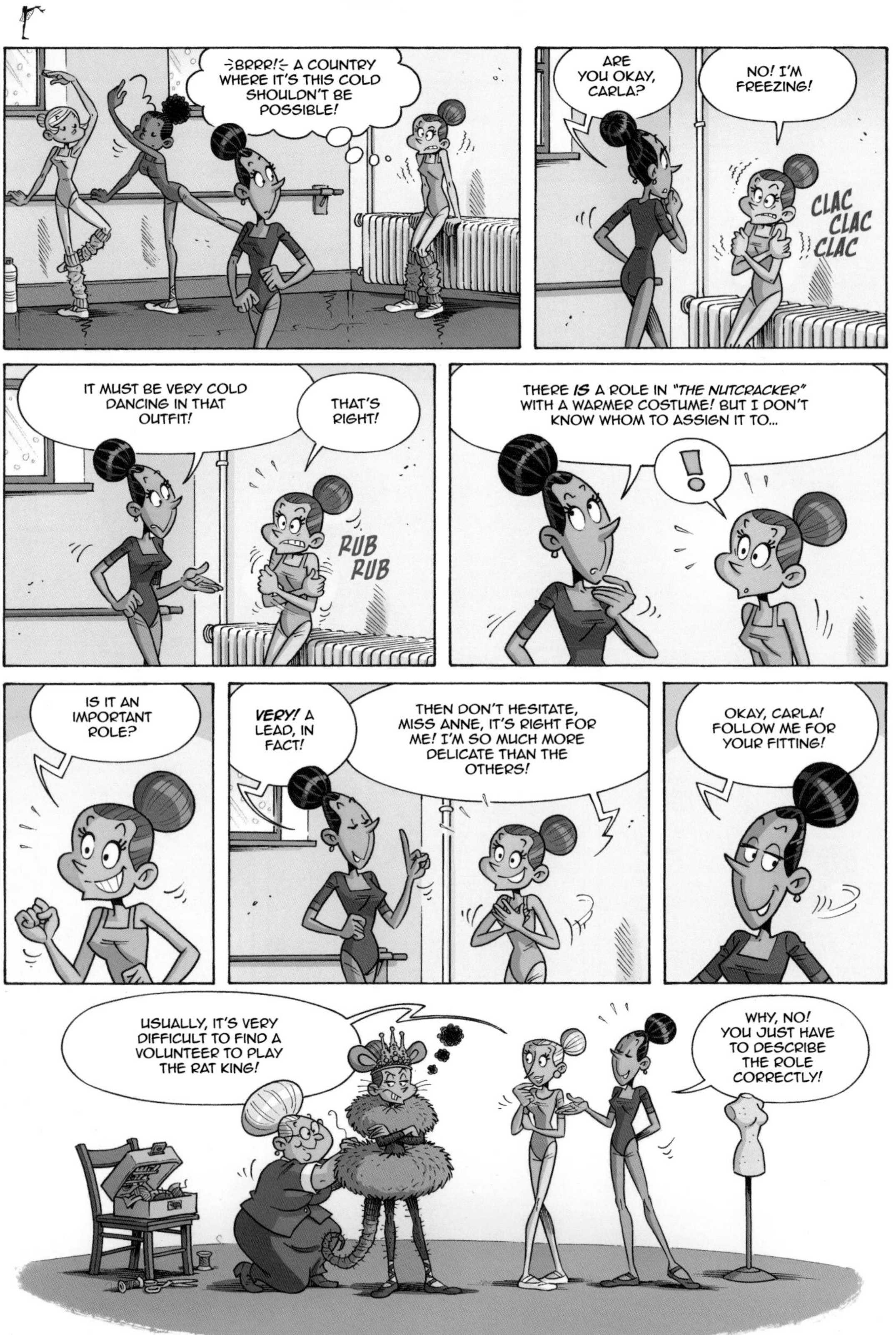
BRRR! A COUNTRY WHERE IT'S THIS COLD SHOULDN'T BE POSSIBLE!
ARE YOU OKAY, CARLA?
NO! I'M FREEZING!
CLAC CLAC CLAC
IT MUST BE VERY COLD DANCING IN THAT OUTFIT!
THAT'S RIGHT!
RUB RUB
THERE *IS* A ROLE IN *"THE NUTCRACKER"* WITH A WARMER COSTUME! BUT I DON'T KNOW WHOM TO ASSIGN IT TO...
!
IS IT AN IMPORTANT ROLE?
VERY! A LEAD, IN FACT!
THEN DON'T HESITATE, MISS ANNE, IT'S RIGHT FOR ME! I'M SO MUCH MORE DELICATE THAN THE OTHERS!
OKAY, CARLA! FOLLOW ME FOR YOUR FITTING!
USUALLY, IT'S VERY DIFFICULT TO FIND A VOLUNTEER TO PLAY THE RAT KING!
WHY, NO! YOU JUST HAVE TO DESCRIBE THE ROLE CORRECTLY!

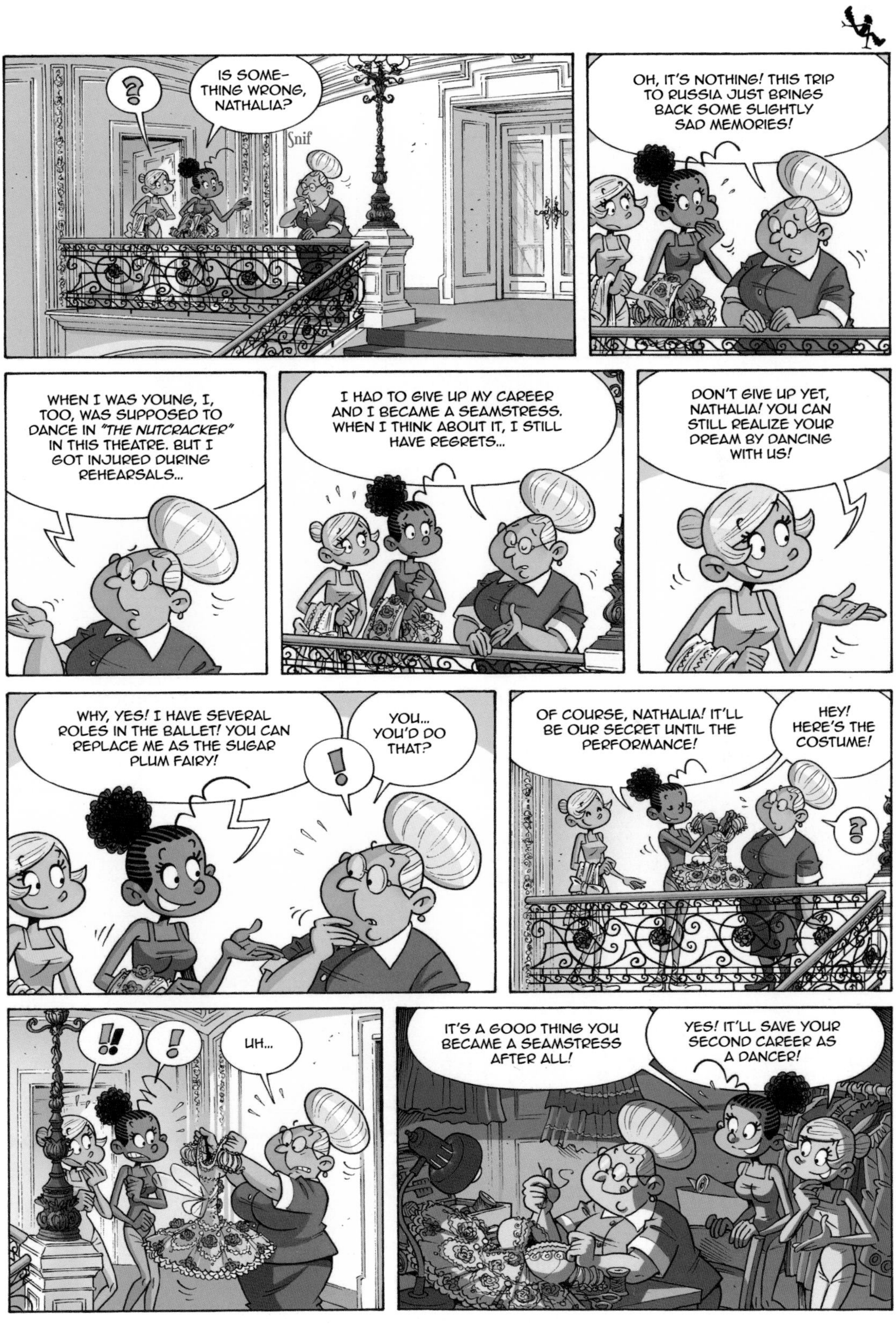
?
IS SOMETHING WRONG, NATHALIA?
Snif
OH, IT'S NOTHING! THIS TRIP TO RUSSIA JUST BRINGS BACK SOME SLIGHTLY SAD MEMORIES!
WHEN I WAS YOUNG, I, TOO, WAS SUPPOSED TO DANCE IN "THE NUTCRACKER" IN THIS THEATRE. BUT I GOT INJURED DURING REHEARSALS...
I HAD TO GIVE UP MY CAREER AND I BECAME A SEAMSTRESS. WHEN I THINK ABOUT IT, I STILL HAVE REGRETS...
DON'T GIVE UP YET, NATHALIA! YOU CAN STILL REALIZE YOUR DREAM BY DANCING WITH US!
WHY, YES! I HAVE SEVERAL ROLES IN THE BALLET! YOU CAN REPLACE ME AS THE SUGAR PLUM FAIRY!
!
YOU... YOU'D DO THAT?
OF COURSE, NATHALIA! IT'LL BE OUR SECRET UNTIL THE PERFORMANCE!
HEY! HERE'S THE COSTUME!
?
!!
!
UH...
IT'S A GOOD THING YOU BECAME A SEAMSTRESS AFTER ALL!
YES! IT'LL SAVE YOUR SECOND CAREER AS A DANCER!

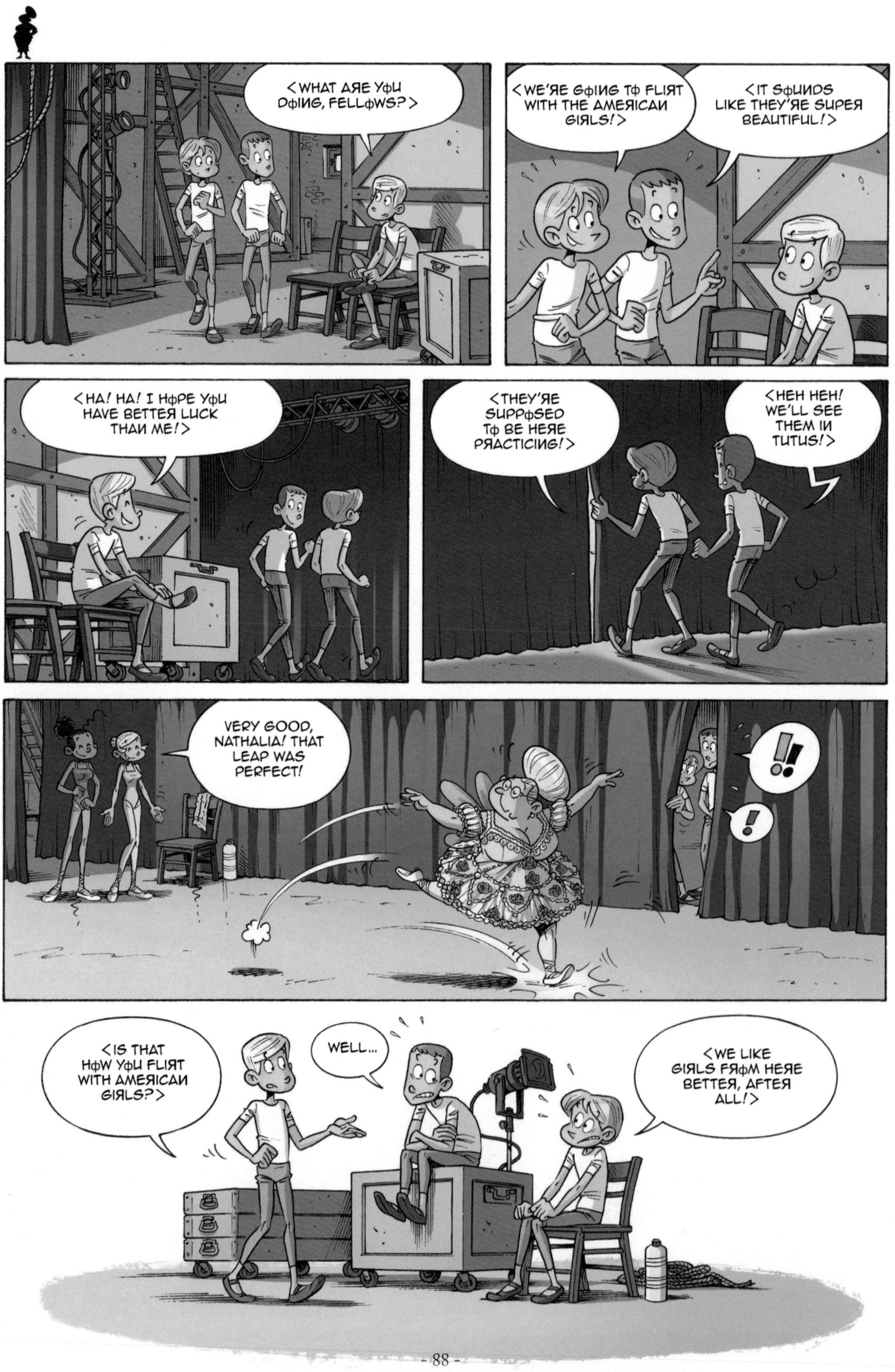
<WHAT ARE YOU DOING, FELLOWS?>
<WE'RE GOING TO FLIRT WITH THE AMERICAN GIRLS!>
<IT SOUNDS LIKE THEY'RE SUPER BEAUTIFUL!>
<HA! HA! I HOPE YOU HAVE BETTER LUCK THAN ME!>
<THEY'RE SUPPOSED TO BE HERE PRACTICING!>
<HEH HEH! WE'LL SEE THEM IN TUTUS!>
VERY GOOD, NATHALIA! THAT LEAP WAS PERFECT!
!!
!
<IS THAT HOW YOU FLIRT WITH AMERICAN GIRLS?>
WELL...
<WE LIKE GIRLS FROM HERE BETTER, AFTER ALL!>

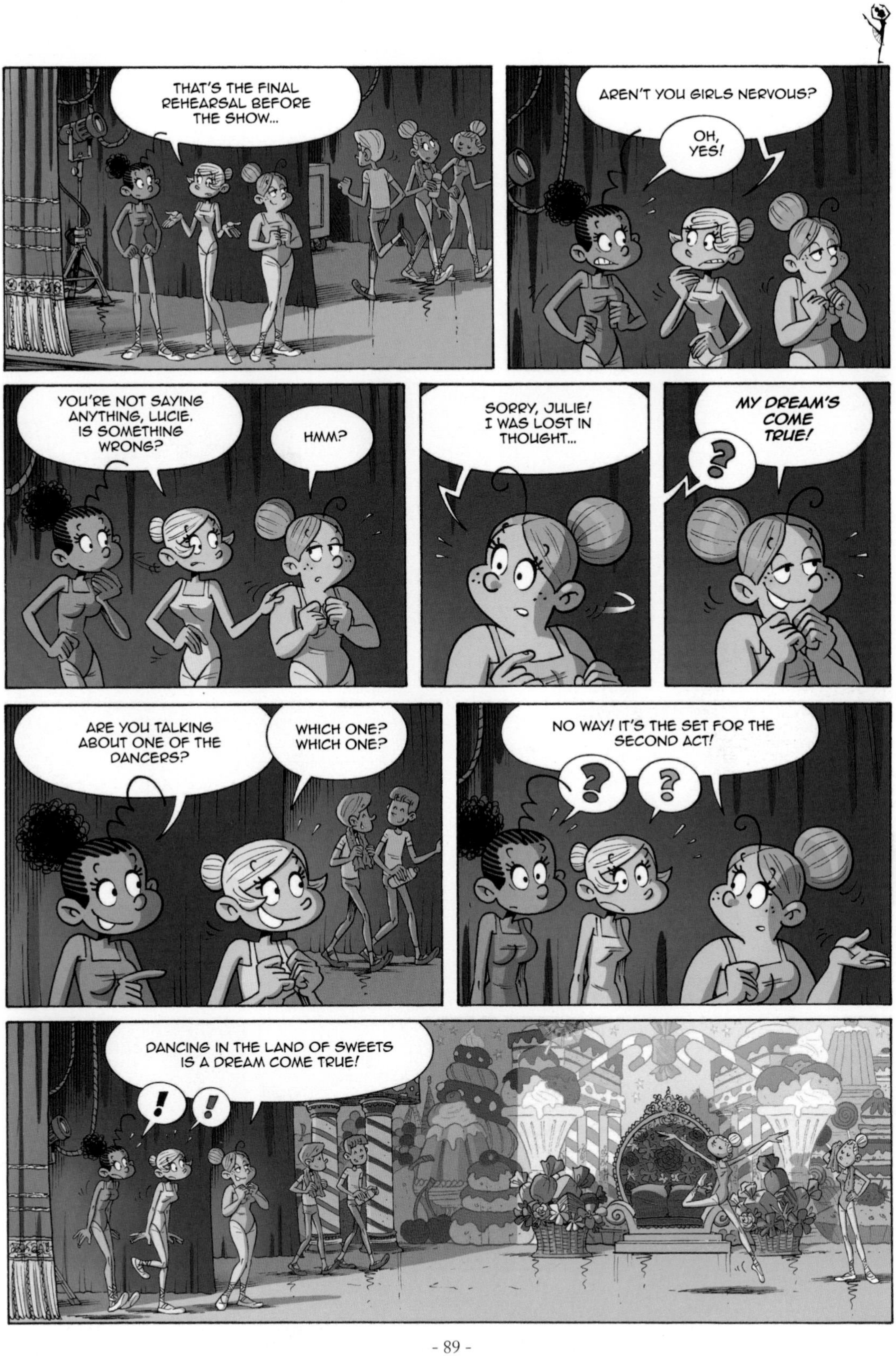
THAT'S THE FINAL REHEARSAL BEFORE THE SHOW...
AREN'T YOU GIRLS NERVOUS?
OH, YES!
YOU'RE NOT SAYING ANYTHING, LUCIE. IS SOMETHING WRONG?
HMM?
SORRY, JULIE! I WAS LOST IN THOUGHT...
?
MY DREAM'S COME TRUE!
ARE YOU TALKING ABOUT ONE OF THE DANCERS?
WHICH ONE? WHICH ONE?
?
?
NO WAY! IT'S THE SET FOR THE SECOND ACT!
!
!
DANCING IN THE LAND OF SWEETS IS A DREAM COME TRUE!

the NUTCRACKER

The Mariinsky Theatre's presents the Christmas Ballet

The NUTCRACKER

Performed by Russian and American dance students

ACT I, Scene One:

IT IS CHRISTMAS EVE. A LITTLE GIRL LEAVES HER BED TO GO SEE HER GIFTS BENEATH THE CHRISTMAS TREE. SHE DISCOVERS THAT ONE OF HER GIFTS IS A WOODEN NUTCRACKER...

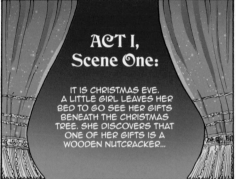

THE RAT KING WILL SOON ATTACK THE LITTLE GIRL, AND THE NUTCRACKER WILL TRANSFORM INTO A PRINCE TO DEFEND HER...

CARLA AND NIKOLAI, YOU'RE ON NEXT!

‹IT'S SHOWTIME!›

SMAK

!

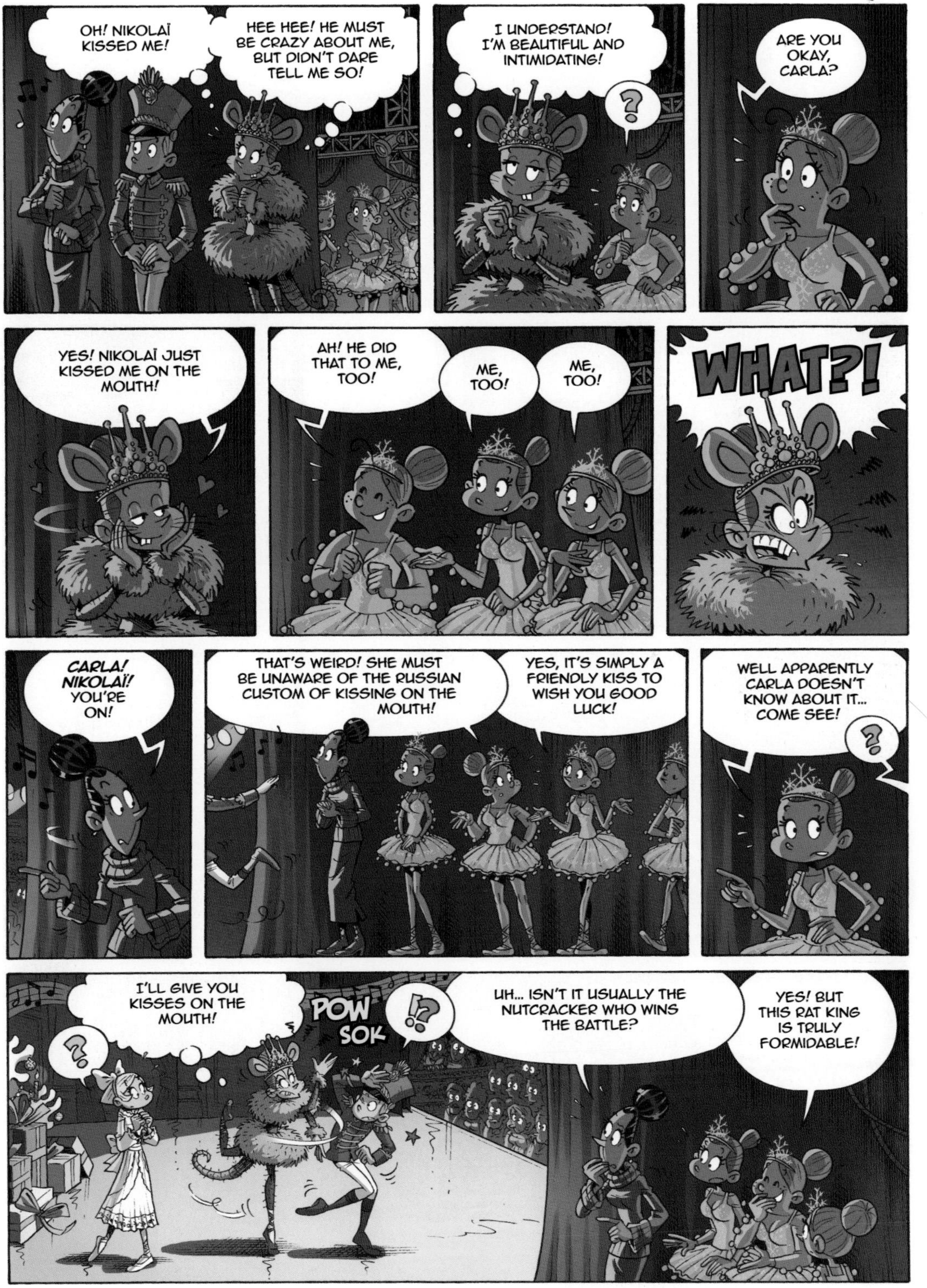
OH! NIKOLAÏ KISSED ME!
HEE HEE! HE MUST BE CRAZY ABOUT ME, BUT DIDN'T DARE TELL ME SO!
I UNDERSTAND! I'M BEAUTIFUL AND INTIMIDATING!
?
ARE YOU OKAY, CARLA?
YES! NIKOLAÏ JUST KISSED ME ON THE MOUTH!
AH! HE DID THAT TO ME, TOO!
ME, TOO!
ME, TOO!
WHAT?!
CARLA! NIKOLAÏ! YOU'RE ON!
THAT'S WEIRD! SHE MUST BE UNAWARE OF THE RUSSIAN CUSTOM OF KISSING ON THE MOUTH!
YES, IT'S SIMPLY A FRIENDLY KISS TO WISH YOU GOOD LUCK!
WELL APPARENTLY CARLA DOESN'T KNOW ABOUT IT... COME SEE!
?
I'LL GIVE YOU KISSES ON THE MOUTH!
?
POW
SOK
!?
UH... ISN'T IT USUALLY THE NUTCRACKER WHO WINS THE BATTLE?
YES! BUT THIS RAT KING IS TRULY FORMIDABLE!

ACT I, Scene Two:

AFTER HAVING DEFEATED THE RAT KING, THE NUTCRACKER PRINCE TAKES THE YOUNG CLARA ON A TRIP TO THE LAND OF SNOW...

LET'S TAKE OUR PLACES FOR THE WALTZ OF THE SNOWFLAKES, LUCIE!

HERE WE GO!

I COULDN'T PARTICIPATE IN THIS SCENE, BUT I'M STILL GOING TO PLAY A ROLE!

HEH HEH! LET'S SEE IF THEY CAN MANAGE TO DANCE IN THESE CONDITIONS!

CREEEEE

SWOOOOSH

SWOOOOOSH

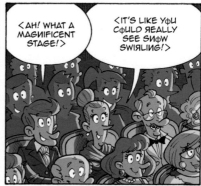

<AH! WHAT A MAGNIFICENT STAGE!>

<IT'S LIKE YOU COULD REALLY SEE SNOW SWIRLING!>

A FEW MOMENTS LATER...

ENCORE! BRAVO!

CLAP CLAP CLAP

BRAVO!

CLAP CLAP

RATS!

CLAC CLAC CLAC

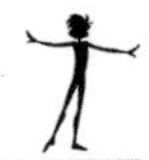

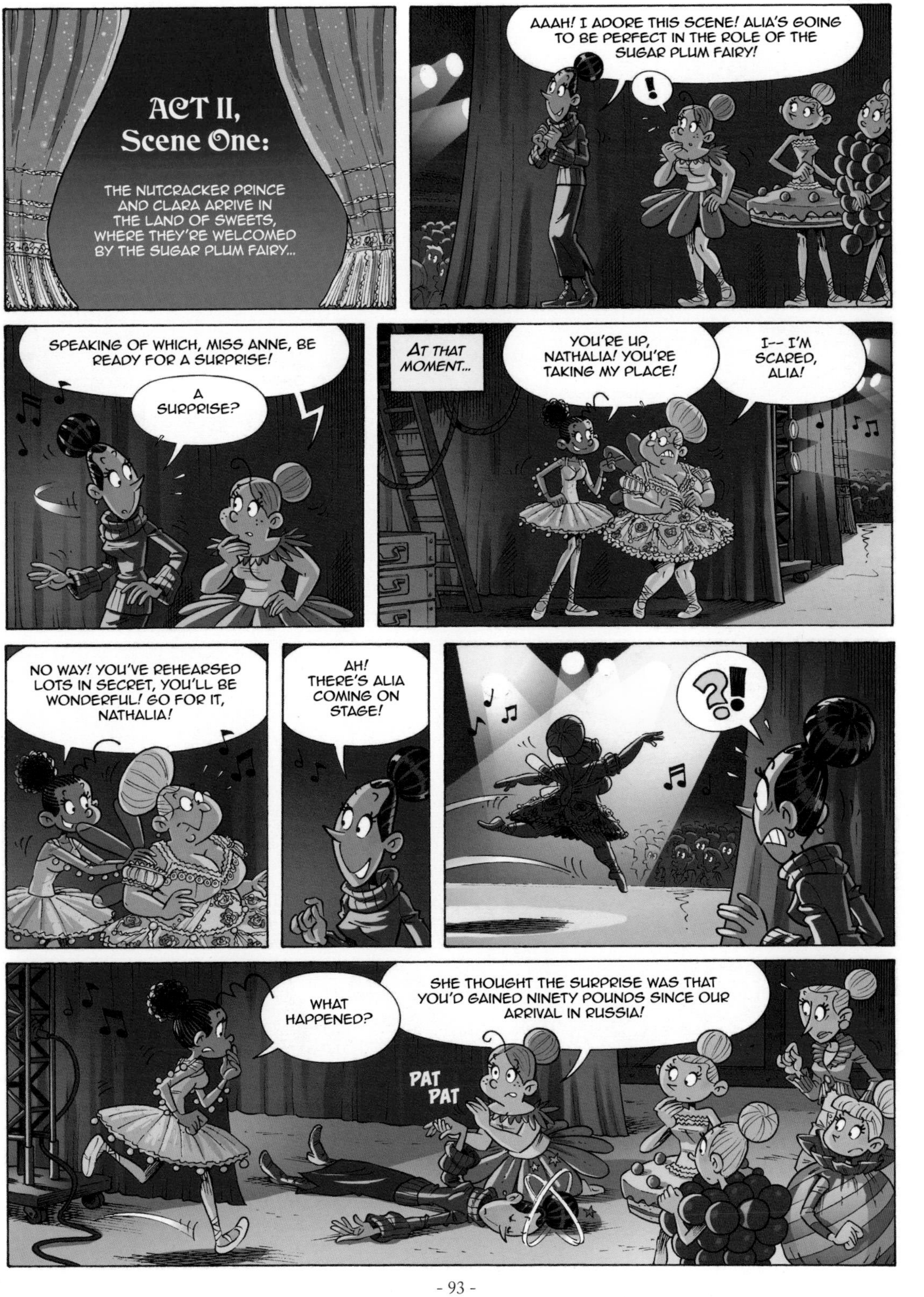
ACT II, Scene One:
THE NUTCRACKER PRINCE AND CLARA ARRIVE IN THE LAND OF SWEETS, WHERE THEY'RE WELCOMED BY THE SUGAR PLUM FAIRY...
AAAH! I ADORE THIS SCENE! ALIA'S GOING TO BE PERFECT IN THE ROLE OF THE SUGAR PLUM FAIRY!
!
SPEAKING OF WHICH, MISS ANNE, BE READY FOR A SURPRISE!
A SURPRISE?
AT THAT MOMENT...
YOU'RE UP, NATHALIA! YOU'RE TAKING MY PLACE!
I-- I'M SCARED, ALIA!
NO WAY! YOU'VE REHEARSED LOTS IN SECRET, YOU'LL BE WONDERFUL! GO FOR IT, NATHALIA!
AH! THERE'S ALIA COMING ON STAGE!
?!
WHAT HAPPENED?
SHE THOUGHT THE SURPRISE WAS THAT YOU'D GAINED NINETY POUNDS SINCE OUR ARRIVAL IN RUSSIA!
PAT PAT

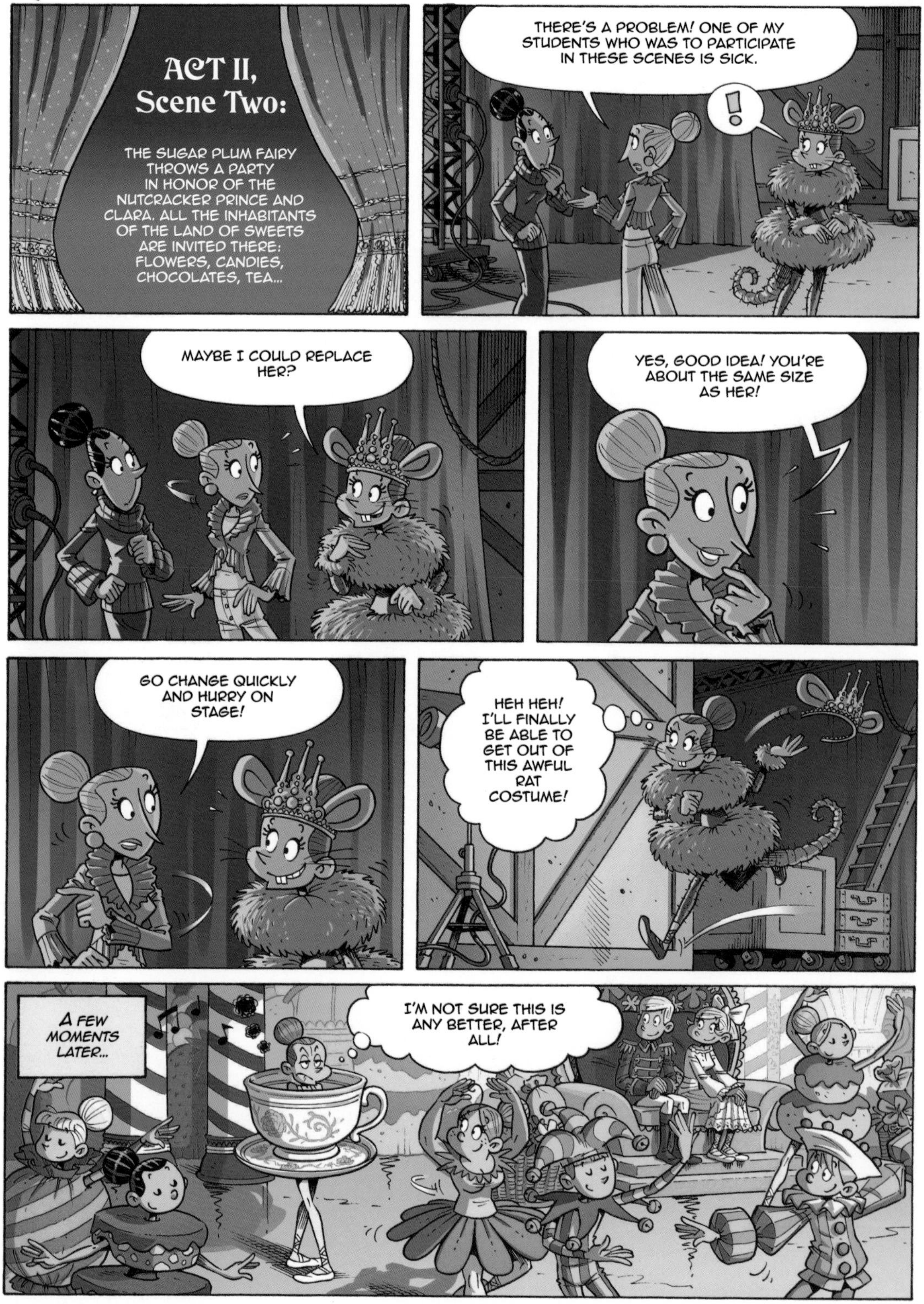
ACT II, Scene Two:
THE SUGAR PLUM FAIRY THROWS A PARTY IN HONOR OF THE NUTCRACKER PRINCE AND CLARA. ALL THE INHABITANTS OF THE LAND OF SWEETS ARE INVITED THERE: FLOWERS, CANDIES, CHOCOLATES, TEA...
THERE'S A PROBLEM! ONE OF MY STUDENTS WHO WAS TO PARTICIPATE IN THESE SCENES IS SICK.
!
MAYBE I COULD REPLACE HER?
YES, GOOD IDEA! YOU'RE ABOUT THE SAME SIZE AS HER!
GO CHANGE QUICKLY AND HURRY ON STAGE!
HEH HEH! I'LL FINALLY BE ABLE TO GET OUT OF THIS AWFUL RAT COSTUME!
A FEW MOMENTS LATER...
I'M NOT SURE THIS IS ANY BETTER, AFTER ALL!

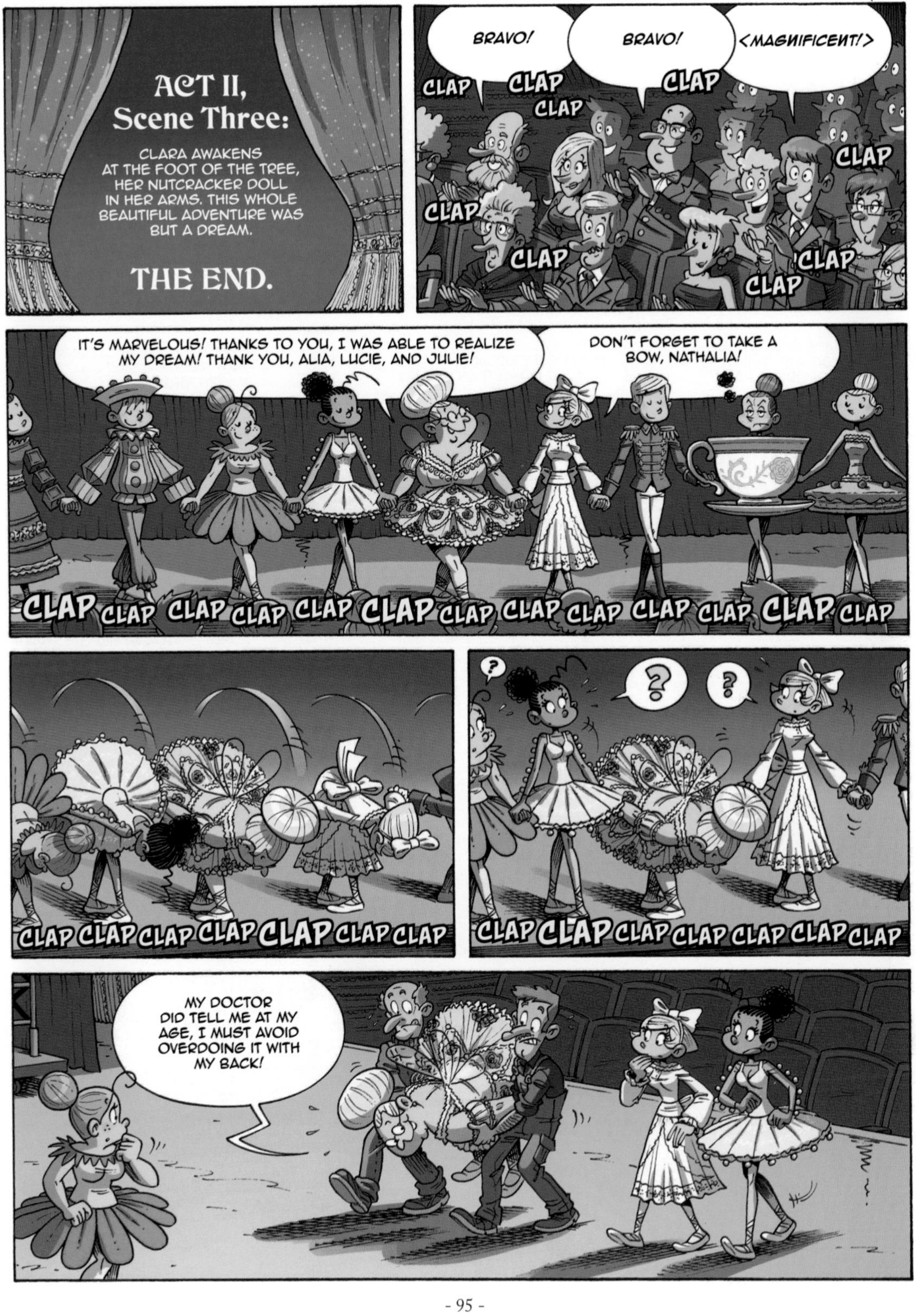

ACT II, Scene Three:
CLARA AWAKENS AT THE FOOT OF THE TREE, HER NUTCRACKER DOLL IN HER ARMS. THIS WHOLE BEAUTIFUL ADVENTURE WAS BUT A DREAM.
THE END.
BRAVO!
BRAVO!
<MAGNIFICENT!>
CLAP CLAP CLAP CLAP CLAP CLAP CLAP CLAP CLAP
IT'S MARVELOUS! THANKS TO YOU, I WAS ABLE TO REALIZE MY DREAM! THANK YOU, ALIA, LUCIE, AND JULIE!
DON'T FORGET TO TAKE A BOW, NATHALIA!
CLAP CLAP CLAP CLAP CLAP CLAP CLAP CLAP CLAP CLAP CLAP CLAP CLAP
CLAP CLAP CLAP CLAP CLAP CLAP CLAP
?
?
?
CLAP CLAP CLAP CLAP CLAP CLAP CLAP
MY DOCTOR DID TELL ME AT MY AGE, I MUST AVOID OVERDOING IT WITH MY BACK!

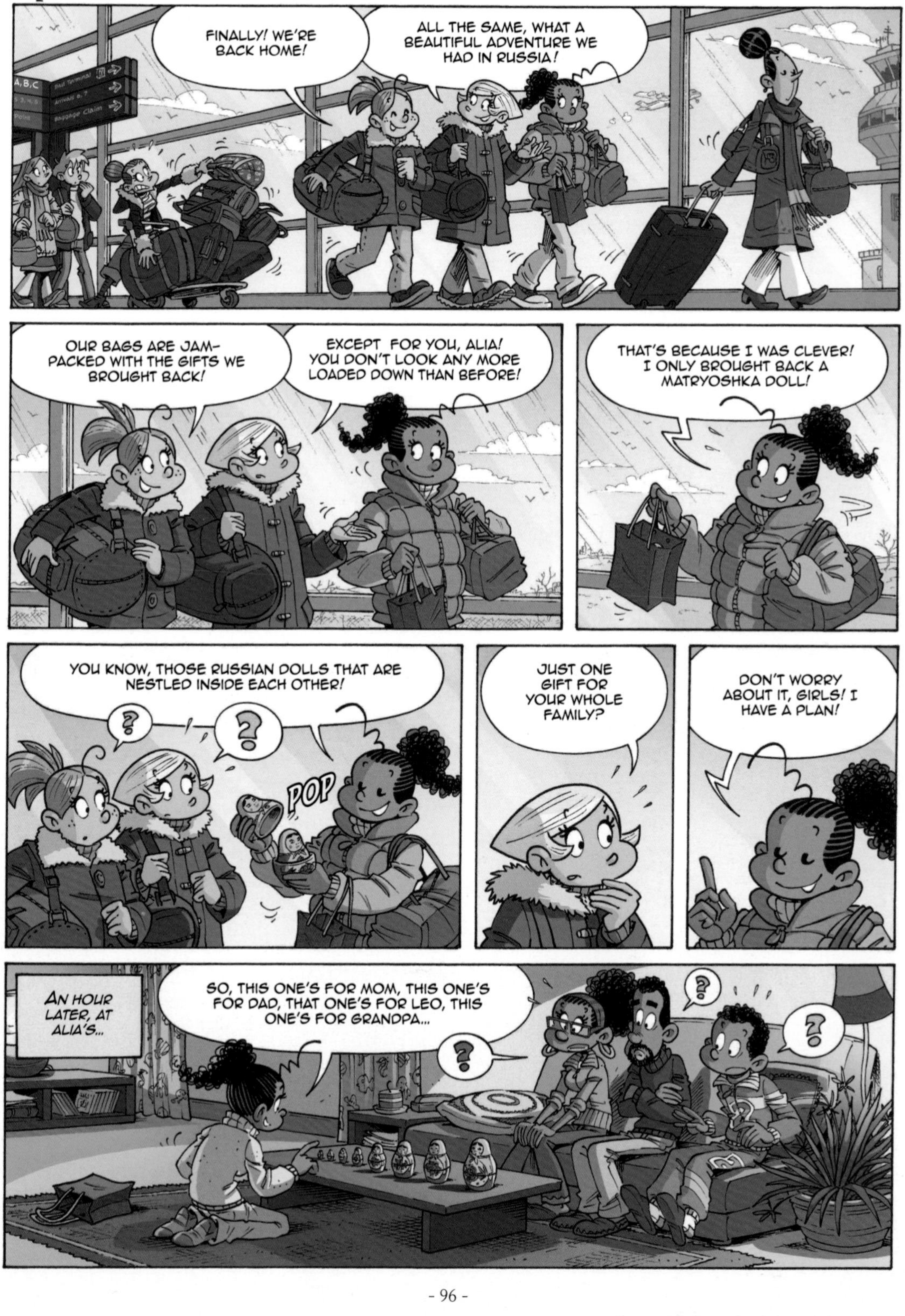
FINALLY! WE'RE BACK HOME!
ALL THE SAME, WHAT A BEAUTIFUL ADVENTURE WE HAD IN RUSSIA!
OUR BAGS ARE JAM-PACKED WITH THE GIFTS WE BROUGHT BACK!
EXCEPT FOR YOU, ALIA! YOU DON'T LOOK ANY MORE LOADED DOWN THAN BEFORE!
THAT'S BECAUSE I WAS CLEVER! I ONLY BROUGHT BACK A MATRYOSHKA DOLL!
YOU KNOW, THOSE RUSSIAN DOLLS THAT ARE NESTLED INSIDE EACH OTHER!
?
?
POP
JUST ONE GIFT FOR YOUR WHOLE FAMILY?
DON'T WORRY ABOUT IT, GIRLS! I HAVE A PLAN!
AN HOUR LATER, AT ALIA'S...
SO, THIS ONE'S FOR MOM, THIS ONE'S FOR DAD, THAT ONE'S FOR LEO, THIS ONE'S FOR GRANDPA...
?
?
?

A Merry Olde Christmas

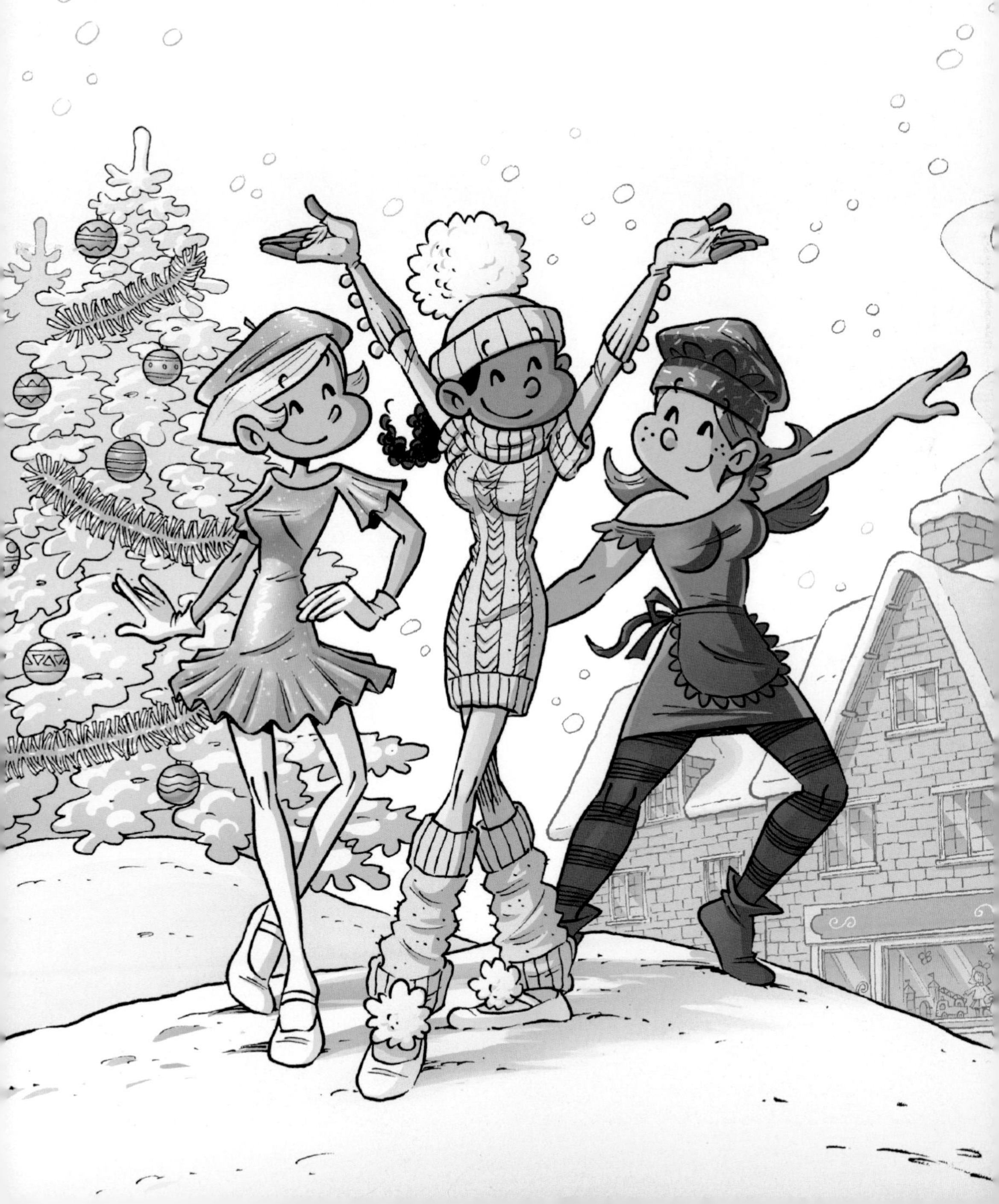

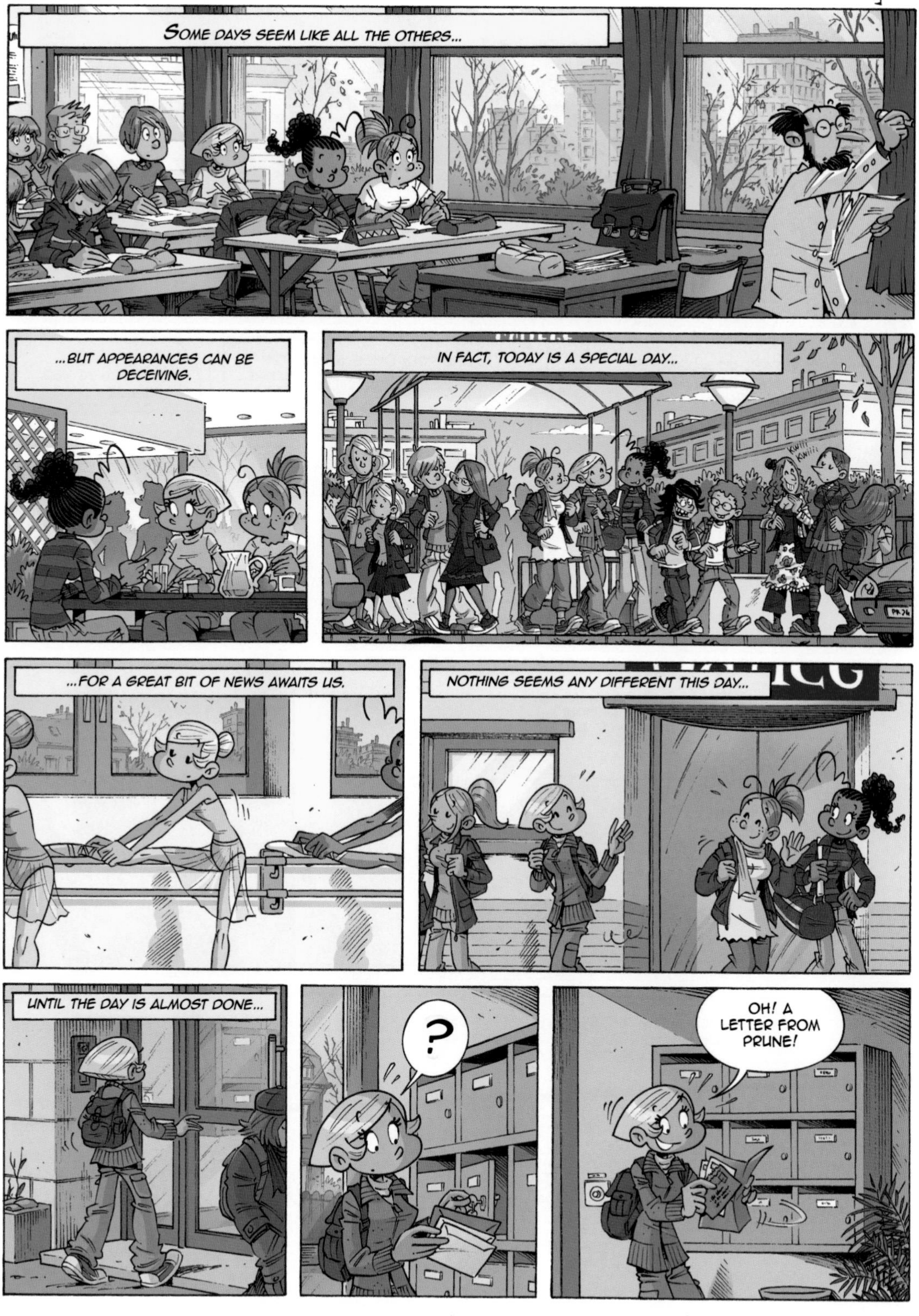
SOME DAYS SEEM LIKE ALL THE OTHERS...
...BUT APPEARANCES CAN BE DECEIVING.
IN FACT, TODAY IS A SPECIAL DAY...
...FOR A GREAT BIT OF NEWS AWAITS US.
NOTHING SEEMS ANY DIFFERENT THIS DAY...
UNTIL THE DAY IS ALMOST DONE...
?
OH! A LETTER FROM PRUNE!

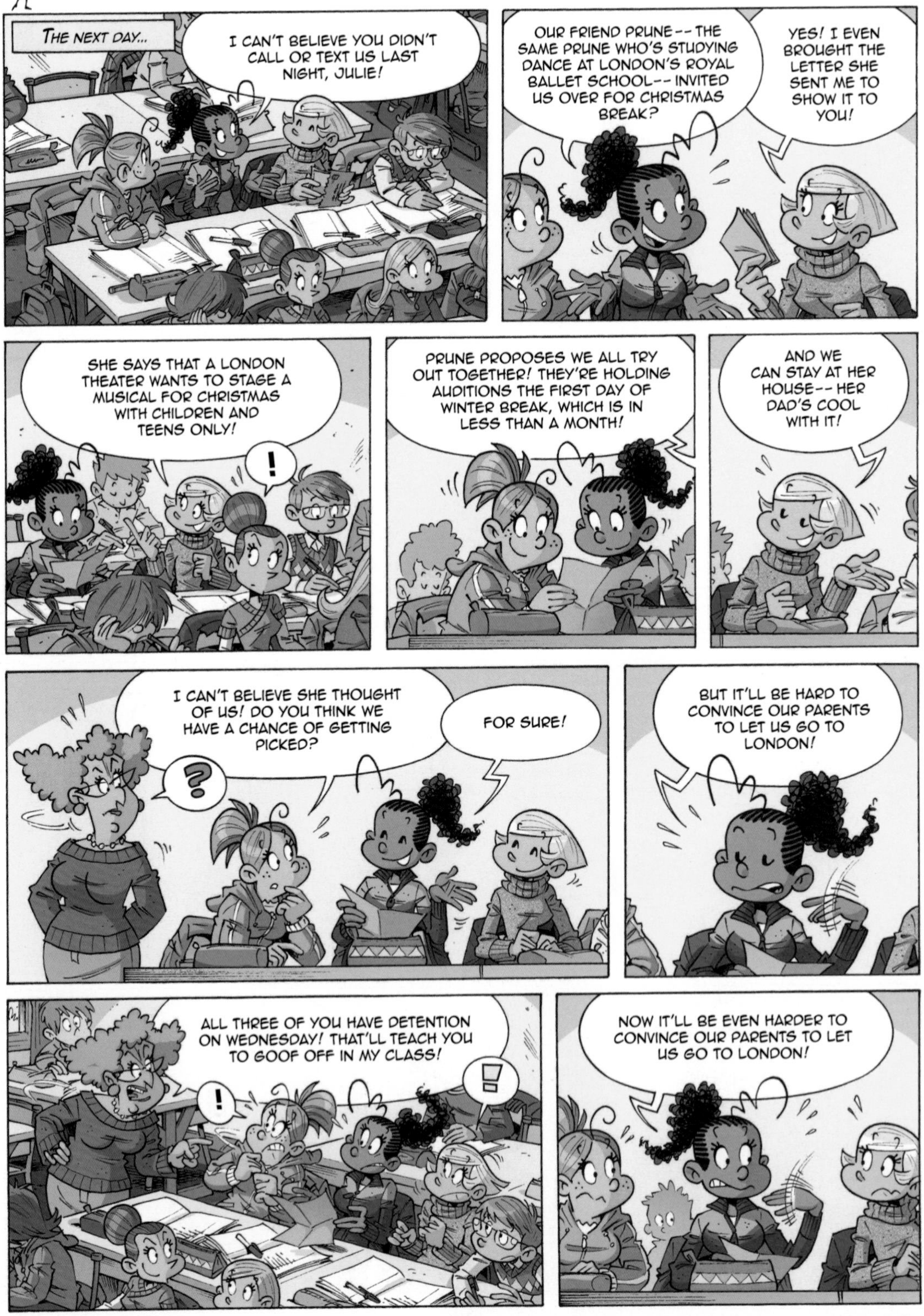
THE NEXT DAY...
I CAN'T BELIEVE YOU DIDN'T CALL OR TEXT US LAST NIGHT, JULIE!
OUR FRIEND PRUNE-- THE SAME PRUNE WHO'S STUDYING DANCE AT LONDON'S ROYAL BALLET SCHOOL-- INVITED US OVER FOR CHRISTMAS BREAK?
YES! I EVEN BROUGHT THE LETTER SHE SENT ME TO SHOW IT TO YOU!
SHE SAYS THAT A LONDON THEATER WANTS TO STAGE A MUSICAL FOR CHRISTMAS WITH CHILDREN AND TEENS ONLY!
!
PRUNE PROPOSES WE ALL TRY OUT TOGETHER! THEY'RE HOLDING AUDITIONS THE FIRST DAY OF WINTER BREAK, WHICH IS IN LESS THAN A MONTH!
AND WE CAN STAY AT HER HOUSE-- HER DAD'S COOL WITH IT!
I CAN'T BELIEVE SHE THOUGHT OF US! DO YOU THINK WE HAVE A CHANCE OF GETTING PICKED?
FOR SURE!
?
BUT IT'LL BE HARD TO CONVINCE OUR PARENTS TO LET US GO TO LONDON!
ALL THREE OF YOU HAVE DETENTION ON WEDNESDAY! THAT'LL TEACH YOU TO GOOF OFF IN MY CLASS!
!
!
NOW IT'LL BE EVEN HARDER TO CONVINCE OUR PARENTS TO LET US GO TO LONDON!

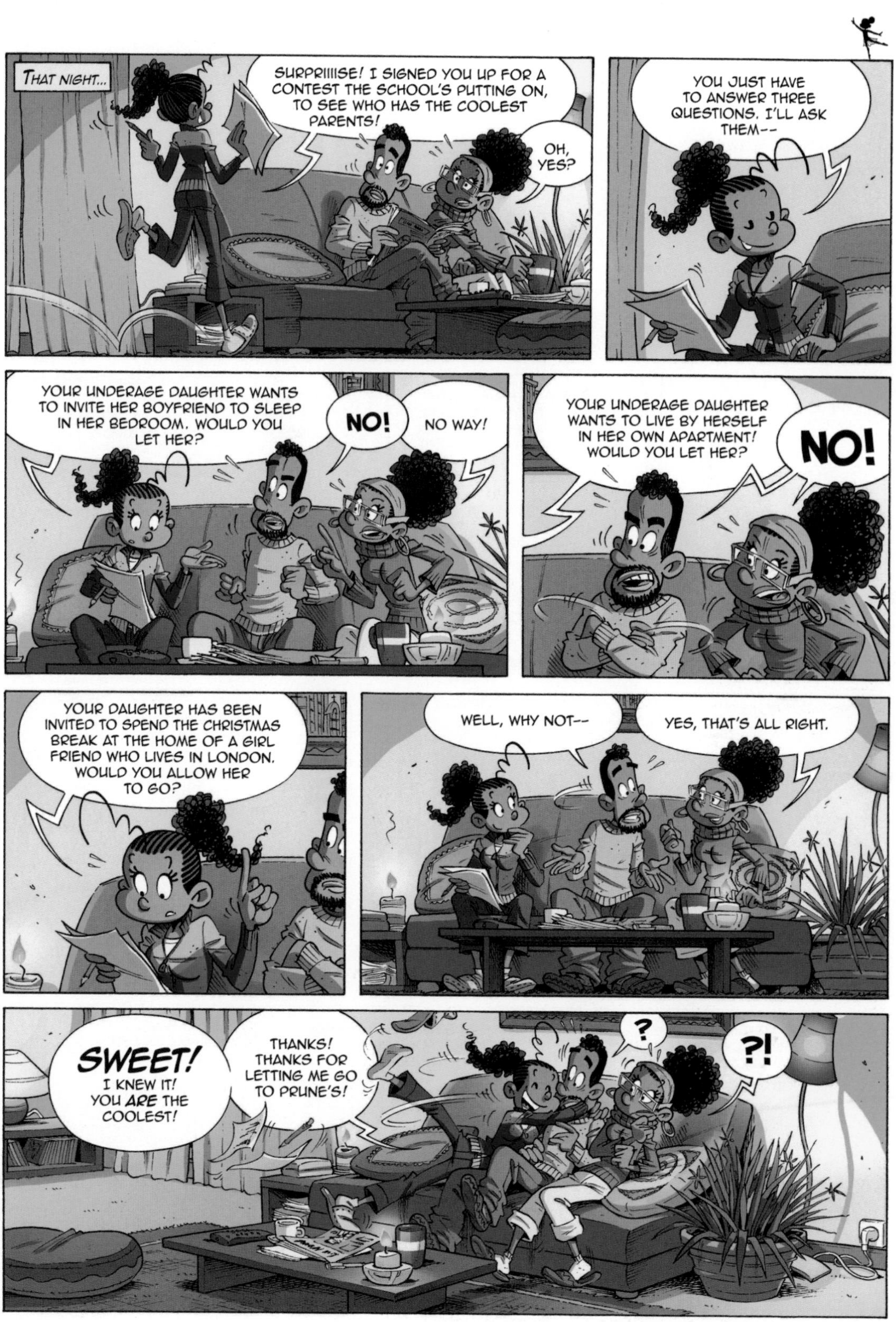
THAT NIGHT...
SURPRIIIISE! I SIGNED YOU UP FOR A CONTEST THE SCHOOL'S PUTTING ON, TO SEE WHO HAS THE COOLEST PARENTS!
OH, YES?
YOU JUST HAVE TO ANSWER THREE QUESTIONS. I'LL ASK THEM--
YOUR UNDERAGE DAUGHTER WANTS TO INVITE HER BOYFRIEND TO SLEEP IN HER BEDROOM. WOULD YOU LET HER?
NO!
NO WAY!
YOUR UNDERAGE DAUGHTER WANTS TO LIVE BY HERSELF IN HER OWN APARTMENT! WOULD YOU LET HER?
NO!
YOUR DAUGHTER HAS BEEN INVITED TO SPEND THE CHRISTMAS BREAK AT THE HOME OF A GIRL FRIEND WHO LIVES IN LONDON. WOULD YOU ALLOW HER TO GO?
WELL, WHY NOT--
YES, THAT'S ALL RIGHT.
SWEET! I KNEW IT! YOU *ARE* THE COOLEST!
THANKS! THANKS FOR LETTING ME GO TO PRUNE'S!
?
?!

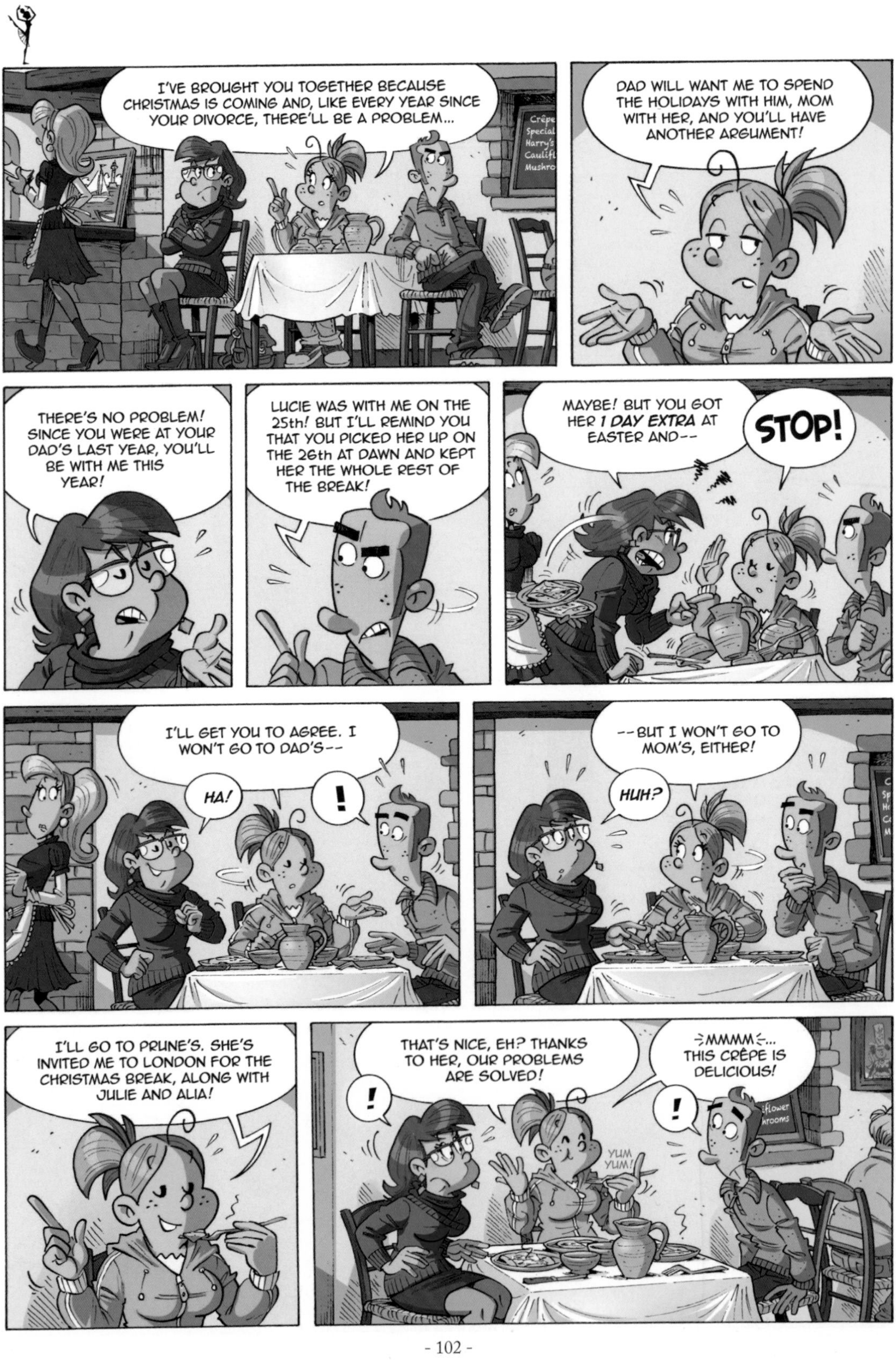
I'VE BROUGHT YOU TOGETHER BECAUSE CHRISTMAS IS COMING AND, LIKE EVERY YEAR SINCE YOUR DIVORCE, THERE'LL BE A PROBLEM...
DAD WILL WANT ME TO SPEND THE HOLIDAYS WITH HIM, MOM WITH HER, AND YOU'LL HAVE ANOTHER ARGUMENT!
THERE'S NO PROBLEM! SINCE YOU WERE AT YOUR DAD'S LAST YEAR, YOU'LL BE WITH ME THIS YEAR!
LUCIE WAS WITH ME ON THE 25th! BUT I'LL REMIND YOU THAT YOU PICKED HER UP ON THE 26th AT DAWN AND KEPT HER THE WHOLE REST OF THE BREAK!
MAYBE! BUT YOU GOT HER *1 DAY EXTRA* AT EASTER AND--
STOP!
I'LL GET YOU TO AGREE. I WON'T GO TO DAD'S--
HA!
!
--BUT I WON'T GO TO MOM'S, EITHER!
HUH?
I'LL GO TO PRUNE'S. SHE'S INVITED ME TO LONDON FOR THE CHRISTMAS BREAK, ALONG WITH JULIE AND ALIA!
THAT'S NICE, EH? THANKS TO HER, OUR PROBLEMS ARE SOLVED!
!
MMMM... THIS CRÊPE IS DELICIOUS!
!
YUM YUM!

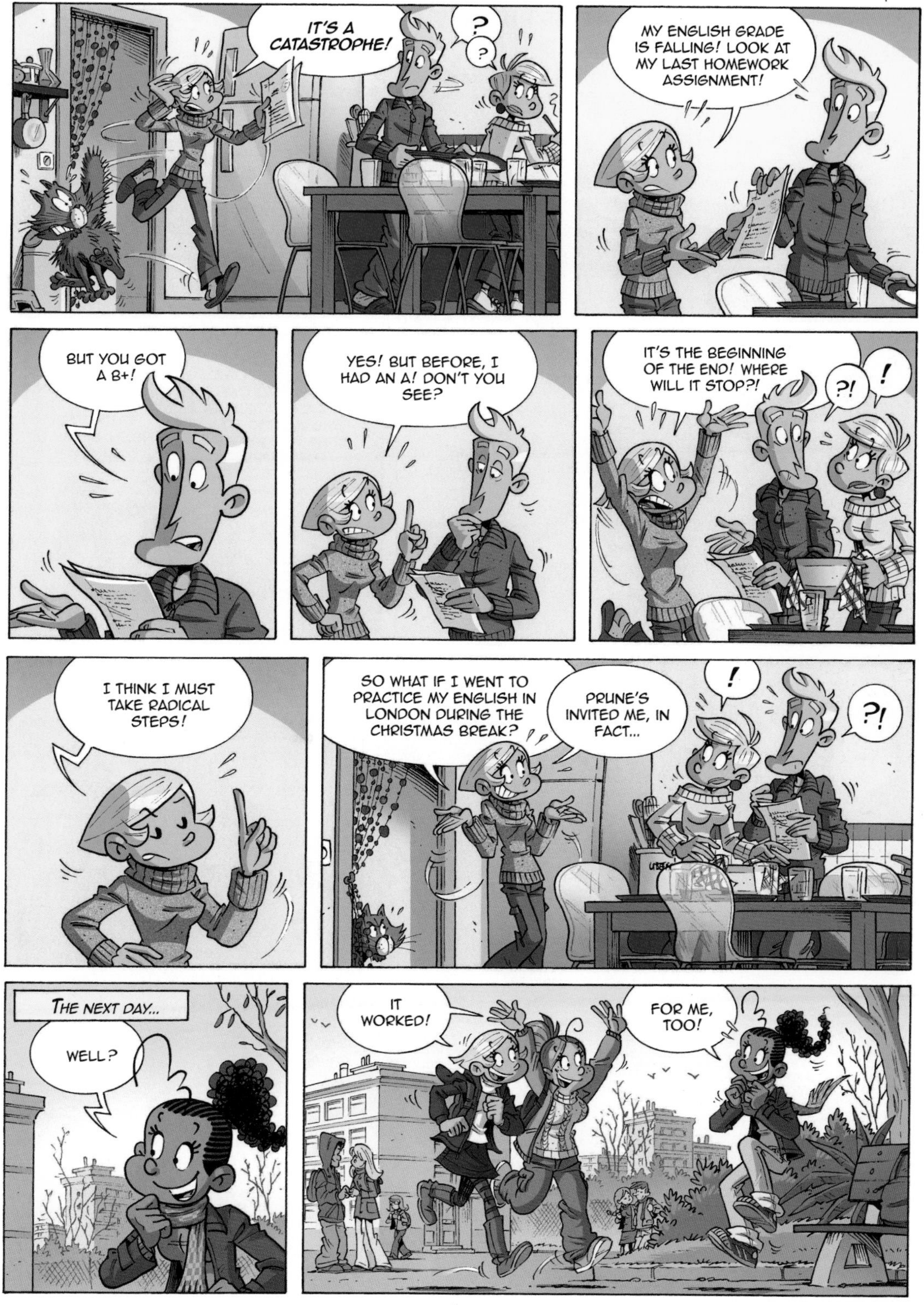
IT'S A CATASTROPHE!
?
?
MY ENGLISH GRADE IS FALLING! LOOK AT MY LAST HOMEWORK ASSIGNMENT!
BUT YOU GOT A B+!
YES! BUT BEFORE, I HAD AN A! DON'T YOU SEE?
IT'S THE BEGINNING OF THE END! WHERE WILL IT STOP?!
?!
!
I THINK I MUST TAKE RADICAL STEPS!
SO WHAT IF I WENT TO PRACTICE MY ENGLISH IN LONDON DURING THE CHRISTMAS BREAK?
PRUNE'S INVITED ME, IN FACT...
!
?!
THE NEXT DAY...
WELL?
IT WORKED!
FOR ME, TOO!

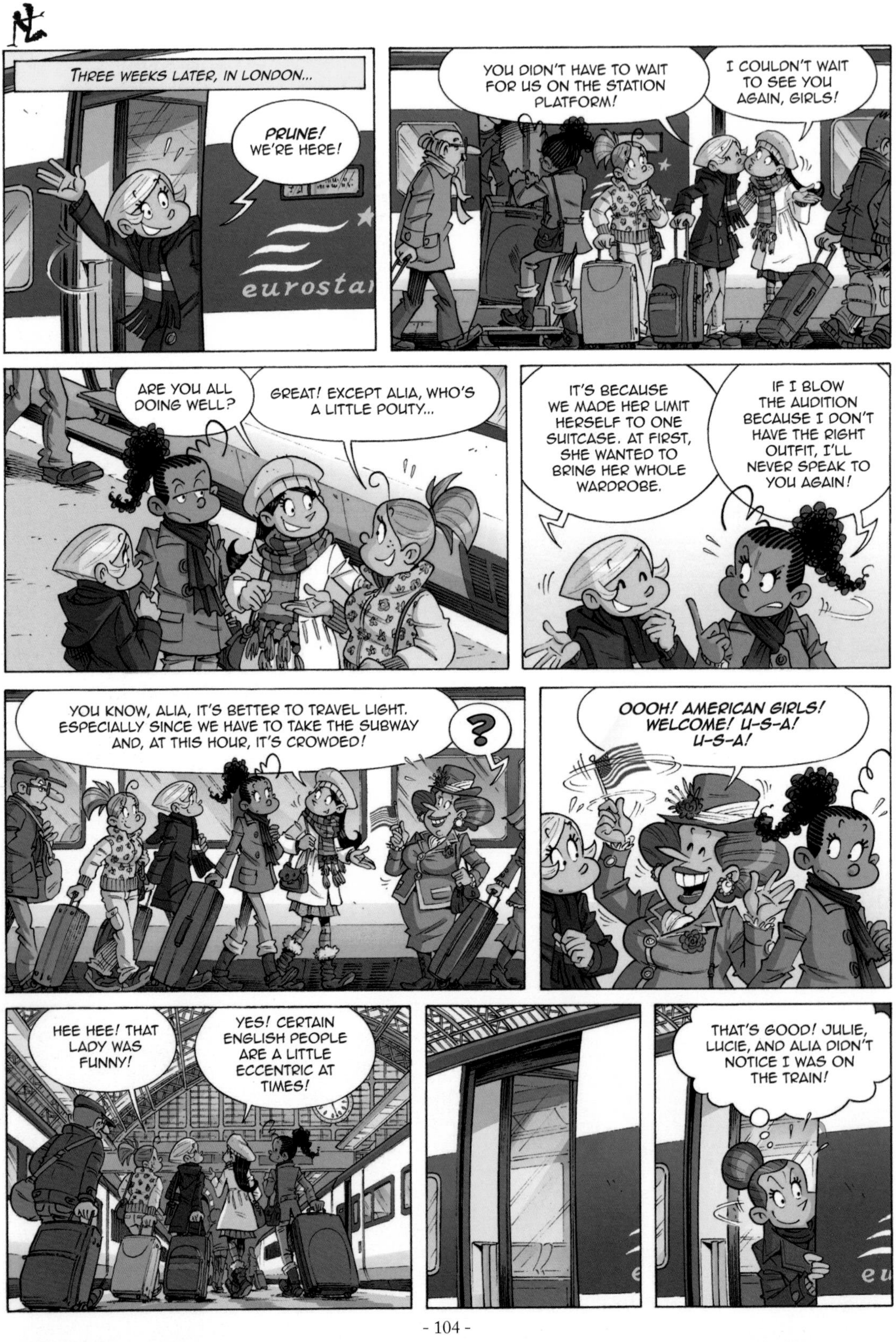

THREE WEEKS LATER, IN LONDON...
PRUNE! WE'RE HERE!
eurostar
YOU DIDN'T HAVE TO WAIT FOR US ON THE STATION PLATFORM!
I COULDN'T WAIT TO SEE YOU AGAIN, GIRLS!
ARE YOU ALL DOING WELL?
GREAT! EXCEPT ALIA, WHO'S A LITTLE POUTY...
IT'S BECAUSE WE MADE HER LIMIT HERSELF TO ONE SUITCASE. AT FIRST, SHE WANTED TO BRING HER WHOLE WARDROBE.
IF I BLOW THE AUDITION BECAUSE I DON'T HAVE THE RIGHT OUTFIT, I'LL NEVER SPEAK TO YOU AGAIN!
YOU KNOW, ALIA, IT'S BETTER TO TRAVEL LIGHT. ESPECIALLY SINCE WE HAVE TO TAKE THE SUBWAY AND, AT THIS HOUR, IT'S CROWDED!
?
OOOH! AMERICAN GIRLS! WELCOME! U-S-A! U-S-A!
HEE HEE! THAT LADY WAS FUNNY!
YES! CERTAIN ENGLISH PEOPLE ARE A LITTLE ECCENTRIC AT TIMES!
THAT'S GOOD! JULIE, LUCIE, AND ALIA DIDN'T NOTICE I WAS ON THE TRAIN!

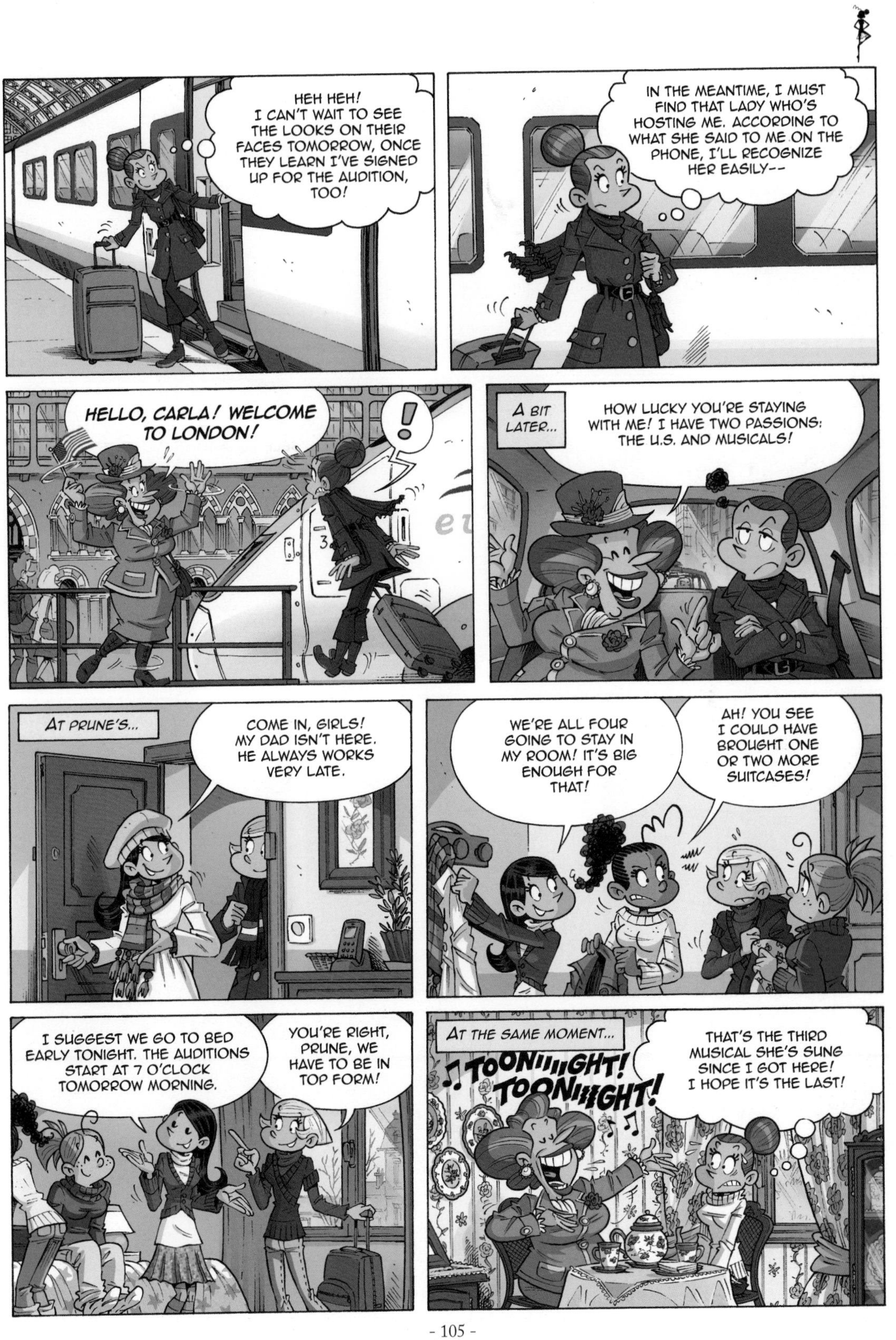

HEH HEH! I CAN'T WAIT TO SEE THE LOOKS ON THEIR FACES TOMORROW, ONCE THEY LEARN I'VE SIGNED UP FOR THE AUDITION, TOO!
IN THE MEANTIME, I MUST FIND THAT LADY WHO'S HOSTING ME. ACCORDING TO WHAT SHE SAID TO ME ON THE PHONE, I'LL RECOGNIZE HER EASILY--
HELLO, CARLA! WELCOME TO LONDON!
!
A BIT LATER...
HOW LUCKY YOU'RE STAYING WITH ME! I HAVE TWO PASSIONS: THE U.S. AND MUSICALS!
AT PRUNE'S...
COME IN, GIRLS! MY DAD ISN'T HERE. HE ALWAYS WORKS VERY LATE.
WE'RE ALL FOUR GOING TO STAY IN MY ROOM! IT'S BIG ENOUGH FOR THAT!
AH! YOU SEE I COULD HAVE BROUGHT ONE OR TWO MORE SUITCASES!
I SUGGEST WE GO TO BED EARLY TONIGHT. THE AUDITIONS START AT 7 O'CLOCK TOMORROW MORNING.
YOU'RE RIGHT, PRUNE, WE HAVE TO BE IN TOP FORM!
AT THE SAME MOMENT...
TOONIIIIGHT! TOONIIIIGHT!
THAT'S THE THIRD MUSICAL SHE'S SUNG SINCE I GOT HERE! I HOPE IT'S THE LAST!

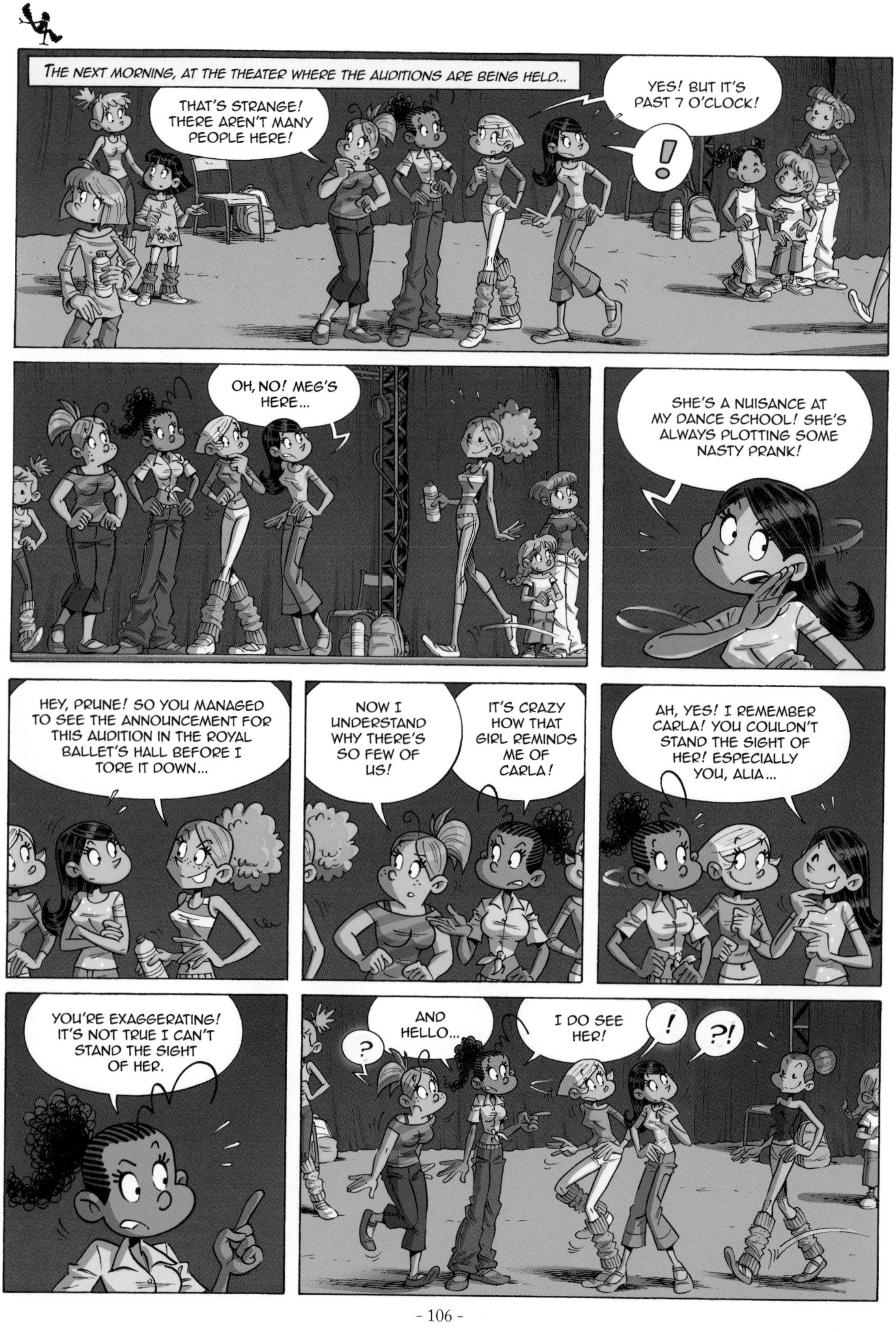

THE NEXT MORNING, AT THE THEATER WHERE THE AUDITIONS ARE BEING HELD...
THAT'S STRANGE! THERE AREN'T MANY PEOPLE HERE!
YES! BUT IT'S PAST 7 O'CLOCK!
!
OH, NO! MEG'S HERE...
SHE'S A NUISANCE AT MY DANCE SCHOOL! SHE'S ALWAYS PLOTTING SOME NASTY PRANK!
HEY, PRUNE! SO YOU MANAGED TO SEE THE ANNOUNCEMENT FOR THIS AUDITION IN THE ROYAL BALLET'S HALL BEFORE I TORE IT DOWN...
NOW I UNDERSTAND WHY THERE'S SO FEW OF US!
IT'S CRAZY HOW THAT GIRL REMINDS ME OF CARLA!
AH, YES! I REMEMBER CARLA! YOU COULDN'T STAND THE SIGHT OF HER! ESPECIALLY YOU, ALIA...
YOU'RE EXAGGERATING! IT'S NOT TRUE I CAN'T STAND THE SIGHT OF HER.
?
AND HELLO...
I DO SEE HER!
!
?!

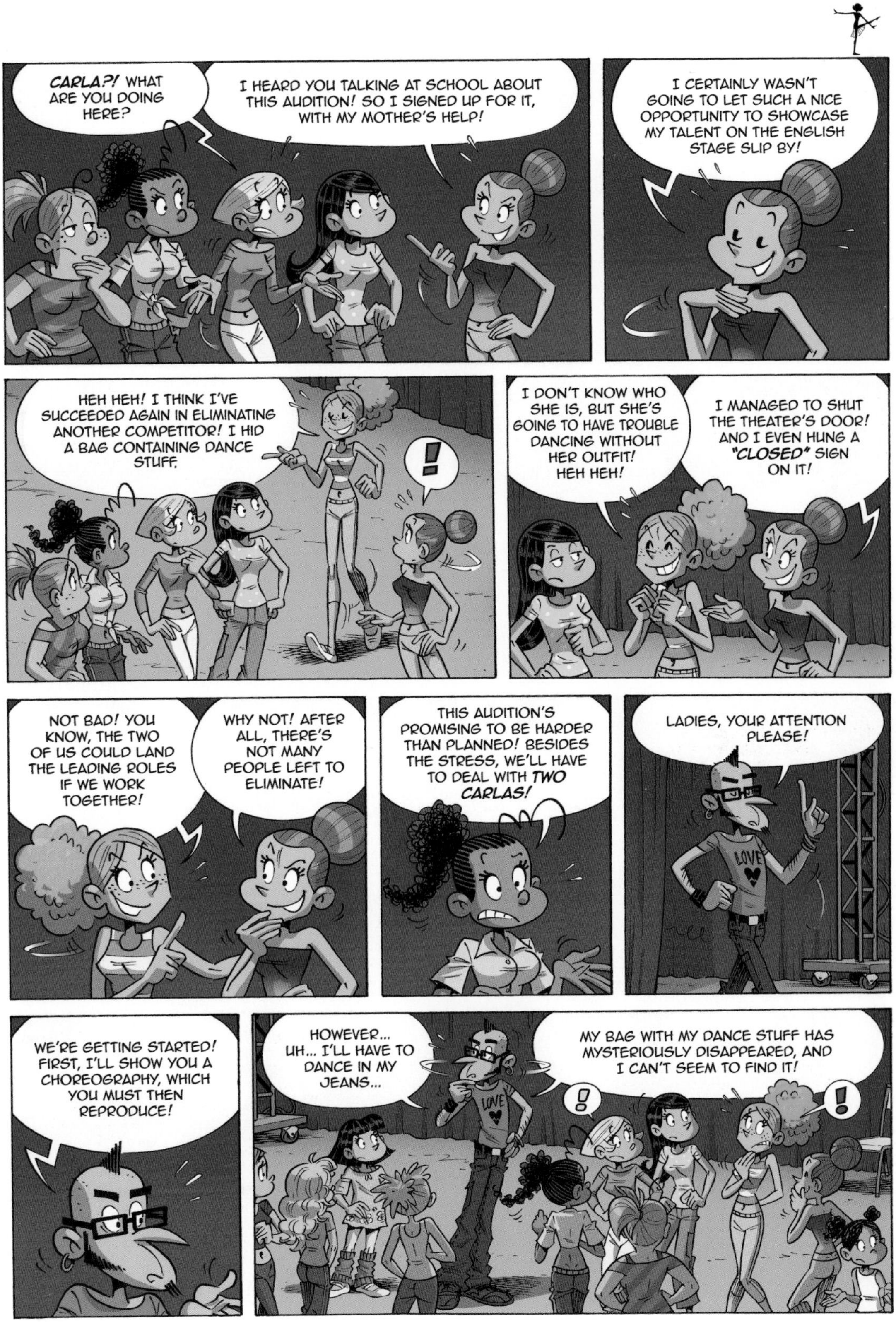
CARLA?! WHAT ARE YOU DOING HERE?
I HEARD YOU TALKING AT SCHOOL ABOUT THIS AUDITION! SO I SIGNED UP FOR IT, WITH MY MOTHER'S HELP!
I CERTAINLY WASN'T GOING TO LET SUCH A NICE OPPORTUNITY TO SHOWCASE MY TALENT ON THE ENGLISH STAGE SLIP BY!
HEH HEH! I THINK I'VE SUCCEEDED AGAIN IN ELIMINATING ANOTHER COMPETITOR! I HID A BAG CONTAINING DANCE STUFF.
!
I DON'T KNOW WHO SHE IS, BUT SHE'S GOING TO HAVE TROUBLE DANCING WITHOUT HER OUTFIT! HEH HEH!
I MANAGED TO SHUT THE THEATER'S DOOR! AND I EVEN HUNG A "CLOSED" SIGN ON IT!
NOT BAD! YOU KNOW, THE TWO OF US COULD LAND THE LEADING ROLES IF WE WORK TOGETHER!
WHY NOT! AFTER ALL, THERE'S NOT MANY PEOPLE LEFT TO ELIMINATE!
THIS AUDITION'S PROMISING TO BE HARDER THAN PLANNED! BESIDES THE STRESS, WE'LL HAVE TO DEAL WITH TWO CARLAS!
LADIES, YOUR ATTENTION PLEASE!
LOVE
WE'RE GETTING STARTED! FIRST, I'LL SHOW YOU A CHOREOGRAPHY, WHICH YOU MUST THEN REPRODUCE!
HOWEVER... UH... I'LL HAVE TO DANCE IN MY JEANS...
MY BAG WITH MY DANCE STUFF HAS MYSTERIOUSLY DISAPPEARED, AND I CAN'T SEEM TO FIND IT!
!
!
LOVE

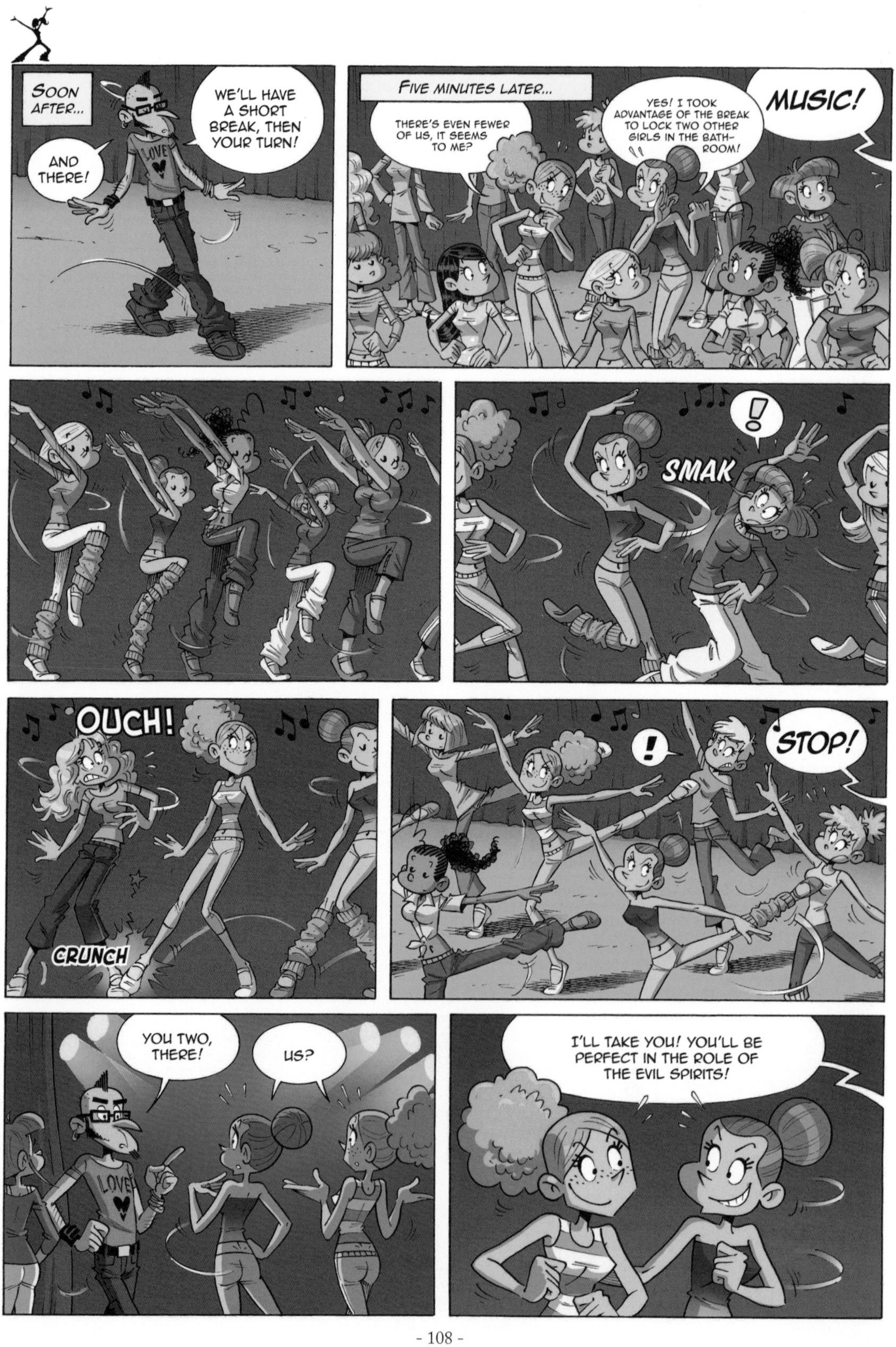
SOON AFTER...
AND THERE!
WE'LL HAVE A SHORT BREAK, THEN YOUR TURN!
FIVE MINUTES LATER...
THERE'S EVEN FEWER OF US, IT SEEMS TO ME?
YES! I TOOK ADVANTAGE OF THE BREAK TO LOCK TWO OTHER GIRLS IN THE BATH-ROOM!
MUSIC!
!
SMAK
OUCH!
CRUNCH
!
STOP!
YOU TWO, THERE!
US?
I'LL TAKE YOU! YOU'LL BE PERFECT IN THE ROLE OF THE EVIL SPIRITS!

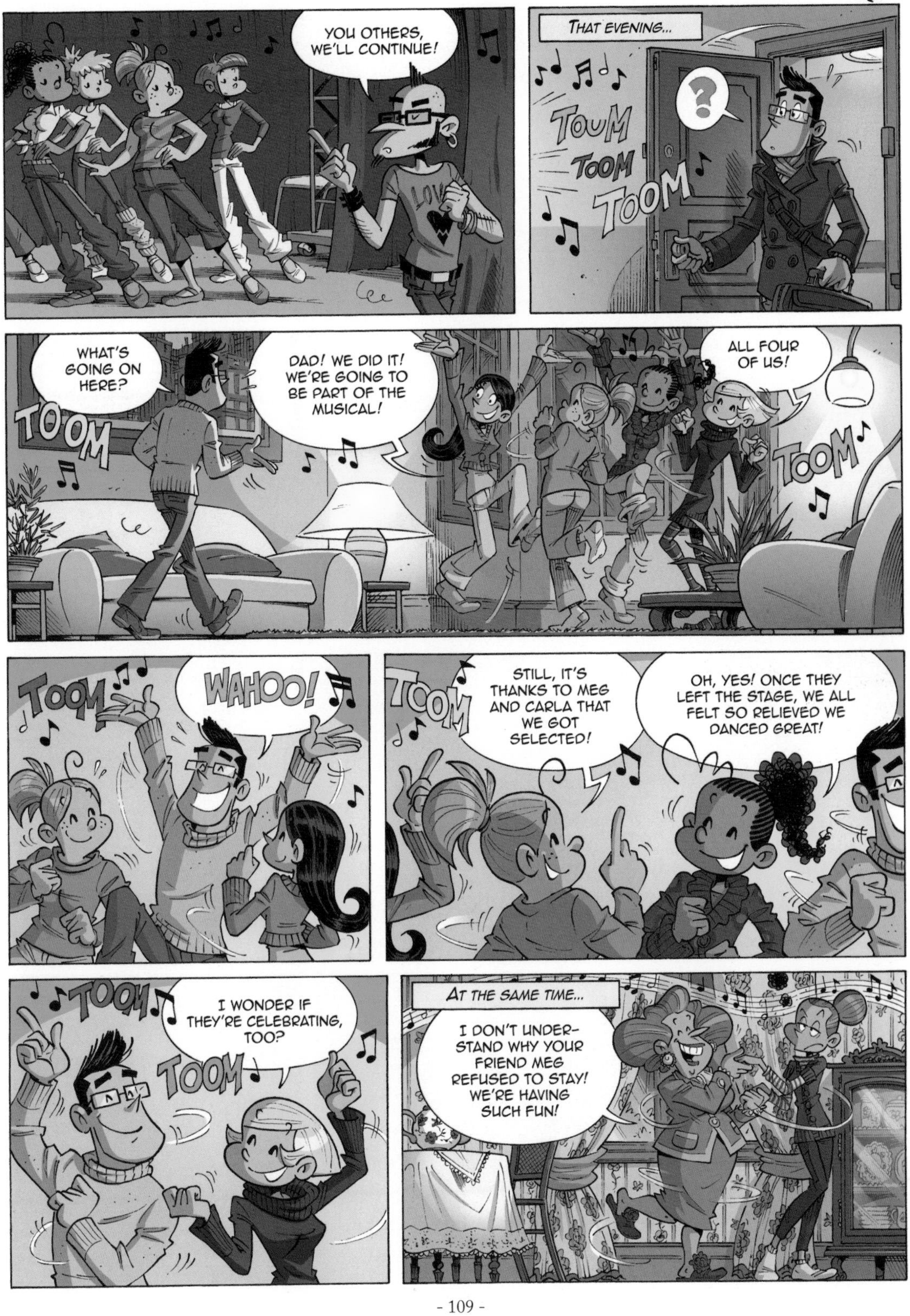
YOU OTHERS, WE'LL CONTINUE!
THAT EVENING...
TOUM
TOOM
TOOM
?
WHAT'S GOING ON HERE?
TOOM
DAD! WE DID IT! WE'RE GOING TO BE PART OF THE MUSICAL!
ALL FOUR OF US!
TOOM
TOOM
WAHOO!
TOOM
STILL, IT'S THANKS TO MEG AND CARLA THAT WE GOT SELECTED!
OH, YES! ONCE THEY LEFT THE STAGE, WE ALL FELT SO RELIEVED WE DANCED GREAT!
TOOM
I WONDER IF THEY'RE CELEBRATING, TOO?
TOOM
AT THE SAME TIME...
I DON'T UNDERSTAND WHY YOUR FRIEND MEG REFUSED TO STAY! WE'RE HAVING SUCH FUN!

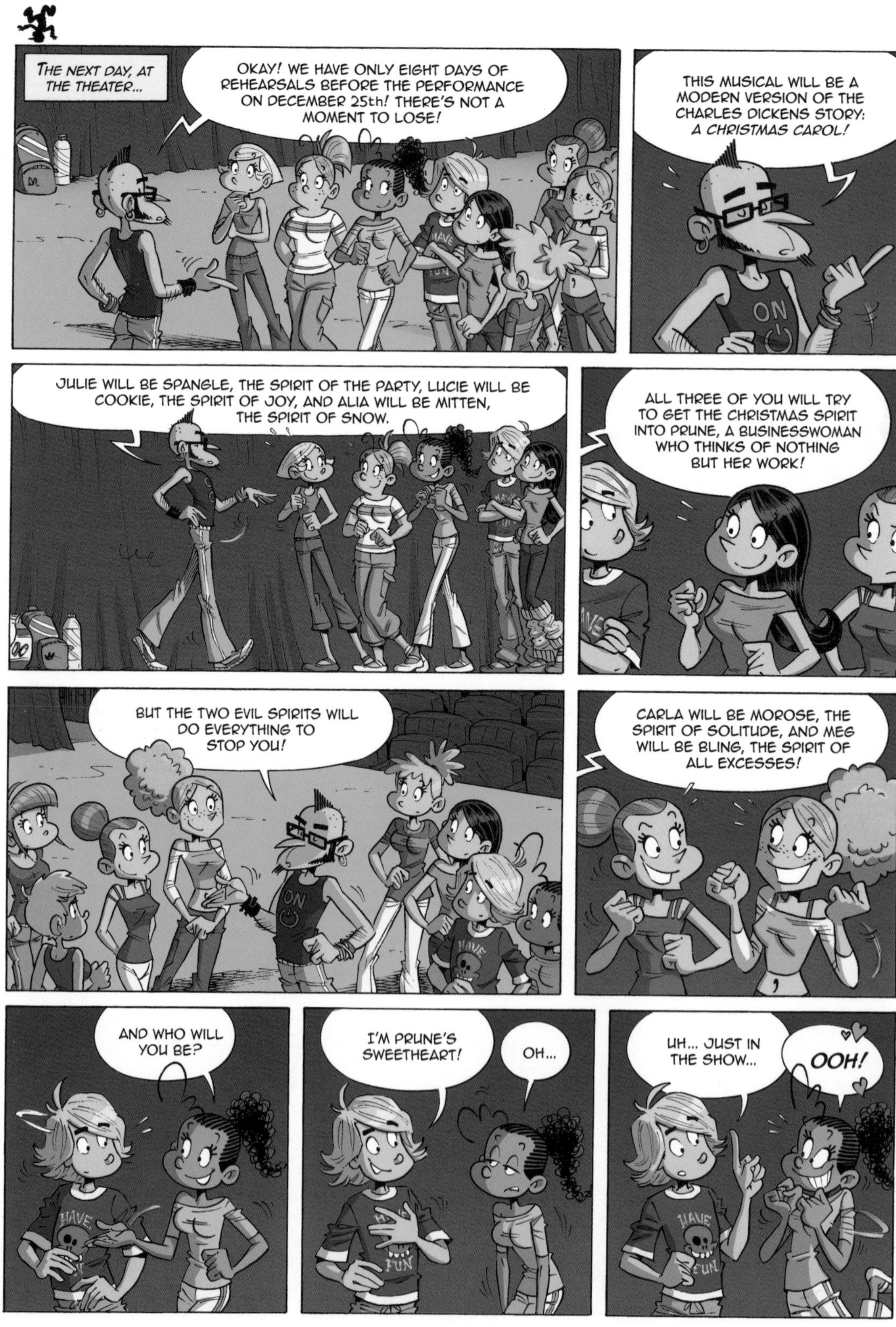
THE NEXT DAY, AT THE THEATER...
OKAY! WE HAVE ONLY EIGHT DAYS OF REHEARSALS BEFORE THE PERFORMANCE ON DECEMBER 25th! THERE'S NOT A MOMENT TO LOSE!
THIS MUSICAL WILL BE A MODERN VERSION OF THE CHARLES DICKENS STORY: A CHRISTMAS CAROL!
JULIE WILL BE SPANGLE, THE SPIRIT OF THE PARTY, LUCIE WILL BE COOKIE, THE SPIRIT OF JOY, AND ALIA WILL BE MITTEN, THE SPIRIT OF SNOW.
ALL THREE OF YOU WILL TRY TO GET THE CHRISTMAS SPIRIT INTO PRUNE, A BUSINESSWOMAN WHO THINKS OF NOTHING BUT HER WORK!
BUT THE TWO EVIL SPIRITS WILL DO EVERYTHING TO STOP YOU!
CARLA WILL BE MOROSE, THE SPIRIT OF SOLITUDE, AND MEG WILL BE BLING, THE SPIRIT OF ALL EXCESSES!
AND WHO WILL YOU BE?
I'M PRUNE'S SWEETHEART!
OH...
UH... JUST IN THE SHOW...
OOH!

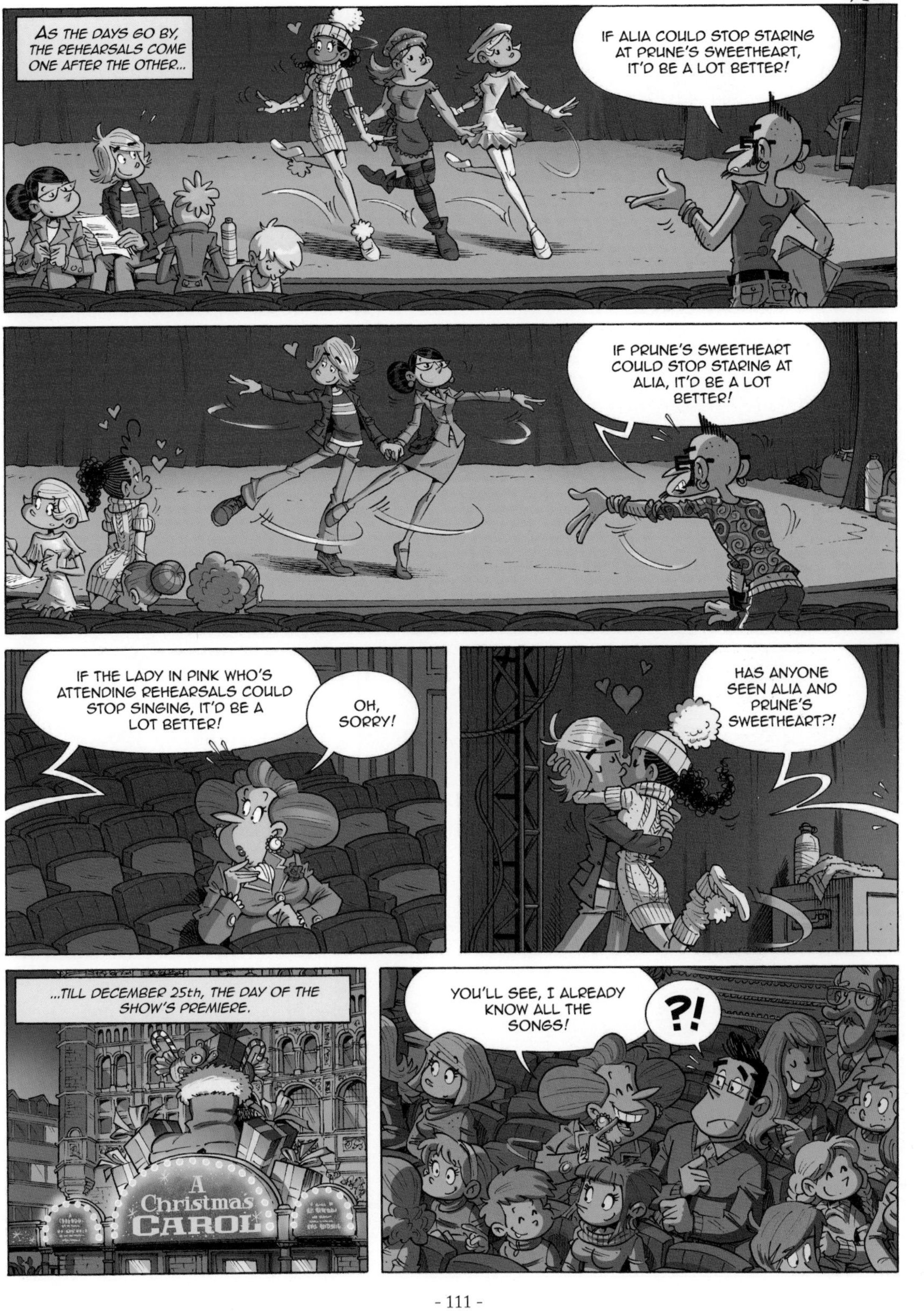
AS THE DAYS GO BY, THE REHEARSALS COME ONE AFTER THE OTHER...
IF ALIA COULD STOP STARING AT PRUNE'S SWEETHEART, IT'D BE A LOT BETTER!
IF PRUNE'S SWEETHEART COULD STOP STARING AT ALIA, IT'D BE A LOT BETTER!
IF THE LADY IN PINK WHO'S ATTENDING REHEARSALS COULD STOP SINGING, IT'D BE A LOT BETTER!
OH, SORRY!
HAS ANYONE SEEN ALIA AND PRUNE'S SWEETHEART?!
...TILL DECEMBER 25th, THE DAY OF THE SHOW'S PREMIERE.
A Christmas CAROL
YOU'LL SEE, I ALREADY KNOW ALL THE SONGS!
?!

LET'S GO, GIRLS!

I'VE GOT FAITH IN YOU-- YOU'RE GREAT!

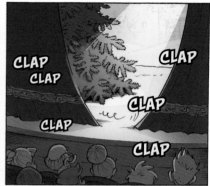

CLAP CLAP

CLAP CLAP

CLAP

CLAP

CLAP

I THINK IT'S TIME FOR US TO GET TO WORK!

YES! WE MUST BRING THE CHRISTMAS SPIRIT TO THE CITY!

FIRST OF ALL, WE NEED SNOW FOR THE SET! IT'S UP TO YOU, MITTEN!

GLADLY, SPANGLE!

SNOW WHITE CLOUDS AND SNOWBALLS, COME AND ADORN OUR HALLS!

THUMP

! ! !!

UH... DON'T YOU THINK THERE IS *TOO MUCH* SNOW, MITTEN?

YES! I'LL GET RID OF SOME!

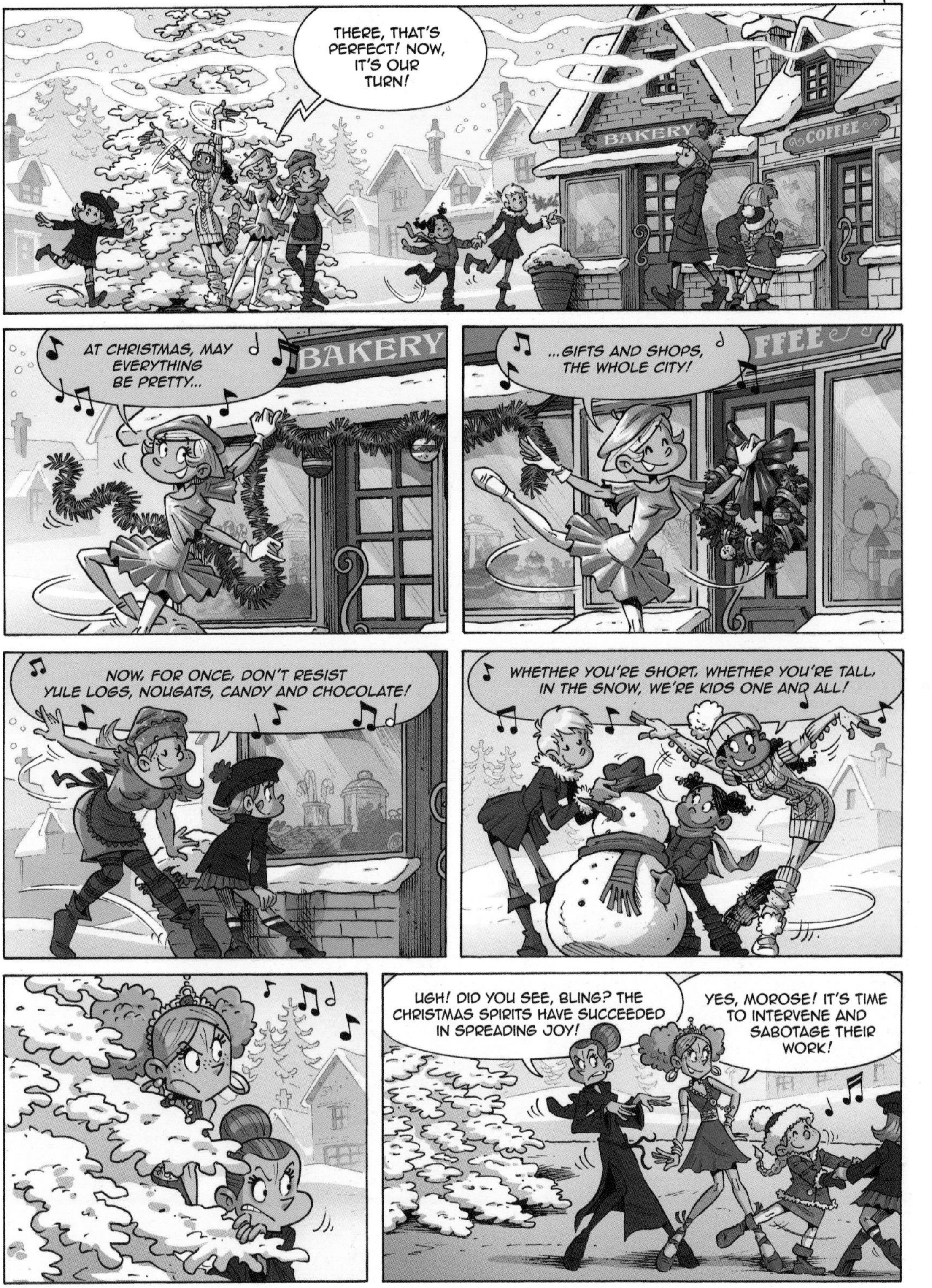

THERE, THAT'S PERFECT! NOW, IT'S OUR TURN!
BAKERY
COFFEE
AT CHRISTMAS, MAY EVERYTHING BE PRETTY...
BAKERY
...GIFTS AND SHOPS, THE WHOLE CITY!
FFEE
NOW, FOR ONCE, DON'T RESIST YULE LOGS, NOUGATS, CANDY AND CHOCOLATE!
WHETHER YOU'RE SHORT, WHETHER YOU'RE TALL, IN THE SNOW, WE'RE KIDS ONE AND ALL!
UGH! DID YOU SEE, BLING? THE CHRISTMAS SPIRITS HAVE SUCCEEDED IN SPREADING JOY!
YES, MOROSE! IT'S TIME TO INTERVENE AND SABOTAGE THEIR WORK!

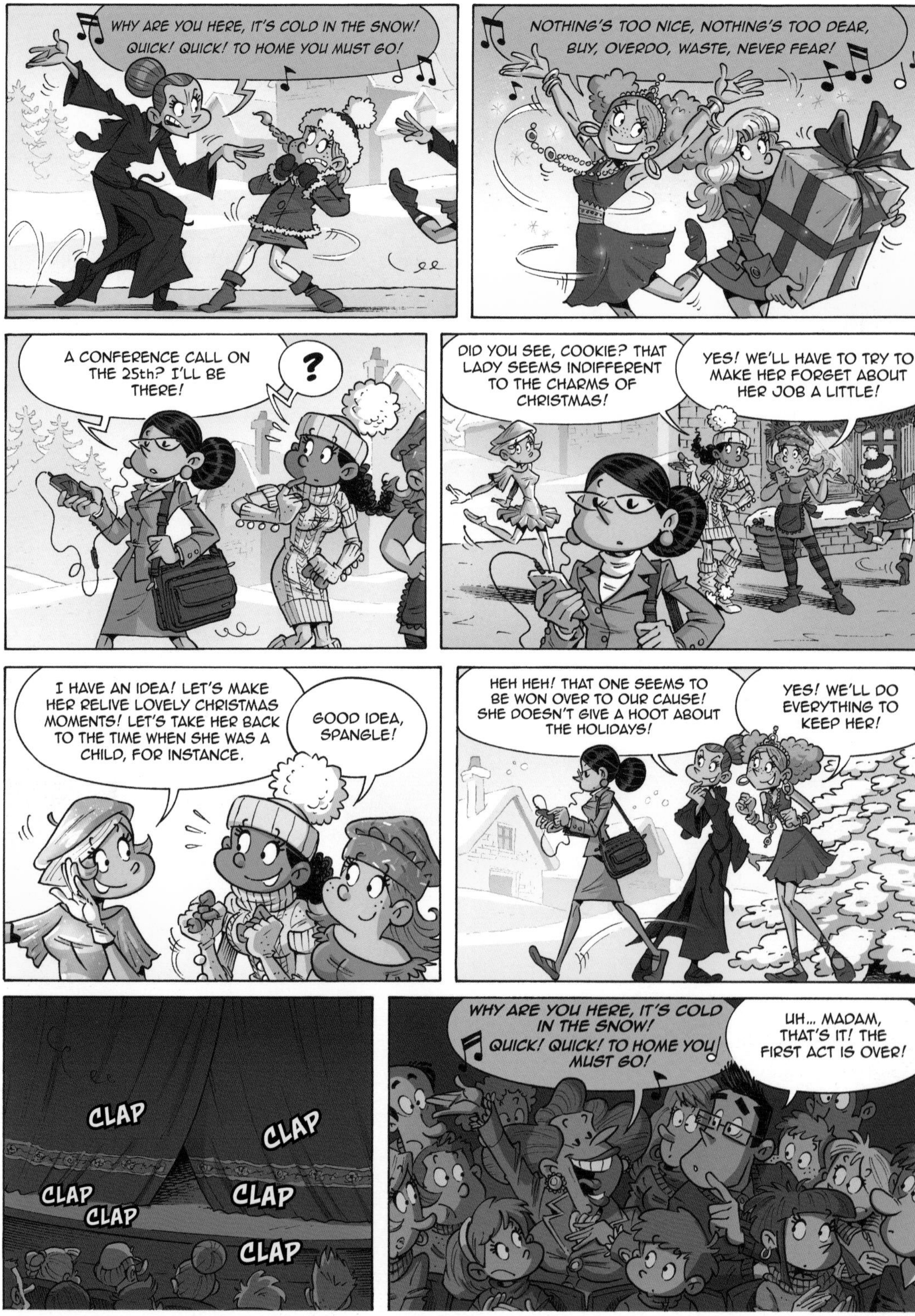
WHY ARE YOU HERE, IT'S COLD IN THE SNOW! QUICK! QUICK! TO HOME YOU MUST GO!
NOTHING'S TOO NICE, NOTHING'S TOO DEAR, BUY, OVERDO, WASTE, NEVER FEAR!
A CONFERENCE CALL ON THE 25th? I'LL BE THERE!
?
DID YOU SEE, COOKIE? THAT LADY SEEMS INDIFFERENT TO THE CHARMS OF CHRISTMAS!
YES! WE'LL HAVE TO TRY TO MAKE HER FORGET ABOUT HER JOB A LITTLE!
I HAVE AN IDEA! LET'S MAKE HER RELIVE LOVELY CHRISTMAS MOMENTS! LET'S TAKE HER BACK TO THE TIME WHEN SHE WAS A CHILD, FOR INSTANCE.
GOOD IDEA, SPANGLE!
HEH HEH! THAT ONE SEEMS TO BE WON OVER TO OUR CAUSE! SHE DOESN'T GIVE A HOOT ABOUT THE HOLIDAYS!
YES! WE'LL DO EVERYTHING TO KEEP HER!
CLAP
CLAP
CLAP
CLAP
CLAP
CLAP
WHY ARE YOU HERE, IT'S COLD IN THE SNOW! QUICK! QUICK! TO HOME YOU MUST GO!
UH... MADAM, THAT'S IT! THE FIRST ACT IS OVER!

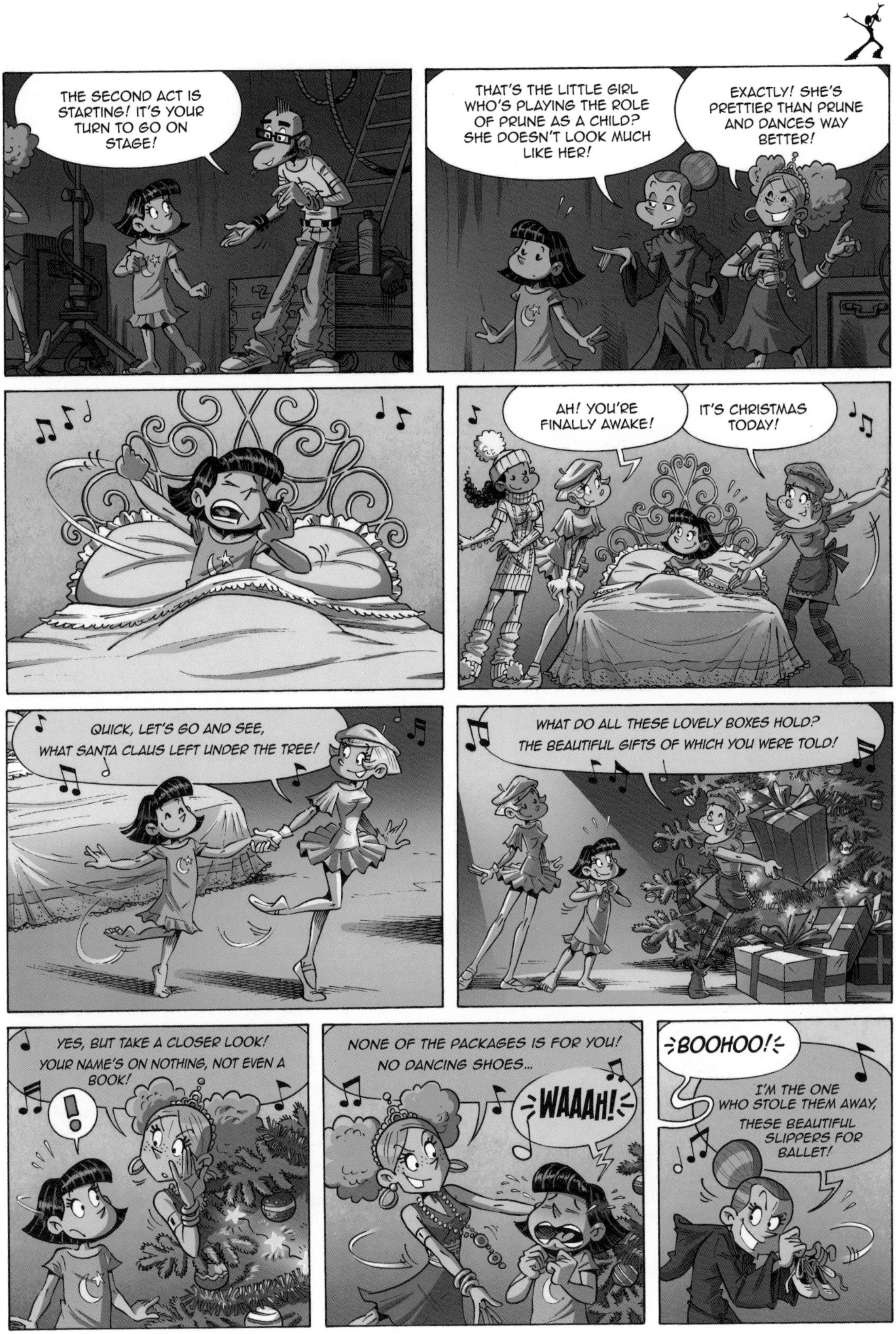
THE SECOND ACT IS STARTING! IT'S YOUR TURN TO GO ON STAGE!
THAT'S THE LITTLE GIRL WHO'S PLAYING THE ROLE OF PRUNE AS A CHILD? SHE DOESN'T LOOK MUCH LIKE HER!
EXACTLY! SHE'S PRETTIER THAN PRUNE AND DANCES WAY BETTER!
AH! YOU'RE FINALLY AWAKE!
IT'S CHRISTMAS TODAY!
QUICK, LET'S GO AND SEE, WHAT SANTA CLAUS LEFT UNDER THE TREE!
WHAT DO ALL THESE LOVELY BOXES HOLD? THE BEAUTIFUL GIFTS OF WHICH YOU WERE TOLD!
YES, BUT TAKE A CLOSER LOOK! YOUR NAME'S ON NOTHING, NOT EVEN A BOOK!
!
NONE OF THE PACKAGES IS FOR YOU! NO DANCING SHOES...
WAAAH!
BOOHOO!
I'M THE ONE WHO STOLE THEM AWAY, THESE BEAUTIFUL SLIPPERS FOR BALLET!

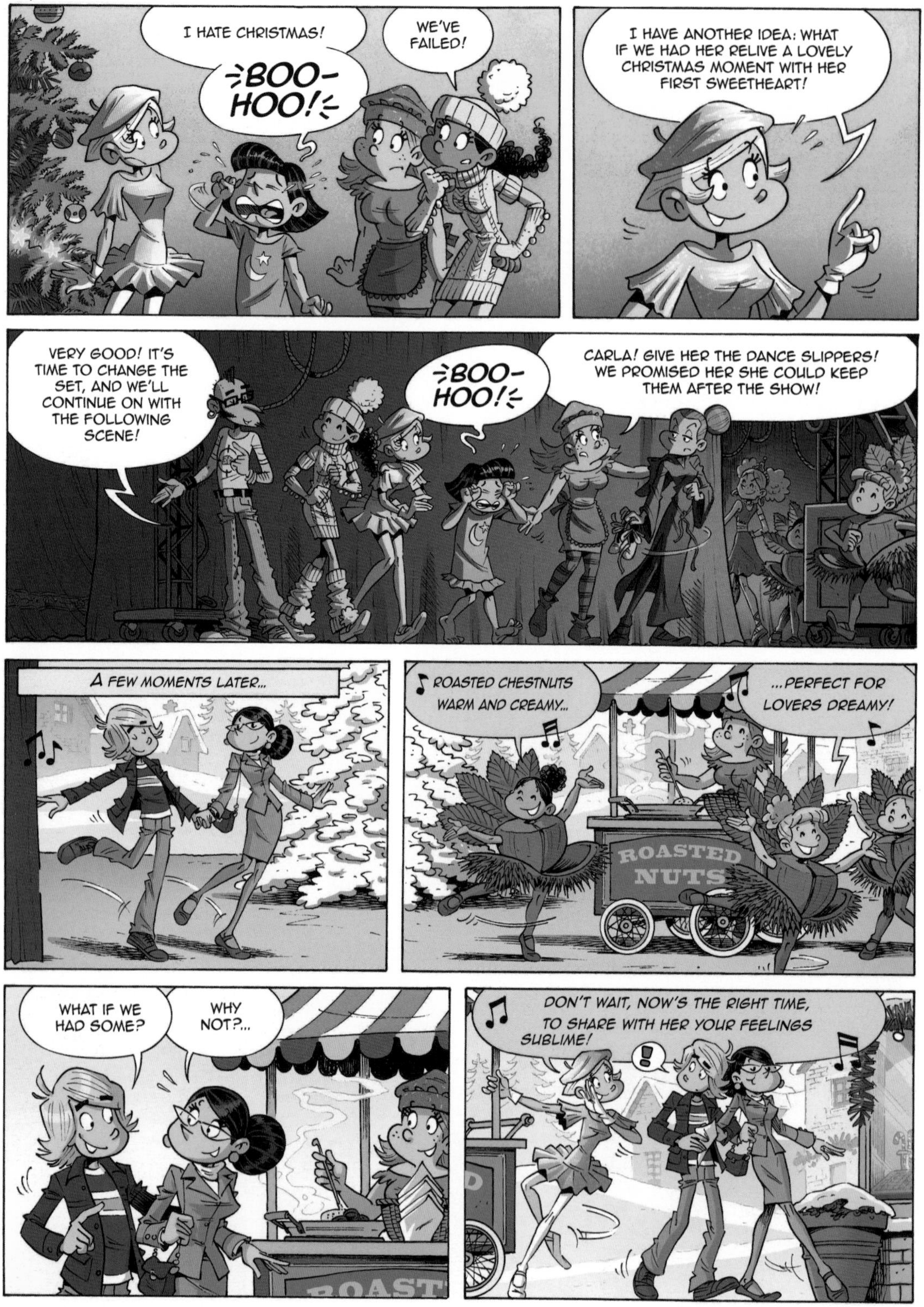
I HATE CHRISTMAS!
BOO-HOO!
WE'VE FAILED!
I HAVE ANOTHER IDEA: WHAT IF WE HAD HER RELIVE A LOVELY CHRISTMAS MOMENT WITH HER FIRST SWEETHEART!
VERY GOOD! IT'S TIME TO CHANGE THE SET, AND WE'LL CONTINUE ON WITH THE FOLLOWING SCENE!
BOO-HOO!
CARLA! GIVE HER THE DANCE SLIPPERS! WE PROMISED HER SHE COULD KEEP THEM AFTER THE SHOW!
A FEW MOMENTS LATER...
ROASTED CHESTNUTS WARM AND CREAMY...
...PERFECT FOR LOVERS DREAMY!
ROASTED NUTS
WHAT IF WE HAD SOME?
WHY NOT?...
DON'T WAIT, NOW'S THE RIGHT TIME, TO SHARE WITH HER YOUR FEELINGS SUBLIME!
!

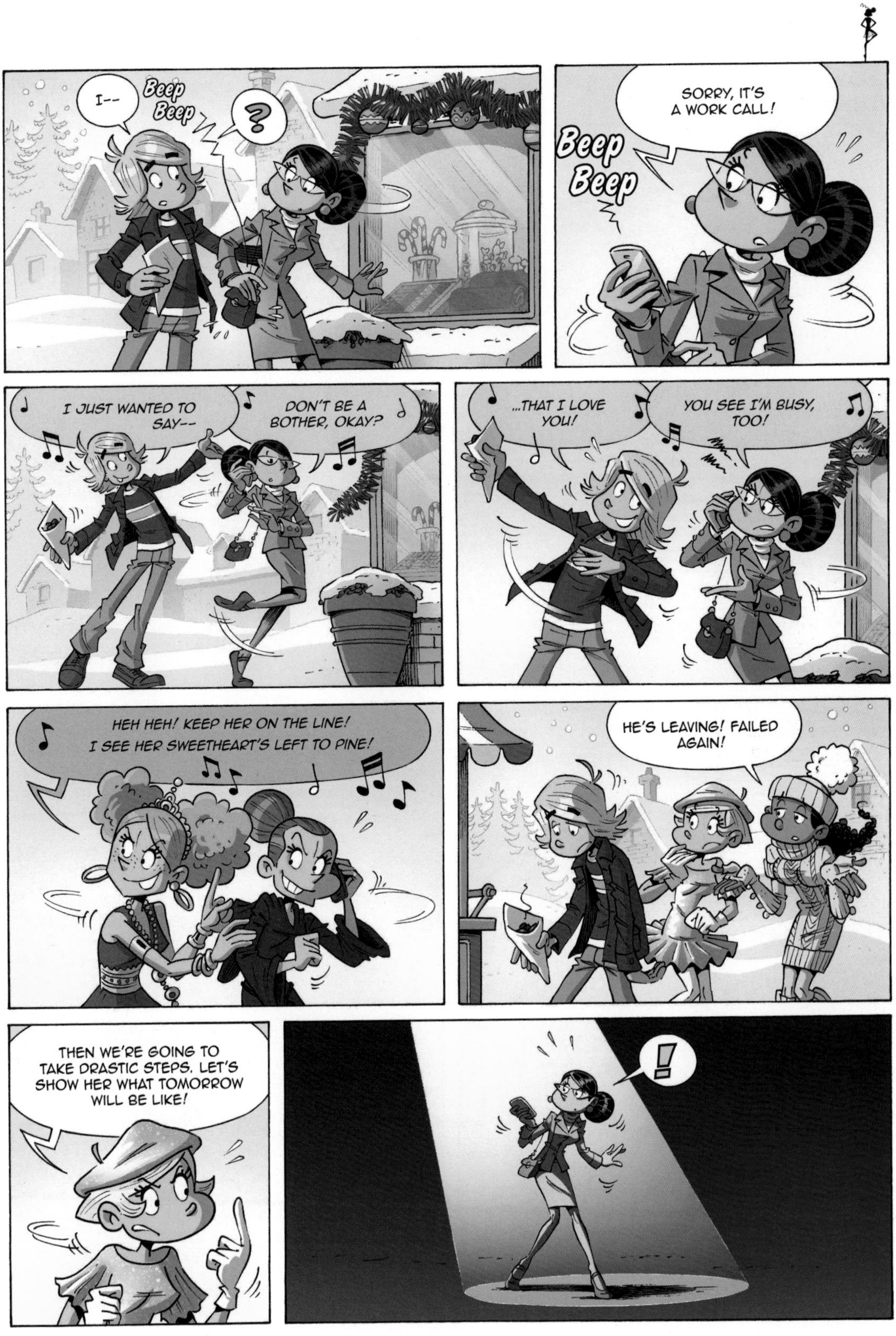
I--
Beep Beep
?
SORRY, IT'S A WORK CALL!
Beep Beep
I JUST WANTED TO SAY--
DON'T BE A BOTHER, OKAY?
...THAT I LOVE YOU!
YOU SEE I'M BUSY, TOO!
HEH HEH! KEEP HER ON THE LINE! I SEE HER SWEETHEART'S LEFT TO PINE!
HE'S LEAVING! FAILED AGAIN!
THEN WE'RE GOING TO TAKE DRASTIC STEPS. LET'S SHOW HER WHAT TOMORROW WILL BE LIKE!
!

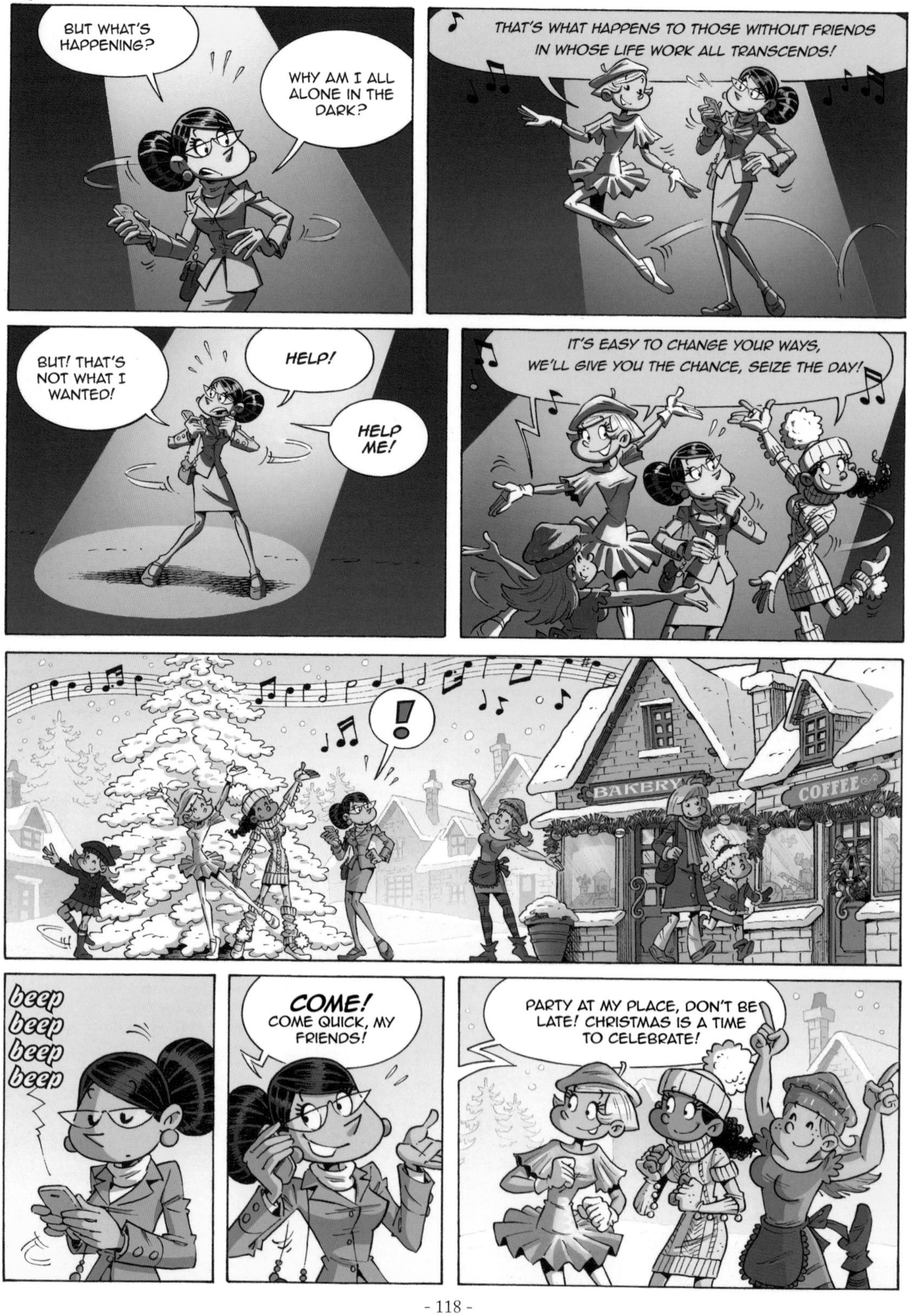
BUT WHAT'S HAPPENING?
WHY AM I ALL ALONE IN THE DARK?
THAT'S WHAT HAPPENS TO THOSE WITHOUT FRIENDS IN WHOSE LIFE WORK ALL TRANSCENDS!
BUT! THAT'S NOT WHAT I WANTED!
HELP!
HELP ME!
IT'S EASY TO CHANGE YOUR WAYS, WE'LL GIVE YOU THE CHANCE, SEIZE THE DAY!
!
BAKERY
COFFEE
beep beep beep beep
COME! COME QUICK, MY FRIENDS!
PARTY AT MY PLACE, DON'T BE LATE! CHRISTMAS IS A TIME TO CELEBRATE!

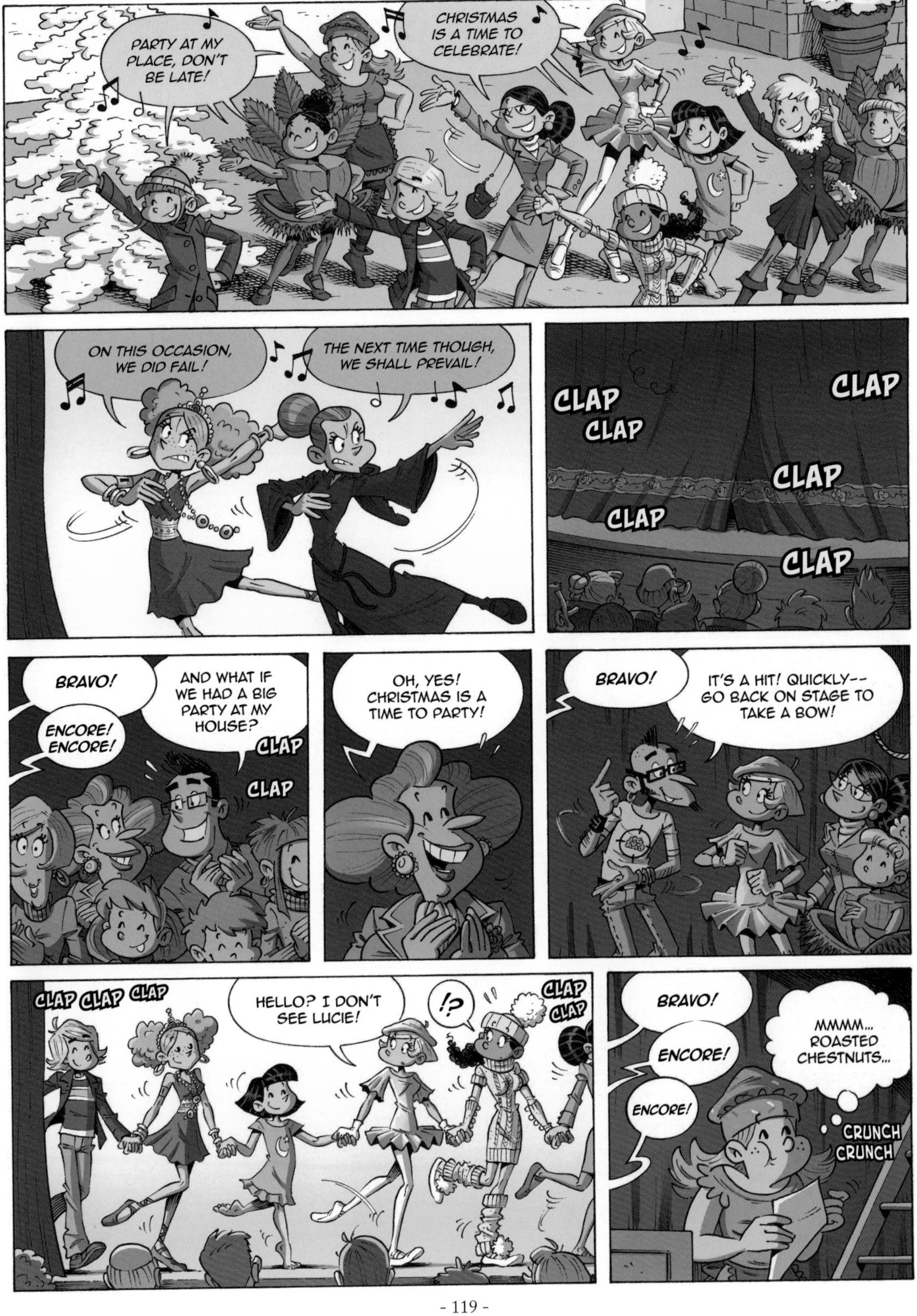

PARTY AT MY PLACE, DON'T BE LATE!
CHRISTMAS IS A TIME TO CELEBRATE!
ON THIS OCCASION, WE DID FAIL!
THE NEXT TIME THOUGH, WE SHALL PREVAIL!
CLAP
CLAP
CLAP
CLAP
CLAP
CLAP
BRAVO!
ENCORE! ENCORE!
AND WHAT IF WE HAD A BIG PARTY AT MY HOUSE?
CLAP
CLAP
OH, YES! CHRISTMAS IS A TIME TO PARTY!
BRAVO!
IT'S A HIT! QUICKLY-- GO BACK ON STAGE TO TAKE A BOW!
CLAP CLAP CLAP
HELLO? I DON'T SEE LUCIE!
!?
CLAP CLAP
BRAVO!
ENCORE!
ENCORE!
MMMM... ROASTED CHESTNUTS...
CRUNCH CRUNCH

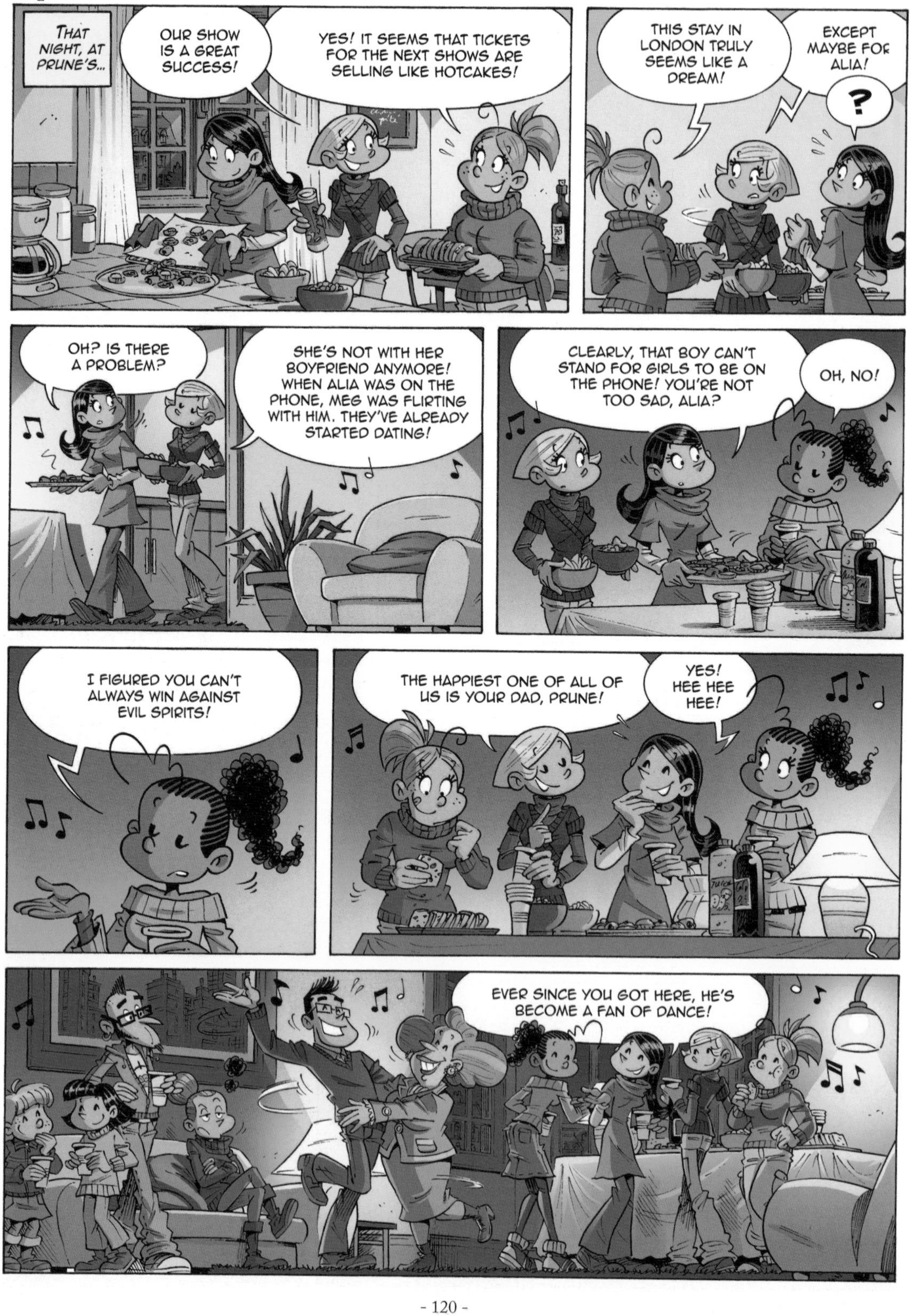
THAT NIGHT, AT PRUNE'S...
OUR SHOW IS A GREAT SUCCESS!
YES! IT SEEMS THAT TICKETS FOR THE NEXT SHOWS ARE SELLING LIKE HOTCAKES!
THIS STAY IN LONDON TRULY SEEMS LIKE A DREAM!
EXCEPT MAYBE FOR ALIA!
?
OH? IS THERE A PROBLEM?
SHE'S NOT WITH HER BOYFRIEND ANYMORE! WHEN ALIA WAS ON THE PHONE, MEG WAS FLIRTING WITH HIM. THEY'VE ALREADY STARTED DATING!
CLEARLY, THAT BOY CAN'T STAND FOR GIRLS TO BE ON THE PHONE! YOU'RE NOT TOO SAD, ALIA?
OH, NO!
I FIGURED YOU CAN'T ALWAYS WIN AGAINST EVIL SPIRITS!
THE HAPPIEST ONE OF ALL OF US IS YOUR DAD, PRUNE!
YES! HEE HEE HEE!
EVER SINCE YOU GOT HERE, HE'S BECOME A FAN OF DANCE!

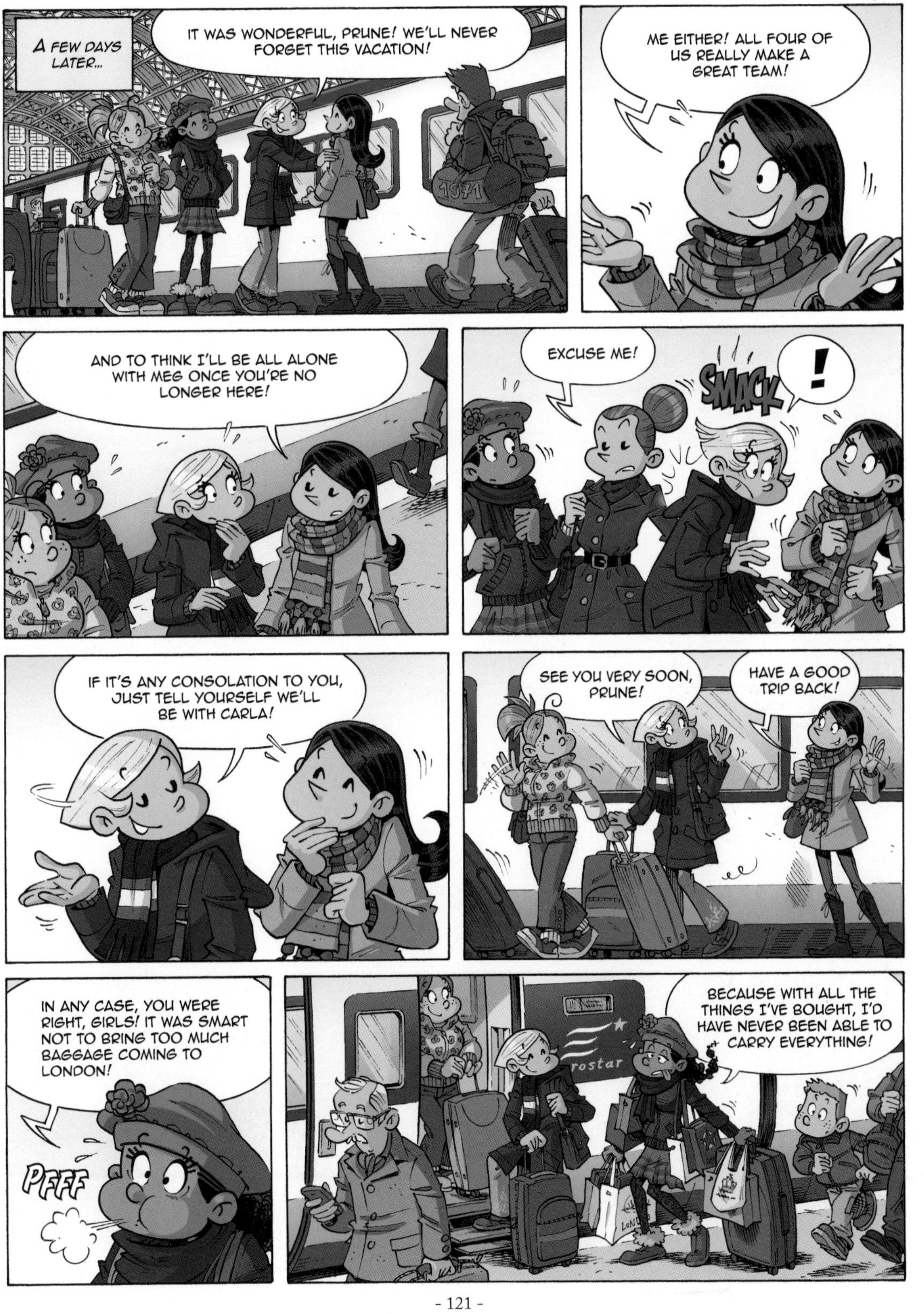
A FEW DAYS LATER...
IT WAS WONDERFUL, PRUNE! WE'LL NEVER FORGET THIS VACATION!
1971
ME EITHER! ALL FOUR OF US REALLY MAKE A GREAT TEAM!
AND TO THINK I'LL BE ALL ALONE WITH MEG ONCE YOU'RE NO LONGER HERE!
EXCUSE ME!
SMACK
!
IF IT'S ANY CONSOLATION TO YOU, JUST TELL YOURSELF WE'LL BE WITH CARLA!
SEE YOU VERY SOON, PRUNE!
HAVE A GOOD TRIP BACK!
IN ANY CASE, YOU WERE RIGHT, GIRLS! IT WAS SMART NOT TO BRING TOO MUCH BAGGAGE COMING TO LONDON!
PFFF
BECAUSE WITH ALL THE THINGS I'VE BOUGHT, I'D HAVE NEVER BEEN ABLE TO CARRY EVERYTHING!

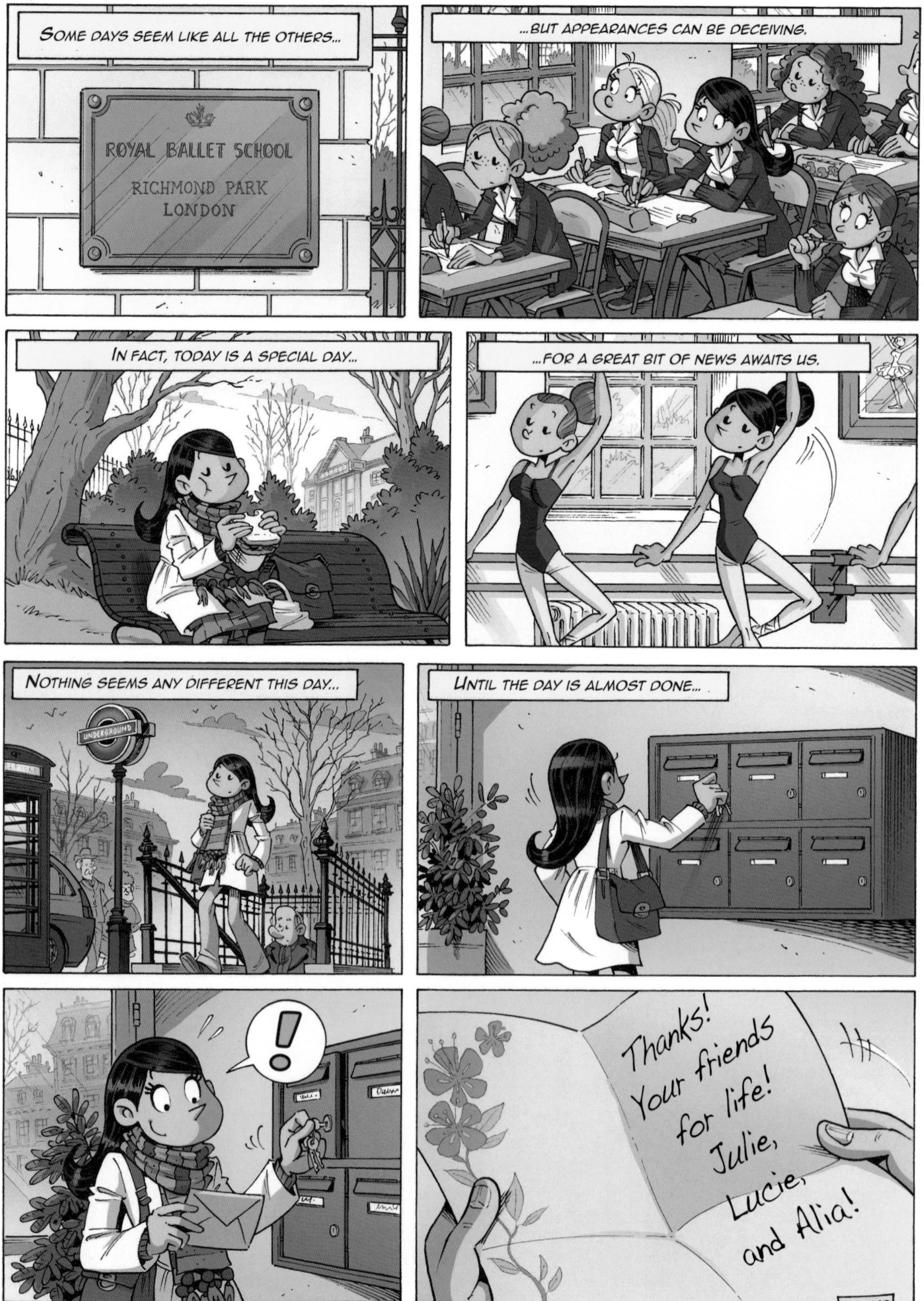

SOME DAYS SEEM LIKE ALL THE OTHERS...
ROYAL BALLET SCHOOL
RICHMOND PARK
LONDON
...BUT APPEARANCES CAN BE DECEIVING.
IN FACT, TODAY IS A SPECIAL DAY...
...FOR A GREAT BIT OF NEWS AWAITS US.
NOTHING SEEMS ANY DIFFERENT THIS DAY...
UNDERGROUND
UNTIL THE DAY IS ALMOST DONE...
!
Thanks! Your friends for life! Julie, Lucie, and Alia!
THE END

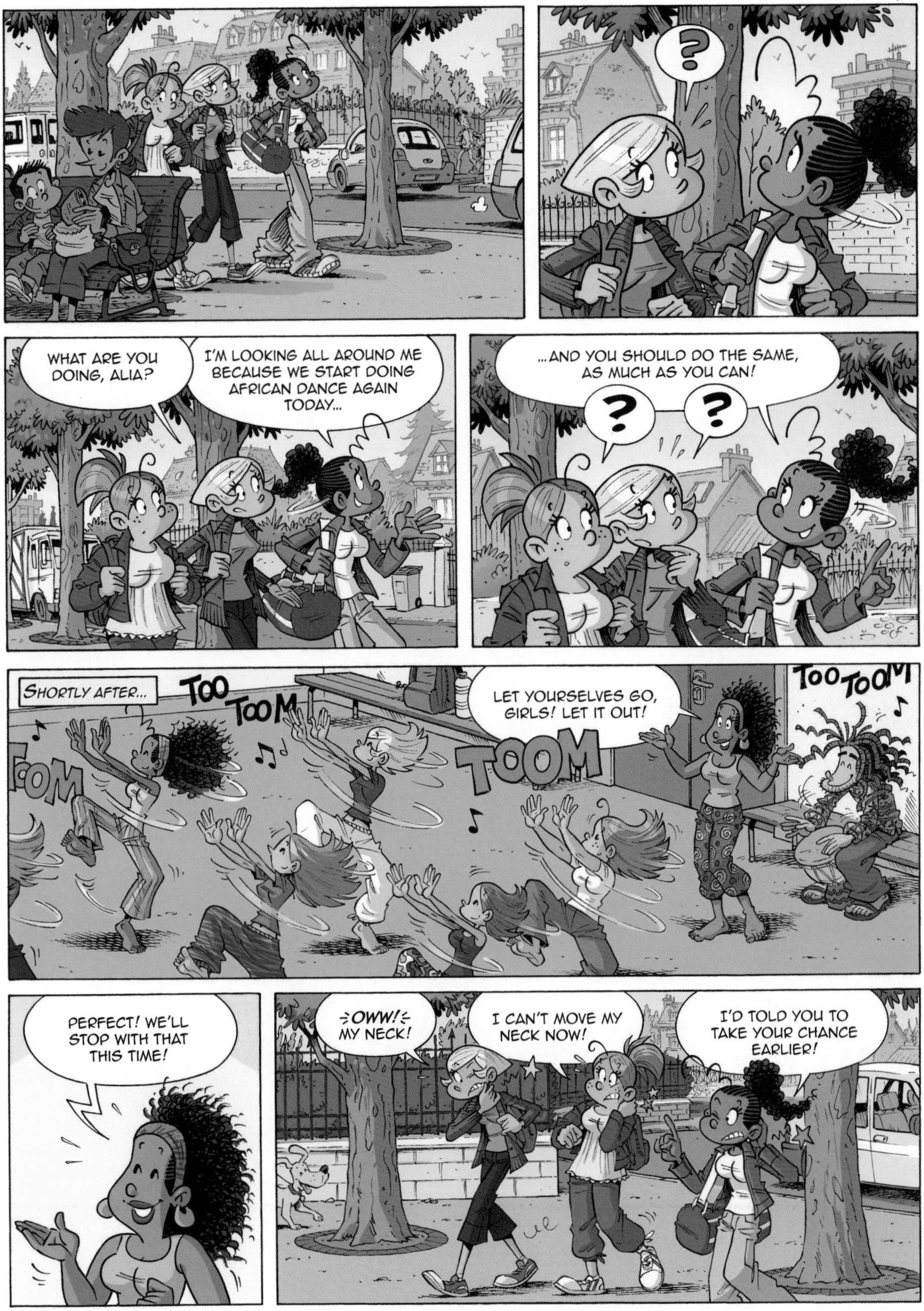
?
WHAT ARE YOU DOING, ALIA?
I'M LOOKING ALL AROUND ME BECAUSE WE START DOING AFRICAN DANCE AGAIN TODAY...
...AND YOU SHOULD DO THE SAME, AS MUCH AS YOU CAN!
?
?
SHORTLY AFTER...
TOO TOOM
TOOM
TOOM
LET YOURSELVES GO, GIRLS! LET IT OUT!
TOO TOOM
PERFECT! WE'LL STOP WITH THAT THIS TIME!
OWW! MY NECK!
I CAN'T MOVE MY NECK NOW!
I'D TOLD YOU TO TAKE YOUR CHANCE EARLIER!

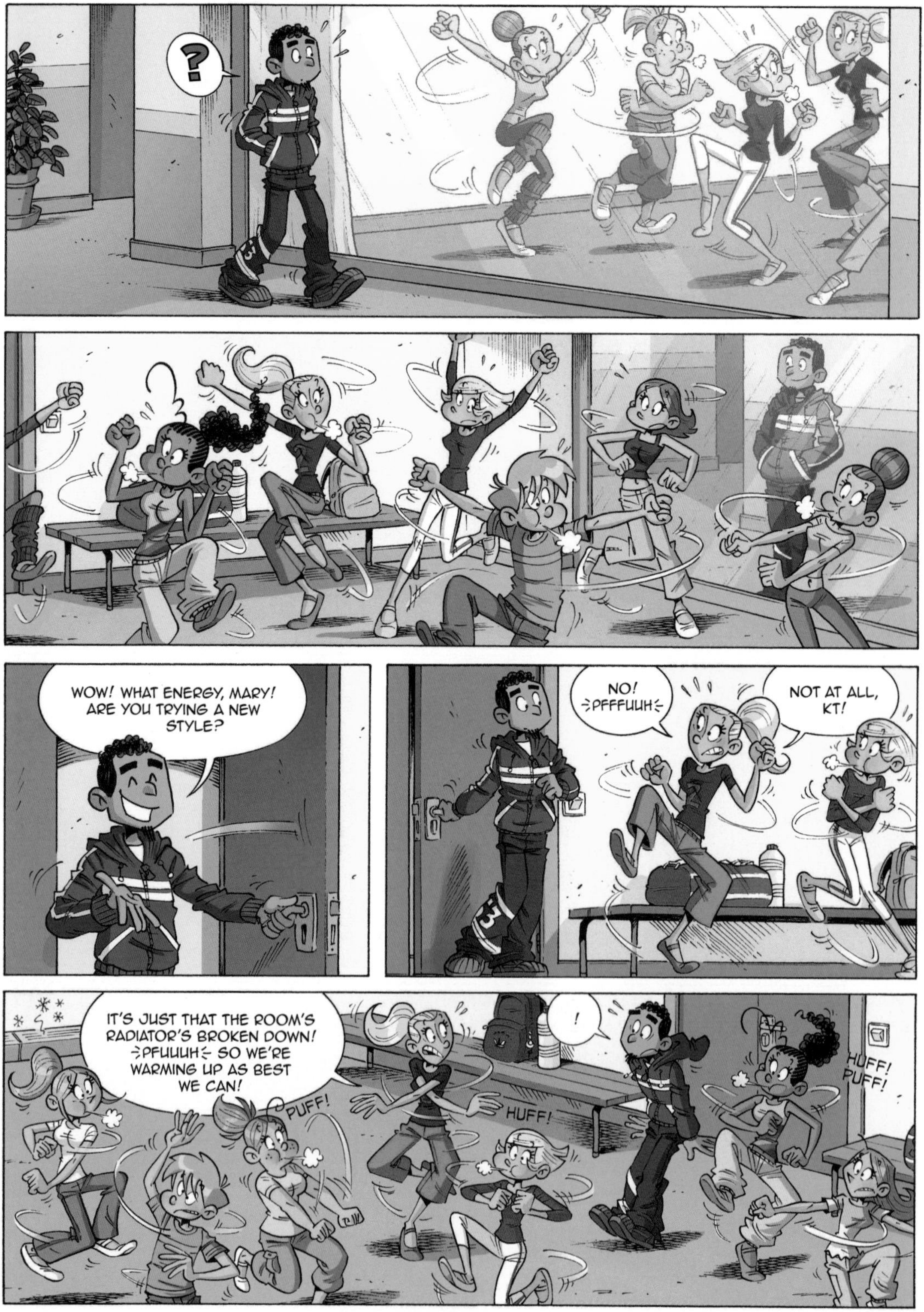
?
WOW! WHAT ENERGY, MARY! ARE YOU TRYING A NEW STYLE?
NO! ⇉PFFFUUH⇇
NOT AT ALL, KT!
IT'S JUST THAT THE ROOM'S RADIATOR'S BROKEN DOWN! ⇉PFUUUH⇇ SO WE'RE WARMING UP AS BEST WE CAN!
!
PUFF!
HUFF!
HUFF! PUFF!

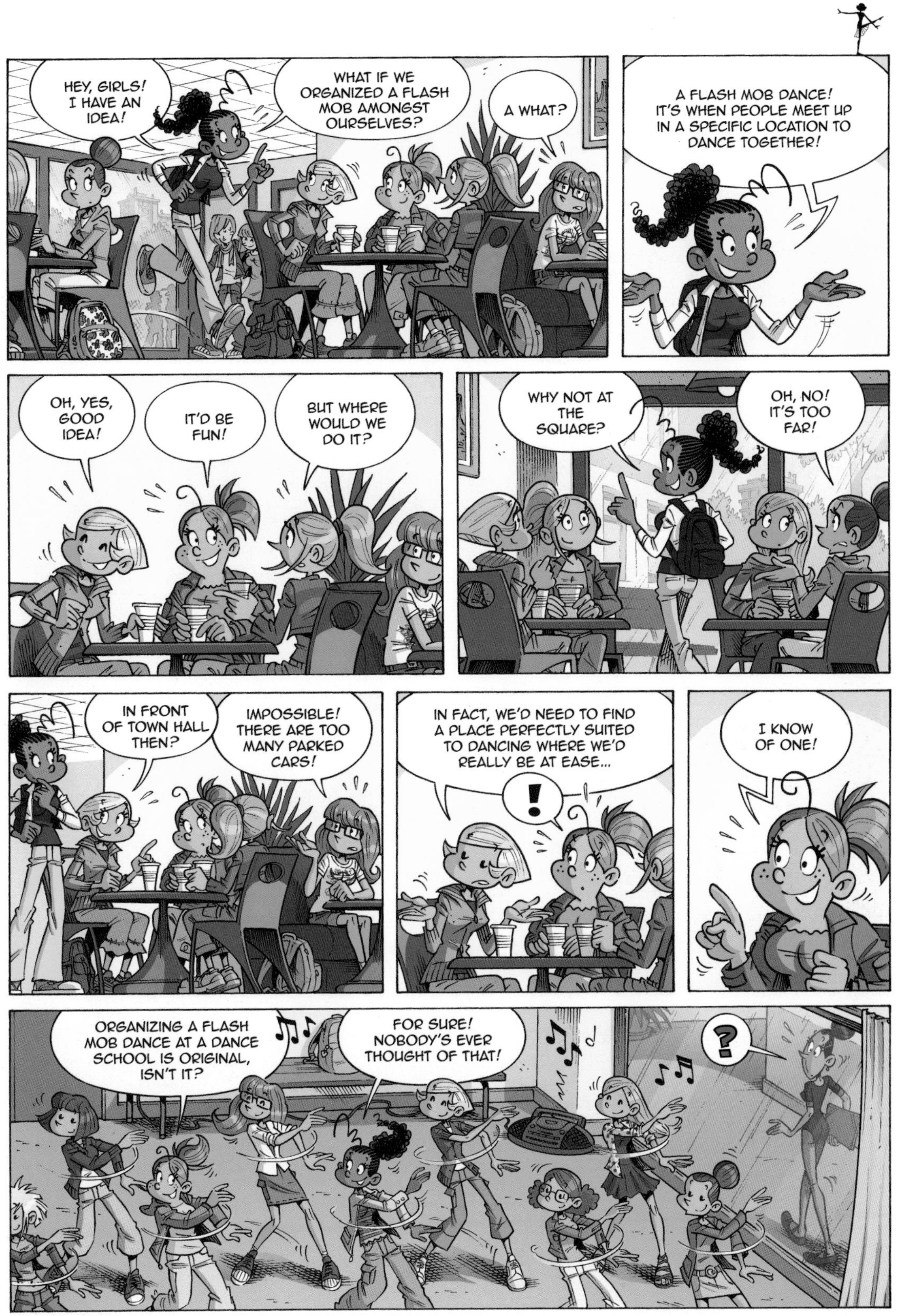
HEY, GIRLS! I HAVE AN IDEA!
WHAT IF WE ORGANIZED A FLASH MOB AMONGST OURSELVES?
A WHAT?
A FLASH MOB DANCE! IT'S WHEN PEOPLE MEET UP IN A SPECIFIC LOCATION TO DANCE TOGETHER!
OH, YES, GOOD IDEA!
IT'D BE FUN!
BUT WHERE WOULD WE DO IT?
WHY NOT AT THE SQUARE?
OH, NO! IT'S TOO FAR!
IN FRONT OF TOWN HALL THEN?
IMPOSSIBLE! THERE ARE TOO MANY PARKED CARS!
IN FACT, WE'D NEED TO FIND A PLACE PERFECTLY SUITED TO DANCING WHERE WE'D REALLY BE AT EASE...
!
I KNOW OF ONE!
ORGANIZING A FLASH MOB DANCE AT A DANCE SCHOOL IS ORIGINAL, ISN'T IT?
FOR SURE! NOBODY'S EVER THOUGHT OF THAT!
?

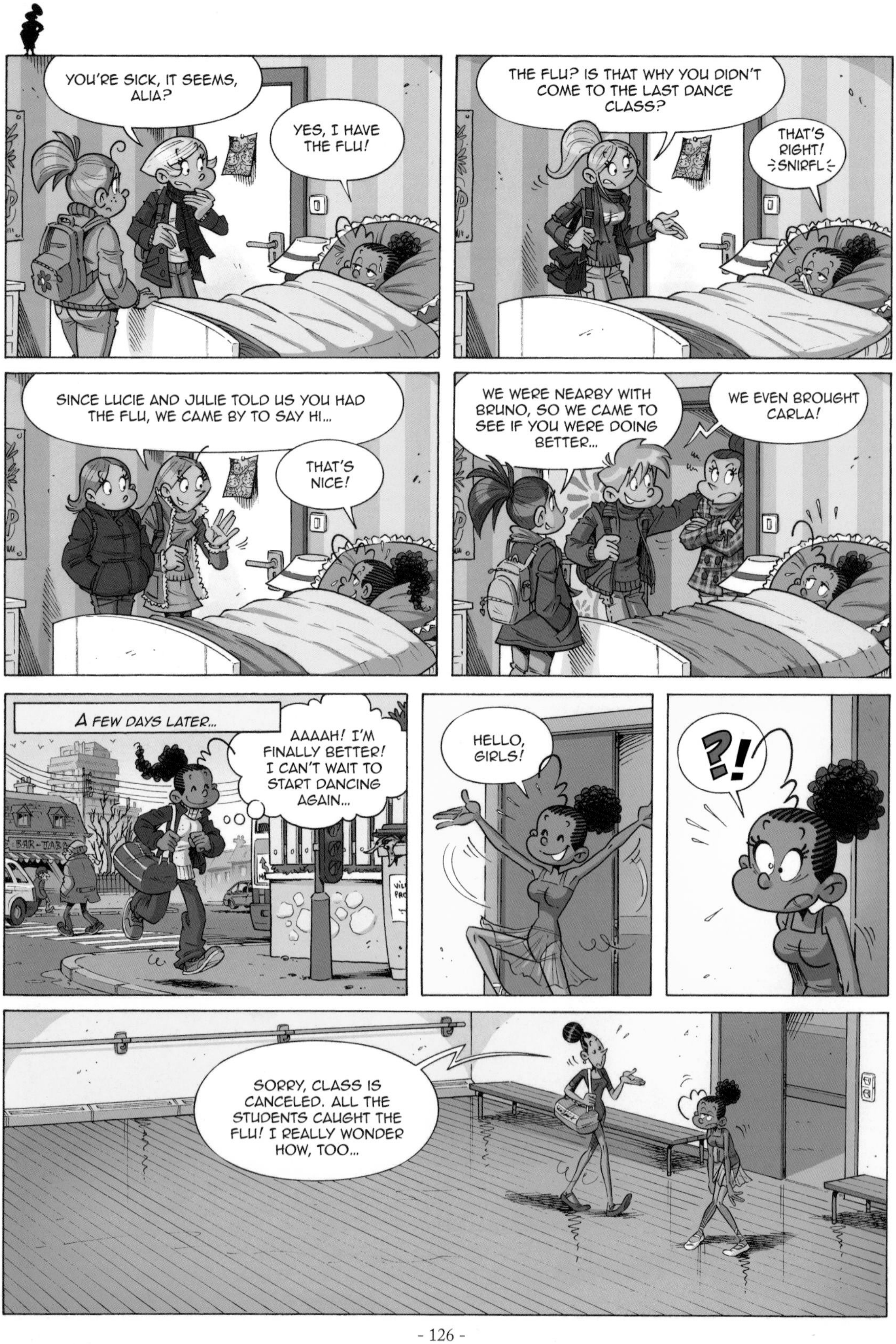

YOU'RE SICK, IT SEEMS, ALIA?
YES, I HAVE THE FLU!
THE FLU? IS THAT WHY YOU DIDN'T COME TO THE LAST DANCE CLASS?
THAT'S RIGHT! SNIRFL
SINCE LUCIE AND JULIE TOLD US YOU HAD THE FLU, WE CAME BY TO SAY HI...
THAT'S NICE!
WE WERE NEARBY WITH BRUNO, SO WE CAME TO SEE IF YOU WERE DOING BETTER...
WE EVEN BROUGHT CARLA!
A FEW DAYS LATER...
AAAAH! I'M FINALLY BETTER! I CAN'T WAIT TO START DANCING AGAIN...
HELLO, GIRLS!
?!
SORRY, CLASS IS CANCELED. ALL THE STUDENTS CAUGHT THE FLU! I REALLY WONDER HOW, TOO...

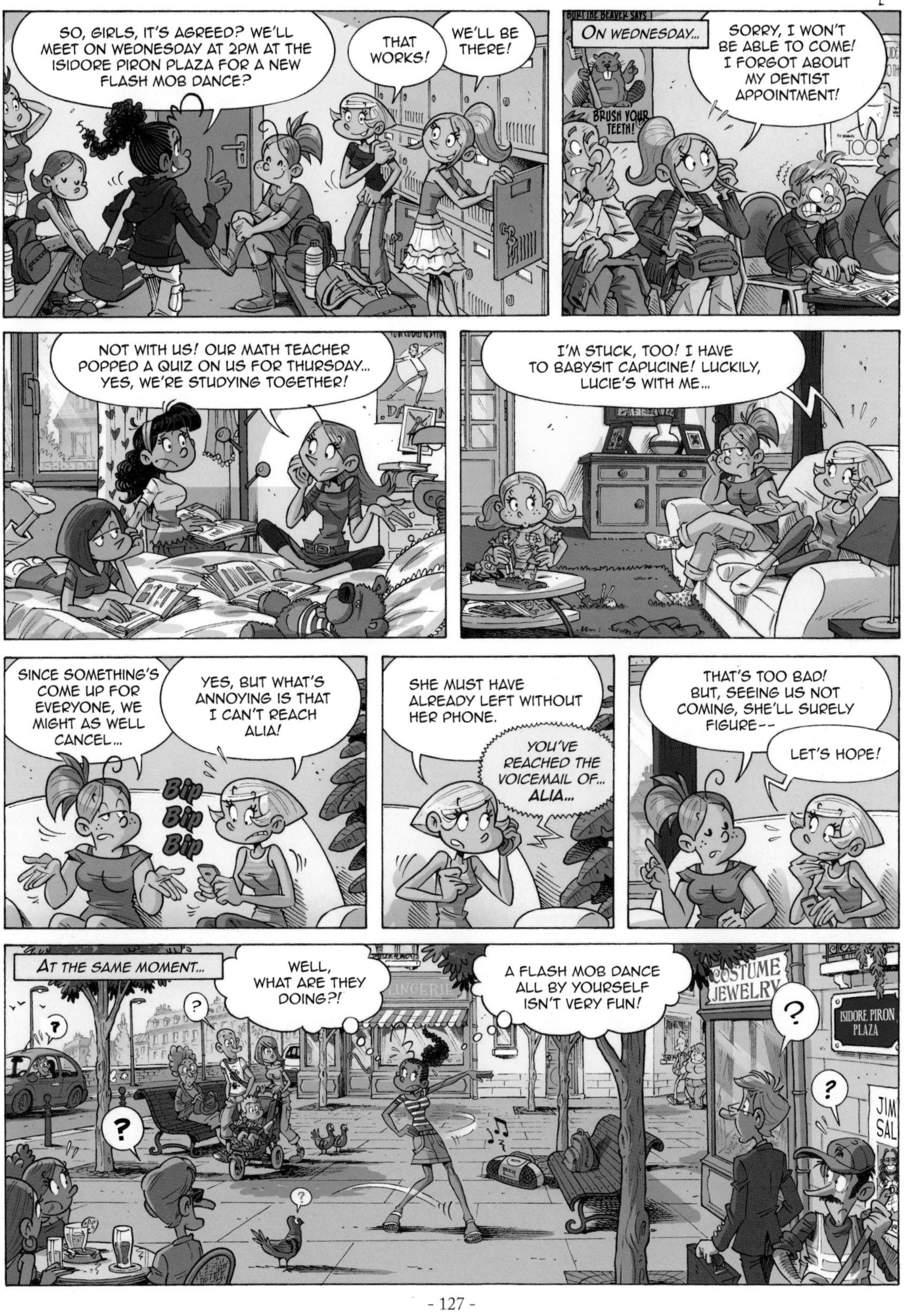
SO, GIRLS, IT'S AGREED? WE'LL MEET ON WEDNESDAY AT 2PM AT THE ISIDORE PIRON PLAZA FOR A NEW FLASH MOB DANCE?
THAT WORKS!
WE'LL BE THERE!
ON WEDNESDAY...
BURT THE BEAVER SAYS:
BRUSH YOUR TEETH!
SORRY, I WON'T BE ABLE TO COME! I FORGOT ABOUT MY DENTIST APPOINTMENT!
NOT WITH US! OUR MATH TEACHER POPPED A QUIZ ON US FOR THURSDAY... YES, WE'RE STUDYING TOGETHER!
I'M STUCK, TOO! I HAVE TO BABYSIT CAPUCINE! LUCKILY, LUCIE'S WITH ME...
SINCE SOMETHING'S COME UP FOR EVERYONE, WE MIGHT AS WELL CANCEL...
YES, BUT WHAT'S ANNOYING IS THAT I CAN'T REACH ALIA!
Bip Bip Bip
SHE MUST HAVE ALREADY LEFT WITHOUT HER PHONE.
YOU'VE REACHED THE VOICEMAIL OF... ALIA...
THAT'S TOO BAD! BUT, SEEING US NOT COMING, SHE'LL SURELY FIGURE--
LET'S HOPE!
AT THE SAME MOMENT...
WELL, WHAT ARE THEY DOING?!
A FLASH MOB DANCE ALL BY YOURSELF ISN'T VERY FUN!
LINGERIE
COSTUME JEWELRY
ISIDORE PIRON PLAZA
?
?
?
?
?
?

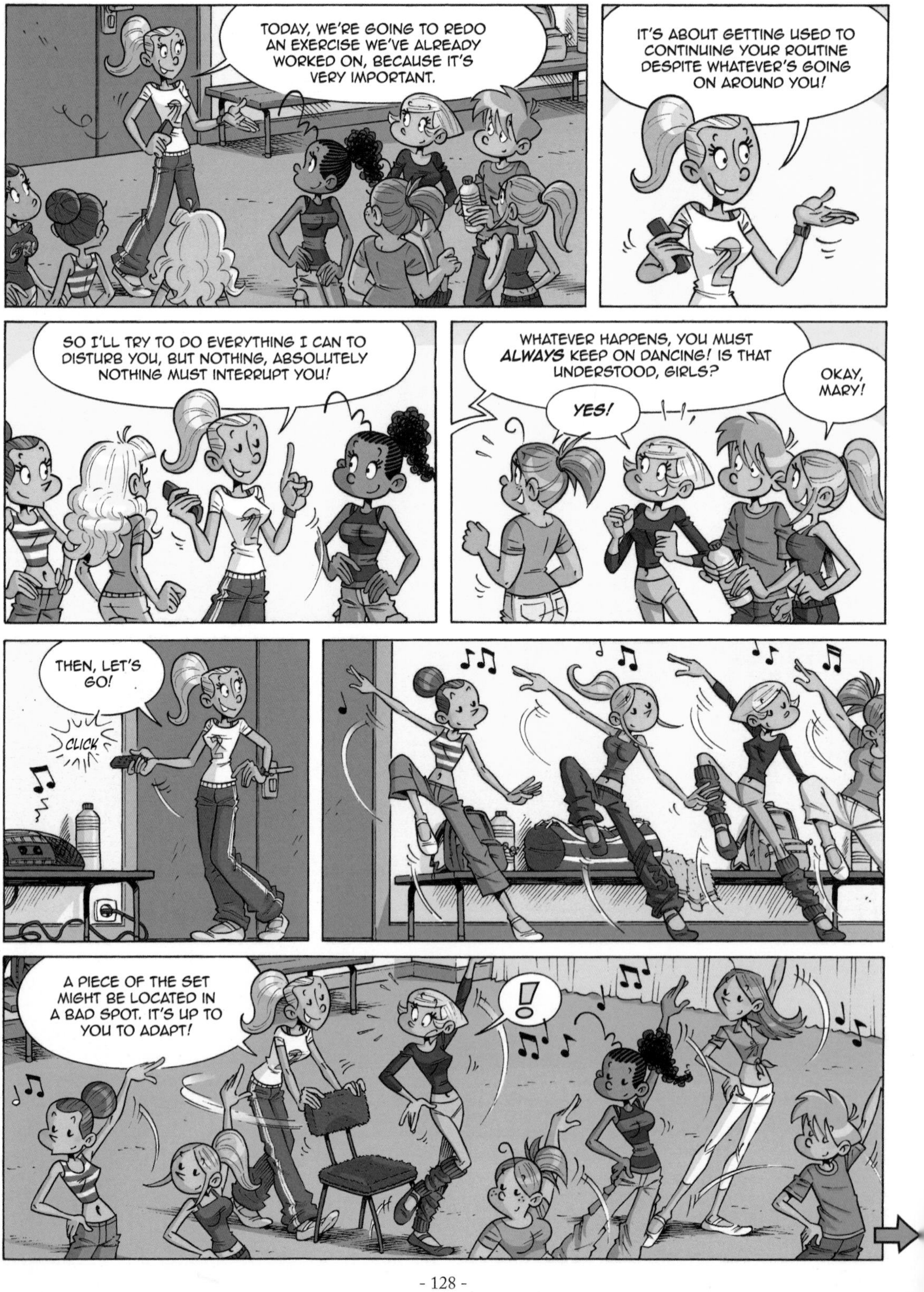
TODAY, WE'RE GOING TO REDO AN EXERCISE WE'VE ALREADY WORKED ON, BECAUSE IT'S VERY IMPORTANT.
IT'S ABOUT GETTING USED TO CONTINUING YOUR ROUTINE DESPITE WHATEVER'S GOING ON AROUND YOU!
SO I'LL TRY TO DO EVERYTHING I CAN TO DISTURB YOU, BUT NOTHING, ABSOLUTELY NOTHING MUST INTERRUPT YOU!
WHATEVER HAPPENS, YOU MUST **ALWAYS** KEEP ON DANCING! IS THAT UNDERSTOOD, GIRLS?
YES!
OKAY, MARY!
THEN, LET'S GO!
CLICK
A PIECE OF THE SET MIGHT BE LOCATED IN A BAD SPOT. IT'S UP TO YOU TO ADAPT!
!

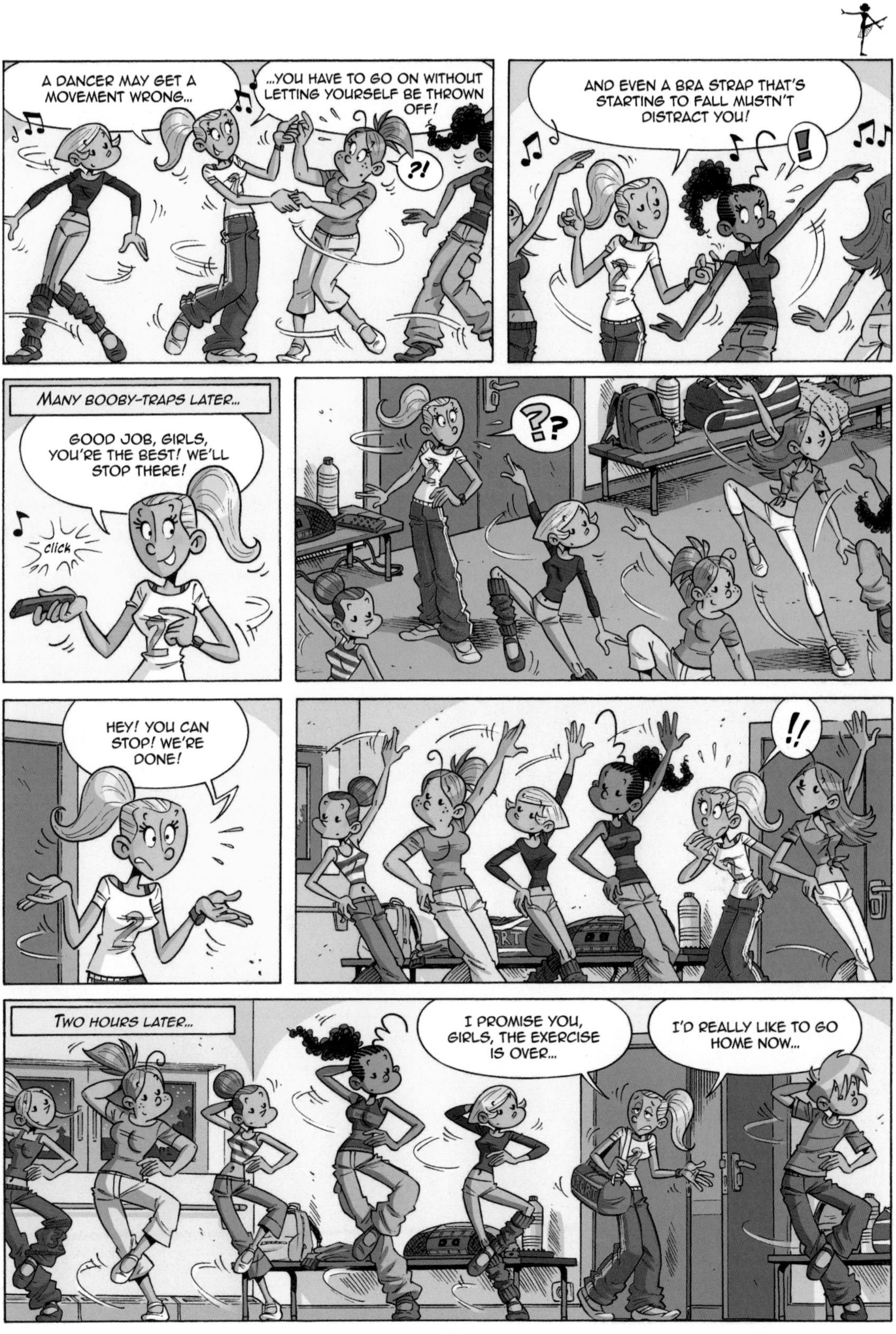
A DANCER MAY GET A MOVEMENT WRONG...
...YOU HAVE TO GO ON WITHOUT LETTING YOURSELF BE THROWN OFF!
?!
AND EVEN A BRA STRAP THAT'S STARTING TO FALL MUSTN'T DISTRACT YOU!
!
MANY BOOBY-TRAPS LATER...
GOOD JOB, GIRLS, YOU'RE THE BEST! WE'LL STOP THERE!
click
??
HEY! YOU CAN STOP! WE'RE DONE!
!!
TWO HOURS LATER...
I PROMISE YOU, GIRLS, THE EXERCISE IS OVER...
I'D REALLY LIKE TO GO HOME NOW...

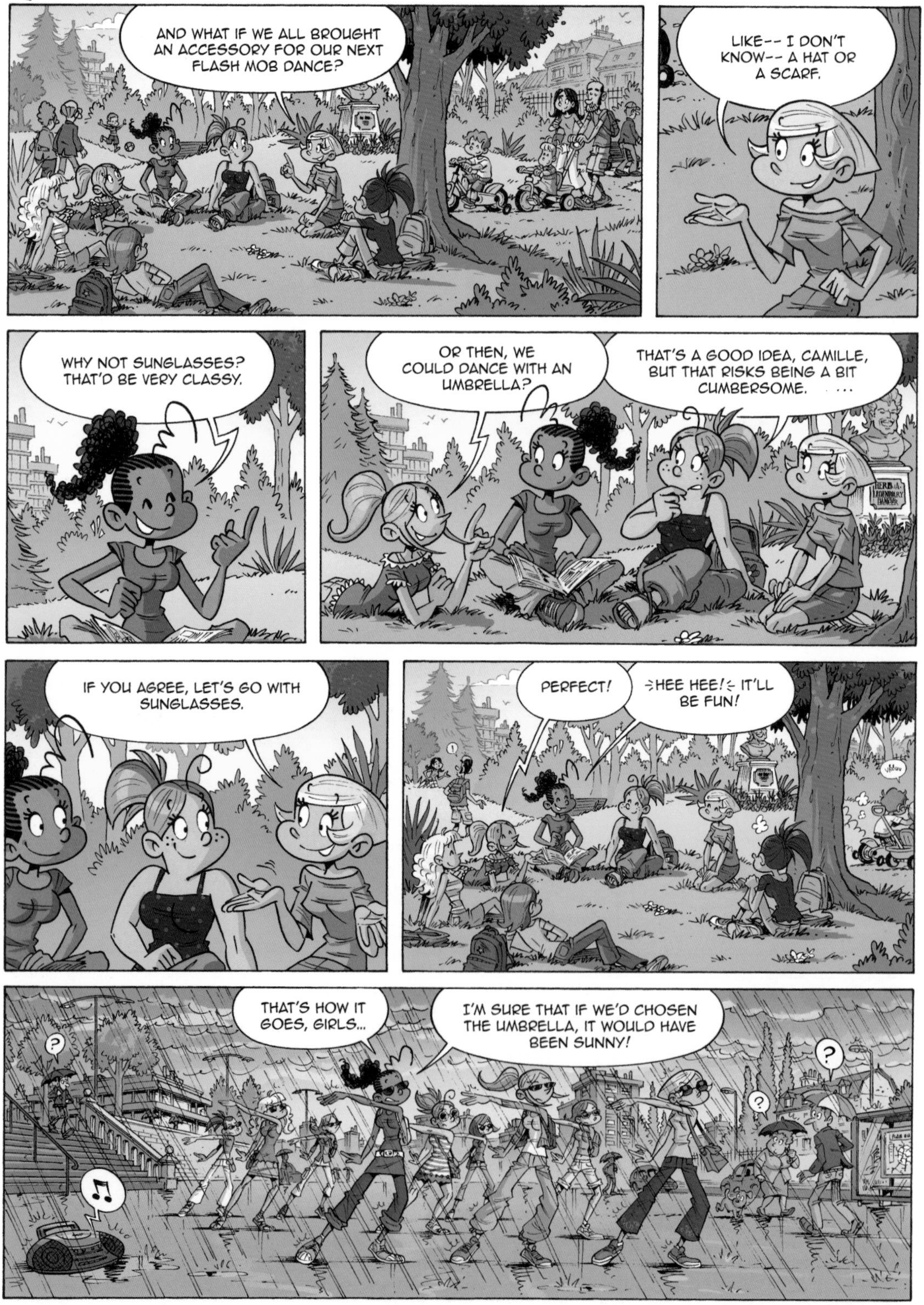
AND WHAT IF WE ALL BROUGHT AN ACCESSORY FOR OUR NEXT FLASH MOB DANCE?
LIKE-- I DON'T KNOW-- A HAT OR A SCARF.
WHY NOT SUNGLASSES? THAT'D BE VERY CLASSY.
OR THEN, WE COULD DANCE WITH AN UMBRELLA?
THAT'S A GOOD IDEA, CAMILLE, BUT THAT RISKS BEING A BIT CUMBERSOME. ...
IF YOU AGREE, LET'S GO WITH SUNGLASSES.
PERFECT!
HEE HEE! IT'LL BE FUN!
THAT'S HOW IT GOES, GIRLS...
I'M SURE THAT IF WE'D CHOSEN THE UMBRELLA, IT WOULD HAVE BEEN SUNNY!

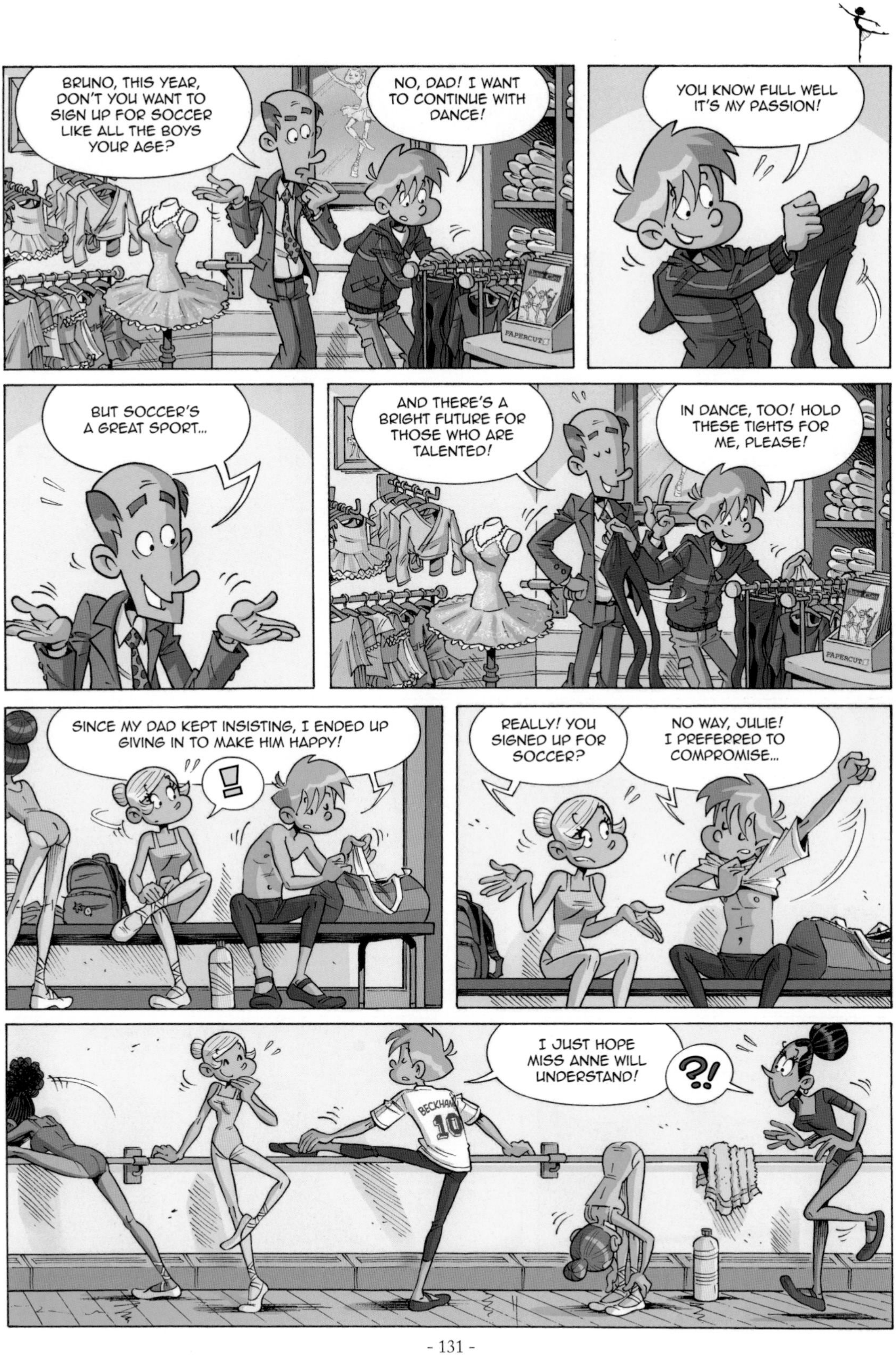
BRUNO, THIS YEAR, DON'T YOU WANT TO SIGN UP FOR SOCCER LIKE ALL THE BOYS YOUR AGE?
NO, DAD! I WANT TO CONTINUE WITH DANCE!
YOU KNOW FULL WELL IT'S MY PASSION!
BUT SOCCER'S A GREAT SPORT...
AND THERE'S A BRIGHT FUTURE FOR THOSE WHO ARE TALENTED!
IN DANCE, TOO! HOLD THESE TIGHTS FOR ME, PLEASE!
PAPERCUT
SINCE MY DAD KEPT INSISTING, I ENDED UP GIVING IN TO MAKE HIM HAPPY!
!
REALLY! YOU SIGNED UP FOR SOCCER?
NO WAY, JULIE! I PREFERRED TO COMPROMISE...
BECKHAM 10
I JUST HOPE MISS ANNE WILL UNDERSTAND!
?!

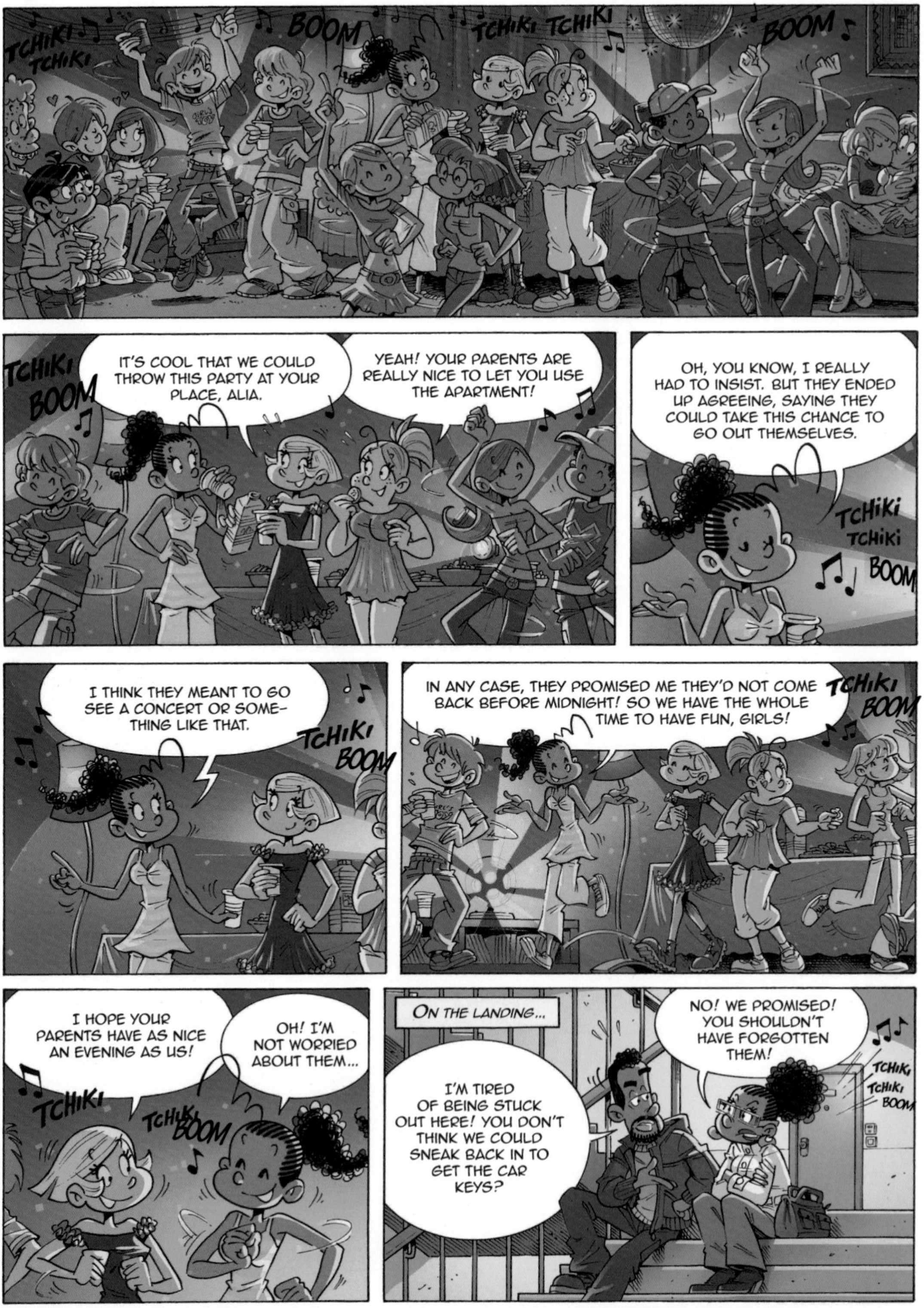
TCHIKI TCHIKI
BOOM
TCHIKI TCHIKI
BOOM
TCHIKI BOOM
IT'S COOL THAT WE COULD THROW THIS PARTY AT YOUR PLACE, ALIA.
YEAH! YOUR PARENTS ARE REALLY NICE TO LET YOU USE THE APARTMENT!
OH, YOU KNOW, I REALLY HAD TO INSIST. BUT THEY ENDED UP AGREEING, SAYING THEY COULD TAKE THIS CHANCE TO GO OUT THEMSELVES.
TCHIKI TCHIKI BOOM
I THINK THEY MEANT TO GO SEE A CONCERT OR SOME-THING LIKE THAT.
TCHIKI BOOM
IN ANY CASE, THEY PROMISED ME THEY'D NOT COME BACK BEFORE MIDNIGHT! SO WE HAVE THE WHOLE TIME TO HAVE FUN, GIRLS!
TCHIKI BOOM
I HOPE YOUR PARENTS HAVE AS NICE AN EVENING AS US!
OH! I'M NOT WORRIED ABOUT THEM...
TCHIKI
TCHIKI BOOM
ON THE LANDING...
I'M TIRED OF BEING STUCK OUT HERE! YOU DON'T THINK WE COULD SNEAK BACK IN TO GET THE CAR KEYS?
NO! WE PROMISED! YOU SHOULDN'T HAVE FORGOTTEN THEM!
TCHIKI TCHIKI BOOM

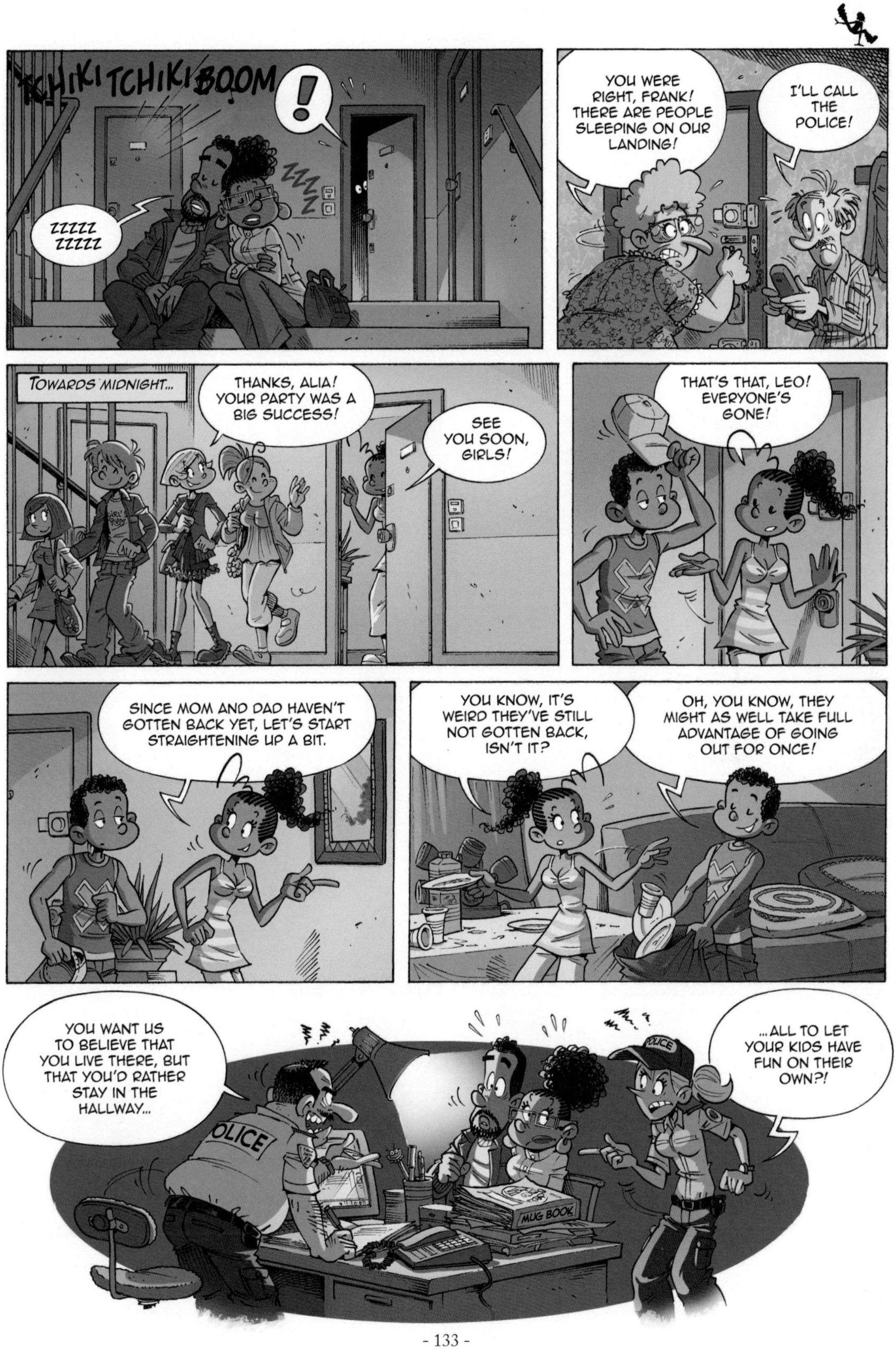
TCHIKI TCHIKI BOOM
!
ZZZZZ ZZZZZ
ZZZZ
YOU WERE RIGHT, FRANK! THERE ARE PEOPLE SLEEPING ON OUR LANDING!
I'LL CALL THE POLICE!
TOWARDS MIDNIGHT...
THANKS, ALIA! YOUR PARTY WAS A BIG SUCCESS!
SEE YOU SOON, GIRLS!
THAT'S THAT, LEO! EVERYONE'S GONE!
SINCE MOM AND DAD HAVEN'T GOTTEN BACK YET, LET'S START STRAIGHTENING UP A BIT.
YOU KNOW, IT'S WEIRD THEY'VE STILL NOT GOTTEN BACK, ISN'T IT?
OH, YOU KNOW, THEY MIGHT AS WELL TAKE FULL ADVANTAGE OF GOING OUT FOR ONCE!
YOU WANT US TO BELIEVE THAT YOU LIVE THERE, BUT THAT YOU'D RATHER STAY IN THE HALLWAY...
...ALL TO LET YOUR KIDS HAVE FUN ON THEIR OWN?!
POLICE
MUG BOOK

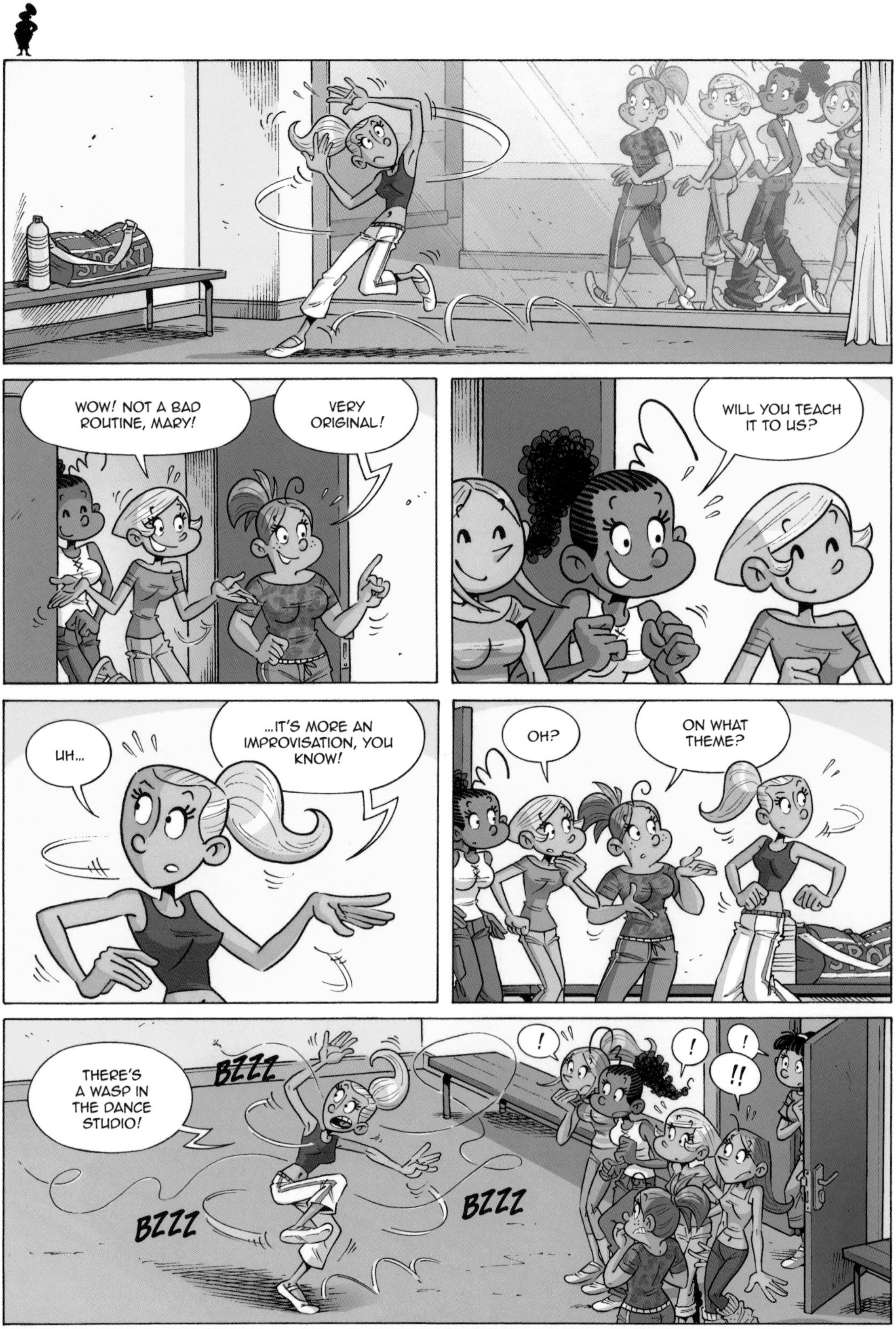
WOW! NOT A BAD ROUTINE, MARY!
VERY ORIGINAL!
WILL YOU TEACH IT TO US?
UH...
...IT'S MORE AN IMPROVISATION, YOU KNOW!
OH?
ON WHAT THEME?
THERE'S A WASP IN THE DANCE STUDIO!
BZZZ
BZZZ
BZZZ
!
!
!
!!

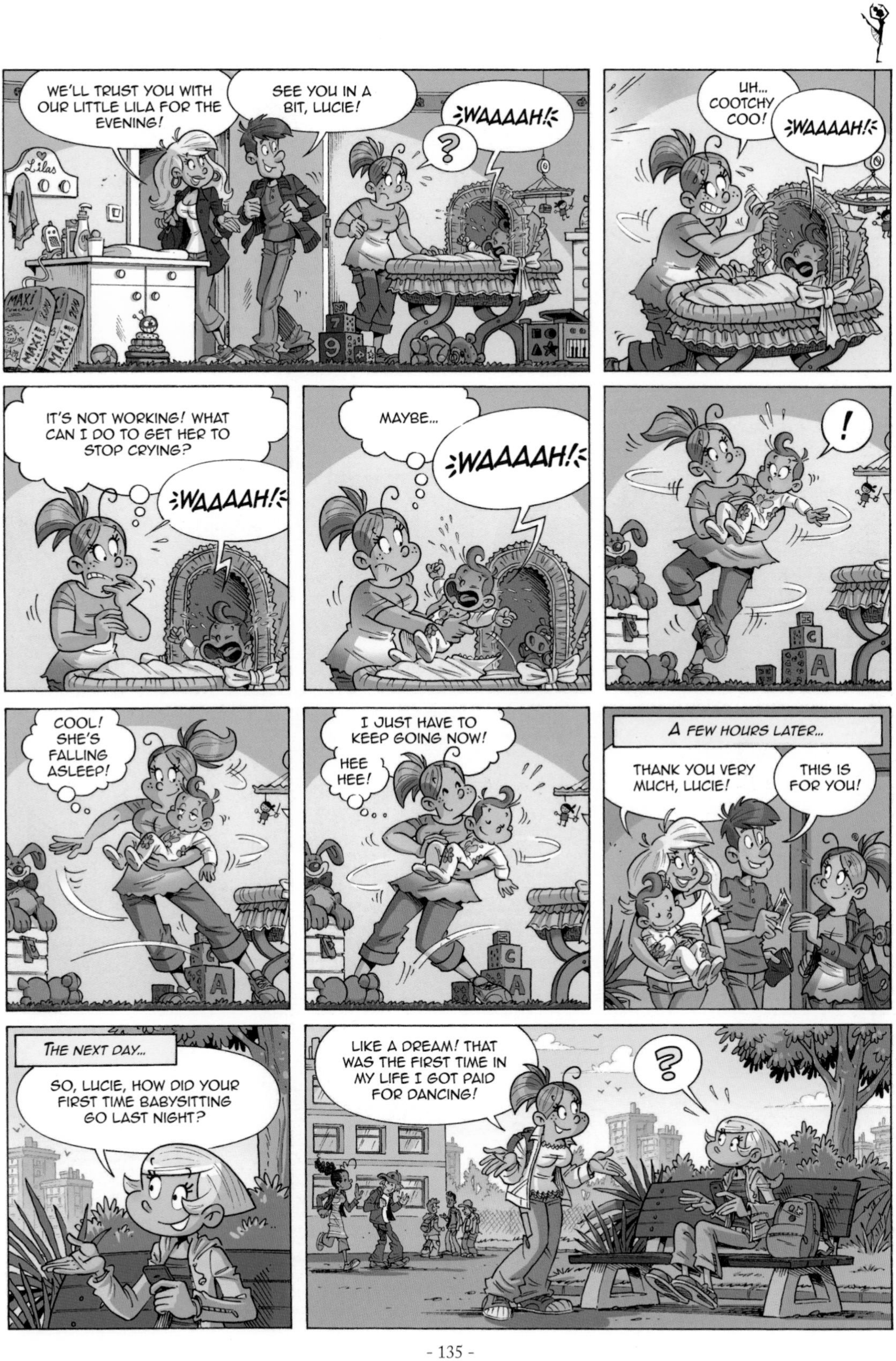
WE'LL TRUST YOU WITH OUR LITTLE LILA FOR THE EVENING!
SEE YOU IN A BIT, LUCIE!
Lilas
WAAAAH!
?
UH... COOTCHY COO!
WAAAAH!
IT'S NOT WORKING! WHAT CAN I DO TO GET HER TO STOP CRYING?
WAAAAH!
MAYBE...
WAAAAH!
!
COOL! SHE'S FALLING ASLEEP!
I JUST HAVE TO KEEP GOING NOW!
HEE HEE!
A FEW HOURS LATER...
THANK YOU VERY MUCH, LUCIE!
THIS IS FOR YOU!
THE NEXT DAY...
SO, LUCIE, HOW DID YOUR FIRST TIME BABYSITTING GO LAST NIGHT?
LIKE A DREAM! THAT WAS THE FIRST TIME IN MY LIFE I GOT PAID FOR DANCING!
?

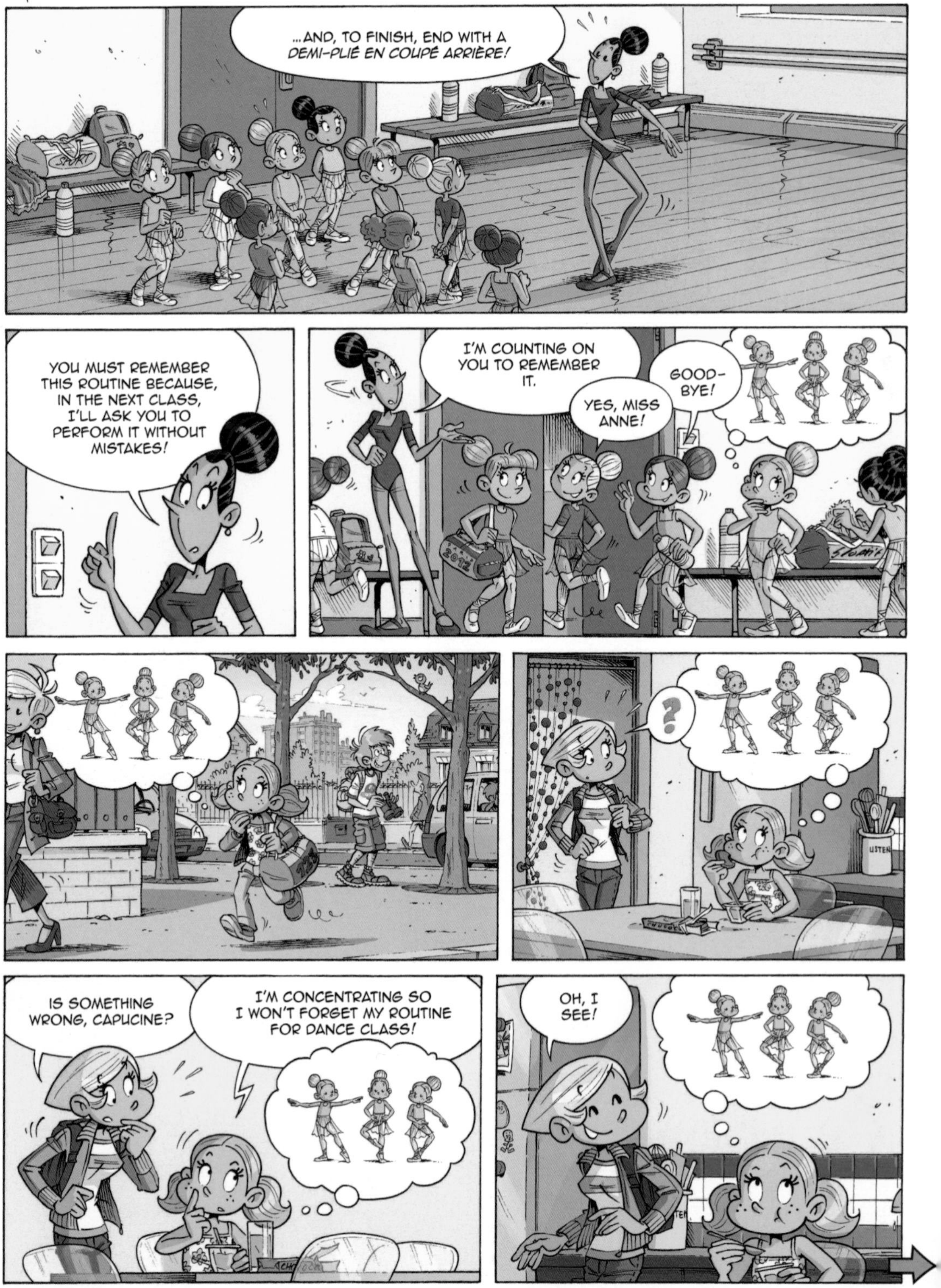
...AND, TO FINISH, END WITH A *DEMI-PLIÉ EN COUPÉ ARRIÈRE!*
YOU MUST REMEMBER THIS ROUTINE BECAUSE, IN THE NEXT CLASS, I'LL ASK YOU TO PERFORM IT WITHOUT MISTAKES!
I'M COUNTING ON YOU TO REMEMBER IT.
YES, MISS ANNE!
GOOD-BYE!
?
IS SOMETHING WRONG, CAPUCINE?
I'M CONCENTRATING SO I WON'T FORGET MY ROUTINE FOR DANCE CLASS!
OH, I SEE!

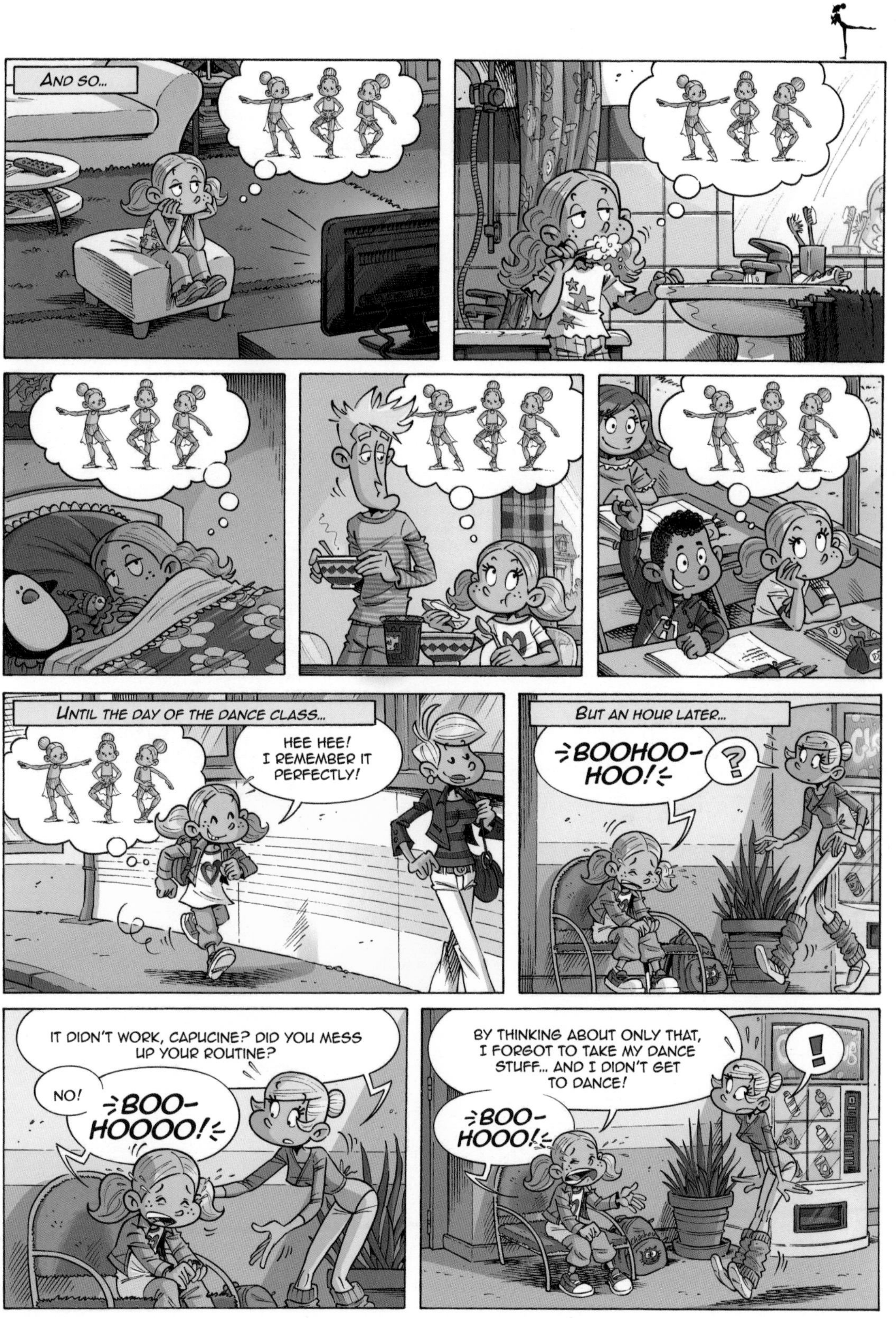
AND SO...
UNTIL THE DAY OF THE DANCE CLASS...
HEE HEE! I REMEMBER IT PERFECTLY!
BUT AN HOUR LATER...
BOOHOO-HOO!
?
IT DIDN'T WORK, CAPUCINE? DID YOU MESS UP YOUR ROUTINE?
NO!
BOO-HOOOO!
BY THINKING ABOUT ONLY THAT, I FORGOT TO TAKE MY DANCE STUFF... AND I DIDN'T GET TO DANCE!
BOO-HOOO!
!

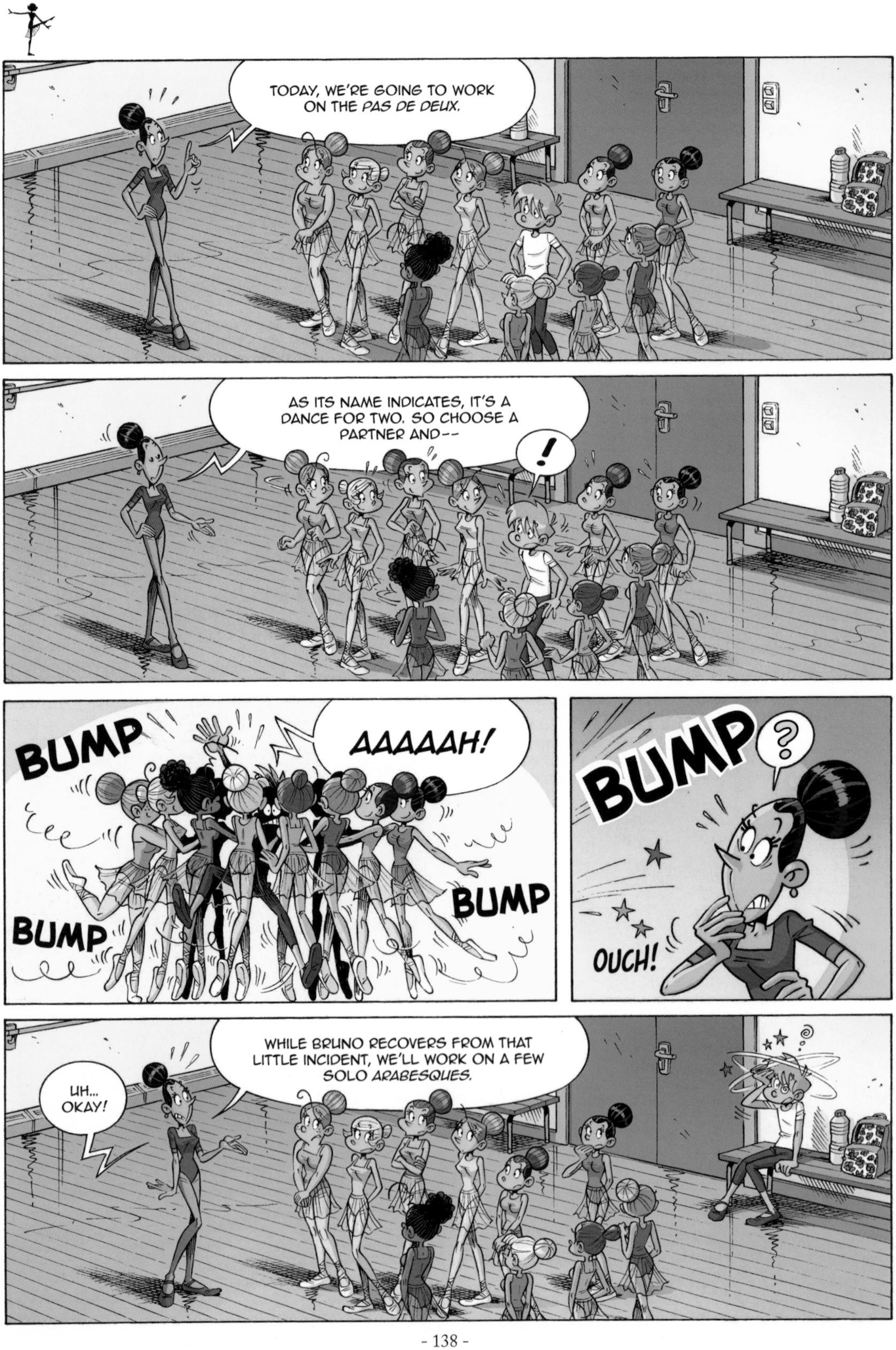
TODAY, WE'RE GOING TO WORK ON THE *PAS DE DEUX.*
AS ITS NAME INDICATES, IT'S A DANCE FOR TWO. SO CHOOSE A PARTNER AND--
!
BUMP
AAAAAH!
BUMP
BUMP
BUMP
?
OUCH!
UH... OKAY!
WHILE BRUNO RECOVERS FROM THAT LITTLE INCIDENT, WE'LL WORK ON A FEW SOLO *ARABESQUES.*

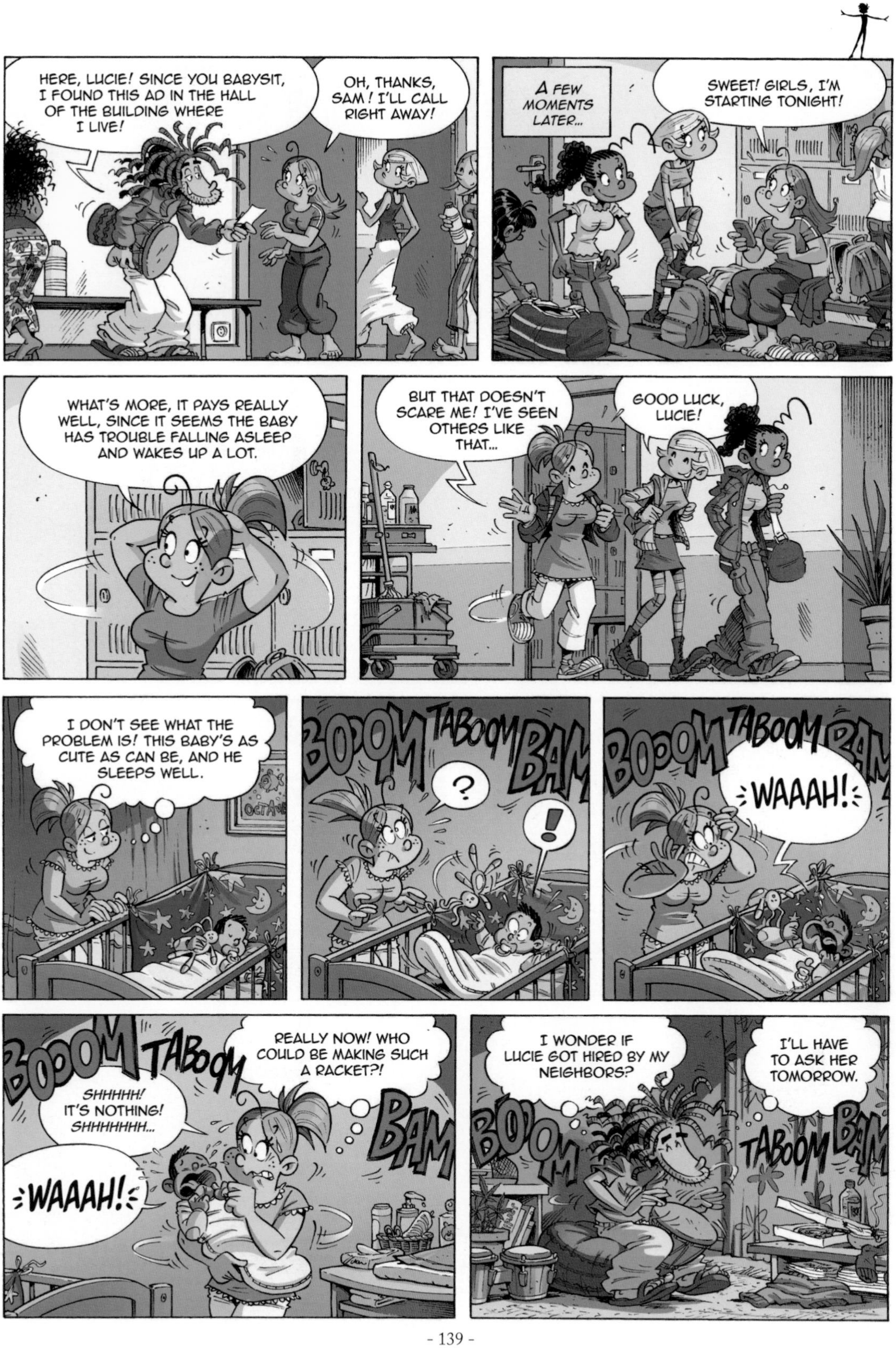
HERE, LUCIE! SINCE YOU BABYSIT, I FOUND THIS AD IN THE HALL OF THE BUILDING WHERE I LIVE!
OH, THANKS, SAM! I'LL CALL RIGHT AWAY!
A FEW MOMENTS LATER...
SWEET! GIRLS, I'M STARTING TONIGHT!
WHAT'S MORE, IT PAYS REALLY WELL, SINCE IT SEEMS THE BABY HAS TROUBLE FALLING ASLEEP AND WAKES UP A LOT.
BUT THAT DOESN'T SCARE ME! I'VE SEEN OTHERS LIKE THAT...
GOOD LUCK, LUCIE!
I DON'T SEE WHAT THE PROBLEM IS! THIS BABY'S AS CUTE AS CAN BE, AND HE SLEEPS WELL.
OCTAVE
BOOOM TABOOM BAM
?
!
BOOOM TABOOM BAM
WAAAH!
BOOOM TABOOM
REALLY NOW! WHO COULD BE MAKING SUCH A RACKET?!
SHHHHH! IT'S NOTHING! SHHHHHHH...
BAM
WAAAH!
I WONDER IF LUCIE GOT HIRED BY MY NEIGHBORS?
I'LL HAVE TO ASK HER TOMORROW.
BOOOM TABOOM BAM

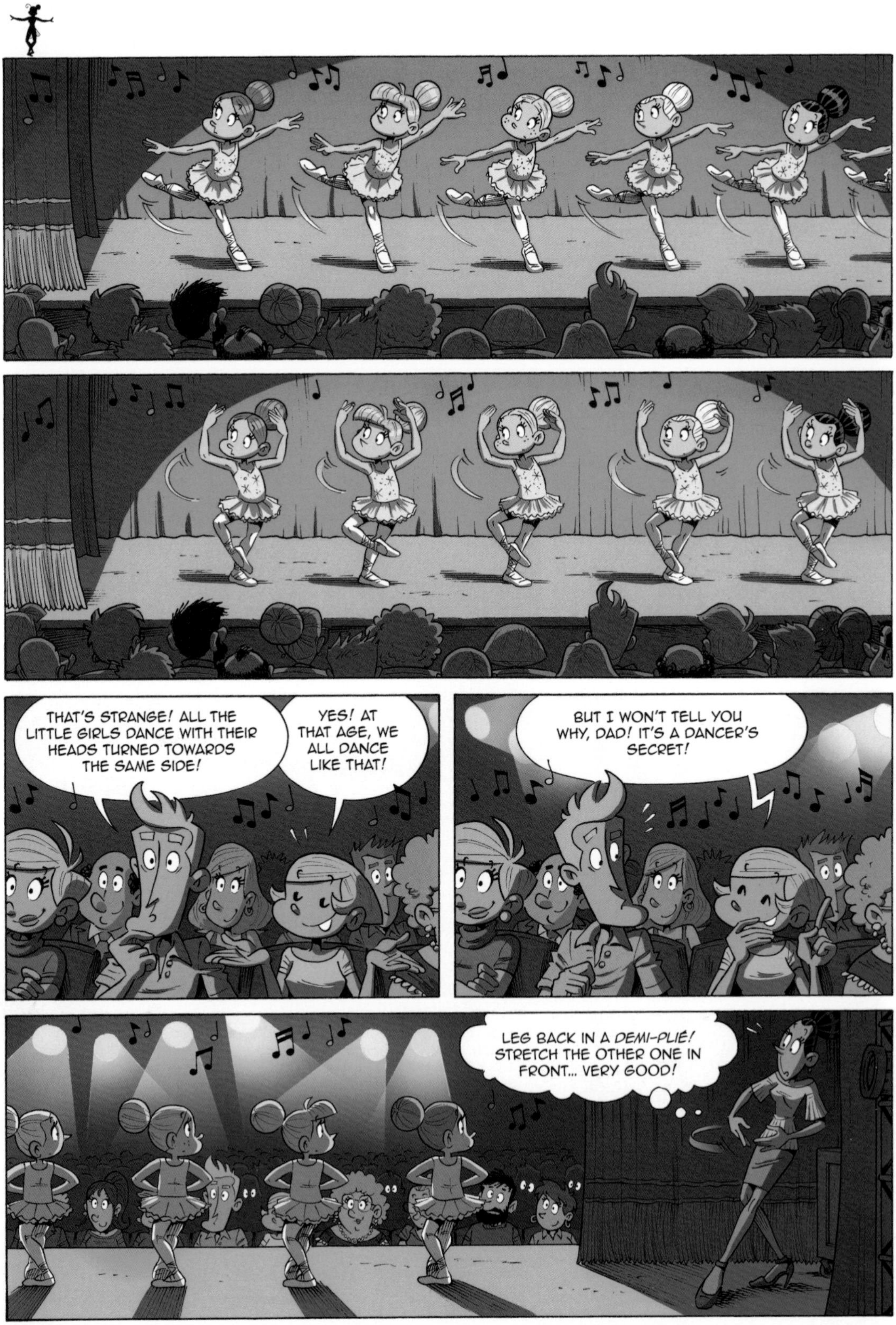
THAT'S STRANGE! ALL THE LITTLE GIRLS DANCE WITH THEIR HEADS TURNED TOWARDS THE SAME SIDE!
YES! AT THAT AGE, WE ALL DANCE LIKE THAT!
BUT I WON'T TELL YOU WHY, DAD! IT'S A DANCER'S SECRET!
LEG BACK IN A *DEMI-PLIÉ!* STRETCH THE OTHER ONE IN FRONT... VERY GOOD!

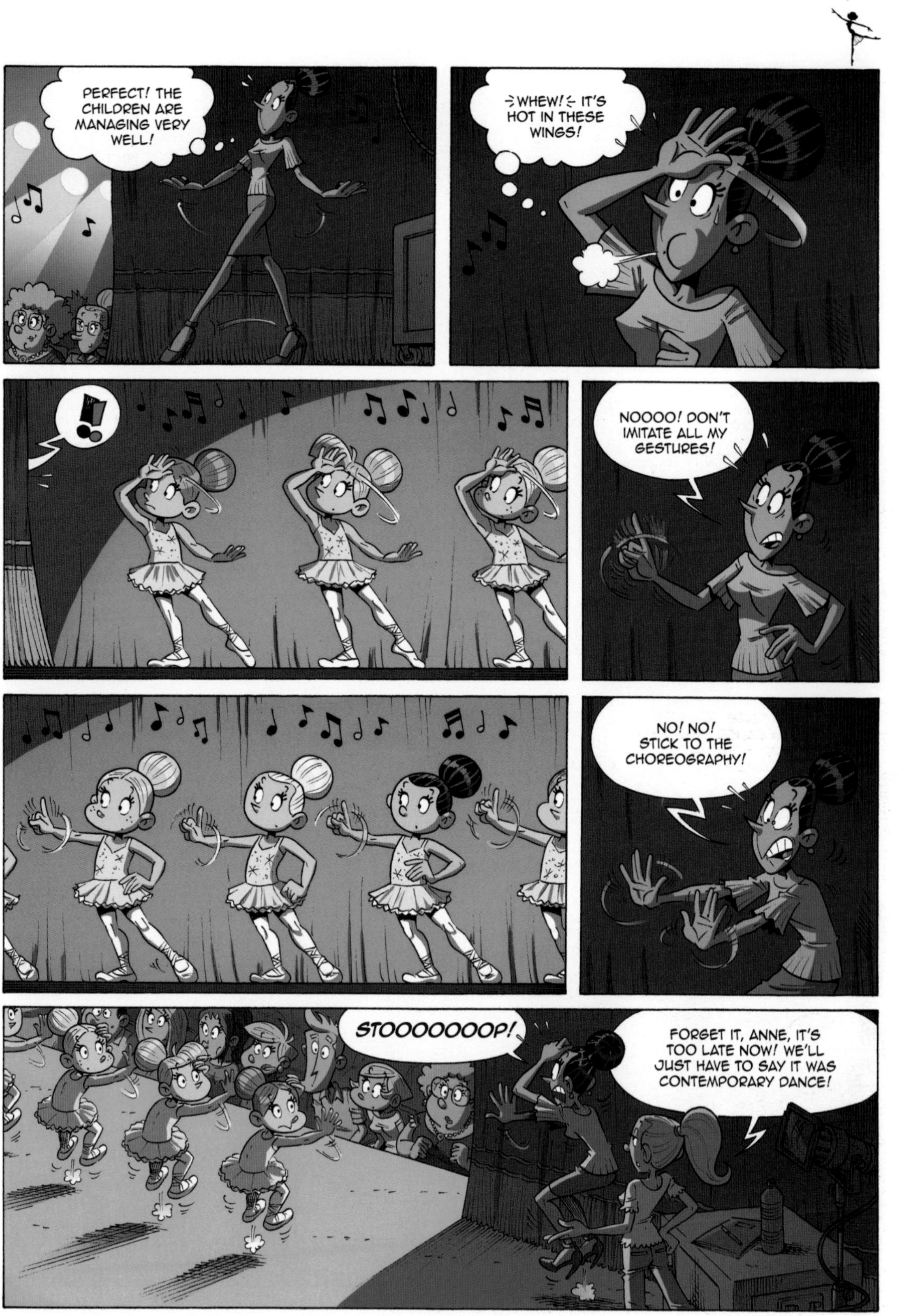
PERFECT! THE CHILDREN ARE MANAGING VERY WELL!
WHEW! IT'S HOT IN THESE WINGS!
NOOOO! DON'T IMITATE ALL MY GESTURES!
NO! NO! STICK TO THE CHOREOGRAPHY!
STOOOOOOOP!
FORGET IT, ANNE, IT'S TOO LATE NOW! WE'LL JUST HAVE TO SAY IT WAS CONTEMPORARY DANCE!

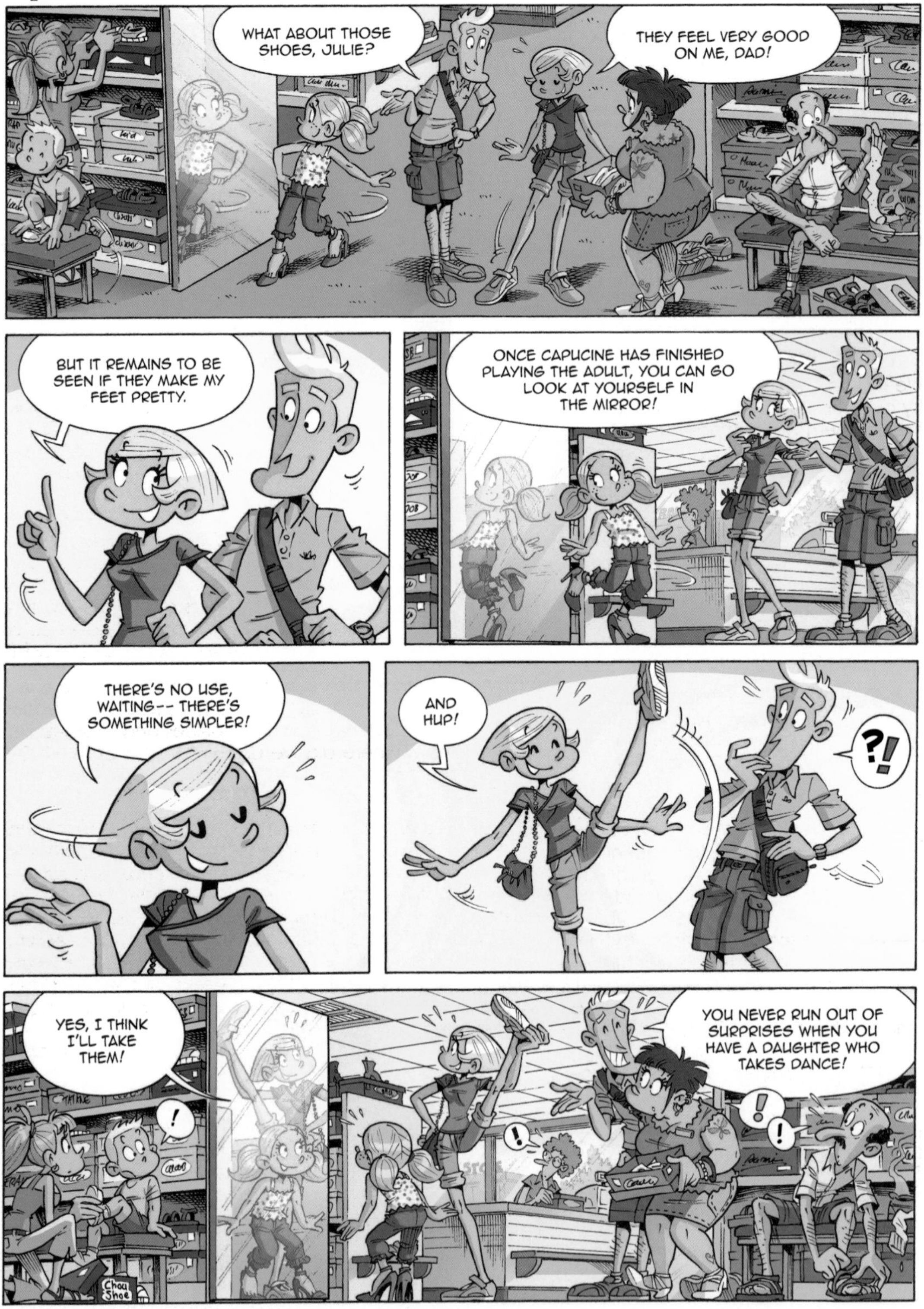
WHAT ABOUT THOSE SHOES, JULIE?
THEY FEEL VERY GOOD ON ME, DAD!
BUT IT REMAINS TO BE SEEN IF THEY MAKE MY FEET PRETTY.
ONCE CAPUCINE HAS FINISHED PLAYING THE ADULT, YOU CAN GO LOOK AT YOURSELF IN THE MIRROR!
THERE'S NO USE, WAITING-- THERE'S SOMETHING SIMPLER!
AND HUP!
?!
YES, I THINK I'LL TAKE THEM!
YOU NEVER RUN OUT OF SURPRISES WHEN YOU HAVE A DAUGHTER WHO TAKES DANCE!
!
!
!
!
Chou Shoe

WATCH OUT FOR PAPERCUTZ™

Welcome to the second (or sophomoric) DANCE CLASS 3 IN 1 graphic novel, by writer Béka, writer, and Crip, artist, from Papercutz, those toe-tapping, wallflowers dedicated to publishing great graphic novels for all ages. I'm Jim Salicrup, the Editor-in-Chief and star of *Dancing With the Scars*. In DANCE CLASS #10 (which is still available at libraries and booksellers everywhere), I told how cat-crazy we are at Papercutz and listed many of the Papercutz graphic novels that featured our favorite felines. Well, in the interest of equal time for canines, we wanted to mention there's an absolutely adorable little doggie in an exciting new series available from Papercutz right now. The dog's name is Dogmatix, and the series is called ASTERIX. It's a really big deal that Papercutz is publishing it, as ASTERIX is one of the biggest-selling graphic novel series in the world. This is big news and was even reported in *The New York Times* and *The Hollywood Reporter*. But regarding Dogmatix, while he does appear briefly—for one whole panel—in ASTERIX #1, it isn't until ASTERIX #2, where he starts to play a bigger role in the series.

Now some of you may not have heard of this Asterix fella, so let's take a quick journey in the Papercutz time machine...

We're back in the year 50 BC in the ancient country of Gaul, located where France, Belgium, and the Southern Netherlands are today. All of Gaul has been conquered by the Romans... well, not all of it. One tiny village, inhabited by indomitable Gauls, resists the invaders again and again. That doesn't make it easy for the garrisons of Roman soldiers surrounding the village in fortified camps.

So, how's it possible that a small village can hold its own against the mighty Roman Empire? The answer is this guy...

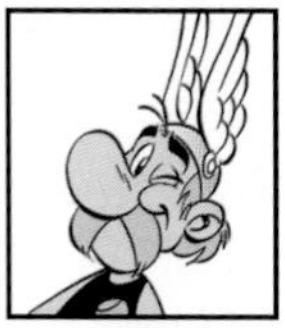

This is **Asterix**. A shrewd, little warrior of keen intellect... and superhuman strength. Asterix gets his superhuman strength from a magic potion. But he's not alone.

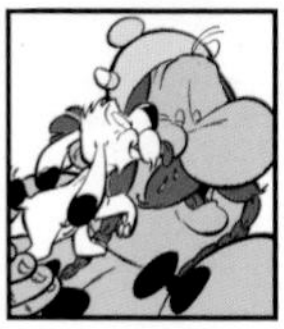

Obelix is Asterix's inseparable friend. He too has superhuman strength. He's a menhir (tall, upright stone monuments) deliveryman, he loves eating wild boar and getting into brawls. Obelix is always ready to drop everything to go off on a new adventure with Asterix. His constant companion (starting with ASTERIX #2) is **Dogmatix**, the only known canine ecologist, who howls with despair when a tree is cut down.

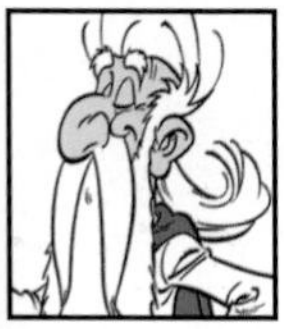

Panoramix, the village's venerable Druid, gathers mistletoe and prepares magic potions. His greatest success is the power potion. When a villager drinks this magical elixir he or she is temporarily granted super-strength. This is just one of the Druid's potions!

And now you know why this small village can survive, despite seemingly impossible odds. While we're here, we may as well meet a couple other Gauls...

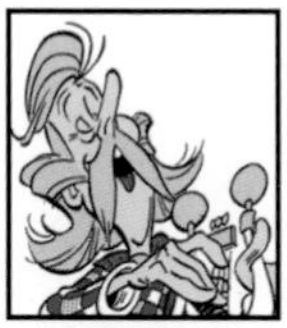

Cacofonix is the bard—the village poet. Opinions about his talents are divided: he thinks he's awesome, everybody else think he's awful, but when he doesn't sing, he's a cheerful companion and well-liked...

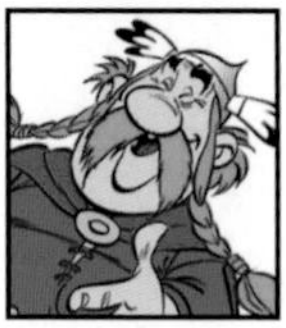

Vitalstatistix, finally, is the village's chief. Majestic, courageous, and irritable, the old warrior is respected by his men and feared by his enemies. Vitalstatistix has only one fear: that the sky will fall on his head but, as he says himself, "That'll be the day!"

There are plenty more characters around here, but you've met enough for now. It's time we get back to the palatial Papercutz offices and wrap this up. Now, where did we park our time machine? Oh, there it is!

We're back. Of course, you may find dogs in other Papercutz titles — Charles in THE LOUD HOUSE and Puppy in THE SMURFS, for just a couple examples—but we're so excited about ASTERIX, we couldn't resist sharing the news with you. And to tie it altogether, at the end of every ASTERIX adventure, the tiny village holds a celebratory feast. And you know you can't really have a party without dancing. Which is just our way of saying, make sure you never miss a DANCE CLASS!

Thanks,

Jim

STAY IN TOUCH!

EMAIL:	salicrup@papercutz.com
WEB:	www.papercutz.com
TWITTER:	@papercutzgn
INSTAGRAM:	@papercutzgn
FACEBOOK:	PAPERCUTZGRAPHICNOVELS
FANMAIL:	Papercutz, 160 Broadway, Suite 700, East Wing, New York, NY 10038

MORE GREAT GRAPHIC NOVEL SERIES AVAILABLE FROM

PAPERCUTZ™

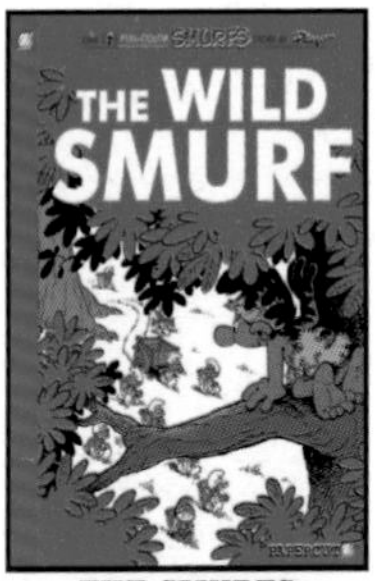
THE WILD SMURF
PAPERCUTZ
THE SMURFS

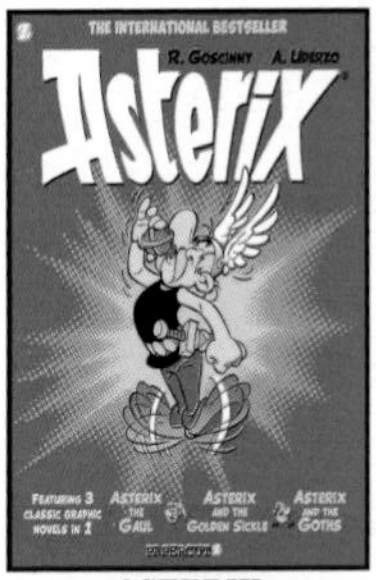
THE INTERNATIONAL BESTSELLER
R. GOSCINNY A. UDERZO
Asterix
FEATURING 3 CLASSIC GRAPHIC NOVELS IN 1
ASTERIX THE GAUL
ASTERIX AND THE GOLDEN SICKLE
ASTERIX AND THE GOTHS
ASTERIX

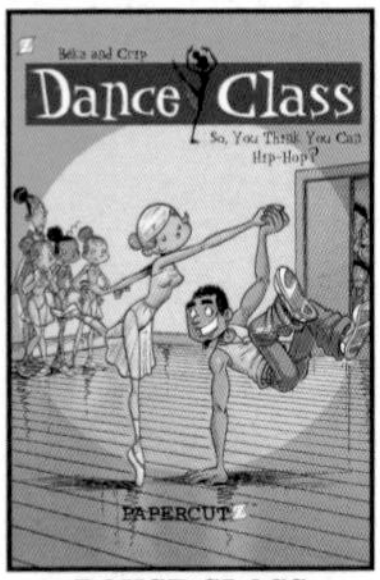
Béka and Crip
Dance Class
So, You Think You Can Hip-Hop?
PAPERCUTZ
DANCE CLASS

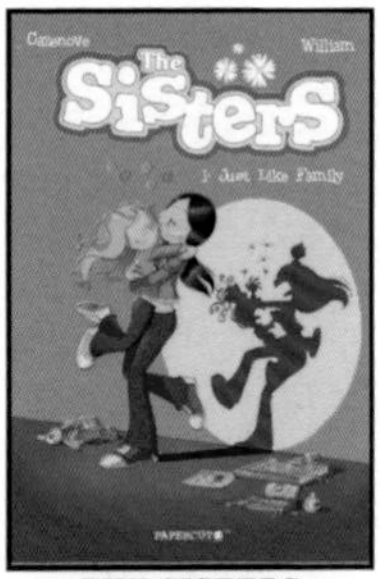
Cazenove
William
The Sisters
I Just Like Family
PAPERCUTZ
THE SISTERS

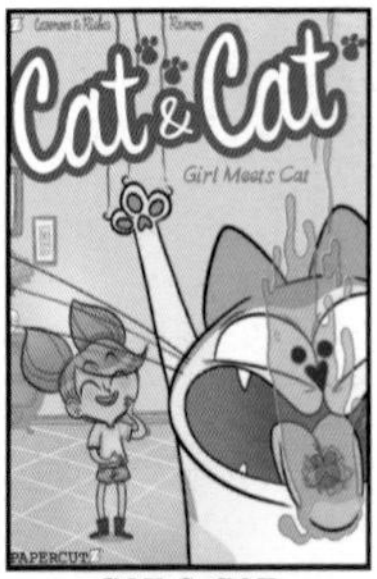
Cat & Cat
Girl Meets Cat
PAPERCUTZ
CAT & CAT

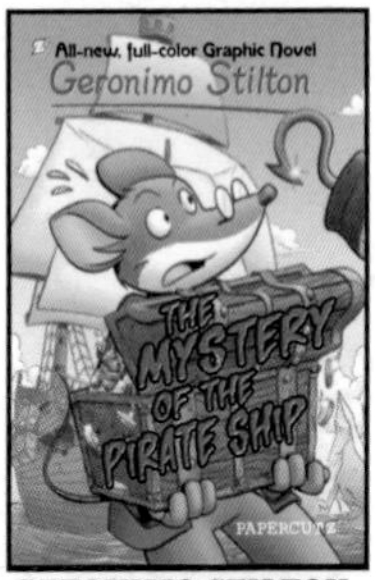
All-new, full-color Graphic Novel
Geronimo Stilton
THE MYSTERY OF THE PIRATE SHIP
PAPERCUTZ
GERONIMO STILTON

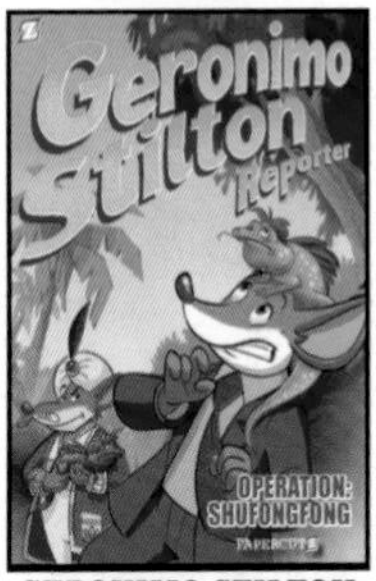
Geronimo Stilton Reporter
OPERATION: SHUFONGFONG
PAPERCUTZ
GERONIMO STILTON REPORTER

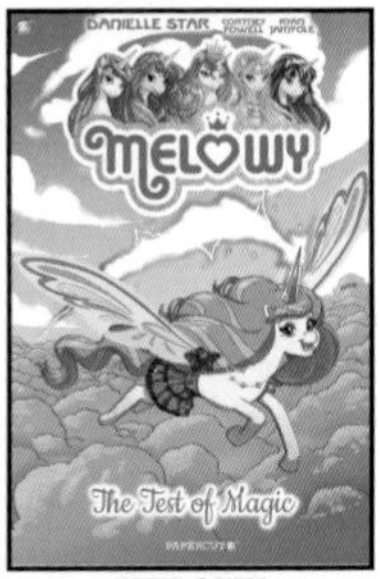
DANIELLE STAR
MELOWY
The Test of Magic
PAPERCUTZ
MELOWY

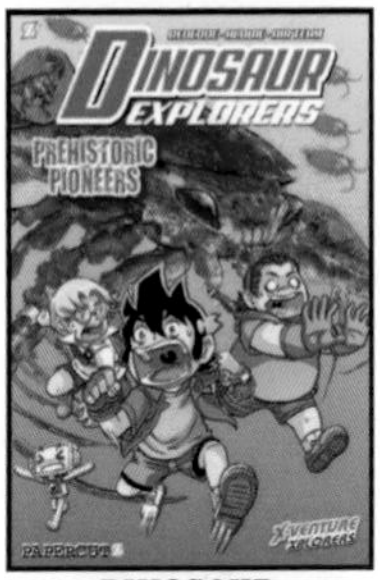
DINOSAUR EXPLORERS
PREHISTORIC PIONEERS
PAPERCUTZ
DINOSAUR EXPLORERS

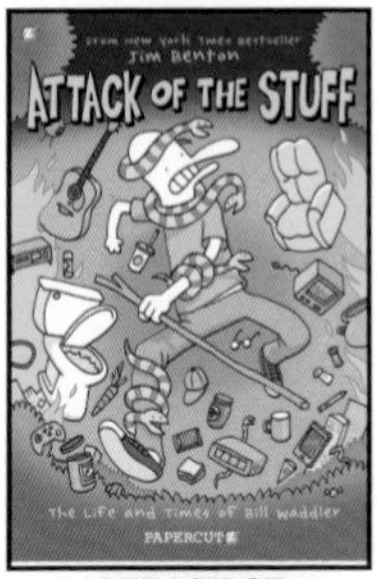
Jim Benton
ATTACK OF THE STUFF
The Life and Times of Bill Waddler
PAPERCUTZ
ATTACK OF THE STUFF

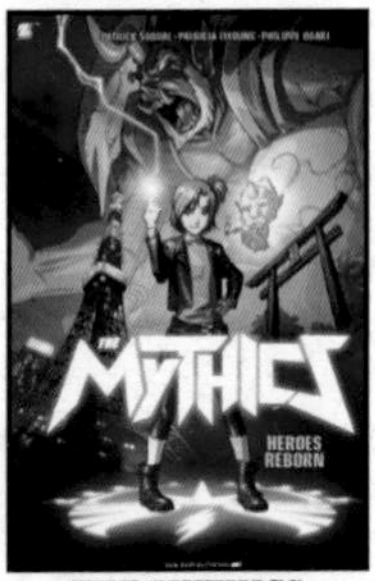
MYTHICS
HEROES REBORN
THE MYTHICS

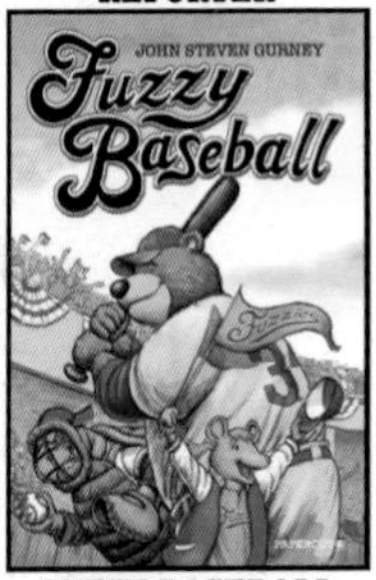
JOHN STEVEN GURNEY
Fuzzy Baseball
PAPERCUTZ
FUZZY BASEBALL

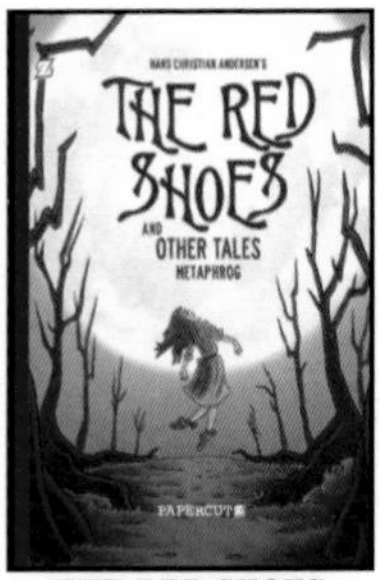
HANS CHRISTIAN ANDERSEN'S
THE RED SHOES
AND OTHER TALES
METAPHROG
PAPERCUTZ
THE RED SHOES

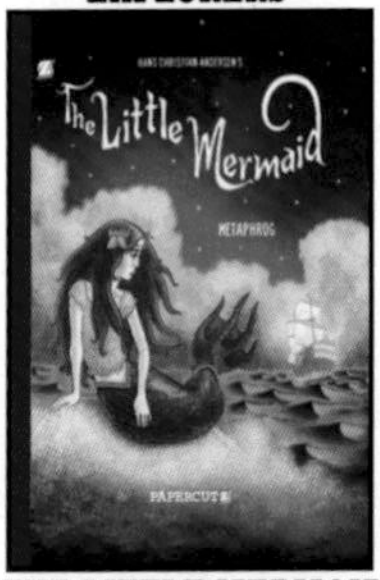
HANS CHRISTIAN ANDERSEN'S
The Little Mermaid
METAPHROG
PAPERCUTZ
THE LITTLE MERMAID

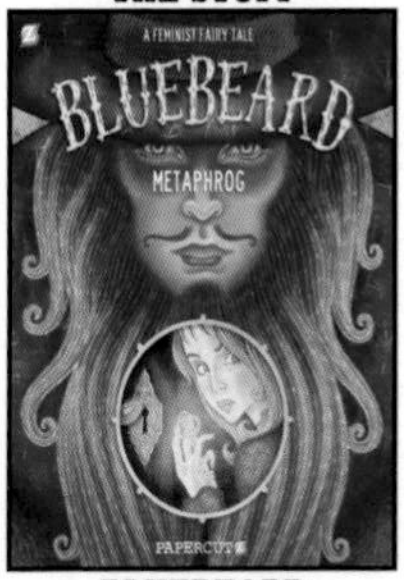
A FEMINIST FAIRY TALE
BLUEBEARD
METAPHROG
PAPERCUTZ
BLUEBEARD

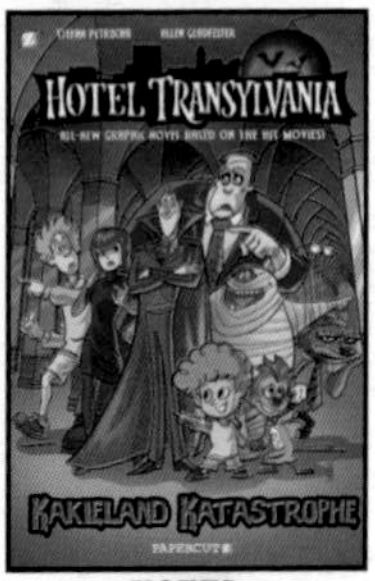
HOTEL TRANSYLVANIA
KAKIELAND KATASTROPHE
PAPERCUTZ
HOTEL TRANSYLVANIA

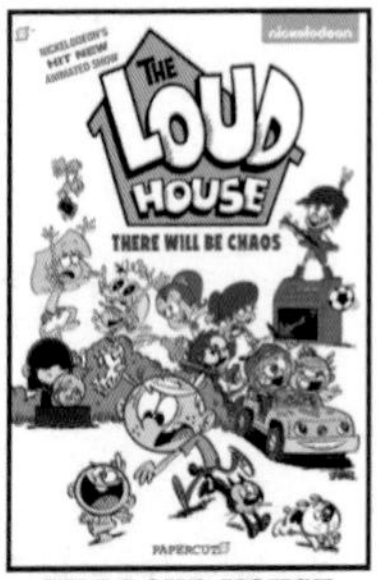
nickelodeon
THE LOUD HOUSE
THERE WILL BE CHAOS
PAPERCUTZ
THE LOUD HOUSE

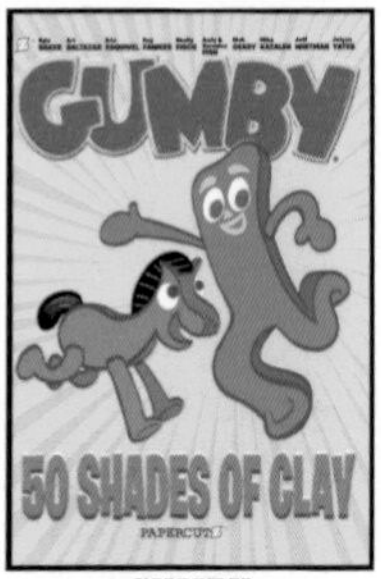
GUMBY
50 SHADES OF CLAY
PAPERCUTZ
GUMBY

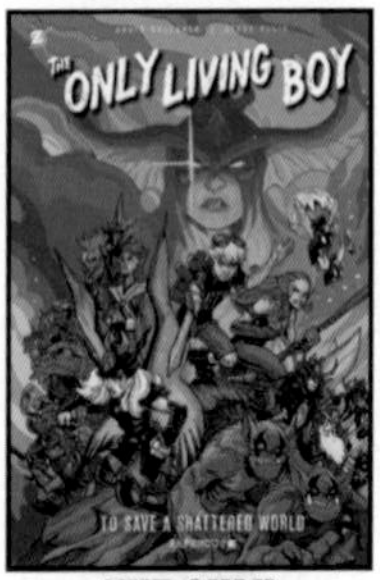
THE ONLY LIVING BOY
TO SAVE A SHATTERED WORLD
THE ONLY LIVING BOY

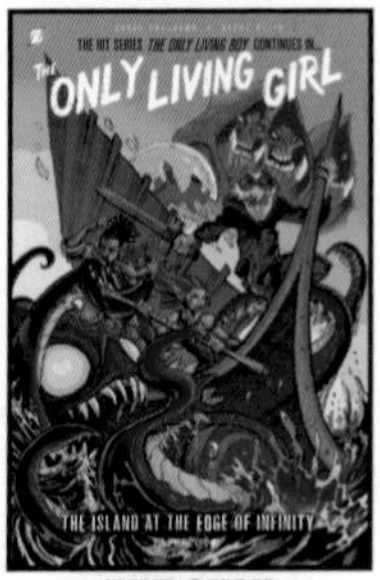
THE ONLY LIVING GIRL
THE ISLAND AT THE EDGE OF INFINITY
THE ONLY LIVING GIRL

Go to papercutz.com for more information

Also available where ebooks are sold.